D1109438

ALSO BY ARTHUR JAPIN

In Lucia's Eyes

The Two Hearts of Kwasi Boachi

Director's Cut

Director's Cut

A Novel

Arthur Japin

ALFRED A. KNOPF
NEW YORK 2010

THIS IS A BORZOI BOOK
PUBLISHED BY ALFRED A. KNOPF

Library of Congress Cataloging-in-Publication Data
Japin, Arthur, [date]
[Droom van de leeuw. English]
Director's cut : a novel / Arthur Japin ; translated from the Dutch by David Colmer. — 1st U.S. ed.
p. cm.
ISBN 978-1-4000-4062-9
I. Colmer, David, 1960– II. Title.
PT5881.2.A59D7613 2010 839.31'364—dc22 2009040989

Manufactured in the United States of America
First American Edition

The author has emended the original Dutch text and revised the translation for this edition.

Signora Vandemberg! From Holland. She was the most beautiful woman in the world . . .

—from "Il sogno del leone in cantina,"
Federico Fellini's last completed footage

CONTENTS

Part One

The Mannequins' Ball

Rome was my idea. The new Rome. The Rome where life is sweet, the place people imagine when they hear the name—that's what I came up with. Just an idea, that's all it was. The city was broken down. She had survived the war but was still suffering from its consequences. There was no work and hardly anything to eat. The cheeky Roman glint had faded from people's eyes, their gazes still marked by the treachery and dying they had been forced to witness. There was too much sorrow lingering in the shade of the cypresses. It bounced off the walls with the heat and got under your skin.

Young and high-spirited, I had left Romagna behind and entered the Eternal City, like a lion tamer stepping into a cage. I settled in the Via Voltana thinking I would first goad the big-city girls and men with my rough wit and then subdue them with my youthful fire. But war broke out and life disappeared from the streets, shrinking back into courtyards and stairwells. That's where people scraped by, and when they finally dared to crawl out of their lairs they had been through too much to let themselves be tempted to play. The lions shrank back and licked their mangy hides with the pitiful gaze of old cats who would no longer let themselves be lured out. Most of them had nothing better to do than hang around the Isola Tiberina, hoping someone might come by with something that needed to be repaired in exchange for a bowl of *trippa* and half a bottle of cheap wine. Sloth dripped from their very being, so much so that at night, when crossing the Piazza Sonnino on your way home, the cobblestones of Trastevere felt sticky underfoot. Every evening, it got harder to scrape off the dejection that clung to my spirit.

One morning it was as if I'd seen her in the street, Rome, the city herself, wallowing in her own filth. She was trying to get herself together among the scraps piled in the gutter after the close of the Porta Portese market. I came nearer and saw that her breasts were shriveled. Flies swarmed around the scars the war had left on her body. Because I could no longer stand to look at it, I helped her to her feet. I shook the dust out of her hair and off her bony shoulders and ran a bath for her. On the *corso* I bought her new shoes and expensive French lipstick. Then I put her in a tight dress and sat her on a gleaming Vespa and told her that hereafter hers would be *la dolce vita*. She believed me. It was just a dream, but she started to live it. For the first time a smile came back to the face of the city I loved. Her self-confidence returned. I gave her that. By lying to her.

I told her not to overdo it. When you've lost something as tiny as your happiness, you shouldn't try to search for it everywhere at once. I told her that her life no longer extended to the piles of rubble along the Via Cassia and that she should stop worrying about the suffering in the Tiburtina tenements. I showed her the Via Veneto and said that's where we'd find what she was looking for. It was a short stretch of road, a few hundred feet, whose buildings had made it through with their grandeur intact. I built a copy in my studio so that she could walk up and down it in high heels, unhindered by reality. I hired a band to play the bossa nova to the rhythm of her swaying hips. I painted the facades of the bars and hotels high-gloss and used a soft-focus lens that made the neon advertisements shine like halos. Finally, I turned a spotlight on her, on Rome. In that beam of light she shone with all the allure of a metropolis and I urged her at all costs to stay inside that narrow circle of enchantment.

It was my fantasy, but the city was dying for something to believe in. And because she was prepared to believe in herself, the rest of the world believed in her too. People came all the way from America to see her with their own eyes and learn something about her new life. Ever since then she's been back on the map. Because I set her limits. The Rome of drinking cocktails in sidewalk cafés, of my friend Marcello, of boisterous paparazzi, of the cool marble fountains. That is the Rome I invented. Because I loved her.

When you lie to a woman, it must be out of love.

That studio is empty now. Except for my bed. It's the old divan that used to be up in my office, where in the last few years I would sometimes rest between takes. They carried it downstairs and placed it in the middle of the studio. It makes a comfortable bed, but I'm lost in this gigantic space. Around me, on the floor, lie the chalk marks from the set of my last production, but there's not a prop in sight. There are no cables or well-thumbed screenplays lying around, not so much as a feather or a sequin from a costume. Even the olive pits and the pieces of salami skin you used to find everywhere after lunch have been swept up. High above me is the iron grid for the lights. It is bare. Someone has packed away the heavy black curtains that muffled the chatter of the extras and made it possible for me to talk to the crew without a megaphone.

The sliding steel doors, which take up a whole wall and can be opened in a trice to reveal the back lot, are bolted shut. Even the birds that nested on the beams below the roof seem to have flown away.

At sixteen I earned my first pay drawing cartoons and caricatures, and I sent them off to magazines in Rome. There, they caught the eye of a publisher of science fiction comics, who for a long time would let me do no more than write dialogue in balloons. It was mindless work. To keep from going crazy, I thought up my own adventures involving Zarco, Commander of the Planet Gomba. As more and more people, trying to support their families, moved away from our area, the manpower in the office fell to a critical level, and I was allowed to develop a few of those ideas. In the end I drew a number of episodes for our regional daily, *Il Resto del Carlino*.

After fixing a piece of blank paper in place, the first thing I did was draw up the lines. Even before I knew what I was going to draw, often before I had a clear story in mind, I would use a ruler to draw the boxes in which the scenes would take place, just as later I often began by determining the frame and filling the shot with extras afterward. Generally, one of those cartoon pages followed a fixed formula, with the first and last pictures the biggest: the first was the introduction, the last one was for the punch line and the tie-in to the next day's episode. Sometimes, however, I would venture using a whole page for a single picture so that I would have enough space to do something bigger: a crowd scene or a panorama. The way to do that isn't to try to fill the whole box at once but to start with a couple of lines and a small, inconspicuous figure somewhere in the foreground.

That describes me lying here on my divan now, a tentative idea on a blank page. This little bed of mine in the bottom left, the emptiness around it contained by the walls of Studio 5, the floor beneath me and the grid above from which the spotlights will soon be hung. Together they form the frame, a lofty hall, which I have to fill completely with my dreams. Above the door to the corridor there is a glass plate with a red light behind it. It just flicked on: SILENCE, FILMING!

When I was a boy in Rimini, many of the most thrilling moments I spent in the Fulgor, our local cinema, were during the last couple of minutes before the film started. Everyone was seated and waiting. They were still talking loudly. The children were howling. My mother smiled and made rustling noises opening bags of candy. The whole theater was so deliciously full of expectation. We were about to see Garbo, Ronald Colman, or the Marx Brothers. For a few days now, I've felt that same way. Except this time the tension is greater, grown-up, like the nervousness I felt when making my own films and walking into Studio 5 on the first day of shooting. There's more riding on it this time.

It still seems most like a lover's embrace. Already you can scarcely move, even as you want to be held more tightly still. The less you can move, the more intense your feelings get. You even have trouble breathing, but you feel secure. When her grip relaxes for a second, you feel like you're going to lose everything, and you hug her closer until she wraps her legs around you and crushes your sides between her thighs. Everything you have to say condenses into sighs. No one understands them, but still you've said it all. Now and then my harsh mistress squeezes her arms tight, almost killing me. She lets me feel my body's limits. "Don't let go," I cry. "Don't let go!" Then she kisses me and smiles, and tightens the belt of her love.

"Put a cork in it, kid," she whispers, "the movie's about to start."

1966

Gala's story has to start with a rose. Lots of roses and tulips too, of course, because as a girl she lived in Holland, surrounded by all kinds of flowers, flowers of every imaginable sort. Yes, the first time we see her, she is surrounded by all the flowers of the world.

Like colorful stains, buds and stems lay strewn across the concrete floor of the auction hall. They had been squashed flat by the trucks driving in and out in the early-morning darkness. Her father strode through the fallen flowers, but Gala was trying to keep her new patent leather shoes clean. So they hopscotched through the mush hand in hand. Sometimes she jumped up, clung to his arm for a second, floating over the ground with her legs drawn up under her until he'd had enough and tried to shake her off, and then she'd leap and race off ahead.

They had almost reached the tall steel doors that granted admission to the immense complex when Gala stopped at a bunch of chrysanthemums. They hadn't been lying there very long and were fresh and relatively intact, but that wouldn't last long with the big trucks still driving in and out. Their headlights bothered the girl. She squinted.

Gala is sensitive to the rhythms of light.

Sometimes, driving down the long tree-lined avenue near their house on sunny days, she had to cover her eyes with her hands to keep from getting dizzy. She hadn't been doing it lately because she was almost eight and had resolved to cure herself of all childish habits before her birthday. In the car she sat on her hands and kept her eyes wide open all the way down the avenue. She ran a gauntlet of light and shade. Three-quarters of the way down the street, she suddenly felt something coming up behind her, like a wave about to wash over her. For a second she thought someone was sitting behind her, a magician, perhaps, with a big flapping cape he was about to wrap around her—she could already see the gleam of the red lining in the corner of an eye. But Gala didn't turn around. A girl who was almost eight was surely old enough to understand that there wasn't anyone there. In that instant the sun, uninterrupted, touched her face. She saw her reflection in the side window, proud that she had withstood this ordeal.

At the flower auction one of the drivers now flashed his lights to warn the girl of his approach. Another rolled down his window to shout something at her, but his voice was drowned out by the heavy rubber tires screeching over the concrete. Gala almost dropped the bunch of chrysanthemums she'd just picked up, in order to hide her face in her hands. But she didn't, because these flowers were for her father. She looked for him, but couldn't find him among the flashing lights. She pressed her eyes shut and felt the wind of a truck catch her skirt as it thundered past. Then, all at once, she knew he was behind her. He came running up out of the distance. A bright beam of light behind him cast a long shadow over the floor ahead of her, quickly growing shorter, smaller, faster, until it coincided perfectly with her own.

Her father scooped her up with one arm, cursing with fright, and didn't put her down again until the entrance of the visitors' center, where he dropped her with a thud.

"What did I do," he snapped, "to deserve a girl like you?"

"Don't ask me," Gala replied, "but it must have been truly awful in God's eyes," and these words of hers were rewarded with an upward curl in the corners of his mouth as the hint of sarcasm that always lingered there briefly moved aside for a genuine smile.

An atmosphere of mutual scorn hung over their family. Gala's father—named Jan, like all Dutch men—always seemed bent on annoying everyone else, on provoking. Fearing that his daughters might not be sufficiently armed against the world, he was anxious to make them as independent as possible, almost rebellious. It was as if he wouldn't rest until they bettered him, and every time they failed to do so his disappointment was renewed. The more tenderly he felt about one of the three girls, or even their mother, the more caustic his rebukes became. And Gala was lucky enough to be his favorite. She loved his cutting words, sure at least he cared about her when he was lashing out. He wanted to get the best out of her, simply because he saw the best in her. All he really did was tease her in the hope of being paid back in kind, but it was a coldhearted game that brought the winner no more joy than the loser.

Before Gala could give her father the flowers she had gathered for him, he snatched them away, and when, looking disgusted, he hurled them, they left motor oil on his fingers.

"Apparently, there are parents who actually enjoy their children."

It was only six thirty, but two busloads of Japanese tourists were already disembarking in front of the visitors' center. Gala's father walked past the waiting crowd.

"Jan Vandemberg," he told the receptionist. "I have an appointment with Professor Dogberry of Yale."

The man they had come to meet was an art historian, like Gala's father, and an authority on the early Siennese Renaissance. Several months earlier, Jan had invited Dogberry to participate in a symposium at the Rijksmuseum, and the better he planned the visit, the more nervous he grew about everything that could go wrong. He had always nurtured a deep respect for Obadiah Dogberry, whose paper on two small panels in New Haven by the virtually unknown Maestro dell'Osservanza had led Jan to a lifelong passion that had defined his career. This respect had suffered a severe blow on the day the man arrived, when he scarcely deigned to look at Jan's meticulous program and informed him that he had set his heart on visiting the tulip fields of the Keukenhof and the Aalsmeer flower auction. It was beyond Jan's comprehension that his plans could be aborted for something so nonsensical.

Jan Vandemberg had taken Gala along with him as if to prove that not everyone can fritter away his time with trifles. Getting up early had put him in an even worse mood, and having to wait for the great authority now did the rest.

"Must have lost his clogs at the windmill."

. . .

Gala wondered whether she had ever gone anywhere this early with her father before. Maybe leaving on holiday sometimes in the car, but then her mother and two sisters would have been there too. Going somewhere alone with her father was unusual.

During the week, Jan took the train into the city to teach and didn't return until late at night. He spent most of the rest of his time upstairs in his study. Children were not allowed, and any who dared venture there would be eaten.

"Every last scrap," Gala's father warned his three little girls regularly, adding credibility to his threats by baring his teeth and growling ferociously. Mara, the youngest, retreated to the corner of her playpen, while Francisca invariably burst into inconsolable tears. Gala was the only one to defy him by brazenly trying to stare him down. She was no less scared than her younger sisters, and yet she loved it when the dangerous man showed his fangs and slowly crept closer and closer until finally their noses were touching. She squealed with fright and fought to resist her terror. It was like climbing out of a roller coaster that had just had you screaming and sick to your stomach with fear and immediately wanting to get back in line for another ride. The tension Gala felt in these moments was addictive, and when her father backed off, forgoing the horrors he had just been threatening, she was more angry than relieved. As soon as he turned around and forgot to be dangerous, Gala felt slighted, as if he were convinced that she wouldn't overdo it and considered her too inconsequential to bother with. She couldn't bear for him to think that she wasn't a worthy adversary. Enraged, she would grab whatever happened to be within reach and hurl it at his head. It could be a colored pencil or a napkin, but it might just as well be a book or a plate of hot food. Sometimes he simply threw it back, and if he hit her he would cheer as other fathers do at a football match. More often, though, he deemed her unworthy of his attention. He left the business of punishing their daughters to his wife—who, like all women in low countries, was named Anna. At moments like these, Gala felt a strong desire to provoke him even more the next time, to actually hurt him, and to keep it up until he finally did more than just show his teeth.

To push him over the edge, she marched into his study one afternoon when she was sure he was concentrating on his work. Without looking up, he asked her again to leave, which only made her more determined. First she crawled under his desk, then behind it, then climbed up on top of it, pushing aside a pile of essays to make room. He swung at her the way you swat at a fly, but after missing, he ignored her, forcing Gala to take it one step further. As soon as he had finished adding his comments to a page of the essay he was reading and had placed it on the pile of work he had already marked, she took it off again and assumed her version of a reedy, affected voice to read out the things he had just written in red pencil. Then she deliberately put the page back: upside down on top of the unread pile.

The first time he acted as if he didn't care, returned the sheet of paper to the correct pile, and kept working. The second time he responded in exactly the same way, but when Gala picked up a green felt-tip pen and started to draw a little man on the third page, he slid his work aside and watched carefully until she'd finished. She took her time, giving the figure a moustache, a briefcase, and wings, and finally adding a hat with a flower with a center like a shining sun.

"Fine," Jan said, taking the piece of paper from her and calmly studying it, "here we go." He put the essays away in a drawer, then slammed it shut with tremendous force. The mocking expression disappeared from his face in that same instant.

"Just remember, you brought this on yourself." For a few seconds he stared at her, making Gala tremble somewhere deep inside, a trembling she had never known before. She was angry with him for trying to impose his authority and happy that in the whole world there was nothing else vying for his attention. When she heard him growl, she did not know what she longed for most intensely, to bite or to be bitten.

This was no longer a game, she felt that. It was quite possible that it might forever change everything she had ever known. Maybe she had set off something that was more dangerous than she suspected, but if it destroyed her, she would take him with her. She was no longer a fly to be shooed away with a wave of the hand.

Suddenly he leapt, throwing himself atop her like a ravenous animal. The girl disappeared almost completely beneath him and his weight bore down on her so heavily that she felt it crushing her chest. She tried to escape his grip, screaming, but he squeezed his nails into her arm and refused to let go. She fought back but couldn't breathe and felt his fingers deep in her muscles. She planted her feet in his groin and pushed him away. His nails scraped along her arm until he was only holding her by her dress. It tore when she scrambled up onto her feet and suddenly shot free, hitting her shoulder hard on the jamb. She ran out onto the landing but saw the way downstairs blocked by her mother, who was coming to see what was going on. Behind her, in his study, her father jumped up now as well. Gala ran upstairs with the grown man following close behind. In the attic she leapt over boxes and old furniture—obstacles he cleared with considerably less ease—and reached the dormer, where she took cover behind a rafter. The sunlight shining in through the window scattered on the dust billowing up from the old bags and crates that Jan kicked out of the way one after the next. Gala saw the man approaching slowly through these shining clouds. Her breathing was shallow and the whole scene reeled before her eyes. When he was almost upon her, with just the rafter between them, she saw his lips quivering, and every quiver pushed more blood up out of a split in the corner of his mouth. It was as if his injury calmed her. As she imagined his pain, her tension drained away. She wanted to tell him she was sorry and that she loved him, but something in his eyes told her that it might be too late.

In the same instant the man recognized his own blind fury in the girl. Was he really willing to hurt her to make her invulnerable? Suddenly afraid, his eyes made a small movement toward the window. Was he directing her thoughts or were her thoughts directing him? Almost at once Gala was up on the window seat, and two or three desperate kicks later the rotted window was out of its groove. The glass broke and a shard cut her leg as she stepped into the gutter. Her pursuer didn't hesitate for a moment and followed her out. Gala heard her mother shriek and run downstairs, and a little later saw the woman running around in the garden with her arms stretched out as if to catch her. The gutter only ran to the corner of the house, where Gala had to choose between leaping to the flat roof of the pantry or clambering up even higher. Behind her she heard the dull sound of her father's footsteps on the tin roof. She put a foot on the first tile—it wobbled but held—a foot on the second, until she felt the whole row slipping. She grabbed hold of a tile above her, but her weight made it tilt, just as she felt an iron grasp around her ankles. She lost her balance, smacked into the tiles chin first, and fell. She fell with her full weight upon her father, who wrapped his body around hers, and together they landed two meters below on the gravel of the pantry roof.

Gala lay there in her father's grip. Screaming with laughter, just as he was, she knew that he had distinguished himself forever from all the rest of the world's fathers. His hands, broad, strong yet still soft, were holding her tight. A shudder passed through his whole body, and when she looked at him, she didn't know whether his eyes were moist from relief or anger.

"That's what you get," he sighed, before his voice had time to properly gather itself, "when someone loves you."

A powerful smell wafted out over Gala when her father opened the door to the flower auction. She could smell millions of flowers and tried to imagine the hundreds of thousands of bunches arranged in vases all over the world by nightfall.

Along the entire length of the complex, some two kilometers long, a catwalk was suspended above the market floor to allow visitors to look down on what most resembled a moving sea of flowers. The American professor was already there, looking out over the activity below. When he saw Gala and her father, he raised a hand and, even before the girl had a chance to say hello, took a photo of her with one of three cameras dangling against his enormous belly. The flash hurt her eyes and, as if the light had become sound, reverberated inside her skull like the striking of a gong.

The American was friendliness itself, and Gala couldn't understand why her father, so much stronger and better looking, had been nervous about his encounter with this gnome. He had urged her several times in the last few days to make a good impression on Obadiah Dogberry. That was something he always did when he was afraid that he himself would fall short. Gala knew what was expected of her: it was time for her to do her tricks again.

They walked over a field of sunflowers that was passing under the catwalk like a small train on its way to the auction sheds. The girl leaned out with the rail against her waist to watch the rattling carts curving over the points. To the rhythm of the wheels, Gala mentally rehearsed the proverbs she would soon be asked to rattle off for her father's guest. To astonish him. In Latin.

Sunt aliquid manes, letum non omnia finit. * *Alia voce psittacus, alia coturnix loquitur.*† To her they were nothing but sound, and she memorized them the way she memorized foreign songs at school—*Hava nagila, hava magila. Kalinka kalinka kalinka moya*—by melody and rhythm alone, but the effect they had on her father's acquaintances was always the same.

"A child of eight. Incredible! Jan, your daughter is a prodigy!"

She had been performing this trick since she was five, and in that time her father had expanded the arsenal with Greek proverbs, poems by Catullus, and passages from the *Odyssey.* Sometimes she got bored with it and hid when her parents were hosting yet another dinner party, but generally she let her father have his fun: when the reactions were enthusiastic he positively beamed. It was only when she made mistakes—and she really did do her best not to, but still, sometimes, especially with people she didn't know—then . . .

At that moment the sunflowers stopped to let a procession of pink gerberas cross their path. Like the silenced wheels, the sounds in Gala's head jolted to a halt in the middle of a poem by Martial.

She tried to pick it up from the last line, but without the help of the rhythm she stumbled again. She went back to the start of the poem, just as she sometimes repeated it to herself at night in bed before falling asleep, but she already feared the worst. She tried to shut out all the unfamiliar noises around her to follow the conversation the two men were having behind her in English so that she could work out how much time she had left before her father wanted to show her off. She could not disappoint him.

The previous autumn a circus had appeared before Gala's house, materializing out of the ether on the field at the bottom of the hill. Like a colorful hot-air balloon that had chosen to land on her favorite playground. Coming home from ballet the evening before, there hadn't been any sign of it, but the next morning she woke to the sound of

* *Spirits do exist; death does not end all things.* (Propertius)

†*Parrots make a different sound from quails.* (Erasmus)

trumpeting elephants and a trombonist who was practicing a bass line. She threw her curtains open with surprise and saw cheerful lights twinkling through the bare trees at the end of the street.

On the way to school she got off her bike at the fence to watch the horses in the outside ring. They were trotting in opposite directions, circling a young woman who was standing straight-backed in the middle ground. She held her head so high that her chin was pointing up in the air. She barked out commands that made the animals stop, rear, and turn on the spot, but, just to make sure they obeyed, she was holding a whip behind her back. Now and then, when one of the grays was about to come up with ideas of his own, she cracked the whip, not to hit him: just to remind.

Gala was late getting to school and had to stay after, but on her way back home she stopped at Circus Rinzi again. This time it was much livelier. Inside the tent, the matinee was in full swing. A band was playing. Acrobats in glittering costumes were walking around outside and a tightrope walker was practicing splits on a steel cable strung over a caravan. Gala gasped with admiration, but the woman, whose eyes were fixed firmly on a point in the distance, didn't even wobble. Through a hole in the rhododendrons, which the girl knew about from having played there so often, she was able to get into the circus enclosure. She was behind the caravans looking for wild animals when the shining lights around the mirror of a makeup table attracted her attention.

A clown was putting on his face. He had already smeared his cheeks with red grease and drawn a mousy little black mouth in the middle of his lips. Now he started doing big eyes. One was radiant, with eyelashes like a sunburst. No longer young, he needed to spread his skin smooth with the other hand to draw straight lines. The second eye was completely different. It wasn't really an eye at all, just a vertical stripe that bisected his eyebrow and went down over his eyelid to the middle of his cheek. Then he practiced a look of resignation in the mirror, slowly raising his shoulders, eyebrows, and the corners of his mouth—all at the same time. When the call came for his first number, he pulled an enormous coat on over his suspenders and ran off in outsized, baggy trousers, disappearing through an opening in the side of the tent.

Gala followed him. Peering through that same opening, she could just make out part of the ring. She saw the man standing next to the stands, unnoticed by the audience until the spotlight touched him and drew him into the middle of the tent. He stumbled over the sawdust. He fell. He was beaten by an arrogant white clown, who began by asking him to do the impossible, then ridiculed him when it proved too much for him. He looked miserable, wretched—an outcast. He reminded Gala of cartoon characters who get trampled by crowds until they are as flat as a pancake but always haul themselves up again, hammer out the dents, and walk on, crumpled but unbroken. This clown was exposed to ridicule, blows, and contempt, but he took it all in good cheer, amused and amusing. Over and over again, he gave that apologetic grin, with his eyebrows and the corners of his mouth raised and his shoulders up to his ears. And each time, the audience had no choice but to forgive him for whatever he'd done. If only I could just touch him, thought Gala, who had never imagined that such extraordinary creatures could exist. This man was stupid yet invincible.

Suddenly someone grabbed Gala hard by the scruff of the neck and dragged her away from the tent. A plump woman with long blond hair had her in a tight grip. A fat snake was wrapped around the woman's neck, resting its head on her ample bosom.

"No ticket, huh?" she snarled, and when Gala shook her head, the woman pretended she was going to kick her in the pants. "Come back tonight with money, and you can watch as much as you like. Now beat it." She took the snake off her shoulders like a scarf and held it in front of Gala's face. "Otherwise I'll feed you to Ennio."

Gala ran home nonstop through the rain without once remembering that she'd left her bike at the circus with her schoolbag on the carrier.

When she rushed, panting, into the living room, she found herself standing eye to eye with the Reformed pastor, who was visiting her parents with his wife.

"Hello, child." The man had a high voice, probably because his tight white collar was strangling him.

"We were just talking about you," Jan said, while the pastor's wife took Gala by the wrist and pulled her onto her lap.

"We were getting worried," she said, the girl bouncing on her knees like a rodeo rider.

Gala's father shot her a look that said that all would be forgiven if she acquitted herself well in the next twenty minutes. The Vandembergs were descended from a long line of clergymen, and, although Jan delivered most of his lectures as if from a pulpit, his decision not to follow in his father's and grandfathers' footsteps had always been resented. He just hadn't dared, he was too much of a doubter himself, and the awe he felt for pastors was not motivated by piety but from the way they could, by choosing their words, either put the fear of God into a whole congregation or choose to comfort them or burden them with guilt. These old-fashioned shepherds possessed the power of the word: a treasure that seemed so valuable to Jan that he had spent his whole life searching for it. Secretly he hoped to refine Gala's verbal skills so much that one day, in this changing world, he might see her standing in the pulpit, with him in the front pew, quaking at her fire and brimstone.

"Your father tells me that you possess the miraculous gift of the word."

"Miracles," said Gala, still bobbing up and down on the knees of the pastor's wife, "seem more like your line of business."

The pastor clapped his hands.

"Goodness, Jan, I believe you've sown a talent here."

"She's only little," Gala's mother tempered their enthusiasm. "Let her play now, while she still can."

"If only she were a miracle," said Jan. "Miracles come ready-made, but Gala has a gift. And a gift like that is an obligation. It demands a lot of hard work. But still, *dandum etenim est aliquid . . .*"

*". . . dum tempus postulat aut res,"** his daughter concluded. The pastor's jaw dropped, and his incredulous mare abandoned her attempts to buck Gala.

"That's nothing," said Jan. "Her little sister can do that too. What I am saying, our youngest comes close to babbling Cato in her cradle. No, Gala's latest passion is Homer, isn't it, honey? I recite it for her at night as a bedtime story and when she gets up in the morning she just rattles it off."

"Well, with a week or two of droning and drilling," said Gala's mother, who had had enough of the whole performance. She liberated

* *Give when the time or situation demands.* (Cato the Elder)

her daughter from the grip of the pastor's wife and asked her where she had been.

"Who wouldn't forgive a father's enthusiasm," crowed the pastor, "when he has such an extraordinary child? It's just . . ."

At that moment Gala remembered her bicycle. And her schoolbag on the carrier!

"Tell me, O Muse . . . ," said Jan, looking hopefully at his daughter. In just a few minutes he would ask her for her lesson book so that he could show his guests her wonderful marks, but right now it was in her saddlebag, soaking up the rain.

"Tell me, O Muse, of that ingenious hero . . . ," Jan persisted, already a little impatient, *"that ingenious hero who traveled far . . ."*

"Far away . . . ," Gala said, "against the fence." She wriggled out of her mother's arms.

"Which fence?" asked the pastor's wife expectantly, confusing Homer with a nursery rhyme. But Gala knew what she had to do.

"The circus fence. I have to go."

"The circus!" bleated Jan, as if she had just said something ridiculous. He couldn't understand how the pastor could find a remark like this as entertaining as the words of Cato the Elder, and when the clergyman slapped his knees and exclaimed, *"Sunt pueri pueri, pueri puerilia tractant!"** Jan thought he was scoffing at him. He snapped at Gala to recite the first lines of the *Odyssey* in the original Greek. The girl's hand went to the pocket in the seam of her dress where she kept her bike key, and she realized she hadn't even locked her bike. And her autograph album was in her bag, and so was her diary, and the sketchbook with the new Caran d'Ache pencils that smelled so good when you opened the box.

"Really, Jan," said the pastor's wife, while clicking open her handbag, "it doesn't matter. Just be grateful for the sparkle in her eyes." She bent over to Gala and slipped her a banknote. "Maybe Daddy will let you go see the elephants tonight." But the smile fell from her face when she looked up at Jan.

"Sometimes I don't know whether you're being contrary or if you're just plain stupid." He'd gone red in the face and tears of shame

* *Children are children, and do childish things.*

welled in his eyes. "She knows it. Come on, Gala, don't show me up like this. You know it. *Andra moi ennepe Mousa polutropon hos mala polla . . .*"

Gala heard the sounds, and they seemed familiar. They spun around inside her head, whizzing past like horses on a merry-go-round that was too fast to jump onto. When she shrugged, she did it the way she'd seen the clown do it, with her eyebrows and the corners of her mouth going up as well, in the hope that it might make the others laugh.

"What stupid children I have!" sighed Jan, just before Gala ran out of the room.

In the auction hall the carts full of flowers had started rolling again. Purple dahlias and salmon orchids rattled over the points and squeaked on the rails, but up above, Gala remained stock-still on the catwalk, searching for words. Lately she had more and more difficulty catching them. As if they were too fast for her. She pictured them the way she had that first time with the pastor, whizzing past on a merry-go-round while she stood in line waiting to get on. As long as she concentrated on a single point, she couldn't make any sense of it, but by quickly following the direction of movement with her eyes, she was able to catch a few sounds, a few syllables at a time, but never a full sentence.

These were the first signs of the disease manifesting itself in Gala—words melting, lights shooting past, sounds bulging—but the child didn't realize it was something to worry about, something she should warn her parents about in the hope of preventing disaster. But when the words started dancing with the shadows, Gala watched them like vivid dreams that come right before you fall asleep. At most, she chided herself for making such a fuss—there was no need for her to get nervous before she was asked to do something. When her father wanted to teach her new poems, she didn't tell him that she couldn't do it anymore; instead, she tried to please him by making an even greater effort to learn the sounds by heart.

If I were just a bit more courageous, she told herself, if only I dared to jump onto that merry-go-round one more time, then I'd get back in control of the words again. But more and more often, they slipped out of her hands, running circles around all those strange ideas inside her head.

. . .

Just as furiously, the market's big clock spun back and forth. The hand shot over the dial that formed the heart of the flower auction as the auctioneer, just as quickly, called out each lot number and the bids for the different consignments of flowers that passed by unrelentingly. The buyers sat, two by two, on a steep stand opposite the auction clock. There were Dutch farmers with faces as round as cheeses, but also dealers from the Middle East, some in turbans and others with black velvet skullcaps. You saw Chinese, and a black man in a blue djellaba was just visible through the thick cigar smoke of two Cubans in army uniforms in the row below him. A place of honor was reserved for the Vatican envoy, who came once a week to purchase flowers for all the altars of the Catholic world and today had set his mind on calla lilies and bargain-priced snow-white petunias. The squat Mediterranean priest had to share his seat with a gigantic Scandinavian woman who leapt up every time something that appealed to her came by, bending forward dangerously to bellow at the auctioneer.

"I want it all," she yelled, "all of it, the whole lot!" The other bidders looked up in annoyance and forgot about the telephones they had held pressed to their ears all morning to ask their mothers back home which scent they wanted to fill the country's bedrooms and living rooms that evening.

At the very top of the stand, behind the last row of bidders, a guide explained the system to Jan, his daughter, and his guest. The lower the price of a consignment fell, the more people wanted it.

Gala wasn't listening. The rhythm of the clock and the calling of the prices formed a cadence in her head and gave her thoughts something to latch onto. In the falling price of carnations she recognized a Catullian meter: *"Passer mortuus est meae puellae,"** she began, and took a few steps away from the others to try to concentrate. *Passer mortuus est* . . . dancing sounds that meant nothing more to her than little gifts to please her father.

To avoid any distractions, she stared down at the floor, where, from her child's perspective, she discovered something peculiar that the adults didn't seem to have noticed. Beneath the benches ran a gutter, as steep as the stand itself. The men and women sat above it on iron grills,

* *My mistress's sparrow is dead.*

through which they dropped all the things they no longer had any use for. From left and right, spilled coffee trickled down along with brown cigarette butts, disposable cups and balls of paper, pieces of stale bread and bits of eel skin. Everything fell into the broad groove and descended to the depths. Who knows, maybe the men and women were so scared of wasting their valuable time that they even defecated there, like cows in a cowshed. There was a whole battery of these sewers, one under each column of seats, and water flowing down them carried away all the rubbish. They were tall slides that you couldn't see the end of. Water was constantly gurgling down the steep gutters, water with its own tempo, gushing water with its own rhythm, interrupted by the splash of falling trash. This wasn't like any meter Catullus ever wrote, and Gala got stuck in the middle of the third line of the second stanza.

It was as if she could feel the blood squeezing through the veins in her temples. No wonder the words have let me down, she thought. There are too many of them, and now there's a blockage. She could feel them jostling even trying to get through first.

"It's just a game," Gala repeated the words her mother had used to comfort her after the pastor and his wife left. "Daddy plays his games, and he's a worse loser than any kid I know."

Jan had forbidden Gala from going to the evening performance of the circus, especially after hearing why she was so keen.

"Of course," he growled, "a clown is all this household needs. Your mother trains the dogs and the monkeys, but I'm the ringmaster. I'd rather be in charge of something with a little more class, but it's my cross and I'll bear it as elegantly as I can. When I step into the cage, I will be obeyed, and anyone who thinks otherwise will feel the whip." Hearing himself rage like this cheered him up so much that the smile returned to his lips. "That's how a lion gets the best out of its cubs, by biting them in the scruff of the neck and shaking them till they squeal. A godforsaken circus, that's what it is, dammit, and the next time someone comes to visit, I'm going to charge admission."

In bed Gala heard the distant, festive music. Her mother lay down next to her to read to her, but stayed there for a while after she had finished.

"I usually let Jan win," she said suddenly to her daughter, calling her husband by his first name as if discussing him with a friend. "And when he struts around with a big smile because he thinks he's the best, that he's got the sweetest wife and the smartest kids, I see that as my reward. The winner isn't the little boy with the trophy, but the person who gets to present it. It's like that with the poems in your head too. They're the prizes in a big game. They're yours. Daddy would love to have them, but he has to earn them first. When you feel like it, you can hand them out, but remember, you can keep them back as well. And the circus, ah, sweetheart . . . It'll come back next year."

Finally her father came to say goodnight as well. With his back to her, he looked out of the window, listening to the music in the distance.

"I'll have to get them to explain that to me in the hereafter," he said pensively, "how people can laugh at bloody clowns."

Something went badly wrong inside Gala's head. She felt it happening while the big auction clock showed the flowers diminishing in value second by second. She listened to the water in the gutters. The words flowed together meaninglessly. They swirled around, then suddenly disappeared into the depths as if being sucked down a plug hole. She had no time to try to recapture the poems her father had drilled into her; it was all she could do to keep her own language under control.

Just then Jan beckoned her. The tour went on, but he and Professor Dogberry hung back, as if expecting something from her. It was time for him to show her off. He wouldn't be able to; Gala felt that clearly enough. She ran up to him and grabbed his hand. The men smiled. Jan lifted her up for a moment, the way he always did. Gala didn't play along. She tugged at his arm and opened her mouth to warn him, but the words on the tip of her tongue made no sense. She immediately let go again. She stood quiet and hunched over to avoid attracting any attention and, as soon as Jan had stepped onto the catwalk with Dogberry, she ran back to the stand.

She had no prizes left to hand out. The only thing she could do for her father now was spare him her defeat. But not a second later and her father was following her.

"What's the matter, sweetheart?" he called out, worried. "Sweetheart, what's wrong?"

In a panic, Gala ducked under the stand and crawled farther away under the benches when she saw his legs approaching. He bent down and looked for her in the shadows under the iron grills. She didn't know how she would ever be able to explain her strange behavior to him. She would rather die than have to tell him about the chaos inside her head. She crawled away farther until one of the refuse gutters blocked her path.

"All of it," she heard the gigantic blonde call out to the auctioneer. "I'm up for everything. I want it all!!!"

When Gala sat down on the slide, she felt the cold water soak up through her clothes. With a shiver, she let herself go. Passing beneath the feet of the bidders, she slid toward darkness. She dropped quickly at first, but soon the gutters curved and headed off to the left and the right. With gentle curves, they seemed to carry Gala crisscross through the market, where the magnificent flowers were lit by the flickering light of flashing cameras. In the middle of the big shed, she shot over the shunting yard between the little trains, touching the bulging cargo with her face and hands and releasing all the smells. Green and yellow, magenta, purple, scarlet and blue petals wafted up into the air. More and more petals dislodged from their stems and mingled with buds and blossoms to form patterns of such intensity that the girl was forced to close her eyes. At that moment, it was as if she'd gone flying off the end of the slide and burst through everything she knew, while all the words in her brain exploded together with the flowers.

"Ahhhhh!" the girl screamed with relief. "*That's* how they fly all across the world!"

And through that whirlwind of color, Gala Vandemberg entered my dreams for the first time.

She lay motionless in the hospital bed. There were small bald spots in her thick black hair where electrodes had been attached to record her brain activity on a long sheet of paper that kept rolling out of a machine.

According to the doctors, cerebrovascular accidents were very rare in children her age and usually caused either by a congenital weakness in a capillary or a small clot in the bloodstream. The stroke had taken place in the left side of Gala's brain and might have been brought on by an epileptic fit. Until Gala regained consciousness and was able to tell them exactly what she had felt, there was little more they could say about it.

The first day her father and mother sat by her bed holding hands, too tense to cry. They were silent, afraid that even one word of superficial solace would reveal the depth of their despair. After Gala had made it through the first night without complications—long hours in which Jan and Anna were obsessed by the demented scratching of the EEG recording the uncontrolled activity in Gala's temporal lobe—Jan managed to convince his wife to go home: the other two girls needed her love as well. But he himself refused to leave Gala alone for even a moment. For two days he sat up straight next to her bed without closing his eyes. He ran every meter of paper that came out of the machine through his hands in the hope of gaining some insight into what his child was thinking. When he suddenly stood up on the morning of the third day, the printout was up to his knees. He left the room and took the bus into town, where he strode into a party shop. Just over an hour later he astonished the nursing staff by reappearing in the neurology department with an enormous, bright yellow flower and a red clown's nose.

"Surely you don't think," he announced, "that Lazarus would have changed his mind if Jesus hadn't convinced him that were still some laughs to be had somewhere." Whereupon he reentered Gala's room, kissed her gently on the forehead, and whispered in her ear that she should hurry up because Auguste the Clown was waiting for her. Less than two minutes later, he fell asleep on the chair for the first time in fifty-six hours, feeling calm and snoring loudly under his clown nose.

For another three long days he stayed by her side, as doleful and lost as a comedian without an audience. Despite his wife's and the doctors' entreaties, he refused to take off the clown nose, even in the presence of visitors he would normally bend over backward to impress. Finally, when Obadiah Dogberry arrived with the head of Jan's faculty to say a polite goodbye on the eve of his return to Yale, the two men discovered the professor of art history at his daughter's bedside, deep in conversation with her favorite bear, which waved a cheerful paw at the two men in three-piece suits. Jan ignored all their questions, even when his boss snapped that he should show some respect for his position and get ahold of himself. When the visitors were about to leave, however, he did say his goodbyes, in the form of three big squirts from the yellow flower on his lapel.

Soon after, the most erratic lines on the EEG calmed. Gala's breathing grew stronger and the specialists assured her parents that she had survived the critical stage and would definitely recover, provided she had absolute rest. Both parents, but Jan in particular, were strongly advised against staying in her room, and, when that proved insufficient, their presence was simply forbidden. In the end Jan nodded, removed the nose, and shuffled off, leaning on his wife's arm so heavily that the porter took him for a patient and refused to call a taxi without authorization from the ward sister.

The next morning Gala opened her eyes. She had been unconscious for almost a week, but it felt like no more than twenty seconds. The first thing she noticed was something black in the corner of the room. The sun was shining on the closed curtains so brightly that, to her sensitive eyes, it looked like a white glow emanating from the fabric, and yet there, a little to the right of the middle, was a spot as black as ink. When she was able to move her eyes, the spot moved with them, and when she was finally able to move her head again, she discovered that it remained in the same place in her field of vision no matter where she looked, always off to one side, so that the edges were always a little vague. At first, it seemed to be moving, undulating, as if the defect were still fluid, but eventually it calmed down and solidified as a rectangle, a small black window that was constantly hiding part of whatever Gala happened to be looking at.

Oh no, she thought, when she began to suspect what had happened, how terrible for Daddy!

Taking Gala in her arms—her daughter still unable to move a single muscle from the neck down—her mother was overcome by emotion. She smothered her with kisses and was reluctant to loosen her grip when Jan wanted to hug his little girl as well. He squeezed her tight, fiercely, without saying a word, and, when he finally let go, it was only to grab her again, briefly, as if he had forgotten something. Then he laid her back on the pillows. He carefully arranged her limp arms by her sides, but was still at a loss for words. Even after they'd sat down and her mother had told her how they'd got through the last few days, Jan remained silent with one hand in his pocket, fingering the flower and the nose, the nose and the flower, unsure whether or not to pull them out. The flower. The nose. He didn't do it. When the duty nurse came half an hour later to tell them they had to leave, he bent over Gala.

"So, little lady, congratulations," he said in a strict voice, "you've outdone yourself once again. You've let me down so many times, I didn't think you could possibly come up with a new way to disappoint me."

It earned him a poke in the side from his wife and, a little later, in the corridor, an indignant remark from the nurse, but in her room Gala was beaming. She realized that it was only a matter of time before everything would be back to normal.

One fine day a professor doing his rounds with a group of female students came up to her bed. The students bemoaned the fate of the pretty little girl being kept in semidarkness and took turns at testing her reflexes, some of them pinching her hand or cheek in encouragement while doing so. The professor raised her eyelid and shone a penlight into her pupil. In long, well-turned sentences, he reassured the young women. When they heard that Gala would probably make a complete recovery, apart from a minor impairment of her vision, several of them sighed so deeply that the top buttons of their well-fitted white coats popped open.

Gala remained like that, motionless in bed, for weeks, for months on end, alone in the bare room. And always that dark window was floating in a corner of her consciousness. There were times when she was scared of it. Scared perhaps that it might get bigger, but also scared that creatures of the night might unlock it and crawl through it to sit down on her bed, knowing she was powerless to defend herself.

But the longer she lay there and the clearer it became that she was not going to regain any more of her eyesight, the more curious she grew about what was actually behind that window. As long as you don't know what something is, thought Gala, it could be anything. On sunny days, for example, when the nurses had cranked up her bed to give her a better view of the outside world, Gala virtually ignored the activity outside on the street corner. Instead she was all the more fascinated by the part of the panorama hidden behind her blind spot. On gray days, she imagined that there, where she couldn't look, the water of a sunny pond glittered, and when she missed her mother or wanted to play with one of her sisters, she simply fantasized that they were there with her, but playing hide-and-seek in the one place she could never find them.

In this way, Gala was seldom alone when confined to bed during the long months of her convalescence. Whenever she wanted to leave her prison, she escaped through her secret hatch to wherever she wanted to go. The things that hid from her there almost always seemed more beautiful and more exciting than anything in her field of vision. And, eventually, just thinking of what she couldn't see was enough to console her for the things she could.

This story is light.

In the telling it must be full of the effects to which Gala's eyes are so sensitive. Our dreams are composed of nothing else. From the radiance of a candle to hallucinogenic halogen: light sets images on fire. Each ray casts a magic glow and is a source of wonder, adding or erasing, enriching or diminishing, emphasizing or dissolving. It makes fantasy plausible, renders the grayest reality translucent, and shimmers like a mirage on the horizon. Light is the tool I have used to create worlds and my own life. Who wouldn't seek to postpone its dying?

1976

"Ah, movement," she said. *"Twirling round and round, what a delight! Can you imagine a greater torture than remaining motionless, like a rock, year upon year?"*

Life composes the facts more brazenly than fiction would ever dare. Later, when this story is coming to an end, Maxim will find it hard to believe that these really were the first words he ever heard Gala speak. One day he will look it up in a well-thumbed script and discover that it was like this:

Gala was sitting still. She spoke slowly and carefully, as if she had been forced to keep silent for months and her lips were still unaccustomed to words. It wasn't until later that afternoon that he realized that this lethargy infused all her movements.

"To be free! To flit from place to place! I would give my life for a night like this. To move!" Keeping her elbows on the arms of the chair, she raised her left forearm as if it were heavy and looked on with astonishment as her own drooping hand began moving in relaxed circles and came to life. *"I cannot imagine that this night will ever pass,"* she said. *"The mere thought is enough to drive me mad!"*

The first reading of *Bal Manekinów* was held in the home of a famous elderly actress who was going to direct the play for Amsterdam's student theater. Her name had drawn quite a crowd. Maxim, always insecure in groups, felt a growing sense of panic as he looked at the other first-year students sitting in a circle in the living room. He didn't know any of them. They were all so busy saying and doing things to make an impression that any urge Maxim may have felt to do the same immediately vanished. What most confused him in social situations was that he always saw people doing one thing while clearly thinking another. He wondered whether he was the only one who noticed this, or if others did too and then pretended they hadn't. In company he felt like a traveler in a foreign country, curious about the customs and annoyed by his own inability to fathom them. At the same time, there was something safe about Maxim's aloofness. He had time to gauge people's intentions calmly, before they did anything. Even when sitting opposite someone, he still felt as though he were observing from the sidelines, half-hidden, and in fact most people were so busy talking about themselves that they didn't really notice Maxim.

He had an unerring eye for which students had enrolled for the summer project to escape their cramped student housing and which had genuine acting ambitions. The latter did everything they could to make an impression on the great actress. She herself was most interested in her huskies, who never stopped barking and pissing on everything close to the ground. Now and then the old woman stopped abruptly in front of someone to stare at them silently with her big childish eyes, until she had just as suddenly had enough, whereupon she resumed pacing and called out from the hall a little later which part he or she should have. In the middle of the room, her assistant took notes. She had a lazy eye and wore a fur draped over her shoulders.

"Ven I vas little, I vas Polish Shirley Temple," the assistant repeated every time someone came in, and then added, sighing deeply, as if all were now lost, "Und das Universitätstheatrum is already booked for ze end of September." It was early May.

Gala showed up thirty minutes late. She appeared in the doorway in a long purple skirt with three flounces and a T-shirt with a conspicuously low neckline. Instead of apologizing, she smiled. That smile alone would have been enough to forgive her for a double murder. One of the coolest guys there surrendered his chair for her and sat down on the floor. The Pole gave a speech about the playwright and his significance to futurism and socialism in the 1920s. Then she handed out the scripts, and the elderly actress, who had gone outside to do some gardening, called through the open doors that the newcomer should read the lead.

"Yes, her in purple, that tasty, voluptuous one!"

Gala turned to the first page. She scrunched up her eyes, as if blinded by the paper. She had a strange face. Her cheekbones were broad rather than high and her face would have looked flat except for the small upturned nose that gave it a classic touch. As if the others weren't sitting there waiting for her, she calmly read through the lines that opened the play. At last her lips parted. They were full and her lipstick was flaming red and the corners of her mouth had a natural tendency to curl.

"Ah, movement," she said languidly.

The play was a dated satire of the bourgeoisie's contempt for the masses: on the eve of Mardi Gras the mannequins of a Parisian fashion house come to life. When a congressman stumbles upon them, they behead him. One of their number puts the human head on his shoulders and goes to the ball of the industrialist Monsieur Arnaux, where he wreaks havoc amid the intrigues of Parisian high society. In the end, he prefers his own wooden head to a human head that is constantly scheming. He gives up his freedom and becomes a mannequin again. In other words, the whole story could have been told as a five-minute sketch. The reading took two and a half hours, interrupted once for a coffee break and once because one of the huskies pissed on the student who had give up his seat for Gala. Even before the unfortunate had dried off, he was informed that, on second thought, instead of the lead role that had been allocated to him at first, Monsieur Arnaux, he would now be playing Mannequin 2, a supporting part.

"Make Arnaux the tall one with that head!" shouted the elderly actress, who was taking the opportunity to clear out a built-in cupboard full of manuscripts from her glory days.

"Which head?" The Pole scanned the circle.

"That one," the actress answered, pointing at Maxim, "leaning back like that, as if he's looking down on everything."

Finally someone came by to show sketches of the set, or what had to pass as one, given the budget of 450 guilders. In the doorway the famous actress announced in a quavering voice that, as an old woman, she had reconsidered, not feeling strong enough for a project with youngsters and therefore delegating the direction to the Polish child star, whereupon everyone said a dazed goodbye and fanned out over the enormous square.

In the passage that cuts under the Rijksmuseum, Maxim was overtaken by a cyclist. It was Gala. Just as she was passing, she turned toward him and called: "See you Tuesday!" She saw Maxim inadvertently look around to see whether she was talking to someone else and, since she didn't know his name, added, "*À bientôt,* Monsieur Arnaux!"

"Oh," he called back, casting about for something smart to say. "Yes, yes, Tuesday!" But Gala had already left him behind. Never before had Maxim seen someone wiggling her hips on a bicycle. He quickened his pace to prolong his study of the way Gala's full buttocks slid slowly from left to right over her bicycle seat. He was eighteen, so in his thoughts he was already sitting naked on her carrier with his hands on that flesh.

That Tuesday evening Maxim arrived three-quarters of an hour early. The rehearsals were being held in a sterile lecture hall on the university island. He waited between the rows of seats, which sloped up like an amphitheater. The small stage backed onto tall windows through which the monumental facade of a diamond factory was visible on the other side of a broad canal. An advertising boat shaped like an enormous diamond had just pulled in to dock. On it you could read the factory's slogan in glittering letters: THE MANY FACETS OF AMSTERDAM.

At home, Maxim had thought up a complete arsenal of witty replies to anything Gala might possibly say to him, but she wasn't there. Gala never arrived early anywhere. She never even arrived on time. The standard fifteen minutes between classes at the university was never enough leeway for her, and, as a result, all lectures, rehearsals, and other gatherings fell silent just after they'd started, because she'd come in. She never said or did anything disruptive, but it was still impossible to avoid being distracted by the sight of her making her way to a seat. Boys and men stared at her with their tongues between their teeth, much to the annoyance of most of the women, who scowled at each other, convinced it was deliberate. It really was hard to believe that the beautiful young woman could be completely unaware of the impression she made. For minutes after she took her seat, a trail of something yearning, misunderstood, and disturbingly feminine lingered where she had walked. Only in old movies do people make entrances to such effect, but then it's more emphatic, slowly descending a long staircase or being drawn in by a team of naked slaves. With Gala, you had to see it to believe it. And the only person who didn't see it was Gala herself. It was as if the black spot that had always remained in her field of vision prevented her from ever seeing herself. That probably attracted more attention than anything else: how naturally she evaded any semblance of posing. Disrupting things by arriving late annoyed her, but she was simply so indifferent to time that she found it impossible to take account of it.

"Everyone is constantly making things run smoothly," she would say, "so there's absolutely no reason for me to worry about it." And whoever got to know Gala had to admit that, despite all her delays, she never missed anything important. Schedules and timetables, diaries and agendas, all seemed to arrange themselves to suit her, instead of the other way round.

"Ah," she laughed when someone mentioned it, "rules are only a problem for people who follow them."

They ran through a couple of scenes that evening, spending most of their time on the choreography at the start of the play, when the mannequins first realize they can move. All the students were allocated a place and a movement to rehearse while saying their lines. Oddly enough, their wooden acting did not make them more plausible as dummies.

It was only in the last fifteen minutes that it was the turn of Gala and Maxim, who had to seduce her. He had never seduced anyone before and it would have taken him years to pluck up the courage, but now he could hide behind someone else's words. He held them in his left hand while wrapping his other arm around Gala's waist and pulling her up against him. She didn't seem surprised to find her lover standing behind her and offered no resistance, laying one hand on his. She slumped back, turning her face to rest against his chest. Her hair brushed his cheek and her buttocks pressed against him. Maxim's breathing quickened as if it were really happening, though the thought that he was only playing a role nudged him on. He pushed his hips forward and felt his stage lover react. He glanced at his script, then spoke his next lines while bowing forward to kiss her on the throat.

"You checking a turkey at ze butcher's?" the Pole interrupted, then spent the last minutes of the rehearsal on a cursing, sighing, and mocking attempt to stimulate the two young actors to show a little more intimacy.

After rehearsal, the whole company adjourned to the bar in a cinema across the road. Gala even got held up crossing the street, and Maxim, who had been the first to enter, thought for a moment that she wasn't coming, but in the end the Pole ordered everyone to move up so that Gala could sit next to her.

Maxim never went to bars on his own account, and he found it hard to understand what others saw in them. He saw people laughing, moderately or effusively, but saw even more clearly that they weren't enjoying themselves and were desperately trying to avoid admitting it. If they didn't come for their own enjoyment, what was the point? Maxim heard them fill entire evenings prattling about themselves, who they were, what they did, what they thought, but he had never felt any urge to do the same. If someone so much as asked him how things were going, he was usually surprised and lost for words, as if he had never given a thought to something so futile. In fact, he just didn't want to talk about it. He had always thought that this was because he didn't consider himself and his thoughts important enough, but since finishing school he had felt stronger. Now he had started to believe that his thoughts might actually be too precious to expose to strangers. Just look at the way they treated them! Unlike most people's, Maxim's ideas and dreams had not been sculpted through interaction with others, but arduously constructed in isolation. He judged them too fragile to withstand the verbal violence that erupted in social situations. After all, most people hogged the stage by vocally hacking away at the words of others, with loud blows and not really listening, whereas they themselves had a great need to be heard. That was why they were so often delighted with someone who didn't strive to contribute an opinion. In company, Maxim seemed like the ideal listener. By always looking people in the eye and nodding his head at appropriate intervals, he encouraged others to dissect their own souls.

He now noticed that Gala was a listener too. She was being monopolized by the Pole, who was capitalizing on the attention of the young men who had slid their chairs up toward them. She provoked them with sexual innuendos and asked Gala insinuating questions as well, hoping she'd play along and turn the men on even more. But Gala's almost invariable reaction was an enigmatic smile that could be meaningless just as well as it could be meaningful. When finally forced to say something, she never said more than a couple of short sentences that promptly brought everything back down to earth and elicited smiles from the men, who were anxious to show that they had joined the table for her and not the middle-aged Shirley Temple.

Maxim had made sure to sit far enough away to avoid being drawn into the conversation, but no less than three times he thought he noticed Gala looking at him. Twice their eyes met after one of her quips, as if she were trying to reassure herself that he had heard it. The third time was around eleven thirty. The bar filled up with people who had seen the second showing of the film, and the theater club was crushed into a corner. Some of them thought it was time to leave, but a small group stayed behind and ordered a bottle of wine. Maxim watched Gala give two guys the brush-off, firmly, almost bluntly, but strangely enough with a smile that seemed almost to promise the opposite, so that they slinked off hopeful rather than disappointed.

Maxim had a train to catch. He had stood up and was waiting for a lull in the conversation to say goodbye, when Gala caught his eye for the third time. Her mood seemed to have changed completely from one moment to the next. Deeply sorrowful, she sought his support, as if no one else would understand. "How far we are from all this, you and I," Maxim read in her eyes, and although he told himself at the same time that he was deluding himself, he hung his coat up again, slid his chair closer, and poured another glass of wine.

Gala wasn't the main reason he decided to miss his train. While hanging around in the bar, toward midnight, he felt a rising sense of freedom. If this was what people sought in places like this, maybe he could understand it after all. As long as he could remember, Maxim had cherished the idea of a grander life to come. As a child, he would lie in bed listening to sounds and voices, imagining a party in full swing somewhere in the big house. He didn't go out and look for it, because the idea that he was expected there was enough of an adventure. This disquieting expectation had sustained him throughout his childhood. Whenever his character and circumstances prevented him from participating in real life, snatches of consolation from everything that was still possible reached him like distant music through an open window. It had always been an abstract passion, formless, without a name and without an end, but tonight, for the first time, he felt he had recognized someone who had also been invited to that future celebration. In Gala he saw something he had probably known forever: how exciting it could be to feel alone when gaiety was all around.

When he was shown the door at closing time, Maxim was completely plastered. While the rest of the group said goodbye, he tried to read his watch.

"Ten minutes ago, and I would have made the night bus," he mumbled to no one in particular, and the next thing he was sitting, without knowing exactly how he got there, on the back of Gala's bicycle, seasick from the view and feeling somewhat unsure about how fast he seemed to be catching up on life.

He tried to find something to hold on to, but didn't quite dare to seize the flesh bobbing up and down in front of him. Earlier that evening, he had simply pulled those same buttocks up against him, as if he did it every day. Obviously it didn't matter how you acted something, he thought, as long as you were convincing, and he clamped his fingers around the steel frame.

"Sometimes," Gala said, "people bore me so much with all their talk that I can no longer restrain myself."

"I can always restrain myself," Maxim replied. "Yes, if you have anything that needs restraining, I'm the one."

"There's no reason for all that . . . Don't you know that? People are so full of themselves they can't possibly believe you're not interested in them."

"What most surprises me is how heavy their words are. The lighter they are, the more they weigh me down."

"It's like they make you dirty, as if their stupidity sticks to you."

"But you still stayed till the very end."

"It only looked like that. I was miles away."

There were potholes in the road and Gala was too heavily laden to dodge them. Maxim had to grab on to her waist. It wasn't as soft as it had been earlier. Under his hands he felt her flanks harden and relax in turn, as she strained against the pedals.

"Shut up, I shout, when their lips just keep chattering, shut up, you're driving me up the wall, but they don't even notice. Sometimes I imagine slapping them in the face. You should try it, it's such a relief."

"And what if they keep going?"

"Then I scratch out their eyes." Gala clawed the air with one hand. "I have to. If I don't follow my whims, they'll explode. In the end I see them babbling away with their skin hanging in shreds from their bloody faces." Gala laughed. Just to be on the safe side, Maxim decided not to say another word.

The last bus was still waiting at the bus station, late for no reason, but just as they rode up, the driver started the engine and took off at full speed. Gala didn't hesitate for a moment, turning her bike crossways and forcing the driver to stop.

"It never needs to get boring," she sighed as the doors slammed between them, and then louder, "The possibilities are endless."

When Maxim raised his hand, he thought he saw her pursing her lips to blow him a kiss, but he couldn't be sure because he could see his own reflection in the window as well, and, when the bus drove off, he immediately lost his balance and flew backward down the aisle.

Ah, movement!

In Amsterdam in the seventies, two people cycling off into the night together could only mean one thing. At the next rehearsal, Maxim noticed the other young men looking at him with envy. Although his prestige was unearned, he still caught himself feeling a certain pride, as if he had come a little closer to Monsieur Arnaux. When Gala finally arrived and they were able to rehearse their scene, the kisses he planted on her neck were calmer, so prolonged that they no longer reminded anyone of a poultry inspection.

Slowly but surely over the following weeks, Gala and Maxim grew comfortable with each other's bodies, but only in the roles of Solange and Monsieur Arnaux. One night, when he ran his hands over her breasts, he felt her nipples responding under the black crepe of her dress.

THE MANY FACETS OF AMSTERDAM, screeched the neon letters on the facade of the diamond factory, which flicked on behind the actors every night at this time. Somewhere inside the amphitheater someone giggled, but the two actors had eyes only for each other.

Gala spoke her lines as they were written, and a little later Maxim delivered his speech without a moment's hesitation, even though his fingers had gone back to those same places, as if they couldn't believe what they felt there. It made him dizzy with pleasure, not only from the power with which his heart was driving the blood to his loins, but above all because of the violence of the realization that he, *he,* had been able to evoke a reaction like that. It moved him. Perhaps, yes, perhaps, for just a moment, it wasn't so much that his excitement moved him, as that being moved excited him.

Maxim wanted to disappear.

Maxim wanted to let himself be seen.

That was why he wanted to act. He saw acting as the only possible way to unite the forces conflicting inside him. It was a childish longing. A lineless drawing. An idea, nothing more. He was full of such ideas, grand but vague, and he trusted them like friends, while he saw facts as enemies. As long as you don't focus on something, he thought, there's still a possibility that it can become anything you want. In that same shapeless way, he felt he carried other lives inside him. He had so many desires and they were so extreme; they could never possibly fit into his own image of himself. Now he thought that this was the actor's paradox: hiding yourself behind your own possibilities.

So it was tonight, at last, running his hands over the curves of Gala's body, that he broke through his own limits for the very first time. Maxim felt bigger, stronger, more brazen than usual, and Gala sensed it too. Her body responded to his dream. When others believed in him, he believed in himself. Here was Maxim's ecstasy. Tonight more people could see him than ever before. In his role, for just a moment, he had disappeared.

. . .

The following Tuesday, during the seduction scene, Maxim was wooden and inhibited. All week he had been dreading it. The sweeter that moment became in his memory, the less enthusiastic he grew about trying to perform the same trick again. When the evening arrived, the idea of someone as shy as himself trying to play a seducer seemed completely absurd. Even the Pole's psychological approach—"So grab ze rutting beach, you are a dog, so take her!"—failed to help him.

It took a few weeks before he dared to rest his fingers on her breasts again, but when they finally reached them, now lingering longer and more emphatically, no effect was discernible. Gala had now repeated her lines so many times that she no longer heard them. Even her intonation was almost unchanged from one rehearsal to the next. In the absence of any significant response from Maxim, she felt no need to draw on her emotions and lose herself in her performance. She went through the motions as if they had been fixed from the beginning. The underlying passion was gone.

Maxim was shocked. First by her coldness, and then by his own ferocity. His sense of betrayal at her indifference was as intense as if she were cheating on him. He was angry, he was saddened, disgusted, and he could no longer bear having her body pressing against his own; viciously he shoved her away. On the sidelines the few people who were watching snapped to attention. He slapped her bottom as hard as he could and immediately took another swing at her, now at her face, but she blocked the blow with her arm.

"Ow," screamed Gala, "ow!"—but it was Solange who turned around slowly as if to spit fire into his face. Maxim went back to the start of the scene. Their words ricocheted through the lecture theater. He pulled her up against him again. A man like Monsieur Arnaux, he decided, does *not* allow himself to be betrayed a second time. From now on, he would be less restrained. He would rub her nipples between his fingers until they were hard. He didn't have long to wait. Solange gasped for breath.

Their concentration did not wane again. No matter how many rehearsals followed, one of them always succeeded in provoking the other by being brazen, taunting, shameless . . . Some of the pinches and groans remained secret—when she nipped his earlobe or when his tongue shot out to lick the salt from under her arm—but otherwise Maxim and Gala played their excitement openly to the auditorium, where the other students sat and watched politely as if they were learning something. Only the Polish Shirley Temple seemed to have figured out what was really going on. She didn't mention it during rehearsals because the unsolicited eroticism added a little zest to her directing, but afterward she sometimes looked at Maxim and Gala while sardonically raising the eyebrow over her walleye.

"Dat shows de real amateurs," she sneered one day. "They don't know where de life starts and de acting ends."

Strangely enough, the complete lack of restraint that Maxim and Gala displayed was confined to the rehearsal room. Beyond it, Maxim's shyness descended like a bell jar. Even his breathing became shallower, as if to preserve the air he had left. On the way to the bar on the other side of the road, he sometimes walked beside Gala, but once inside they invariably sat apart and sometimes at different tables. None of the people there suspected that Gala and Maxim were still feeling each other out from a distance. Generally they would both listen to someone else's conversation while Maxim practiced the kind of quips that came to Gala so easily. With the odd word and an amiable smile, he tried to master his boredom. At first he would glance at his female lead to harvest a smile after each triumph, just as their eyes met now and then in search of support when someone had said something incredibly dull. At times like that they both felt so withdrawn that they might as well have been floating up from their chairs to gaze down on the others. A glance, a gesture, a few nails clawing the air was enough to acknowledge their complicity. And eventually they were so attuned to each other that they could drop the nods and winks. They were so convinced they could read the other's thoughts that they no longer needed confirmation.

This intimacy was much more important to Gala than physicality. It excited her more than the moments during rehearsals when they were entangled in each other's arms and his arousal was pulsing against her body. Then she'd just give a naughty smile and brush against him with a hip or thigh, because that happened to be the role she was playing. It was only teasing and meant almost nothing to her. But the idea that someone could be so taken with her thoughts as to harmonize his own thinking with them—that excited her. It stirred her senses and kept her awake at night, as if he were always somewhere nearby and might lash out again at any moment. It spurred her to stay one step ahead of him in everything she did. She was determined to keep surprising him.

After that first night, Maxim never missed the last train again. He left on time, often before anyone else, disappearing wordlessly, if possible. Outside he caught his breath, relieved to have his own thoughts to himself again. The cackles and guffaws tumbling through the bar's open window reassured him, just as the sounds in the big house had reassured him years before: there was a party somewhere!

Gala watched him go, but he never waved, at least not as far as she saw, not before he disappeared behind the black window in the corner. No doubt, he turned back once he was there. To make him jealous, she leaned a little more heavily on the student who played Mannequin 2.

At home in his provincial town, Maxim closed his eyes, called Gala to mind, and took pleasure in her image as young men do. Then, while recovering, he tried to reconcile his image of himself with everything that was happening to him.

One day toward the end of June, Maxim's dreams suddenly gathered momentum. It was Mannequin 2's birthday, so instead of adjourning to the cinema bar after rehearsal, the whole troupe headed off to his place, nearby, above the old diamond factory warehouse on a lane ending abruptly at the canal. There were no chairs or sofas in his attic, only cushions and shabby mattresses. The Pole held out her arms and flapped her hands until two men lowered her onto the cushions. She kicked off her shoes, slid the straps of her top down a little, spread out the fur she invariably wore draped over her shoulders during rehearsals, and lay back like a baby on a bearskin.

Everyone crawled around wearing blankets and lengths of fabric, whipping up clouds of dust that hung over the candles and incense pots like stuffy halos. While a circle loudly formed, Maxim opened one of the wooden skylights. When he turned back, he saw Gala lying on her stomach beside Mannequin 2, who rested his head on the small of her back as if he had just received his first birthday present. Maxim had to brace himself and urge three people to move along a little before he succeeded in sitting down next to Gala, determined to do everything in his power to stop Mannequin 2 before he started unwrapping.

When the hash was passed around, Maxim considered joining in. It would have fitted his idea of living a life that teemed with forbidden pleasures and sensual abandon, if only the dope smokers he had known hadn't seemed so small. They didn't smoke because they, like him, wanted to experience something unprecedented, but because they had already abandoned all hope of anything unprecedented ever happening in their lives. Mannequin 2 sucked back like that as well. The way he enjoyed himself was flaccid and listless. He passed the joint to Gala. She took it and studied the filter through her lashes, as if reluctant to give in without a struggle. Then she pursed her flaming red lips, sucked, and closed her eyes. She handed the joint to Maxim and, keeping her eyes on him, opened her lips to let the smoke spiral up out of her mouth.

Maxim played his role as best he could. Since he had never smoked, the usual slapstick ensued—mouthing the joint, sucking, holding in the smoke, coughing and trying to hide his choking—but by the fourth or fifth toke, he had the knack of it. He held his breath until Gala looked at him. Then he opened his mouth the way he had seen her do it. A little later she seemed to dissolve behind the smoke escaping from his lungs.

He came to because Gala was shaking him. Urgently. A couple that had been going at it in the corner quickly gathered their clothes and rushed off. Mannequin 2 leapt around over the cushions.

"What kind of idiot opens a window?" he shouted while throwing a bucket of water onto a length of tulle that was being consumed by flames. The wind had blown one of the curtains too close to an incense pot. The Pole noticed it first and attempted to douse the flames with her whiskey. Finally she was forced to sacrifice her fur, which Mannequin 2 now used to attack the smoldering cushions. He had almost conquered the fire, but he was no longer in the mood for a party.

Outside with Gala, Maxim realized that this time he wouldn't even make the night bus. Gala ran in the opposite direction, toward the water at the end of the lane. She stepped onto the dock and took a few deep breaths.

"I'm dizzy," she said. "I have to lie down."

"We shouldn't have smoked." He put his arm around her shoulders. He was shocked by how suddenly the smile that always lingered around her lips disappeared. She wobbled and grabbed hold of him.

"I'll take you home," he said, although he could see that it was too late for that.

"It's not the smoking."

All at once Gala's knees buckled and she lay down flat on the planks. Maxim looked around, as if expecting to find someone standing by with instructions. A stiff breeze was blowing over the water and pushing up cold and damp between the planks. All Gala had on was a thin skirt and a sleeveless T-shirt. He sat down next to her.

"Come on," he said gently, "this is no place to lie down."

"It's fine." Her voice sounded clear. She knew what she wanted. "I'll just rest a little, then I'll be okay again." She scooped up some water and splashed it on her face. Startled, she sat up. "Although . . . headache," she said, "you need to be careful not to hurt yourself."

"Always," said Maxim with growing uncertainty, "and everywhere." Now he *really* wanted help. He would have gone to fetch some if he hadn't been so scared that Gala would tumble into the canal if he let go. She looked around. She tried to see what was hidden in her blind spot, and when she turned her head far enough, the advertising boat appeared, in the same place where it had been tied up the whole time.

"Oh," she exclaimed, beaming like a child, "the diamond!" The discovery seemed to revive her. "Yes, the diamond, how beautiful!" She wanted to get to the boat and tried to stand up, but when that was too much for her, she crawled over on all fours. Her skirt caught on a nail and tore. Maxim jumped up and tried to stop her, pulling her up onto her feet. She reacted like an angry child and lashed out with both hands, as if he were trying to keep her from a treasure she had spent years searching for.

"I have to go there. I have to go there now!" she shouted, and Maxim, having no idea what to do, let her go.

It was only a small boat with a glass superstructure. The cheaply mounted panes of glass were designed to imitate the shapes of a cut stone, ending at a blunt point where the name of the factory was written in glittering letters. The pane that served as a door hung on rickety hinges. Gala had no trouble jerking it open and sat down on the floor of the glass cage, sheltered from the wind.

"And now we set sail," she shouted.

"Yes," Maxim answered to accommodate her. "It's just like we're about to set sail." The boat almost shot out from under him when he stepped into it.

"No," intoned Gala, as if the adventure ahead demanded her utmost concentration, "not *like* we're about to set sail. We're going."

"We can't," Maxim tried, and, when she insisted, he added, "We'd need the ignition key!"

Gala stood up impatiently and started untying the thick rope with her small hands. "Now. Now." He helped, and while they disentangled the hawser their hands touched. Finally he put a foot against the dock and pushed off. They shot off toward the middle of the canal, where they were picked up by the sluggish current caused by the nightly opening of the locks around the city. Drifting on the fresh polder water that was flushing the canals, they passed under a high brick bridge on their way into the old city.

"They always make me mournful, these houses." Gala was lying on the bottom of the boat with Maxim beside her. The imposing facades along the side of the canal were only partly visible and distorted by the glass panes of the diamond advertisement.

"Mournful?"

"The way they'll be in three hundred years, the broken windows, the crumbling walls." She squinted. "The damp has got under the canvases and in the wind they crack even more. Rooms stripped bare, only the marble mantel still in place. I can't stand it."

"Why should they fall apart? They've been here for centuries."

"Can't you see?" Baffled, Gala sat up and pointed at the sky. "There, what's left of a chimney. Splinters of broken rafters against the moonlit sky!"

Maxim was still hoping that it would turn out to be a game, something like shapes in clouds or, for his part, a Strindberg monologue, but when her voice started to quiver and he noticed a fat tear in the corner of an eye, he knew he was in deep trouble.

"And the quays, crumbling, caving in." And sure enough, now she really was crying. "Slowly the sand is carried off to the sea." She stared at him again with that bizarre, intense look, the way old people can stare at a child, as if they'd like to suck the life out of it.

"I thought everyone saw that."

Maxim shook his head cautiously.

"No," she went on, "how could they? Those girls on bikes there . . . They're already being eaten away. Like skeletons, people sit in their regular spot behind the window. The advertisements have blown off the walls. The neon lights shatter on the shop fronts. Only a few old, thick cables are left hanging, dangling in the wind. They could fall any minute now. Dear God, why doesn't anyone see it? I always thought everyone could see that."

"Yes," said Maxim. "Oh yes, now I see it." But of course he couldn't see anything. His heart was in his mouth. He deeply regretted the whole adventure. Living life to the full placed exaggerated demands on people. Wasn't there some way of plunging in one foot at a time instead of immediately going under?

To his relief, he discovered a paddle under the seat. They were bobbing up and down in one of the widest canals, not far from a houseboat that was within paddling range. But just when he was about to get up, Gala turned around to face him and laid her head on his chest. Suddenly calm, she briefly raised her upper body so that he could wrap his arm around her.

"It won't be long now," she said. "Take care of me. You'll take care of me. Promise? Promise you'll take care of me!" He promised and she grinned, open, radiant. "It's going all right, isn't it? I'm still talking. I am, I can hear myself. Maybe it'll drift over."

The floating home was already behind them when the advertising boat threatened to get caught behind one of the basalt titans bearing the piers of a bridge from the thirties. While a nest of grebes stared at them, Gala and Maxim bobbed up and down in the filth that had gathered in the backwash. But finally they caught a faster current away from the center of town and passed the tall somber figures with their heads bent under their heavy load.

"I'm only scared when I'm alone," Gala said, slurring her words, "but I'm not alone, am I? Weird, isn't it? Alone, alone, alone, alone." She laughed. "What a strange word it is, alone, simply ridiculous: alone, alone, alone . . ."

"Not at all," Maxim said, "I'm with you."

"Yes." Gala beamed like a child that has been given a present. "Yes." She pointed at her mouth and said, "Spri bilissiti?" Since he didn't understand, she pursed her lips and pointed at them. Her eyes were now locked onto his. Her eyelids were drooping. She looked at him urgently from under her lashes, fragile.

"Spri bilissiti!"

She opened her mouth and pointed at her tongue. Maxim knew that something was about to go seriously wrong. He tried to free himself to paddle, but Gala wouldn't let him. Her fingers clawed at his chest, as if she were afraid she was going to fall. Wailing like a frightened animal, she signaled that he mustn't let her go. He felt tension, but no panic. Perhaps because Gala herself relaxed as soon as he lay down again. More than anything else, he felt flattered that she dared to let herself go in his arms. Because she *was* going. Slowly she slid away, Maxim felt that clearly. And while she slipped away from him, he rose up on the wings of her trust. He grew calm. These were the moments that mattered, when everything could be decided in a single second.

She pointed at his mouth, more urgently.

"What is it, darling?" Maxim asked, and it was the first time he had heard himself say the word. But was he talking to a woman or a child? "Just relax, what do you want me to do?" And he was intensely moved that someone dared to put herself in his hands.

"Are you thirsty?"

Gala shook her head. She pointed at his mouth. All he could think of was to kiss her on the forehead. And again. She shook her head and pointed at her mouth. Her mouth! She could no longer speak, but made little groaning sounds, weeping deep within about not being able to make him understand. Then he kissed her, not making a fierce and exaggerated show of it like on the stage, but carefully. First their lips touched without any pressure at all, as if passing by chance and only briefly lingering, but when she opened her mouth to him and he felt her breath in the back of his throat, he naturally went further.

"Oh!" she exclaimed in admiration, beaming.

Maxim moved closer with his legs wrapped around her, the way he'd sat behind her on the bicycle, and when he saw her widely dilated eyes roll back at the start of the epileptic fit, he held her tight with all his strength.

"Let it go, Gala, I'm here, sweetheart, I'm here, aren't I? Gala darling, dear Gala, Gala darling, it'll be all right."

They could have been wrestling with passion, catching each other and then slipping away from each other again, the way new lovers raise each other's body only to press it down again. Shoulders, feet, arms, and legs banged against the bottom of the boat. Sweat began to flow and heavy breathing sounded in the night. If people had been walking along the quay, they would have smiled or felt a pang of jealousy, thinking back on the hours in which they themselves had been snared by that kind of love. The jolting of the young bodies spread over the water in circles that grew until they broke against the banks.

On the bottom of the boat, Maxim measured his strength against Gala's. He was stronger, but for the first few minutes she had the advantage of a madness that stopped at nothing. Even her fiercest swipes seemed involuntary, as if controlled by something beyond her. Over and over he was caught out by the erratic way her muscles contracted, hitting and kicking. Her movements were unpredictable. Dangerous. As if determined to inflict injury. Again and again her head bashed against the ribs of the boat, and whenever he leapt in between to cushion the blows there was always an arm or leg that lashed out with wood-splintering power, cutting and grazing itself in the process.

But finally her body came to rest and rolled back. The muscles that had gone through such contortions relaxed, still quivering from the strain. Maxim leaned back with relief and gently let her slack body sag against his. Now moving only to the rhythm of his breathing, she lay there heavily. One by one, he dislodged the black hairs stuck to her forehead. He stroked her cheek and wiped the drops of blood away from the corner of her mouth. He spat on his thumb to wash away the smudged mascara under her lashes. Then he wrapped his arms around her, felt her breathing, and, for a few moments, felt so intimately linked to this woman that he thought they would never be separate again.

When he became aware of the chafing and burning of his own

injuries, he rested his head. For a long time, he lay there like that with Gala's head on his chest, looking at the moonlight, broken by all the facets of the diamond, differently every time, sparkling and unpredictable, falling inside the boat in countless rays and colors.

The boat had been motionless for quite a while. Maxim opened the glass hatch, lifted Gala out, and laid her down carefully on the sand. They had run aground on a large sandbank just outside the city—maybe this is Amsterdam's beach, he thought, with the sea far away, at low tide, or, if the city doesn't happen to lie on the coast, we'll make the broad, empty flats an excavation for the new harbor. Maxim took off his shirt and soaked it in the water. Then he thoroughly cleaned all those places where she had soiled herself in her trance, including the most intimate. He had never touched a woman there. He did it slowly and gently, but without hesitation or ulterior motives, because, all this time, the only thing he wanted was for Gala to regain consciousness feeling cool and clean and with nothing to be ashamed of.

When she opened her eyes, he was sitting next to her on the ground and dabbing her forehead. It took a while before she could make herself understood. Meanwhile he tried to help by asking one question after the other—"How are you? What's my name? What happened? Can you see how beautiful the moon is on the water? Are you thirsty? Does it hurt? Do you feel like crying? Shall I sing for you? Where are you now?"—not because he wanted answers, but because he was afraid that her attention might drift and she might slip away from him again. Every few minutes, he used his fingers to drip some moisture onto her lips, which were still bleeding in two places.

"Sweet," she mumbled finally, with a swollen tongue that had been caught between her molars on both sides.

"Shouldn't you take something?"

She nodded, but shrugged.

"Forgot."

"How can you forget something like that?"

"It makes me dopey. Don't want you thinking I'm dopey."

"Dopey?" Maxim kissed her on the forehead as easily as he had when she was unconscious. She rolled over onto her side and pulled up her legs; it hurt. He brushed the sand off her back, which was moist with sweat, turned toward her, and snuggled up closer. "Let me reassure you . . . ," he continued. "Dopey, you weren't."

"I'm glad," said Gala, and a little later she added, "I don't want to miss anything, anywhere."

"Me neither," Maxim replied eagerly. Suddenly he couldn't bear the idea of having neglected so many aspects of life. As if he had walked past with his eyes shut. Now that Gala was calm and the tension was ebbing away, he had difficulty restraining his tears. With one ear on the sand, he could hear the waves coming in. The water made a sucking noise as it washed back between the grains. Gradually the realization sank in that, during the whole adventure, he had scarcely given himself a second thought. Just as in his scenes on the stage with Gala, he had done what he had to do without being conscious of himself doing it. He took that for maturity—acting autonomously without having to think about it—and considered the compulsion to take yourself by the hand and ponder the consequences of every deed as something childish, a rigidity he would eventually grow out of. He tried to remember whether he had ever lost himself in someone so completely before. I've got to stick close to Gala, he thought, and learn to see as she does.

"So, she has finally deflowered you, has she?" As charming as ever, the Pole shouted it out from the other side of the lecture theater. Everyone noticed that the tension between Solange and Monsieur Arnaux had disappeared from one rehearsal to the next. Their seduction scene had become somehow self-evident. It was no longer a brazen demonstration of intimacy. Although Maxim still massaged her breasts and Gala writhed as requested, the piquancy of their acting had given way to restrained tenderness, something the director couldn't use at all.

"Darling, I of all people know that de Dutch man needs a helping hand," she said to Gala, "but couldn't you wait until after de premiere? You look like an old married couple!"

Since their night on the Amsterdam beach, Maxim and Gala had seen each other every day. After lectures they popped into a tearoom to eat cakes, one night they went to the cinema, and Wednesday afternoon saw them stretched out on the red plush of the Concertgebouw staircase, listening to a free performance by the renowned resident orchestra. When they wanted to go for a drink afterward, Gala suggested the museum of modern art, whose restaurant lay on the other side of the square, surrounded by a large pond. Instead of walking around to the main entrance, she took off her shoes, tucked the hem of her long skirt up under her belt, and stepped into the water, terrifying a school of carp.

"Come on," she said, wading toward the restaurant, "if you know where you want to go, why take a detour?"

Maxim had never even walked on the grass if there was a sign telling him not to, but he didn't want to be a spoilsport. Encouraged by the people at the outdoor tables, he kicked off his shoes and rolled up his trousers. With Gala he wasn't afraid to show himself anywhere.

Arriving at an outdoor café, they settled down for a long, drawn-out conversation. Others could have squeezed it into half an hour, but Maxim and Gala were so absorbed by each other's company that the urge to talk or ask questions simply faded away. As long as thoughts were enough, words seemed almost inappropriate. Their silences were three parts satisfaction and one part the awkwardness inspired by a misunderstanding, each thinking the other's conversation was more scintillating than their own, and each mistakenly suspecting that the other's silence was given over to the formulation of original thoughts that neither wanted to interrupt. Nothing could have been further from the truth. They both enjoyed the pauses in the conversation, and when one of them finally broke the silence, the discussion was animated because there was nothing they had to do, and nothing either wanted to hold back.

They spent quite a while in this hazy state before they finally got around to the seizure. Gala and Maxim were lying on the grass under an almond tree in the middle of an enormous roundabout. Across the road was a major brewery, and its big copper kettles caught the sun, casting a warm yellow sheen over the branches and the two young people. Gala had to cover her eyes from the glare. She told Maxim about her sensitivity to light and the stroke she had suffered as a child. The consequences had been limited to the black spot, which she tried to explain, and more or less regular seizures.

"I'm a little careless with my medication," she said, as if that were an achievement. "And when I do take it, I don't follow the directions that strictly. Not at all, if you ask some people. No drinking, no smoking, early to bed. Am I supposed to live like an old lady?"

"But aren't seizures like that dangerous?"

"Something could always rupture." Smiling, she snapped her fingers against her temple. Maxim wondered why her nonchalance annoyed him.

"I don't understand why you would take that kind of risk."

"Is that any way to live, playing it safe?" asked Gala, surprised. In the silence that followed, she looked at him with big eyes. It reminded him of the way she'd stared at him on the beach, like an animal caught in headlights. He felt such a powerful emotion that he thought he might burst into tears. Instead he bent over and started to kiss her, carefully at first, like the first time, before he knew what was wrong with her, but when he felt her tongue shoot into his mouth, he threw himself on her, licking, biting, and sucking as if for dear life.

They lay there entangled on the grass all afternoon and deep into the evening. Passengers in the trams that circled the roundabout struggled to catch a glimpse of the kissing couple rolling entwined among the narcissi. Whatever the Polish woman thought, this was the first time either had felt the love of another body. Now and then, breaking free of the embrace and looking up, Maxim saw the faces of the tram passengers. Children with their noses pressed flat against the windows waved, a plump woman going home from the market winked at him through the leeks in the bag she had propped on her knee. All these people were going about their business as if they knew what everything was all about. A group of boys encouraged Maxim with obscene gestures, and one of the tram drivers saluted the couple by doing a whole extra circuit, ringing the bell exuberantly all the while. Gala and Maxim burst out laughing, but weren't distracted. On the contrary. Displaying himself shamelessly before the eyes of the city only encouraged Maxim. As if being seen were proof that he existed. He still had a chance of joining the party he had dreamed about in his isolation, the party he had always known was going on somewhere else, a little farther down the road, in squat buildings that radiated music and light when you passed them in the night.

"That sure was different from the first kiss," he sighed after rolling onto his back for a moment to catch his breath. His lips were burning where Gala had nipped them. She propped herself up on her elbows and looked at him, squinting a little from the sun.

Finally Maxim realized what she had reminded him of that night on the water: a girl, four or five years old, that he had seen not so long ago at the swimming pool. She couldn't swim and was standing at the edge of the pool with her water wings on, quivering with fear and looking down at her father in the water. He stretched out his arms and gestured for her to jump. Her eyes were glued to his, as if the world outside her field of vision had dissolved. She didn't dare to take a step in either direction and, considering all the options, her face contorted, as if simply standing there caused her physical pain. Her lips started to tremble. Her eyes filled with tears and Maxim felt the tears welling in his eyes too. He was fascinated by the invisible lifeline between the man's and the girl's eyes. He had abandoned her to her fate and yet she still wanted to be with him. He had already betrayed her and now he was asking her to trust him anew. It worked. Drawn only by the pull of his eyes on hers, she moved closer to the water. Her toes were already over the edge when she started to cry, with heartrending sobs, but the man was implacable. Once she realized that there was no way back, she surrendered, swung her arms, and leapt toward him.

"What first kiss?" asked Gala. "Did you kiss me?"

It took Maxim a moment to grasp that Gala didn't remember a thing of what had happened.

"I probably asked for something between my teeth, a bit of wood, or a hankie, so I wouldn't hurt myself, and you thought . . . Man, I could have bitten your tongue off." She seemed to find the idea amusing. She knew, of course, that she had suffered a seizure and that Maxim had looked after her, but she didn't have any memories of it at all. Their most intimate moment, and he had experienced it alone.

"Usually the last thing I remember is this feeling that someone or something is coming up behind me, an enormous wave about to wash over me. Then I don't know a thing until I come to. I remember coming to, I remember that very well. It was somewhere on sand, wasn't it? With you, very peaceful. Yes, I remember that very well, lying there together so peacefully, for a long time. That was it, wasn't it?"

Maxim didn't know exactly why, but suddenly, perhaps because he was so happy, perhaps because he was tired and relaxed, but suddenly he was so moved by the thought of that quivering girl that he began to cry. While Gala kissed the tears from his cheeks, he resolved that he would one day be worthy of the trust she had shown him.

And so I gradually fill this high, empty space. This blank page. I search for big shapes, to make a small effect. I fill the picture with extreme details because each of them hides a facet of the essence. I gather strange butterflies. My white is made up of so many colors. Nobody who has seen my chaotic films will be able to believe it, but I strive for the tranquillity of a Japanese print.

Japanese prints have always fascinated me. Usually, most of the surface is taken up by something insignificant, a branch, the back of a head, blown-up details that for no apparent reason have reached the foreground: an extravagant fan, the grotesque face of a Nö actor. As if they had been caught by chance as they were creeping by. A geisha's shoulder blocking the view of Mount Fuji. An umbrella dominating the chaos of a bustling street scene. The teahouse is less important than the paper lantern dangling from the doorjamb in the wind.

I show life as it shows itself to me; what really matters is hidden behind an enormous thigh that just happened to wobble past. Maybe I could gather all my strength and use both hands to push away that floral dress and reveal the truth, but the truth is so much less attractive. If I don't see something, it doesn't mean it's not there. If I don't show something, it doesn't mean it's not there for all to see.

With the body still, consciousness can go its own way. The flesh is weary, but the soul wants to go on. That's why we dream. The body is not going anywhere, but thoughts take off in all directions. These night visions have always been more important to me than the issues of the day. The memories from my sleep are dearer than the memories of my life. Since the fifties I have kept a diary in which I note down all my dreams and draw the impossible images that appeared in them. They are my escape, and my gold mine. I use them in my films and, transmuting dreams into my work, bring them into my conscious life.

As I wait to start shooting my next film, my days and nights are free for dreaming. Project after project flashes through my mind. Stories, drawings, vistas—I don't know where to begin.

The screenplay for a comedy is taking shape: two elderly music hall artists meet again at a sanatorium on Monteverde after many years. They have both had strokes and are in a hospital. Though they are paralyzed, they discover that they can communicate through their old gags. They drive their doctors mad, but have the time of their lives. Success at last! At last an audience that can't walk out on them.

Coma prima! is a good working title. As soon as I can, I'll travel to Japan in search of backers.

Then there is also a quasi-scientific work that constantly requires my attention. It will be more than just an ordinary consideration of history. It will instead describe evolution as the principle of narrowing possibilities. My thesis is that all progress is the result of limitations of some kind. I'm not entirely sure what that means. But that is how I feel about everything important. So I am more and more convinced that I am on the right path. Snippets of this foolish study flash through my daydreams. All I have to do now is order them. I'm thinking of three sections: (1) God limits man; (2) Man limits God; (3) Man limits itself. That's the story of the world. Once you realize this, you can't understand why you never noticed it before. Mankind only moves ahead when other directions are cut off. As they are now, for me. It won't be that bad. I reinvented Rome; that was surely harder than reinventing myself.

As soon as the war was over, we wanted to start filming. My friends and I wanted to tell of the things we had seen. But the studios of Cinecittà had been bombed. So we recorded what we saw on the street, with the sun as our spotlight. The people walking past became actors. And that is how a style was born: because there were no other possibilities.

My characters have remained realistic. They walk on by: real people with their buttocks, breasts, and grimaces, looming up out of the crowd. But you only see part of them. That makes them seem larger than life, extreme. That's how I draw, trying to evoke the life that is hidden behind their outsized appearance, like the teahouse behind the lantern.

My friends and I spent our evenings in front of the Moviola studying the footage we'd shot on the streets in the daytime: scene after handheld scene, all silent. That's the best way to watch a film, even now: in a small dark room without sound, forcing the little picture on the monitor to tell the whole story.

Later critics sometimes claimed that I couldn't show real people, fully developed, flesh-and-blood creatures—that I am too baroque, that I resort to caricature because I am afraid of the psyche. Nonsense. Every part contains the whole. What do I care about a nicely rounded character, when I notice a gesture while passing someone in the street? A whole life has preceded that casual gesture; it is the outcome, at the instant that I see it, of all those sorrows and emotions. I see them all in that one gesture. Of course, I recognize my own tears too. Both are equally genuine. I see the whole person when I see someone unthinkingly pursing their lips. That gesture is the sum of their character. It is all I know about that person and all I need to know. I collect moments like that. I magnify them. Baroque. Hands, faces, images that tell a wordless story.

That's why my stories seem crowded and my actors experience such wild adventures. Everything I show existed once. I saw it somewhere and quickly whisked it away, because what is reality other than the simple truth? The truth does nobody any good. It can only distort.

Part Two

Les nouveaux pauvres

The essence of Rome, my Rome, the city that moves and excites me, cannot be found in the Forum or in the palazzi, in the immortal works of art lining the walls of churches and galleries. No, the essence of the Eternal City is inconspicuous—spread over the suburbs and the surrounding countryside.

Its heart is not in the history that has been saved from destruction but in the mementos that have disintegrated so much that no one can be bothered with them.

They're everywhere: looking, at first, like piles of rubbish, overgrown mounds of bricks, or pieces of crumbling stucco where *ragazzi* have scratched their names. But look more closely, behind those old newspapers and that tangle of plastic bags from the local supermarket, and you can still make out the curve of an arched vault, a wrought-iron wall clamp, the remains of a window or door. The tile floor has collapsed to reveal the heating system; and the reddish brown, black, and yellow pebbles once formed a mosaic that is now lost forever.

This is the ancient Rome that interests no one. And most of the fragments *are* ugly, hidden away in Campagna Romana, between the modern neighborhoods, beside the highways, and in the fields. They're everywhere, up to Monti Prenestini in the east, the Alban Hills in the south, and the hills of Tuscany to the north, but nobody seems to notice, so many that archaeologists don't give them a second thought. Some were once cordoned off, but even the fenceposts have long since vanished, and the NO ENTRY signs rusted away. The chicken wire has been trampled by children who wanted to play in the ruins, or by couples who couldn't wait to be alone. Only when a new housing project is being planned is a bit of historic cement discovered on the drawings of the land register, causing the developer, who hadn't noticed, to curse heatedly and adjust his plans to make the remains of the racecourse, the gladiatorial barracks, or the nymphaeum disappear behind the waste containers or in the median strip in the middle of the road where they won't ruin the view.

This is where I often linger. Here, in a small way, I touch eternity. I recover something and simultaneously I get lost. Between the modern buildings and the debris of the past, a piece of lead from an ancient water pipe brings tears to my eyes. Why? Who knows? Perhaps because it seems an answer to a question I have not yet been asked.

Rome's entire history is in these pieces of junk. They mean nothing but contain everything. They reduce eternity to its essence. I, at least, feel its extent more keenly when standing next to an overgrown pile of grit behind the gas station at the Cecchignola exit than when faced with the reliefs of Trajan's Column or the chiseled capitals of the Forum, which were carved by the hand of a master. My Rome is more to the point. The dome of the Pantheon demands respect for the mind that designed it, but in a brick I see the handiwork of the mason and the sweat of the man who lugged the buckets of mortar. I smell the urine of the neighborhood boys, the droppings of the sheep that grazed there. Like a stray dog, I rest against the cool marble of a wall that crumbles away a bit more every year, and casts a shorter shadow every spring. This summer, a circus pasted its posters on it. Local residents jog by. They're not interested in eternity. The most they'd do is wipe an oily rag off on it when they're fixing the car, or use it to anchor a wash line. This very dereliction moves me to a sad ecstasy. I shudder, and the girl riding past on the back of her boyfriend's Vespa throws me a suspicious glance. See, the relics say, this is what's left now of the great baths.

. . .

That's how it is with your own memories as well: the stronger they are, the more they get in the way of your own freedom to think. People want to pin everything down, but I say: let it go!

I notice it now that I'm sort of lying about my studio. How much time do I have to get rid of the shapes of everyone who was dear to me? To erase their facial features, the laugh lines, the tracks of tears that turned out so differently from how I intended? Ghosts are my only remorse for my next project.

The more I get to know someone, the less I understand him. This characteristic has always interfered with my relationships. Yet I can read the history of an entire family in an anonymous face in a crowd, imagining it so precisely that I decide that this stranger has a maiden great-aunt called Narda. I see the marks her elbows leave in the plastic tablecloth on her kitchen table and how she reveals the last remaining tooth in her lower jaw when she laughs. I'm that much of a fantasist! I'm even convinced that I know why the old spinster is so entertained, and why her head was resting on her hands so despairingly.

But I can stare into the eyes of my own sister and have no clue to what's going on inside her. This incapacity has caused a lot of grief, but for me it is vitally important. My lack of involvement with those dearest to me allows me to take my full measure of interest in the rest of the world. There's no challenge in something I understand, but things I don't know I can interpret any way I want.

I'm afraid my wife, Gelsomina, never understood my fascination for strangers and could get jealous that she had to compete for my attention with people whose names I didn't even know. This is my excuse: by fantasizing about the lives of the unknown, I hope to better understand mine.

Precisely because the teahouse is hidden behind the lantern I can imagine what it's like.

This characteristic was essential to the conception of my films and is now coming in handy as I strive to complete the screenplay I've been toying with for weeks. I can see more clearly now what the ghosts who have been haunting my thoughts are up to. I fill in their actions with details, absolutely sure of things it's impossible for me to know.

. . .

Now that the building is starting to crumble, I can set to work with the debris. Soon, at last, I'll be free to take the pieces and reconstruct the dreams I saw before life got in the way.

Why should we fear the future? Everything is still possible there. Better to shrink from the past, the place you'd had such high hopes for.

I

Rome in the mideighties.

Halfway down the Via Due Macelli, Gala gives up. The rain pours straight through her umbrella. Water gushes into the deep gutters and washes over the pavement. She takes her shoes off and walks on, barefoot. The street feels warm. The memory of the sun in the paving stones of Rome is enough for the city to survive the first autumn squall.

October is the worst time to come to visit, the only month of heavy rains. What's more, the hotels are crammed with conference-goers. From the Coppersmiths Union to the Association of Head Cooks at Franciscan seminaries, everyone seems determined to gather annually during the Roman storms.

A cloudburst doesn't stop Gala. The Dutch are born with their feet in the water. She laughs at the Italians who flee into doorways at the first drops. The group she just passed were cowering under the awning of a bookshop. Between the women with bags full of fennel from the Via Arcione market and the ladies going to their couturiers in the Via Condotti stands a man with a red scooter he's trying to shelter. Every time he sees a splatter, he wipes it off with his silk handkerchief, cursing and invoking the Madonna all the while. Just then, a taxi speeds through a puddle. A bucket splash of water. Under the awning, the ladies scream. They assess the damage to their clothing. Indignant, Gala does the same. The man is happy that his scooter is still dry, thanks to the young woman who has just taken the brunt of the blast. He watches her flick the mud off her dress. Globs of it glide down her legs. She realizes that it's no use, closes her umbrella, puts it in her purse, and lets the rain stream over her shoulders. She tilts her head back for a moment and stands there with her eyes shut the way a normal person might warm her face in the sun. Meanwhile, the dark patches in the red fabric spread across her body.

This flaunted femininity elicits a snort from one of the working-class women under the awning. How is she to know that Gala never does anything for effect? Or, more to the point, that she has no idea how people react to her? She simply doesn't see them. If only Gala *were* aware of the impression she makes. Even if it robbed her of half of her apparent self-confidence. *Then* she might have noticed the man standing between the women under the awning and the way he was looking at her. After a few seconds, she runs her fingers through her hair and walks on, swinging her hips. Even the swaying of her lower body, which attracts attention even in a packed shopping street, is unconscious and caused by a difference in the length of her legs, a slight aberration, imperceptible to the naked eye.

The man watches until she disappears into the gaping mouth of the traffic tunnel under the Quirinale. With a sigh he puts the handkerchief back in his breast pocket and pushes his *motorino* out onto the street. He looks down sadly at the gleaming metal that will get dirty, but revs the engine and, cursing, rides off after Gala. He makes sure to stay a dozen or so meters behind her, which isn't easy because Gala is walking so slowly he can hardly keep his balance. She has no idea that she is being followed. On the other side of the hill, the sun is already coming out.

The light shining into the tunnel is like a halo around her silhouette.

After getting off the train at Termini, Gala and Maxim walked to a nearby pension that Maxim's mother had recommended. Pensione Gasser, where the woman had spent several happy months, was not only still operating after all these years, but Providence allowed that they could spend their first couple of nights there.

Tomorrow they'll be out on the street. They've spent the whole morning searching for a place to spend the night. Each has covered a different part of the city and they are now meeting around noon, as agreed, beneath the portico of the opera house. As soon as Maxim sees Gala, he rushes up to meet her. They kiss.

"I told you this was no weather for walking!"

"Only the barbarians came to Rome to stay indoors."

Arms around each other, they cross the square to a bench, where he lays her out to dry with her head on his lap. He takes her shoes out of her bag and wipes off the mud.

"Did you bring another pair?"

"I thought Italian fashion was developed enough that I might find some shoes here."

Maxim laughs. He puts the wet shoes out in the sun, then removes their map of Rome from the bag. It's dripping wet and tears when he unfolds it. He spends a while flapping the two halves back and forth in the hope of drying them.

"I did the whole length of the Via Nazionale," he says. "No rooms anywhere."

"I tried every hotel I passed."

"We can't afford a hotel."

He dangles the bunch of grapes he bought at the market over Gala's face. She snaps at them, but he pulls them away. Growling, she sits up and snaps again. She's got them now and tears away at her spoils.

"Wait," says Maxim, "I have to wash them." But Gala bursts the fruit open between her bared teeth. The juice runs down over her chin. She tries to lick it up, but it's already dripping down her neck. He wipes the drops from her chest and licks his hand clean.

The opera employees are streaming out the stage door on their way to lunch on the Piazza Gigli. Two elderly ladies nudge each other.

"Aren't you the gentleman who asked the manager about Signor Sangallo?" one of them asks.

"Yes," Maxim replies, "but no one seems to know him here."

"Ah, tastes change so fast. One year it's in to be stylish, then it's out again. This winter, God willing, he'll be back for a revival of *La Clemenza,* and then who knows? We all get old. Nowadays the opera is in the hands of youngsters like yourself. But you, at least, have not forgotten the maestro. Is he a friend of yours?"

"In a way."

"Here's his old address. I wrote it down for you. And his telephone number, but that might have changed."

She's scribbled it on a scrap from an old pattern. Maxim tries to find the street on one of the quadrants of the map. The woman's friend takes her by the arm. "If you see him, give him a kiss from Estrella. Now those were costumes! When you sewed them, it felt like little angels were holding up the fabric!"

Maxim wonders whether to drop in on the elderly opera director or announce his arrival in advance. It's been three years since he last saw him. There's a pay phone on the corner of the square, but a man has been using it the whole time they've been sitting there.

Gala's shoe leather is stiff as he forces her shoes back on. They agree to meet at six in the little hotel near the station where they can stay for one more night. They kiss again as they leave. It's a ritual, but not an altogether natural one. Their lips seek each other's and cling briefly.

Before turning the corner, Maxim waves. He almost knocks over the red scooter of the man who is still standing there, on the telephone. The man grits his teeth but shows his back until Maxim is out of sight. He looks over the top of his sunglasses at the young woman, who throws the strap of her bag over one shoulder and heads off for the Forum. Her heels are so high she has to tilt her pelvis to walk.

Gala had promised herself Rome.

Halfway through her second year in college, she and Maxim had such fond memories of *The Mannequins' Ball* and were so fed up with classes and discussions that they applied for the theater school. The day before the auditions, Gala went home to break the news to her parents. She told Maxim she thought her father would respond by faking a coronary, lamenting his fate, and sucking furiously on his pipe, then locking the liquor cabinet because you can't trust actors. Instead, Jan Vandemberg didn't get up to any of his usual antics. He seemed at a complete loss. The blood drained from his face and the strength from his muscles.

"Aren't you going to let me have it?" suggested Gala uncertainly.

"Choices like these are beyond us." He slumped down on a chair and stayed there, so lethargic it seemed he'd sink into the cushions and disappear. "It's your life. Your mother and I gave it to you. It's not up to us."

Then he asked to be left alone until dinner. Rather than demonstratively staying away as everyone expected, he arrived, forcing Anna to hurriedly set a place for him, doing his best to seem cheerful and participate in the conversation. Over cognac, he asked Gala to perform the monologue she'd prepared for her examination. Standing in front of the fireplace, she acted out an excerpt from Lorca, and when she had finished he broke the silence by applauding with wide flapping arms.

"Just look at that," he said to his wife, "just look at that, you spawned an actress!"

The next morning, when Gala appeared before the admissions committee, she could still feel the heat of the embers on her back. And while she tried to summon up the stifled rage of the spurned woman, all her passion was extinguished by the thought of the benevolence in her father's eyes as he did his utmost to be encouraging.

Although the results wouldn't be in for two weeks, Gala left the audition room knowing she wouldn't be admitted. She spent a night with Maxim drinking and swearing, dancing and crying, but when he appeared beside her bed the next morning with warm croissants, freshly squeezed orange juice, and Alka-Seltzer, she had already adjusted her plans. She'd finish her undergraduate degree, she wouldn't disappoint her father again, but then, she told herself, "our accounts are settled and my life is my own." She liked that idea. It excited her to postpone things. Suddenly she could visualize her freedom, like a light shining more brightly at the end of a longer tunnel. One day, many years later, she would bathe in it. She eventually graduated with honors, and none of her professors suspected that the only thing that kept her going was the thought of the freedom awaiting her.

Gala passes through the shadows of Emperor Trajan's Market. Each of the old shops in the semicircular gallery is lit up by sunlight from the high windows. The wind of time has polished the travertine so that the sunshine reflects and scatters into every gloomy corner. Walking down the marble passage, Gala appears as a specter in the light and a smudge in the shadows. A specter in the light, a smudge in the shadows. The click of her heels echoes through the low stone rooms. What *is* it about that gait, so slow you want to hurry her along, tell her to get moving, even though you'd never dare? But the languor of a woman inspires more awe than annoyance. She has eternity on her side; haste is all we've got. Gala saunters past the deserted stalls. How tempting to mistake this calm for confidence.

"Nowhere else I know so evokes the atmosphere of ancient Rome." The man is standing eyes shut in the middle of Trajan's Forum. Gala hadn't noticed any other visitors.

"With a little effort, you can see them on their way to the baths, mothers coming from the market with their whining kids behind them."

Gala smiles and walks on.

"Try it," the man insists, "close your eyes."

"Don't need to. I can imagine it like this."

"Then you must be an artist." He opens his eyes and looks at her as if seeing her for the first time. "Or a magician, of course."

Gala ignores him. In the two days since she got to Rome, he's the eighty-sixth guy who's tried to pick her up. In her mind, she starts running through the brush-offs which, together with the conjugations of "to be" and "to have," form the basis of every Italian course back home in Amsterdam. But the man doesn't try to follow her. He has closed his eyes again, standing there as if he finds the dead more important. Of course, Gala is relieved that she won't have to give him the brush-off. But for an instant so brief she hardly notices it, her stomach shrinks at the thought that she's somehow proved inadequate. That she has disappointed him. Soon, on her way out, she is once again fascinated by the floor mosaics. She hasn't even reached the street when, studying her map, she bumps into someone. It's the same man. He asks where she's going and offers her a ride.

At that moment, Maxim is ringing the bell of the apartment on the Villa Ada. Sangallo has to stop and think when he hears the visitor's name through the intercom. Actually, the viscount buzzes him up without a clue who he could be, but as soon as the elevator doors open on the young man, he sees him once again on the Amsterdam stage in his *Ariadne,* with long flowing hair, his youthful body shining through the tight taffeta, one hand on the gilded dagger at his hip, and swathed in meters of crepe de chine that the viscount had flown in from Nanking at exorbitant cost, just to drape around Maxim's shoulders.

In each of his operas, Filippo Sangallo had one or two favorites. He never forgot them. When he returned to Rome at the end of the run, they played new roles in the productions of his dreams. Sometimes one of them would visit him, as Maxim is doing now.

Reality is always a disappointment.

"Your neck is too long for short hair," is all the old man says. No greeting, no invitation. He turns on his heel and disappears into the shadows of his apartment. Maxim is unsure whether to follow, but then the shutters are thrown open inside.

"Look!" Sangallo is in his study, bent over the fifteenth-century chest of drawers that he uses as a drawing table. On the back of a set design he sketches Maxim's face in a few lines, the deep-set eyes, his neck, the curve of his chest.

"That face: handsome but arrogant. It seems almost disconnected from your trunk. But let your hair grow"—he sketches it the way he wants to see it—"and the Olympus from which you look down on us mortals from under your eyelids becomes linked to your body. It makes you gentler. For you, long hair is like a frame around your face. I told you before, I'll tell you again now. The intangible enclosed in a frame. The head and the heart unified. Is that too much to ask?" With a grand gesture he pushes the charcoal and the sheets of paper into a corner of the marble drawing board. "But now, life itself. Have you eaten? Have you ever tasted the sun in the honey of Piedmont?"

"Without extras," Filippo Sangallo was fond of saying, "people would fall asleep from boredom halfway through life." For years, these young men and women, each decked out more brilliantly than the singers, had been the most expensive part of his productions. In the old days, when he was Luchino Visconti's partner, there wasn't a theater manager alive who would dare deny his extravagant demands, but when Filippo decided to continue directing after the death of his lover, he ran into more and more resistance. The biggest opera houses were the first to close their doors. His productions were too expensive and his ideas outmoded. Dissatisfaction grew among the singers as well, whom he still arranged as tableaux vivants at a time when other directors were letting them scream and roll around on the floor. Finally, all he had left were minor companies in countries and states so small that they needed to subsidize their culture. For the audiences in such places, as undiscriminating as they were, his name still recalled the glory days in which he toured the world with Maria Callas.

Filippo saw exactly what was going on. He drew up a list of works in which he still wanted to create the images of his dreams. He had no intention of compromising his vision in any way, even though he was more and more frequently obliged to forgo his own fee to achieve it. His most important exigencies invariably involved the extras. Each was like a brushstroke in a painting inside the frame of the stage.

But it went beyond rehearsals: he surrounded himself with extras outside the theaters as well, young people he had plucked from the rabble that appeared at auditions. He chose them for a look in their eyes, a gesture, a shadow of a memory, the curl of a lip, anything that let him glimpse the kind of beauty sometimes captured in old paintings. All were enthusiasts at the start of their careers, still free of professional jealousy. He bloomed in their presence. After rehearsals, he took them to exhibitions or bookshops where he bought them expensive gifts, solely to nurture their interest in the arts. He could always spot the ones who hung around for the material benefits alone, and gave them even more expensive gifts, just to make them feel uncomfortable, and then excluded them from the dinners he held for the rest of the group in the city's best restaurants. He insisted that everyone try all the dishes, knowing that these youngsters earned little and were used to eating badly. They worshipped him, needless to say. Most had never met a man of his caliber, and to this day it's easy to point out the artists who were inspired by him.

During the meals, he entertained everyone with poems or scenes from old movies, and his own life was a source of incredible anecdotes, the most roguish of which he acted out in different languages and strange dialects. Although a melancholy expression came over his face whenever he felt completely at ease, he clearly enjoyed the attention. When someone caught one of his cynical interjections, which were mostly lost between his jokes, a grateful smile appeared on his somber face, as on that of a child who has briefly forgotten why exactly he was crying.

These meals were even more colorful around premieres, when the viscount flew in old friends from abroad to show them his dreams. For those who had known him in happier days, he hosted intimate dinners, where he would be accompanied by whichever extra he happened to be most fond of at the time. After a premiere in Scheveningen, for example, Maxim once ate in a *chambre separée* at the Badhotel with Louis Jourdan and James Baldwin, and they endlessly tried to outdo each other with tales of their sexual escapades. Soon after, he found himself sitting across from a thin elderly woman in Amsterdam's Amstel Hotel. Wearing a silk turban and hidden behind enormous sunglasses, she hardly said ten words all evening, and as a result it wasn't until midway through the second course that Maxim realized she was Marlene Dietrich, whereupon he became so nervous that he forgot to keep eating. By dessert, she could bear it no longer. She slid a plate of confectionery over to him.

"And now," she said, "it is eat or die."

The viscount is tall and heavy as a bear, yet his massive body is as nimble as his mind. It's hard to believe that someone who seems to weigh so upon the earth can zigzag through a room like a dragonfly. He shuffles along so quickly that it's hard for a young man in sneakers to keep up with him. Now he's standing on the balcony, picking some basil from a pot and drawing it through a plate of honey. He holds it up to the light and watches the golden liquid drip off the leaves. Then he puts them in Maxim's mouth as though feeding an infant. When his fingers touch Maxim's lips he is suddenly embarrassed, afraid he's gone too far. He puts down the plate and peers into the distance at the heavy clouds over the cypresses of Villa Ada.

"We shall have to discover Rome anew," he says after a while, "nothing else for it. Come Sunday morning and I'll have a car."

Maxim is already in the hall when Sangallo asks him to write down the number of his hotel.

"I'll only be here one more night. Everything's full. I don't know where I'll end up."

"Just give me the number where you'll be tonight. In case something comes up. Oh, and put your name with it, otherwise I'll lose it." The viscount slips the piece of paper with the name that's eluded him the whole time into his pocket without looking at it. He gives the young man an umbrella with a walnut handle, a paper bag full of grapes, a couple of sprigs of basil and the jar of honey he liked so much, a bound edition of Goethe's *Italienische Reise,* an opened bottle of vin santo, and a lithograph of Cola di Rienzo's *Flight to Castel Sant'Angelo*.

Arms full, Maxim stands in the elevator. For a moment Sangallo studies his face.

"Yes," he sighs, then presses the button and slams the iron grate shut between them. "That's what's exciting about beautiful things. They know when enough is enough. A blink of the eye and it's gone!"

Gala proves the opposite, Maxim thinks. She emerges from the bathroom with her hair wet, as beautiful as ever. Or is beautiful even the word? Nothing about her resembles classical beauty. Her nose, if you look at it closely, is too flat. Her head is too square. It's almost too big for her body, and her features are irregular. But still, there's not a man who doesn't feel attracted to her and longer than the blink of an eye, longer than a night, longer than the years Maxim has known her. No, Gala's secret is anything but fleeting.

Her body is crooked as well. Legs and hips, as mentioned, but especially her back. It hurts after a long day's walking. She drops onto the bed and rolls over onto her stomach with difficulty. Maxim straddles her on his knees and rubs her aching muscles.

"He seemed nice."

"A man who just comes up to you on the street?"

"He wasn't pushy."

"Well, thank goodness for that."

"Ouch!"

Maxim plants his thumbs between Gala's shoulder blades and moves them in little circles, constantly changing the pressure, as he follows her backbone. He can trace two curves. The first, gradual, runs almost the entire length of her spine, and then right at the bottom is a sharp little kink, just above her buttocks. This area has grown more sensitive over the past few months, but no matter what Maxim says, Gala insists on high heels.

"What do *you* suggest?" she asks. "We have to move somewhere tomorrow morning. That count of yours is no use."

Maxim pours her a glass of vin santo. He dips some basil in the honey.

"Bite first, then rinse."

Gala tastes it and says, "I take it all back. The man is priceless."

Maxim searches through her bag for the other half of the map.

"Don't worry," Gala reassures him, "we'll find something. We could live off the wind in a land that makes things like that."

He spreads the two halves of the map out over the bed and Gala, who is still lying on it. He tries to fit them together on her back.

"And the house that guy was talking about . . ."

"Gianni is *not* just a guy. You'll see, he's very much a gentleman."

Every time Gala breathes, the city splits open, revealing a strip of skin between the streets. Redness shows where Maxim pressed too hard.

"What's the area called where that house is?"

With its embassies and galleries, Parioli is one of the best neighborhoods in Rome. The houses were built in the nineteenth century on the slopes of the Valle Giulia, and most of the gardens back onto the park of the Villa Borghese. The Via Michele Mercati turns out to be on one of the quiet streets behind the National Gallery of Modern Art.

Gala strides from one gate to the next looking for the number Gianni has given her. Maxim follows with his pack and her suitcase. He got up this morning without waking her. First, he went out to change money and get some bread, then he paid the hotel bill and packed their things so that everything would be ready before Gala opened her eyes.

These are small tasks that Maxim always takes upon himself. That's how things have turned out. If he doesn't do them, no one else will. They're practical matters, and Gala has no interest in them. They simply don't seem to exist for her. She assumes that everything will turn out fine. And it always has. For years. Maxim doesn't even know if she realizes how much he does for her. He doesn't care. He likes doing it. It makes him feel good. Like a father looking after his child, Maxim doesn't expect anything in return. It feels warm. It feels like love. It's enough just being part of that carefree life of hers, which gives him so much hope.

Number seventeen is scarcely visible from the street. The moment Gala steps onto the drive, a watchdog starts to bark. Maxim hesitates.

"Why would someone offer us a house like this?"

"Why not? We're not in Holland anymore. Anyway, it's only a room."

A young man is sitting on a rhododendron-shaded bench at the side of the house smoking a cigarette. When he sees Maxim and Gala, he immediately makes himself scarce.

The house is run-down.

"Angels! There you are. Angels, descended among my flowers." A woman has thrown open the shutters on the first floor. "The front, go round to the front." She gestures frantically, leaning dangerously far out of the window. "I come as fast as I can. The big yellow doors. You can't miss them. For you, I'll open them. Just a second."

She only comes up to Maxim's navel and seems as broad as she is tall. The coarse material of her black dress is tight at the seams. One moment she's wringing her hands, the next she's running her fingers through her gray hair and pushing loose strands back into her bun. She introduces herself as Geppi, the concierge, and seems to have been expecting her two guests, so much so that Maxim is afraid she's mistaken them for someone else.

"Not at all. Signor Gianni called me. Two shining North Stars. She is as seductive and beautiful as a panther, and him . . . Well, he's big and blond and taller than seems humanly possible. And straight. Up into the sky like an obelisk."

Her eyes are gentle but too nervous to hold your gaze for long. To conceal her insecurity, she chatters away nonstop about the adventures of the forgotten cartoon character she was named after, Geppi, la Bimba Atomica.

"Did you tell this Gianni what I look like?" Maxim asks in the meantime, but Gala shakes her head. Geppi takes a bunch of keys and leads them down a narrow hall beneath the grand staircase. There are no windows here. The only light comes from under the doors. There is life in some of the rooms. The rays are interrupted by people moving around inside. At the end of the hall, the concierge opens a room with a bathroom en suite.

"This is too expensive for us," says Maxim.

"Heavens," laughs Geppi, "if we measured our happiness in money . . ." She opens the shutters. There is a small, round window, set high in the wall. The room is sunk below in the garden, which slopes up toward Monte Pincio on this side of the house. For people inside, the path and the trunks of the rhododendrons are at eye level. Two pin-striped legs walk by.

"What's more," Geppi continues, "it's up to Signor Gianni to decide what things cost. Of course, you have the use of the furniture, and that's quite something. This wardrobe, that bed, and just look at this magnificent clock. It's the kind that's only right twice a day, but who could expect more from something so gorgeous?" She helps Maxim take off his backpack and throws it onto the bed. Then she lays her hands on his shoulders and stands on her toes to look into his eyes.

"How big they are, and how blue, sainted innocence, it's going to be mayhem! Crick, crack, I can already hear the first heart breaking. Boom, bang, my ears are hurting. Don't let it get you down, son, the first heart's always the noisiest. Afterward they just fall softly, plomp, ploff, like newborn sparrows falling dead onto the moss."

"It's a whorehouse," Maxim says, refusing to unpack his things. "You can see it, you can smell it. What's behind all those doors?"

"We'll ask," says Gala. "In an hour we're having lunch with Gianni at the tennis club."

"Tennis club?" Maxim feels his resistance wobbling. "We're having lunch at a tennis club?"

Only Gala can talk about completely unknown places as if she's frequented them for years with the rest of the jet set. God, how he loves the unexpected. How he loves her for attracting it.

"Thank God you're here," says the man, introducing himself to Maxim as Gianni Castronuovo. He's just showered and his hair is plastered wet against his skull. Small droplets are dripping down onto the shoulders of his elegant suit. "I was so worried that I might have offended you by offering you such a shabby room, but it's all I have, everything else is taken."

The tennis courts are wedged in between the ancient Muro Torto and the road through the park. In the outdoor café their voices mingle with the traffic noise echoing off the high wall. As food and wine are served, Gianni puts a thick book down in front of the Dutch couple.

The names, biographies, and addresses of everyone in Rome who has anything at all to do with the film industry.

"It's a beautiful city, but you can't keep wandering around until you're old and gray. You want to live here, don't you? Then we'll have to get those careers of yours off the ground as soon as possible."

"Do you work in cinema as well?" Maxim leafs through the book.

"Ah, if only. But I've done my bit. Yes, when I was your age I put on a miniskirt and stood there behind Ben-Hur with the lions. Who didn't in those days? But later . . ." Gianni lowers his eyes, not out of modesty, but to look up again with more effect while revealing his triumph. "Yes, later I worked with Snaporaz."

"With Snaporaz?" A passing waiter looks up at the sound of the name. A woman at the next table turns around in the hope of catching the rest of the conversation.

"With Snaporaz. Twice." The dapper gentleman searches the air with his hands as if to recapture the shape of a memory. It's touching how he's forgotten himself. His eyes gleam.

"His classic scene on the forecastle of a ship. Right next to the lifeboat, the man in the bathing tights, that was me."

The woman at the next table can't resist. "The blue-striped bathing tights?"

"The same."

"How amazing, meeting like this!" She slides over her chair. "Did you have any lines?"

"Lines? No, I didn't have any lines. I didn't have any action either. But I had my personality."

"And your bathing tights," says the waiter, coming over to stand by their table. "We shouldn't underestimate that. Those blue-striped bathing tights are etched in everyone's memory."

"Nonsense," the woman snaps, "this gentleman would have stood out even without the tights."

"It might not have been a big role," says Gianni, "but it was the crux of the whole film."

Gala, who has been looking through the film almanac, now finds, to her astonishment, Snaporaz's address.

"That a man like him is simply listed . . . ," she says. "Telephone number and all!"

None of the Romans bats an eye.

"Via Margutta," they exclaim together. The waiter disagrees with the woman about the house number. According to a ball boy who runs past collecting strays between the tables, they're both right: one door leads to Snaporaz's office; the other to his home.

"Closed doors, yes," Gianni adds triumphantly. "Anyone can stand in front of them, but to be asked inside . . . Well, that's a different story."

The conversation falls silent. Gianni bites his lips like a child, beaming as if a secret he can't tell is burning the tip of his tongue. Gala catches Maxim's eye and gives him a quizzical look. He has to admit that Gianni seems pleasantly naive rather than cunning, as expected.

"Why are you helping us?" he asks, going straight to the point.

"I have my house. I live off it. Plenty of actresses live there. And actors. You'll meet them. Americans, French, a model from Hungary. One month they have work, the next they live on credit. It's in my own interest for you to start earning as soon as possible, because come the end of the month, I want to see the rent. If I were a developer, I'd discuss building projects with you. As it happens, I know some film people. Not the real big shots, but it's a start." From his inside pocket, he pulls out a list with names. Some have two stars after the telephone number, others, less important, just one. "Maybe my name will help you to get a foot in the door. That's all. The rest is up to you. Every day I kiss the hem of the Madonna's robe in the hope that she will send me youngsters with talent, so that I won't go hungry."

"May I have a look at that list as well?" asks the woman at the next table.

"Out of the question," snaps Gianni.

"Maybe I could do something in the movies too."

"Not until the day blandness comes into fashion, madam."

After lunch he escorts Maxim and Gala to the exit. While shaking their hands, he looks them over again from head to toe.

"Very serviceable," he says contentedly. "The kind of thing people here are looking out for. I'd bet my *motorino* on that. What an adventure is in store for you two, what a world of possibilities!"

Maxim and Gala walk into the park. When they glance back, Gianni salutes them briefly before plunging recklessly into the stream of traffic, bolt upright on his red scooter.

. . .

By evening, Maxim and Gala have settled into the house in Parioli. They are sitting on a big bed surrounded with hundreds of pictures of themselves. There is a glossy portfolio with an extensive selection of both of them. It starts with photos of the two of them together: embracing, fighting, entangled. Then a series of each alone. Neither had considered making a separate portfolio. This adventure is theirs together. They also make folders for all the agents and directors who seem in any way important. Gala slips two portraits into each, one with glamour and one with character. Maxim has borrowed a typewriter from the concierge. He has it balanced on his lap and is busy putting together their curriculum vitae. One by one, they tally up their film and television roles and their achievements in Dutch theater. It's quite a list. There's not enough space to mention everything. That's convenient, because the less there is, the more impressive it sounds.

"The Mannequins' Ball," says Maxim. "I don't need to say that it was a student production, do I?"

"Of course not, that doesn't mean a thing to people here. What have you got now?"

"That we had the lead parts."

"We did."

"Yes, honesty is the best policy."

"And mentioning that it was in the University Theater," says Gala, "information like that just confuses things."

"Is 'theater, Amsterdam' enough?"

"Or maybe 'Amsterdam Theater'?"

" Wouldn't 'National Theater' sound better?"

"National?"

"It definitely wasn't international."

"True, that's no exaggeration."

"Fine. Make it 'Teatro Nazionale,' for the sake of clarity. And the number of performances?"

"Ten? How many were there, maybe twelve?"

"Ah, it doesn't make that much difference, does it?"

"None at all. A role is a role."

"Just the year then?"

"I'd just put the season."

"That covers two years."

"Exactly."

Every new environment casts a new light on things. It gives the past another chance. What better reason could people have for moving?

In the hours that follow, the cheap wine in the Coke bottle they filled themselves in the Via di Ripetta adds to their euphoria. As soon as they've put together the list of directors, agents, and casting agencies that can look forward to a visit in the coming days, they fall backward. Lying close to each other, they draw their campaign plan in the air with grand gestures, excited as fresh troops embarking on an expedition.

"It's weird," says Gala suddenly, "there's something sad about it as well."

"As if we have to put something behind us, that's what it feels like."

"Although we've been looking forward to it for so long."

"It's weird how people hope their dreams will come true."

"Really very strange, and incomprehensible."

They've just fallen asleep when Maxim wakes with a start. In the bathroom he searches through her makeup and his shaving gear for Gala's epilepsy medication, tablets she has to take twice a day. He counts them. There are two too many, the two she should have taken that evening. He presses them out of the silver strip, runs the tap until the water's cool, and fills a glass. The night is warm. Before waking her with a gentle caress, he watches the beads of sweat well up between her shoulder blades.

2

The big house stays dark late into the morning. Still, some people are up. The sun forces its way through the chinks in the shutters. Gala turns over to make the real window emerge from behind the black window in her field of vision. Yesterday everything seemed possible, but from now on everything that happens to them will have to press its way through this room.

Whenever she'd had to spend a long time waiting on the set of some Dutch film or other—because even as a student she sometimes caught the eye of a young film director—Gala killed time by watching the lighting technicians. She loved how shadows slipped by. Most fascinating of all was the increasing intensity of the big lights. With all four metal shutters open, you hardly notice the effect of one of those spotlights. It lights the whole scene, but leaves little impression. Only when the light is adjusted, the shutters closed, the rays narrowed and directed, does the beam become powerful. Suddenly, it gives things depth. Everything becomes sharper. Black and white.

In the dark rooms of the house in Parioli, Rome slips through a few slats of wood. The city becomes even more radiant.

"Tiruli, tirula," someone sings.

"That's him," says Gala. She's standing with Maxim in the middle of the Via Margutta in front of Snaporaz's house. One of the first-floor windows is open. Through it, they see a bit of wall and the corner of a painting. That's all. Maxim shrugs. He can't believe anyone this famous could be so easy to find.

"Pitipo, pitipa."

Gala doesn't dare to say another word, afraid to disturb the great man in song, but she squeezes Maxim's arm.

The bar on the corner of the Via del Babuino and the Piazza del Popolo has a telephone on the wall. Maxim's bought some *gettoni* and underlined Snaporaz's number in the thick book. He's almost done it three times now and can't wait any longer. He dials.

"Ma chi è?" A breathless, female voice, maybe a secretary.

Gala presses her ear to the side of the receiver. Her forehead is resting against his. When he talks, his voice reverberates in her bones. Half in Italian and half in French, Maxim explains who and what they are, actors.

"Yes, yes. And what do you want?" It's a good question. Maxim doesn't have a quick answer.

"I'm sorry, *il signor Snaporaz non c'è.*" She hangs up. Gala's head moves away from his.

The same bar, hours later: there are no outside tables, but the owner has put two kitchen chairs out on the sidewalk for them. The carrier of a parked scooter makes a serviceable table. On it are empty cups, the big casting book, and assorted paperwork. Maxim and Gala take turns watching the Via Margutta while the other hogs the telephone, calling one casting agency after another. They pour handfuls of tokens into the phone. There is an amazing demand for foreigners. Tall? Blond? In the next few days the two *attori olandesi* can come introduce themselves everywhere. Then they pluck up the courage to call the directors whose numbers are listed in the book: Pasquale Squitieri, Castaldi, Celentano, Marco Bellocchio, Dario Argento, Franco Brusati . . . They take a personal approach, opening with an admiring remark about each director's latest masterpiece: a bluff, because Dutch distributors seldom take risks and Gala and Maxim have seen hardly any of their films. A few are crazy enough to let themselves be talked into an appointment.

Finally Gala and Maxim reward themselves with a bottle of spumante. Maxim neatly writes out their list of appointments. On the torn map, he plans out routes past all the places where their careers could take off at any moment. They're all over the city. Now they just have to decide where to begin.

"Skylight," he says after puzzling it out, "Via Angelo Brunetti. That's just on the other side of the square."

The elevator to the top floor, where the casting agency is located, is a small brass cage. Maxim and Gala stand close together. The old apparatus creeps its way up the elevator shaft. The travertine steps of a wide staircase wind around it.

"Maybe we shouldn't have had so much to drink," says Maxim.

"Fortuna demanded a libation."

He wipes a hair away from the corner of Gala's mouth and gives her a kiss of encouragement. With her thumb she wipes a smudge of lipstick from his chin. They both look up. Stomach to stomach they approach a milk-white skylight through which the fierce daylight is shining.

"Impressive," says the casting agent. He has their CVs and the portfolio on his lap. "Yes, indeed, this is really something." He leafs through the photos without looking at them. Instead he keeps his eyes fixed on the young actors. "This really is something we can work with. I've been in the business for years, and you develop an eye for it. Great material. A very productive conversation."

He just wants to see how the light catches their cheekbones. He wants to see them one by one in the next room. He opens the door to an adjoining office and asks a secretary to hold his calls. He'll be busy for a while.

"Bit of a weirdo," whispers Gala.

"No one ever reacted to us like this in Holland."

"That's why we would have suffocated if we'd stayed there."

"Yes," says Maxim, "suffocated and dried out."

Fulvani, that's the man's name, sticks his head around the door. All the charm has fled from his face.

"What are you saying?" he asks suspiciously. A second later, he's smiling again. "I'm going to do for you what I did for myself." He tosses a photo onto the table. In it he's a young man with his arm around

Charlton Heston. "Ben-Hur. My first role. An instant success. Seen it? I was one of the lepers."

He takes Maxim into the side room first. It's a terrace, closed off with glass to form an annex to the office. Fulvani presses a button. Automatic blinds descend on all sides. He flicks on a lamp and aims it so that the light hits Maxim's face from the side. He studies his eye sockets from near and from far. His nose and the line of his jaw. Then he adjusts the lamp and checks the shadows on the other side of his face the same way.

"Your eyes are deep set. Always keep your chin down, otherwise you'll look like a skull. But those cheekbones will make your fortune. High cheekbones are a lifelong gift."

He opens the blinds with a snap, grabs a camera, and takes a few shots.

"Now a few without your shirt."

Maxim displays his chest. The other man squeezes his arms and looks at his back muscles.

"Are you a gymnast?"

"No," answers Maxim. "I have a big heart. It presses the lungs apart. That's why my ribs are so spread out."

"Some people get it all on a silver platter." Fulvani takes a few more photos.

"You fuck her?"

Maxim thinks he's misunderstood him.

"Is she your girlfriend," Fulvani explains, "that girl in there? *Fate l'amore*?"

"Does that make a difference to the roles we get?" asks Maxim curtly. He puts his shirt back on. Fulvani shakes his hand.

"Welcome to Italian cinema."

"Whatever happens, you're not going in there alone," Maxim tells Gala in Dutch as he comes back into the office.

She doesn't react.

"I believe I'm about to do something I've never done before," says Fulvani. He paces back and forth in his office. Weighing the pros and cons. Sighing, he runs his fingers through his hair. "But since everyone knows me, they know I'd never bother them without good reason and they'll have to take it seriously." Without another word he disappears into the adjoining room. He consults the secretaries.

"Careful not to rub him the wrong way," says Gala. "He's going to do something for us."

Fulvani comes back, picks up the telephone, and dials.

"Nobody gets straight through to Snaporaz. They have to get past Fiamella first." He covers the receiver with his hand. "Once she was his lover, now she's his Cerbera."

"You're calling Snaporaz?" asks Gala.

Fulvani shakes his head, slightly annoyed. "To reach Fiamella, first you have to get past Salvini."

Just look how reliable and well informed he is, says the glance Gala tosses at Maxim.

Someone answers.

"Salvini? Salvini, good afternoon! I've got something here. Fiamella must see it. What do you mean, who from? From Fulvani, of course! Look, I'm doing you a favor. Sollima and Bertolucci are casting as well, shall I call them? Yeah, I think I will. First one, then the other. Fiamella will be furious . . . Call back? Why should I give you the pleasure? Make trouble now, and later take all the credit! Five o'clock then. At five thirty I'm offering these gifts to Bertolucci. Seven, and woe betide you if you don't tell everyone where you get your stars from. At Skylight we pluck them straight out of the sky!"

They're back at seven o'clock sharp.

"He still hasn't called." The rasping voice coming through the intercom is Fulvani's own. The secretaries have gone home. "What do you want, come upstairs and wait a little or try again tomorrow?"

"Tomorrow," Maxim hisses to Gala in Dutch.

"How unfriendly," says Gala. The door opens with a buzz.

"Say 'Holland' and every Italian will say 'Petrus Boonekamp.' "

Fulvani can't believe that Gala and Maxim have never heard of the delicacy. He pours some for them.

"Not for me," Maxim says, but Fulvani insists. "You can't sell it if you don't know what it tastes like."

Fulvani has arranged an audition for them for a Petrus Boonekamp commercial.

"Tall, well built, blond, just the Viking they're looking for. Ten a.m. tomorrow in De Paolis. And then, at two, a test for the Fiat Lancia Christmas lottery. Repeat after me, *'Puoi vincere!'* "

"Puoi vincere!"

"The job's in the bag," laughs Fulvani. "And don't forget, I get twenty percent of everything, okay? I only ask fifteen from amateurs." Then he turns to Gala. He rests an encouraging hand on her back. "Your friend is lucky. He stands out here. Since the days of the Normans, men like him have been rare below the Alps. But you, my beauty, you could just as easily be Neapolitan. A pearl in the crown of that city, true, but still, there are others to be had. Have you considered dying your hair?"

Gala looks sideways at Maxim. She bends down to pick up her bag. He knows what she wants to get out of it. He shakes his head. Fulvani notices, picks up their portfolio, and starts to leaf through it.

"Wonderful material," he says after a while, shaking his head. "It has it all, but still, I miss something . . . something to grab the attention of those men, the kind of thing that would appear among the thousands of photos a director gets on his desk and make him jump to attention."

Gala's hand slips into the bag.

"I wouldn't," Maxim says urgently. Gala looks at him. Caught. Like a child who has to hand over her toy, she pulls a face at him, ugly, pretending to be angry. Fulvani is sitting right there and can see everything, but that seems to have slipped her mind. As if everything that disappears behind that black window really were gone.

Maxim shrugs. She's already pulled the slides out of the envelope and is holding them in her hand.

"Perhaps you ought to look at these."

He takes the transparencies between thumb and index finger and holds them up to the sun, which is setting in the suburbs across the Tiber.

"Please, children," he says amiably, "not so formal."

Eight slides. Eight fairy tales with Gala in the lead role. As many days' work went into them, sparing no trouble or expense. A new set was built for each scene, each employing stylists to arrange the expensive fabrics and props. In the middle, Gala. As Snow Queen and mermaid, selling matches and wearing a red riding hood, in Ali Baba's cave and in the clouds of Magonia. The editors of *Bunny* really went to town. The thousand and one nights of Gala Vandemberg!

She had just made an outrageous movie with a rising Dutch filmmaker and, as an up-and-coming starlet, she was in no position to make too many demands. The money wasn't the point. The one thing she insisted on was Maxim's presence at every photo session. She was unsure about the whole adventure and wanted his opinion on every detail. The first morning, he'd intervened a few times. Concerned that in her nakedness she should look as unattainable as possible, portraying her as the master of the situation, not as a slave. But even before the lunch break, he sensed that it was a lost cause. When Gala came to him, on the verge of tears, to show him the thick blue eye shadow the Spanish makeup artist Pedro had deployed to transform her into Cinderella, he disguised his aversion and reassured her. What else could he do? She'd signed the contract. There was no way back. The most important thing was to avoid making Gala more insecure than she already was. He insisted willy-nilly that it suited her, that it went with the general atmosphere, and that it was particularly tasteful. He kept it up. Even the next morning, when seven horny dwarves with fake beards and pointy red hats were waiting for them.

A dejected Maxim sat off to one side through the remaining sessions. After all, it was what she wanted. They'd discussed it extensively beforehand. When Gala caught his eye, he smiled supportively and otherwise tried not to think about it.

On a lazy Sunday, years earlier, when Gala was listening to a sermon on the radio with her father, her mother had asked Maxim to go for a walk in their garden with her. Just for him, she opened up her rose house to show him the special varieties she was growing for an exhibition. She taught him to distinguish scent groups with his eyes closed, just by the fullness of their bouquet. He gradually managed to pick out various spices in the faint smell: bitter first, then pungent and fresh, and eventually even a hint of apple. Just when he was starting to enjoy it, she asked, "Do you understand, Maxim, why we can never completely enjoy the things we love most?"

To avoid answering, he closed his eyes and hid behind the petals of a *Rosa tomentosa*. He recognized cinnamon.

"Always afraid it will be taken away from you." Suddenly Mrs. Vandemberg grabbed both his hands. "Will you watch over her?" she asked imploringly. Shamelessly. "For God's sake, will you watch over her?" Without giving him a chance to respond, she continued, with the clarity and passion of someone who knows she'll never have this much courage again. "She trusts you. We don't ask what she does or who with. I don't have to know, if I can be sure you care about her. Will you look after her for us? Please. Her pills. I think of them every morning and every evening. But what's she thinking? Does she remember to take them? Oh God, you have no idea, every morning, every evening. A child is just one more vulnerability. It makes you so sensitive that you feel you don't have so much as your own skin protecting you from the outside world." The moment she heard how she was letting herself go, her courage subsided. "Who else can I ask? You love her."

Tears ran down her cheeks. He wiped one away with the back of his hand. That helped her regain her composure. She turned away, took a handkerchief from her sleeve, and dried her eyes. She pulled out one of the low wooden drawers and removed a pair of shears. Facing away from him, she started cutting off rose hips. Her hand was unsteady. Now and then, as discreetly as possible, she sniffled. Finally, she straightened up and weighed a few flowers in her hand.

"We'd save ourselves a lot of sorrow if we kept to ourselves."

She cut a full, round flower off under the bud and stuck it through Maxim's buttonhole.

"I'll protect her," said Maxim, "I promise." It felt like a solemn oath. Like the promise he had once made to Gala. And sincere. "I'll do everything in my power."

Gala's mother removed her gloves and held the greenhouse door open for him.

"Pleasure," she said, "is something people can only derive from things that don't really matter to them."

By the end of the day, the heat from the spotlights made the photographer's studio almost unbearable. Maxim woke from his daydreams with a start. He jumped up. Now that he was finally striding across the room, he felt the air moving over his sweaty skin. He resolutely positioned himself between Gala and the lens. From her perch on the beanstalk that had wrapped its tendrils around her, Gala looked at him with surprise. The moment had come for Maxim to intervene. His eyes glided down her body. It was dizzying. So much courage, so little shame! The crew stood waiting on the sidelines. Gala a naked goddess, an unattainable idol.

"Your nipples," he whispered. Gala smiled at him, as grateful as a child, fully confident that Maxim would never let her look a fool. As her hands were fixed above her head in the plant's tendrils, she turned her breasts toward him. He squeezed the nipples until they were hard and pointing straight at the camera again.

The telephone rings. Fulvani reluctantly puts down the last fairy tale. He looks at Gala and Maxim openmouthed, as if he needs to recover. Annoyed, Maxim snatches the slides off the table.

"That was Salvini," Fulvani explains after he's hung up. "Fiamella wants to see you." He pulls out twenty thousand lire and sends Maxim off to the bar in the Via di Ripetta for a bottle to celebrate their achievement. "Italian cinema can breathe again. You kids bring luck. At last: Snaporaz is preparing a new film!"

Not until he's out on the street, with the slides drumming against his breast with every step, does Maxim become uneasy. Overwhelmed by the general jubilation, he has left Gala alone with Fulvani. He stops in midstride and is about head straight back, but how can he explain returning empty-handed? He sprints to the end of the street. He can see the bar from there. He looks back one last time.

"Does he sleep with you?" asks Fulvani.

"Why?"

"He guards you like a lover."

Maxim is out of breath. He's back at Skylight with the first bottle of wine he saw. He rings the bell. Waits. Rings again. The third time he keeps his finger on the button until something happens. The intercom. Fulvani, "Not now, Maxim. Come back in half an hour. Be a good boy: we don't need you right now."

Maxim is too astonished to answer. For a moment he thinks it's a joke and presses against the door. It doesn't open. He pushes the button again. The same voice. Angry this time.

"Are you dense? You know what's going on. Fuck off."

Maxim rings yet again. His blood seems to drain into a reservoir that has suddenly opened inside him. The light on the intercom dims. He can push the button as much as he likes. The system is switched off. There is no response.

Maxim tries to get hold of himself, concentrating on the dizzy feeling in his head. Then he runs back to the corner. He races across the Piazza del Popolo to the bar where he made the calls that morning with Gala. He phones Skylight. Fulvani answers.

"I want to speak to Gala."

"She doesn't want to speak to you."

"I'll call the police."

He hears rummaging in the background. Then bumping. Are they struggling? He screams into the receiver. Then Gala's voice comes.

"It's all right, Maxim," she says in Dutch. Then in Italian, "Do what he says." And, "It's nothing terrible." Then he's cut off.

Maxim calls the police. He tells them everything. Stumbling over his words. Actors. *Bunny.* Nude fairy-tale characters. Snaporaz. They don't take him seriously. He can come into the station. Tomorrow morning. Preferably with the slides.

He runs back to the Via Brunetti. He kicks the door. People look out of windows. Some swear at him. He keeps it up, kicking, cursing, hoping some neighbor will call the police. But the shutters all close. Someone shouts down at him to go away and sleep it off. He's still holding the bottle he bought with Fulvani's money. His fingers are blue, tense with fury. He relaxes. Leans against the wall. Enraged, sobbing, he slumps to the ground.

An old lady walks by, followed by her maid.

"It must be that time again," the old lady says when she spots the young man next to the door.

"Snaporaz?" her maid asks with a sideways glance at Maxim.

"He only has to think of a new film and actors start migrating from all over the world, like birds that have caught a whiff of spring." The lady shakes her head. "The scientists are mystified."

In front of the big door of the palazzo, the maid puts her plastic bags down to look for her keys. Maxim jumps up. The heavy wooden door slowly closes behind the women. He blocks it with a foot. The elevator stops on the third floor, halfway up. Maxim waits until he can't hear anything in the stairwell: no footsteps, no keys, no doors. He walks up to the fifth floor, creeping up the last flight. He saw that in a movie once. It's ridiculous, because once he reaches the door of the casting agency, he has to make them hear him. He shouts.

"Gala!"

He tries the doorbell, but it's turned off here as well.

"Gala! Gala!" he yells, hurling himself against the door with all his might. And again. Roman doors are sturdy. Since the Visigoths first arrived, Romans have secured them with an iron bar. Then he realizes: there was one downstairs at the back of the front door too. He could use it to force his way in. He takes the elevator down to get it. Halfway between the fourth and third floors he hears something. Someone is walking down the travertine steps above him. In a hurry. Suddenly the elevator stops. Maxim tries the alarm, but the electricity has been cut. He's dangling halfway down the shaft in a brass cage.

The blood is churning through his temples. The impotence raging inside him is so fierce that he is afraid he might faint. He feels the tension in his every fiber, as if his will were about to erupt through his skin. Amid all this fury, he hears her. She's calling him. As silent as it is, he hears it very clearly. He tugs at the sliding iron doors, in vain, then discovers a hatch above his head. He shoves it open, hoists himself up, steps up onto the mechanism, and kicks open the door to the floor. Then he runs downstairs, grabs the iron bar, and walks back up slowly and thoughtfully to muster his energy. On the top floor he jams the iron bar into a crack and levers it like a crowbar. In that same instant, Fulvani opens the door.

"Thank God!" he says. "You've come at last!" He's in such a panic that he even seems relieved to see Maxim, grabbing him by the shoulders and pulling him in. "Hurry up. She's in my office." Then his astonished gaze moves from the crowbar to his door.

"But, what . . . ? Are you *both* insane?" While Fulvani tries to push the splinters back into the wood, Maxim goes into the office.

Gala is lying on the floor. She tries to prop herself up on her elbows, but her muscles scarcely react. Finally Maxim is calm. He has a minute, maybe one and a half, before she loses consciousness. He kneels beside her. She probably still recognizes him because she smiles at him, open and beaming, and starts describing the incredible things she can see. It's little more than a baby's babbling. Maxim listens intently, as if it meant something.

Fulvani comes in, nervous as a sinner before the throne of God.

"Nothing happened, honest, we were just having a nice chat and ka-boom, suddenly . . . I tried to get her to come to . . ." He slithers over to the cupboard where he keeps his booze and pours himself a double Petrus Boonekamp.

Maxim lays Gala's head on his lap, takes his handkerchief, rolls it up tightly, and opens her mouth with one finger. Her tongue reacts immediately, curling around his fingernail. He pushes it down and clamps the cloth between her jaws. They wait it out like this. Together.

Are these two lovers, or aren't they? Many have asked the question, but their curiosity has never been satisfied. Even I never got to the bottom of it, and I saw them together at close hand. Familiarity and a lack of inhibition can indicate indifference just as well as devotion. Who can understand someone else's love life? Who understands his own? A song in Trastevere dialect has this to say about it:

> *Forget about the truth, Fanfulla!*
> *Guessing flutters free from Coeli to the Borgo,*
> *Knowledge lies under the bridge, a stone around its neck.*

They have kissed, often and, above all, long. They necked in all the discotheques and public gardens of Amsterdam. On long summer evenings, they rolled under the bushes in front of Gala's parents' house and over the field where the circus pitched its tent when she was little. There is no spot on either's body that the other hasn't kissed. But is that what makes two people lovers?

In sickness and in drunkenness, they've cleaned up each other's vomit without gagging and then crawled back into the dirty bed to spend the rest of the night dabbing feverish sweat from breast and brow. But whatever else they did in bed, convinced they were holding their dearest in their arms, they did not engage in sexual love.

They went much further. They told each other every intimate detail. How they made love, or wanted to, with others, how that felt, and how they could help each other to conquer others. They seemed to be trying to outdo each other in caressing the other's naked back. Every tear, every word they shared, brought them both closer to and farther from each other. It melted their hearts to hear these fragile revelations; when they were at their most vulnerable, each new disclosure felt like acid dripping into an open wound.

Isn't that what lovers do?

But they never said the one thing they wanted to say. They didn't expect to hear it, either, since they were sure they knew each other's thoughts completely enough to be able to fill in the gaps themselves. They preferred to stick their tongues down each other's throats rather than talk about apparently obvious things. So in all those years, they had never spoken a word about their love, but great loves don't need that. Longing is safer than fulfillment. So if they're not lovers . . .

Fanfulla, Fanfulla,
Forget the truth.
Hope keeps you alive,
Having is only for Death.

On the other hand, they *are* actors. It's always possible that they're simply acting for each other, so convincingly that they've started believing it themselves.

Gala comes to in an iron bed in an enormous ward in the Fatebenefratelli Hospital. Fulvani called them in a panic, and the brothers refused to let Maxim fob them off. They strapped her onto a stretcher and took her to the island in the Tiber for blood tests and an EEG.

The first things she sees are the wooden beams of the sixteenth-century nave. Waves of light surge over the dark rafters. It's always difficult to know where madness stops and reality begins. It takes her a while to realize that the space is a ceiling, and that the reflection comes from a beam of light. One spotlight, aimed at the ancient bridge outside the hospital, shines onto the fast-flowing water of the Tiber. Then things speed up. Within a few minutes, she understands what must have happened. But it takes almost two hours before she is freshened up, able to carry on a conversation, and steady on her feet. Her head hurts, but she insists she doesn't want to go straight home.

"I need to see some life," she says.

With their arms around each other, the two foreigners walk off the island, out of the spotlights, and into the darkness of the night.

"Look, I really don't know," Gala says. She sips her sambuca. Maxim is trying to figure out whether she's really forgotten what went on between her and Fulvani. The seizures can rip whole chunks out of her memory. But he's skeptical. She won't look him in the eye. Maybe she just doesn't want to talk about it.

In the rear of the establishment, the only place to eat in Trastevere past midnight, the lights go on over a small stage. A young woman clambers onto it. She is fat. It's hard for her to get up there. Two musicians take their position behind her, an elderly accordionist and a young boy with a tuba.

Gala lays her hand on Maxim's and shrugs.

"Maybe it'll come back, maybe it won't."

The woman on the stage plants her fists on her hips and bursts into song. Gala and Maxim don't understand a word of her Roman dialect.

"What kind of person would just throw those slides on the table?" Maxim asks eventually.

"You're the one who always says I shouldn't be ashamed of them."

"You shouldn't. But there's a time and a place."

The singer is followed by an elderly couple. The woman's costume is trimmed with ostrich plumes. The man makes a show of casting off his cape and reveals a gold lamé body stocking. Now and then the woman calls out something, whereupon her husband twists his wiry body into a pose. He maintains it for a few seconds, in the utmost concentration, as if performing a superhuman feat. Then he relaxes, skips on the spot, and calls, "Hop-la!" He does the discus thrower, the rape of the Sabine virgins, and something that looks like a dying Gaul.

The novelty soon fades. Sniggering, Maxim looks aside at Gala. She is crying.

"I did it for you," she says, "stripping for those photos. Why else?"

They watch the movements of the man in the gold long johns.

"How can you say that?" Maxim asks without looking at Gala. "You do things like that because *you* decide to. The craziest things."

"Insane," she agrees. Her voice sounds completely serious. "Completely bonkers!" As if she's summing up their whole life and has now finally reached a conclusion. "The two of us are completely insane."

"Things nobody else dares to do. You just do them. I see you doing it and I think, 'God, I love that lunatic.' " Maxim is now tearing up too, moved by the idea of daring to deviate from what other people expect.

"You were only too happy to come to Rome with me," says Gala coolly. "Those photos made it possible. I always saw them as our tickets here. I flung them into the fray because I thought they might help us."

The magazine with the nude fairy tales had been out for two days when Maxim laid it on Gala's parents' table. He came with her because he was scared Jan Vandemberg might attack her. It wouldn't have been the first time. Her father's urge to protect her was so strong that he was inclined to slap her around to spare real injury. Once he had grabbed a piece of burning wood from the fireplace and flung it at Gala's head because she refused to wear a helmet on a scooter.

This time he did not react at all.

"You could at least have a look," said a disgruntled Gala.

"As far as I'm concerned, that magazine is an open coffin," Jan replied, without raising his eyes from his newspaper. "There's no point looking. The damage has been done."

The magazine lay there untouched until it was time to clear the table for dinner. When Gala picked it up to make room for the place mats, Jan snatched it out of her hand. For a while, all they heard was the sound of his turning of the pages and puffing on his pipe. Only when Gala was called into the kitchen did he glance at Maxim over the edge of the magazine.

"Well, sir, a lot of men will enjoy this. One could even argue that it's noble of you to show the world what you could have kept for yourself."

Before Maxim could react, the family came in and sat down. Jan immediately rose, ripping the photos out of the magazine one by one.

"Look, Anna," he said, showing his wife, "this is what we produced. Fairy tales." He walked over to the fireplace, threw in the pictures of his daughter, and watched the flames until the last piece of flesh had turned to ash.

"The hope of the old goes up in smoke to provide clouds upon which their children can build castles."

He picked up the carving knife. Before plunging it into the roast beef, he closed his eyes and said grace. "Lord, bless this meal and watch over the woman I love and the strange creatures that accidentally crept out of her. Amen."

Laocoön is wrestling with a rubber snake. The man in the golden tights wraps up his act.

"A true artist," the owner of the trattoria says tenderly as he lays the bill on the table. "Used to be world-famous. A body like Apollo. He could do classical poses without a net. High on the trapeze, swaying back and forth on the tightrope. No one else was up to it. He's too old to fly now, but he can still do the poses."

"Impressive," says Gala. She really is moved, but the man doesn't believe her. He shrugs and snatches the notes from the saucer in a huff.

"Even out of water, a fish gasps for air. Or should he give that up too?"

Entertainment's not cheap. The surcharge is so high that Maxim and Gala have to dig out their last telephone tokens to pay for the meal. They don't have any lire left for the bus, but so what? This is Rome. They've been ripped off, but the night is warm. Cheerfully they turn down the first lane toward the Tiber. Gala glances up and sees the sign with the name of the street. Just in time. She sees it in a flash, before the lights go off. In this street, in the adjacent streets, in what looks like the whole neighborhood.

. . . . .

I always tell the truth, but who would believe it? All my life I've been told that I exaggerate, whereas I only record what I see. People smile and shrug as if I'm joking. They shake their heads in disbelief, because they don't see the interconnections in their own lives. Are they unable to do it, or just unwilling? They call my reality fantasy. It used to annoy me, but now I understand that there's no point in getting upset about it. They just don't see what I see. We listen with the same radio, but my receiver is tuned to a different station. I pick up other sounds, but that doesn't make them any less real. For years, to accommodate others, I've even tried to dampen things. In reality, people are actually much more grotesque than I portray them; the things they experience are infinitely more extreme, less credible. They just don't want to believe it.

So the street Gala and Maxim are walking down when the blackout occurs is called the Via della Luce. Why should I make that up? My story would be more plausible without it. I should have made up another name. The only reason I don't is because it is an example of the coincidences that meet Gala at every turn.

"Did you see that?" she asks, bursting out laughing. "Did you see the name of the street?" Delighted, she throws her arms around Maxim's neck. She's always more astonished by things like this than he is. Over the years, Maxim has learned to accept that coincidences like this happen when Gala is around. It's one of the things he loves about her. More than anything else, it makes him stand in awe of her. Minor details shrink from her presence to allow life's essential themes to shine through. It reminds him of the frescoes in the city's oldest churches: the colors have faded, leaving only the grooves of the original drawing in the plaster.

. . . . .

Along broadly sketched lines like these Gala will cut straight through the indescribable anthill of Rome to cross my path at last. That's what's so wonderful about the truth: it does things we wouldn't dare make up. No, the only thing that's really unimaginable, that might seem like something I've invented, the most incredible thing of all, is that people don't see that I portray them accurately, showing their world as it is. We experience exactly the same things, in the same reality, but simply pick out different details.

Lying naked on her stomach on the downy back of Andersen's flying swan, Gala had seen exactly what was going on in Maxim's eyes. They were making a fool of her, and he wasn't warning her. The photographer asked her to tilt her pelvis a little. The lighting men aimed the spotlights to banish the last protective shadows. Along the sidelines were a few members of the editorial team who had chosen this day to see something of the sessions they were paying so dearly for. They were hot. An assistant slid a window open. The big bird's feathers moved in the draft. Again the photographer instructed her to tilt her pelvis. This time he sounded even less patient. "Come on, babe, a little further, people want to see something." One editor sniggered. Maxim was sitting between them. He must have heard it as well. But he did nothing. He just sat there with his legs crossed. Watching. He was ashamed. There was no doubt about that. Gala caught his eyes. Insistently. Her expression very clearly asked him to intervene, to help deliver her from this position. A few words would have sufficed. Then she could have grabbed a bathrobe and walked away from the set, but all he did was give her a reassuring signal with his eyes.

It was only a quick flicker of his lashes that broke the contact between them, but Gala suddenly felt abandoned. She wanted to scream with fear, but she knew that no one would hear her, and decided to save her energy, even though she had no idea for what.

Just as a calm certainty grows within a drowning man when he realizes that the last hope is lost, an awareness arose within Gala that compared to the struggle ahead the present conflict was unimportant. For a second, enduring this trial even seemed worthwhile, just to see how she could possibly survive it. Now Gala found an unsuspected source of strength, and a new consciousness was born somewhere deep beneath the waves of her abandonment.

The eyes of all the men who surrounded her—the photographer, his technicians, the makeup artist, the editors, and Maxim's eyes as well—glided over her body, becoming entangled with the wind blowing over the canal and entering through the open basement window. They swirled through the room, playing over her throat, her flanks, buttocks, feet, calves, blowing up between her thighs and chilling her sex. The eddies caressed her skin, making the hairs stand up suddenly, shocked by the watery chill, only to immediately relax and lie down again, as if an invisible hand had smoothed them over.

With a stab, Gala experienced the menace of the male in its full intensity for the first time; she was astonished, as if the danger came from a completely unexpected source. She shuddered to think of the depths behind his mask. She did not fear the sorrow, the insecurity, or the pain a man inflicted by loving you—child's play, compared to this unnameable something. She shuddered at the realization of the true perversion, the loneliness of the role men have to play, the part that everyone, themselves included, expects them to play with such abandon that if they have to they will destroy you to make you believe it. In a flash, Gala became aware that this natural, insurmountable inequality renders impossible any hope of fully abandoning oneself to the other.

This must be why every woman discovers sooner or later that, together with love, this menace has forced its way into her unnoticed.

When the photographer urged her for the third time to tilt her pelvis, his voice was anything but friendly. Gala let the tone sink in, as if letting the humiliation strengthen her, as if the memory of this moment would give her a weapon she could one day use to defend herself. The weapon was contempt. Like a magic spell it instantaneously robbed the men of their magic. "They're using me," thought Gala, "but they need me too. I can and I will turn the tables." This was a powerful observation, but it was hardly a conscious formulation, anything but a strategy: it was a realization with all the innocence and openness of a newborn, shocked and bawling at the unknown.

She wrapped her arms tightly around the swan's neck, pressed her abdomen against the feathers, and tilted her pelvis back as far as she could. She even raised her lower body to give the men a better view of her sex. Their breathing quickened. They slid back and forth against the walls uneasily. The camera didn't stop clicking. Flashes of light shot over her retina. With these fireworks Gala celebrated her triumph.

"What were you actually thinking?" asks Gala. She's still standing there in the same dark street. By the flame of his lighter Maxim has discovered a box of Asti Spumante in the courtyard of the trattoria that just overcharged them for their dinner. The kitchen door is open. Inside, people are running back and forth between the arrested refrigerator and the oxygen cylinder for the lobster-filled tank.

The coincidence goes to Maxim's head and makes him reckless. He tries to open one of the bottles with his teeth.

"What was I thinking about what?"

"When you were looking at me in the photographer's studio."

His teeth scrape the neck of the bottle. He swears.

"There are two sides to everything, you know," she continues, "in front of the lens and behind the lens." Her voice has a sudden urgency. We're both a bit drunk, Maxim thinks, but we still make more sense than anything about this day. He replaces the bottle, then picks up the whole box, weighs it in his arms, and decides they have a right to it. He puts away the lighter. Suddenly Gala grabs him. She shakes him. He feels her nails digging into his arm through his shirt.

"From now on, we're on the same side of the camera, okay? The two of us. The same side of the camera, promise? Promise me!" Her grip is so tight that he almost drops the box. The bottles clink against each other.

"Chi è? Chi è?!" Someone comes running out of the kitchen. But Maxim and Gala are already walking on through the night. He puts the box on his shoulder so that he has one arm free to wrap around Gala's waist. Her stilettos click out a melody on the cobblestones of Trastevere.

"I thought," says Maxim, "we already have so many dreams. Those fairy tales are just a few more."

. . .

He can't sleep once he's finally in bed. Of all the extraordinary things that happened that day, one, the most innocent of all, haunts him. He didn't mention it to Gala and now he wonders why not. It was this: a little girl walking barefoot down one of the hospital's long white corridors. She is wearing shiny silk pajamas. When she passes the bench where Maxim is waiting for the neurologists to finish with Gala, she pauses, holding her head a little to one side and looking at him. She wonders why he's so gloomy when everything else is bathed in light. When he smiles at her, she dashes off. In the distance she grows smaller and smaller.

A little later two nurses run up. They're searching for her.

"Every day it's the same," pants one.

"It's an addiction," the other swears. They open doors left and right and peer into the wards.

Something about their tone makes Maxim decide not to help them. Instead he starts looking for the child himself. He walks down the hallway, looks back briefly, then quickens his pace. At the end he discovers two new corridors. These lead to others. He takes a few wrong turns, but quickly retraces his steps. It's almost as if he knows where to look. At last, he sees her, far away, facing a large window. The light shining in is so bright that he can only see her as a black silhouette staring out the window. The spotlights that illuminate the island in the Tiber for the tourists are as powerful as film lighting. One is aimed at the old hospital. The girl stares obsessively into the beam while slowly moving her hand back and forth in front of her face. Even when Maxim's running footsteps approach over the marble floor, she doesn't look up or around.

"What are you doing?" he asks.

"A game."

"What's it called?"

"Looking into the light," she says. She makes up the name on the spot. "Looking into the light and seeing things."

"What kind of things?"

"I don't know. They're always behind me."

"Behind you?"

"I feel them coming. I look around but . . ."

"But then you're already falling."

"I knew you knew what game it was," the girl rebukes him.

She moves her hand back and forth in front of her eyes ceaselessly, compulsively. The shadow flies back and forth over her face.

"Aren't you afraid to fall?"

"Course I am."

"Why bring it on then?" Maxim grabs her arm in annoyance. Now she looks at him. Disturbed. She angrily wrenches her arm out of his grip and starts again.

"Because it feels good," she says.

When Gala notices that Maxim can't sleep, she crawls over the big bed toward him and takes his hand.

"Tiruli, tirula," they sing until they fall asleep. *"Pitipo, pitipa."*

3

"One breath: that's how long beauty lasts. The rest is either memory or repetition." Sangallo's eyes are wandering over Maxim's hair, studying how the light falls on it. "One breath, at the most, and even then only if we happen to be lucky enough to notice. A single moment of inspiration makes the body blossom; afterward, the worms know what to do."

This will be the third time in a month that the viscount has taken the young man to show him the city. And for the third time he's offered him the same long, black leather coat, draping the garment over his shoulders almost casually, as if trying to concentrate on the other things he needs for their excursion: an old map, a silver fruit knife, a bag of mandarins to perfume the car, and two crisp *rosette* with mortadella. He seems far more interested in these things than in the black coat.

It is an unusual article of clothing, shiny as an oilskin. The leather looks as stiff and rugged as a uniform, but it's actually very light, so supple you forget you're wearing it. It's extremely well made. Molded pads accentuate the shoulders, and the waist is cut to make the hips seem narrower. From there, the wide-gored flaps hang so far that, even on someone as tall as Maxim, they reach the calves.

"It's too hot today to play dress up," Maxim grumbles. He is annoyed with the old man, though he doesn't know why.

The first time Sangallo tossed the coat over to him, he wasn't sure what to do with it. It was early November. There was a fair chance of a shower, but only a fool would have wrapped up like an old salt in a westerly gale. Sangallo didn't notice his hesitation and had apparently forgotten the coat until the car pulled up in front of the building and they stepped into the elevator.

"Go on, put it on."

"Maybe later, if it starts raining."

"You've got to try everything once."

"Fortunately we still have plenty of time."

"Please," insisted Sangallo, "in the interest of science." His eyes smiled so sadly that Maxim didn't dare refuse. He had hardly slid his arms into the sleeves before the old man's face lit up like a praised child's.

"Don't forget the bottom button," he added. "Keep the belt loose and turn the collar up a little." He showed no more interest in it that day, but a week later, for the second outing, he held the coat out again, his eyes averted to a monograph about Piazzetta, whose painting *Giuditta* was on their program for the day. This time, Maxim threw on the garment without grumbling. It was airy enough. It was no bother, and if it was important to the old man, why not?

Now, the third time, Maxim has the coat on before he stops to think. He only reconsiders it once the viscount goes off on his pet topic.

"How can anyone enjoy something permanent?" Sangallo asks. "Something that is still attractive at a second glance, after that first sigh, is boring."

Maxim hurls the coat into a corner. It's mid-December and quite warm.

"If it's all so fleeting," he says, amazed by how sulky he sounds, "the shine must have gone off this by now as well."

"Boredom bears a close resemblance to beauty," Sangallo replies imperturbably. "It's all that's left when you cage something beautiful."

Sangallo's tours of Rome are wild journeys of exploration. They shoot through the streets like boats tossed by rapids. Hour after hour, they cross old squares and ancient forums, following the inscrutable plan that the viscount abandons again on the slightest whim. He can unexpectedly change course, screaming for his driver to stop while already throwing open the door. The car has hardly had time to lurch to a halt before his tall, heavy body is shooting down an alley or through a gate, all as if he's in a tremendous rush, his large, shuffling feet scraping over the pavement at a remarkable pace. By the time Maxim catches up, Sangallo is standing in a church or a ruin, before a mural or a marble statue, pointing at a single detail that moves him. Usually he tells a story or recites something. It could be a poem, a childhood memory, or a discourse on the history of art, but it might just as well be a Charlie Chaplin scene, executed with all the appropriate poses and walks. On their previous outing Sangallo was so moved by the light in one of the forgotten Caravaggios in the Santa Maria del Popolo that it was too much for him.

"There," he said in English, trying to hide his discomfort and nervously undulating his tie between his fingers like Oliver Hardy, *"that's another fine mess you've gotten me into!"*

"That faun." Sangallo points at a statue by Praxiteles. "That's Momo."

"Momo?"

"Momo the faun. A childhood friend."

After having torn through the Vatican museums, this is only the third room in which Maxim is allowed to linger.

"I remember him from the house of one of my mother's friends in Bergamo. He was at the top of the stairs. We stayed there by the lake in the summers. And when I went up the cool marble steps to my room at the end of the day, he was waiting for me with his powerful chest and the muscular arms he only uses to lift the panpipes to his mouth. See how he's inhaling? His sides are puffing. He could start playing right now." The old man lays a hand on the stone midriff. A guard notices, but doesn't think of saying a word. Every museum attendant in Rome knows the viscount.

"One day I saw a fisherman untangling his nets. He was standing up to the waist in the lake. 'Momo!' I called out. That's how much he looked like the statue I loved. I imagined legs underwater, with split hooves and as hairy as a billy goat's. That day I walked into the water. I had just turned twelve."

For others Rome might be a city, Maxim thinks, but for this old gentleman it is an enormous playroom, filled with mementos. Sangallo has moved on. He swings a leg over a cord strung across to keep out the public. Maxim catches up, running down a corridor built around the outside of the museum.

"Filippo? Why are we always in such a hurry?"

"Because time is trying to catch us. This is Rome. Stay vigilant! Today is abandoned before it can even become yesterday. The centuries tumble over each other like children let loose in a bakery, hurling pies at each other. You should have come earlier if you were planning on just plodding around. So I do what I can. I take you along. I point out things that are meaningful to me. If any of it interests you, you'll come back of your own accord. Later. Alone. But at least I'll have done what I could."

An attendant unlocks the entrance to a long narrow hall, which they follow to a dark and indeterminate room where a muffled commotion, like the one behind the backdrop of a film set during the coffee break between shots, has replaced the devotional silence of the museum. It is smoky and crowded. Roman workers are relaxing with water and freshly drawn wine, *pizza bianca* and dishes of tomatoes, grapes, and citrus fruit. Among them are a number of Japanese: some wearing white doctors' coats, others with T-shirts with NIPPON TELEVISION NETWORK printed on them. With surgical masks over their chins and protective goggles on their foreheads, they are bending over a sketch with a small delegation of professors dressed in the latest Milanese fashion. When Filippo joins them, the academics greet him as a friend. A geisha in a business suit bows deeply and offers him a bowl, and he ignores the matter at hand to drink from it with a seriousness appropriate to a tea ceremony.

Only now does Maxim notice the folds in the walls. They turn out to be made of heavy material, hung up like the sides of a circus tent. The small room has been erected inside a much larger space. Here and there, he can make out sections of a construction forming the base of a tower of scaffolding. Far above, at a dizzying height, there is a plank floor. Maxim hears the buzz of hundreds of visitors, immediately behind the cloth walls. He recognizes the bright pink and the pale green in the small corner of the painting still visible far above, between the planks of the scaffolding and the small builder's hoist. He slides the tent cloth aside, slowly, like the curtain of a theater. He steps through it into the middle of the Sistine Chapel, directly below God, who, with a powerful gesture, though clad in a lavender frock, is separating night and day.

While tourists wander past, Maxim takes in the colors of the frescoes. They are deep, warm, and somber on one side of the scaffolding, fresh, cheerful, and brilliant on the other, where Japanese television's cleaning project has already stripped the soot and grime.

Around the ceiling, the vaulting is filled with naked men and women. Young or old, their flesh is voluptuous and comforting. Together they seem like one great naked body that wants to embrace Maxim, the nudes bending toward him, as if to lift him up and rock him in their arms. Full of lust, ruddy, uninhibited as children, muscular as young men, soft as parchment, they cry, run, flinch back, cower, or twist their bodies like contortionists. Shameless. Yes, especially that: they feel no shame.

Maxim's head starts to spin. The pictures fade and then charge back even brighter. Perhaps he's been staring up too long, pinching a blood vessel in his neck. Whatever it is, they are dizzying, but he is enjoying himself so much that he can't bring himself to look away. His eyes shoot left to right across the narrow hips, full breasts, muscular buttocks, fleshy thighs. Arms reach out to each other without touching. He spins round and round, trying to see them from every side, whirling beneath a heaven full of desire. Without the slightest embarrassment. Suddenly, the whole spectacle is illuminated by a flood of light. Maxim stops abruptly, as if he's seen the souls shining forth from inside the bodies, but the surrounding space keeps spinning. For a second, he feels he's about to be lifted into the painting.

The break is over. The spotlights are back on. For the benefit of the restorers, as well as of the sponsor's cameras, recording the whole process, batteries of lights have been set up on all sides as if it's a TV game show. Workers nimble as acrobats on their way to the trapeze ascend the scaffolding.

"It's a stew of nudes!" says Sangallo, who has come up alongside Maxim.

The Japanese shoot up in a lift beside the scaffolding.

"Sinful, worldly, and grotesque, that's what Adrian the Sixth thought of them. He wanted them hacked off. What else could you expect from a northerner?"

Sangallo wants to keep moving, but Maxim, overwhelmed, can't tear himself away.

"Hurry up a little," says Sangallo. "You desperately need taking care of. Pampering."

"A little longer."

"Why would someone want to see everything in one go, if he could see part of it later close-up?"

"Close-up?"

"From very, very close by. 'I'm old,' I told Pietrangeli, 'a chance like this only comes once every couple of centuries.' Carlo is a friend of mine, director-general of Papal Monuments. It just happens that a delegation from the *soprintendenza* is visiting today, otherwise we'd be up there already. Never mind, we'll go up some other time."

Maxim imagines standing eye to eye with Michelangelo's brushstrokes and, as if one thing went with the other, thinks of Gala.

"She has to come with us," he says out loud. "Gala. I'll introduce you."

"Who?"

"Gala, my girlfriend! If we go up the scaffolding, she can come with us, can't she?"

"Pietrangeli hasn't promised anything. He'll call me." Suddenly Sangallo sounds tired. He looks around as if the whole museum, and Maxim too, has suddenly begun to bore him. He pushes his way through a group of Zimbabwean novices toward the exit.

It's not the first time that Sangallo has cut off a conversation the moment Gala is mentioned. Up till now, it happened so unexpectedly that Maxim wondered whether he'd said something inappropriate. Only now does he realize that Gala's name is all it takes to make the viscount uncomfortable, as if the sound alone distracts him from their being together. This annoys Maxim, because it clashes with his image of Sangallo: a rich, free spirit on intimate terms with great artists should be above the envy that dominates petty lives. But though elegant, courteous, gifted with the ability to make life sparkle and charm, Sangallo, of all people, has drawn a line. As if he wanted to be Maxim's sole frame of reference for this city.

For Maxim, discovering Rome is only half his endeavor: the other half is Gala's. Sharing it is the essence of their Italian adventure. Upon returning from his previous two outings with Sangallo, Maxim had immediately gone out with Gala. Until past midnight, they wandered the city while he showed her as many of the secret alleyways and forgotten springs that Sangallo had revealed to him as his memory allowed, trying to deliver the same anecdotes with the same flair, hoping to overwhelm Gala with impressions just as he had been overwhelmed. Even if they spent all their days wandering the city apart, at night Maxim still felt they'd spent all those hours together. He couldn't help it. Whenever he enjoyed something, he imagined her reaction—giggling in surprise with that turned-up nose of hers, pinching his arm when overwhelmed, searching together for words to describe something that could only be felt—and he naturally assumed she felt exactly the same way. That's how these things work. Even when alone, he is an indivisible part of the two of them.

When he finds the old gentleman in the museum shop next to the exit, he goes up to him.

"Listen, Filippo, as far as Gala is concerned . . ."

But Sangallo has already recovered his enthusiasm. Like a child that can't make up its mind in a toy store, he has grabbed all the most beautiful objects. Beaming, he showers them on Maxim.

"As far as Gala is concerned, I want to be clear to you that she and I . . ."

A study on Lysippus's *Apoxyomenos* athlete, a model of Bramante's Tempietto, a replica of a chubby Etruscan cherub sitting on another's lap, a catalog of the collection of ancient sculptures of animals, and a large, professional reproduction of Raphael's *Transfiguration,* before which Maxim had stood studying the epileptic whose cure it depicted. He clamps it under his chin while Sangallo buys another book about the Sistine Chapel before the restoration and one about what it will look like afterward.

"Listen," says the young man, who almost has to crane his neck to look over the gifts in his arms, ". . . that Gala and I . . ."

"Gala and you, you and Gala, I know all that already." Sangallo adds new acquisitions to the pile in Maxim's arms. "You must believe that I can hardly wait until I get a chance to see with my own eyes the delightful creature who has managed to enchant enchantment itself."

He means it.

At least, he says it with the same enthusiasm he musters for an extraordinary brushstroke, but he doesn't stop perusing the tables, presumably searching for a book about the chapel *during* the restoration.

"That must really be something special, Maxim. Gala and you. You and Gala. It only happens once or twice in a lifetime. Cherish it."

This still sounds gruff to Maxim, almost like an order to shut up about it, as if he were really saying, "Cherish it in silence!" If he hadn't been standing there awkwardly, loaded down with gifts, he would have reacted at once. But all he can do is follow the viscount to the car. The chauffeur relieves him of the gifts while listening to instructions to drive them to the Apelles restaurant in Ostia.

"Apelles was court painter to Alexander the Great," mumbles Sangallo. "He painted a portrait of Alexander's concubine Campaspe and fell in love with her. The moment Alexander saw the painting, he realized how much love had gone into it and gave her to him in marriage. More people should accept that other people's passion can be greater than their own."

Now, of course, I could keep pushing, thinks Maxim, and insist on picking Gala up on the way. He knows how generous Sangallo is with guests: "Try a little of this too, just taste this. Let's simply order a plate of everything. So that you will have a full impression of Ligurian cuisine. Come on, just a mouthful . . . If only in the interest of science." Gala, just like him, could use a meal like that. They hadn't brought much money and for the last few weeks she and Maxim had been investing—some might say squandering—it all in their future. Photos, photos, and more photos, big and glossy and with the most expensive finish, for the best possible impression. They had to print business cards and CVs on cream-colored, handmade paper. They bought expensive, stylish folders to put it all in and stamps to mail it. And of course there were the gifts they kept having to buy for agents, cameramen, and directors, who arranged to meet at the most expensive outdoor cafés and always needed to rush off to another appointment, leaving the up-and-coming film stars to pay for the drinks.

After a few weeks, all they have left are the two modest checks from the Department of Social Security that arrive from the Netherlands at the end of the month. It's barely enough to get by. They've already stopped buying the tomatoes and grapes that are their staple diet at the Campo de' Fiori; now, they pick them up in the Via Rasella or at the stalls along the Via del Portico. They've also learned to rely on the farmers who sell basil and onions from their cars near the Porta Portese on Sundays; with a bit of luck, they can find homemade salami and jars of honey for under a thousand lire.

Maxim is keenly aware that he hasn't eaten a thing since last night's salad. Stubbornly insisting on bringing Gala might ruin his chances of a free meal. That would be dumb, especially because he'd also be ruining his chances to go to the famous restaurant on the river in Ostia. One lunch is better than none: he's sure Gala would feel the same way. And before any feelings of remorse can well up, Sangallo orders his chauffeur to stop yet again. He shepherds his protégé into a small print shop on the Via dell'Orso and asks the owner to get out an etching by Bartholomeus Breenbergh. It shows Saint Peter's Basilica before Maderno hid it behind his facade.

With an exaggerated gesture, Sangallo brings the drawing up close to his face to study it.

"See," he says, "this is the chapel we were just in. This is the passage we walked down." He buys the print and, back out on the street, gives it to Maxim.

"So you don't forget the layers under the face of this city."

"Out of the question. No, really, it's too much."

"Breenbergh made these as souvenirs for his countrymen."

"It's too expensive. Magnificent, absolutely . . . but no, I don't deserve it."

"Back then, nobody took this one home. Do the artist a favor. Take it with you, just as the poor fellow always hoped."

When the driver puts the print in the trunk with the other gifts, Maxim discovers the black coat. He looks at Sangallo, who blushes like a child caught red-handed. He shrugs and scratches his head like Stan Laurel when Hardy is about to bawl him out.

You just can't get angry with the man.

"Do you think we can eat outdoors in Ostia, Filippo?"

"They have a terrace," replies Sangallo, "but it is December."

"Exactly," says Maxim. He takes the coat out and slams the trunk. "It could get chilly."

Maxim gets back to the Via Michele Mercati late in the afternoon. Gala's not in their room. He tosses the day's spoils—besides the print and the books, a chunk of ham and a jar of pomegranate jelly made from fruit gathered under the trees along the Via Appia—onto the bed. He looks for a note, but he knows there isn't one. Gala comes and goes without plans or explanations. He wouldn't have it any other way. How he loves how she does whatever she wants, self-centered enough to go out even when she knows he's coming home weighed down with stories. She follows her whims without a second thought. And this afternoon, when he has so much to share with her!

At least he can surprise her with the print. It fits into the collection of the pieces of Rome he and Gala have gathered from all over the city like magpies picking up aluminum. They've dragged all kinds of things back to their nest: marble from the forbidden passages in the Aventine, a lump of red-leaded stucco from Hadrian's Villa.

Maxim tries to hang the Breenbergh so that Gala will notice it the second she comes in, which isn't easy without damaging the aged paper. He slides one corner behind a loose piece of wallpaper, another under some cables, trying a few variations, but the draft keeps getting it, the Vatican curling up and fluttering to the floor. Maxim, who almost never loses his cool, swears out loud. His irritation with the uncooperative paper is mixed with his concern. When did she go out? The least she could have done was to leave a note with her time of departure, so he could know when to start worrying.

It would be easier to handle if concern and irritation didn't create the same nagging pain in the pit of his stomach.

Disappointment was a factor: she wasn't home, and he'd arrived hoping she would be.

He would say that he missed her, if he ever mentioned it, which he wouldn't, at least not to her, because she would laugh at him, and she's never once been concerned on his account.

When the print folds for the umpteenth time, it leaves an ugly crease. For an instant Maxim is annoyed with Gala, worried about the paper; but he immediately pulls himself together.

He opens her suitcase in search of a hairpin or something to attach the print. It goes without saying that there are no secrets between them. Why should you be able to run your fingers through a woman's hair but not her toiletries bag? He dumps it onto the bed, almost at the point of tacking the print to the ceiling with nail varnish. He tosses the items back one at a time—boxes, jars, combs, curlers, powder puffs—no wonder they never arrive anywhere on time when Gala has to put on her makeup. The swirling powders and perfumes give off the scents he knows so well. They calm him down: he sniffs them and sees her before him.

At the same time, he's fidgeting with a small glass jar, shaking it. Pills, but not for epilepsy, and he's never seen them before: an Italian brand he's never heard of. She must have bought them here. Suddenly it occurs to him: clothespins!

In the garden, the concierge is hanging the washing up on the rotary clothesline.

"Signora Geppi, good afternoon, I was hoping to borrow two pegs."

"You were, were you? As long as it's not for anything naughty," she angles hopefully, but he doesn't get it. Brazenly eyeing him over a pair of drawers, she takes two pegs and rotates them around her breasts in ever-decreasing circles until they touch the nipples that stand out under her worn black dress like stems at the bottom of a bag of plums. Opening them a few times, she lets the steel springs click shut, like a Spanish dancer's castanets. Finally, she tosses them into the air and bursts out laughing, shrinking with embarrassment. On both sides of her mouth, she blows spit bubbles out through gaps in her teeth.

Maxim catches the pegs. "It's just to hang something up on the wall."

Geppi is so red that she has to duck behind a row of sheets.

"Do you know when you're leaving?"

"We're planning on staying."

"Of course. They all want to stay. As long as possible. That's why they go."

"I don't quite understand. You mean the rent?"

"Don't worry. Signor Gianni has paid three weeks in advance. It's just . . . He thought you would be going away on a trip soon as well."

"A trip?"

"He thought so."

"Where to?"

"Who knows? It's none of my business. But I'd like to rent out the room while you're away. We can share the takings, so it's good for you too. And it will be there for you when you get back, of course."

"But we're not going anywhere."

"But if you do, even just for a couple of days, even a weekend. It won't be much longer. Let me know at least a day in advance. Our house just happens to be very popular."

"I've noticed," says Maxim, his initial suspicions confirmed. "Very popular. Especially with gentlemen, and never for much longer than an hour."

Geppi pulls down the clothesline to see if he's kidding. Then she lets it pop back up, the wash dancing in the sun.

"It's an offense against Saint Julian to show people the door when there's a room you're not using."

"There's some mistake; we're not planning on going anywhere."

"I just thought you were. But what do I know? It just goes to show. I draw my conclusions. If you've seen one go, you think the next one will too."

"Who on earth are you talking about?" asks Maxim. "Where are they going?"

"Who cares? Short trips. Wherever. And if a couple have gone, you think they're all going. The same old song, I've shot my mouth off again. I've always been reckless. That's what got me my nickname."

"Yes, I know, la Bomba Atomica." Yet another thing that doesn't make any sense, thinks Maxim, who has pocketed the pegs and is searching for a chance to get away from the old fool.

"Not *la Bomba, la Bimba,* the little girl. The cartoon character! Don't tell me you've never heard of her. It was the first story us kids looked for when we got our hands on the *Campanello*. Those magazines were long before your day. She was sweet, but rowdy: Geppi, la Bimba Atomica, much too rowdy. She always meant well, but things got out of hand, and by the bottom of the page she was always in tears. And later I even got her body. Irresistible! Explosive! No wonder the name stuck! A name to be proud of, because that figure of mine . . ." She slides her hands down her dress. For a moment he's afraid she's going to weigh her breasts in her hands, but fortunately she thinks better of it. "That figure of mine . . . Believe it or not, but in my day I looked like a secret weapon with a hair trigger. Which reminds me . . ." Sighing, she bends down to pull the last pillowcases out of the laundry basket, before disappearing into the labyrinth of hanging sheets. "There was a gentleman caller."

"What?"

Geppi tugs on the clothesline, making the laundry spin and fan out in the sun. "Yes, a gentleman caller for your girlfriend. That's what made me think of it, of course."

"What gentleman?" Maxim asks. "Geppi? Geppi!" He heads into the corridors of laundry to find her between the fluttering walls, but she's slipped out and away without a word.

"He's seen our photos!"

"Snaporaz?"

"He's seen them and picked them out."

"What do you mean?"

"Snaporaz has graced us with a glance," Gala teases, giving herself the air of a Grand Inquisitor, "whereupon it pleased him to make further inquiries."

"Is that it?"

"Do you know how many photos a man like that sees every day?"

"Do you know how many people he then inquires about?"

"We're up on the notice board in his office in Cinecittà! You and I. He can't go in or out of his office without seeing us. That's how far we've come."

"How do you know that?" When she pauses before answering, just like when she's forced to admit she didn't take her pills, Maxim's immediate mistrust is confirmed. "Who told you that?"

"You'll never guess."

"No, that's why I'm asking."

"Don't worry, nothing happened."

"Fulvani!"

"Meek as a lamb. When I suggested stopping by his office, he didn't even want me to. We went to Tucci, behind the Piazza Navona. Did you know they have the most amazing *tartuffo*? I'll treat you to some, soon. He kept it purely professional."

"On a Sunday afternoon?"

"I told you, he's scared of me. That seizure taught him once and for all not to mess around with actresses. All I have to do is touch his arm and our Casanova recoils as if I'm a witch who wants to change his sword into a pin."

"Why were you touching his arm?"

"Why not? He had good news. Maxim, sometimes I think you're just not the kind of person open to being surprised by life. Isn't it wonderful? Snaporaz! Face-to-face with Snaporaz ten times a day! He walks by. Sees our mug shots out of the corner of his eye. Stops to have a better look and, today or tomorrow, he'll think, 'I need them, I've got to call them!' "

"I'd just like you to be a little more careful."

"What am I supposed to do? Hang up the phone when someone says he's practically made an appointment for you with Snaporaz, who's casting his new film?"

Maxim shakes his head, aware he's being ridiculous. Only now does the news sink in. He screams so loudly that Gala jumps. Laughing, he grabs her, lifts her into the air, spins her around the room, and smothers her throat and breasts with kisses.

"Come on," he says, throwing her onto the bed and dropping on top of her, "we've got something to celebrate."

Now that she's lying down, she spots the Breenbergh for the first time, still rustling from the wind they've whipped up. She studies it through squinting lashes for several minutes.

"Exquisite! The way he's captured the light. Did you feel this paper? It's almost like it's real!"

"Yes," says Maxim, pulling her up off the bed and out the door, "it's our lucky day."

"Buon natale!" shouts a Father Christmas at the Casina Valadier. The terrace is decorated with Christmas lights, but beneath the pine trees of the Pincio it is still warm. A law firm is holding a reception: ideal for celebrating free of charge.

Maxim and Gala mingle as if they've been invited. Their graceful self-assurance and casual arrogance keep even the most seasoned headwaiter from asking for their invitation. On those rare occasions that one of the organizers comes toward them, Maxim and Gala invariably seem to spy an old friend off in the distance. Surprised, they raise a hand to wave at a stranger on the other side of the crowd, then bear down upon him calmly but resolutely, leaving any awkward questions behind.

One cannot, like an amateur, accept every drink and hors d'oeuvre on offer. After a disdainful appraisal, Maxim and Gala reject almost all of them. Eventually, they request some exotic fruit or liqueur that they are sure cannot possibly be available. Disappointed, they can only make do with the champagne and the salmon canapés doing the rounds, but only as a condescending favor.

The Dutch couple have soon generated so much goodwill that no one raises an eyebrow when Maxim takes a full bottle from the bar, showily reads the label, then wanders off mumbling, "I guess this will have to do." Gala follows, grabbing a dish of stuffed zucchini flowers while wishing Santa *"Buon natale!"* on her way out.

"What do you actually know about this film?" asks Maxim. Looking out over the obelisk of Ramses the Second and the traffic on the Piazza del Popolo, they drink to their future.

"Exactly as much as Snaporaz himself."

"Nothing, in other words."

"That's why he drives producers to despair."

"But he's got to know which direction he wants to go? Hasn't Fulvani said anything? How can Snaporaz choose us if he doesn't know what for?"

"He's got a story. There's not much to it. Two actors. They're old. Probably played by Marcello and Gelsomina."

"Marcello and Gelsomina . . ." Maxim savors the names. He's moved. He takes Gala's hand. "Just imagine."

"Elderly actors. Once famous, now forgotten. They loved each other but lost touch. They meet again in a clinic where they are convalescing."

"The film they could make about us sixty years from now."

"Exactly, Maxim."

"Meager, but moving. That's how it works. The less meat, the more emotion. At the end they dance together, the old actor and the old actress."

"Dancing?" asks Gala. "No one mentioned dancing."

"Completely unsuspecting, they come into the recreation room and find a band sitting there."

"Dancing? Will I still be up to that?"

"Of course. I haven't seen you for all those years. And suddenly you're standing there. Old, but still beautiful to me. Because I see you as you were and not as you are. What should I say? What do you say? No words can express it." Maxim jumps up, a little unsteadily. "But our bodies know exactly what it was like. It all comes back. Every step. Each movement."

Gala plays along, cuddling up as they dance the waltz from *The Mannequins' Ball*. The gravel, crunching underfoot, is all the music they need.

"Buon natale!" calls Father Christmas as he goes by. He's done for the day. He's carrying a red coat under his arm, he's taken off his beard, and he's tugging at his suspenders to lower his thick, quilted trousers.

The waltz degenerates into shuffling. Finally, the tipsy dancers stand there with their foreheads touching.

"Tell me honestly," Maxim begins, "no one's asked you to go on a trip, have they?"

"A trip? What makes you think that?"

"Nothing. Just curious. If anyone had invited you to go on a trip."

"A trip . . . ," says Gala after a while. "Now that you mention it, someone did ask me, yes."

"Fuck! See, I knew it. I knew it!"

Shocked by his intensity, Gala shrinks back, making Maxim lose his balance. He swings his arms as if lashing out at an invisible assailant, loses his balance in his aimless fury, and falls, cutting his hands on the sharp stones. Staring at the injured palms of his hands, he stays on the ground while the dust descends.

"A trip, God almighty, what's that supposed to mean? Who with? Where? And what did you say? Who fucking well asked you?"

"You did," Gala answers, sitting down beside him. "Who else, you fool?" She carefully brushes the grit off his hands and strokes his long fingers. "You asked me to come to Rome with you. We were in the bathroom. Don't ask me why. I was sitting on the edge of the bath, you were on the washing machine. I didn't even have to think about it. It's the best thing we ever did."

"You think so?"

"I feel it. Don't you?"

"Yes, yes, I think I do feel something."

4

The next morning, as soon as his hangover has subsided, Maxim walks to Skylight. Fulvani shouts through the intercom that waiting is the best strategy for the time being. It's almost Christmas, people are going off on their holidays, offices are shutting down, and not much will be happening in the film world for the next few weeks.

When Maxim thinks of their photos on Snaporaz's bulletin board, he feels an energy he finds hard to square with this news. It was only a matter of a few weeks before the edges would start to curl. A disappointed starlet could rip them down in a fit of jealousy; an inebriated cameraman might pull out a felt-tip during the New Year's party and doodle a drooping eyelid on his picture, or a moustache on Gala's.

Where would we be now if Garibaldi had kept bobbing around at sea instead of sailing into Trapani?

That very morning, they take the metro to Cinecittà. From the Istituto Luce on the other side of the road, they observe the comings and goings at the studio gate. Finally, they settle for the most brazen option. They cross the street and stroll in, ignoring the sign telling them to register and waving at the guards instead, like regulars: these guys see young people coming in for auditions all day long. They wave back from behind their newspapers, but emerge from the booth anyway to comment on Gala's provocative hip swinging. The oldest insists he hasn't seen anything like it since the day Sophia Loren arrived holding her mother's hand to report to the set of *Ben-Hur,* where she was an extra in the chariot race. As always, Gala doesn't notice, but their jealous stares make Maxim walk twice as tall.

A real border post stands in the forecourt, marking off the separate city. Gala fishes an Instamatic out of her shoulder bag. To Maxim's astonishment, she wants a shot for posterity.

He didn't even know she had a camera.

He hesitates, but she presses the button before he can get away. Then it's her turn.

After all, in a whole lifetime there's only one first time you enter the land of Snaporaz.

Gala poses.

He takes the photo.

It moves him.

They really are crossing a border.

Gala has never before wanted to record anything.

Along the wide green avenues, there are no signs of the approaching holidays. In the studios, which are marked with large numbers, the movie business is in full swing all around. In the distance, an enormous 5 stands out like a beacon on the famous Teatro Cinque, the studio where, since the fifties, Snaporaz has shot all of his films. They head straight for it, their nervousness growing with every step. The bar, a kiosk in the middle of the grounds, is packed. In between sandwiches, actresses in Western outfits flirt with toothless medieval peasants. Gala worms her way through, orders two shots of vodka, and knocks them back.

"So I can be more relaxed," she says, getting ahead of his criticism.

"More relaxed than who?" asks Maxim.

Teatro Cinque's tall sliding doors are open, but the enormous studio is deserted. The offices are above it. Maxim tucks a few strands of hair in behind Gala's ear and wipes a lipstick smudge off the corner of her mouth. She uses a little spit to tame his recalcitrant eyebrows.

"What do we say?"

"We heard he has our photos."

"We had to be here anyway, and we thought we'd drop by to introduce ourselves."

"And then?"

"Then you say something witty."

"Why me?"

"Because you're so relaxed."

Upstairs, a long corridor stretches the full length of the building. There are doors everywhere, but none marked with a name. They try their luck by knocking on a door and asking for the maestro. A young woman talking on the phone looks up with surprise.

"That's you, isn't it, on the notice board?"

Behind her back, Gala pinches Maxim, who is already having difficulty restraining a shriek of delight, on the bum.

"Yes, that's right," he says, "that's us."

She opens a door—and there they are between lots of others: character actors, carnies, laborers, washerwomen . . .

"He'll be right with you," the receptionist says before leaving them alone.

"He'll be right with you," repeats Gala, shaking her head. She tries to take it all in: the office, the windows overlooking the pines, the sketches on the wall. Maxim reads the production schedules in the hope of learning something about the chapter they're about to write in cinematic history, but the scene and location numbers mean nothing to him.

The wait is remarkably long. At first they're upset, worried they've been forgotten, and then they get bored and calm down. Maxim flops onto the sofa and leafs through the latest *Variety*. Gala drapes herself over the desk like a Pirelli pinup on the hood of a car. She leafs through the in and out trays, moving the photo of an overripe Dane from one to the other.

The man who finally arrives pricks their dreams like a finger pushed into a soap bubble. Not only is he not Snaporaz, he doesn't have anything at all to do with the artistic side, and his job is to discourage, not help. And he's merely the lowest official in the outer circle of a long series of offices and waiting rooms around the inner sanctum.

To film their disappointment, you'd have to dolly in on Maxim and Gala quick enough to zoom out at the same time, so their dismayed faces would get closer while their surroundings recede, so alienating is their abrupt realization that months, not minutes, separate them from their goal.

If they'd acted on their feelings, stumbling over the shards of their ambitions on their way to the exit and the metro, slowly resuming their true proportions as they disappeared down the tunnel, the whole adventure could have ended here.

Instead, they wander numbly over the grounds behind the studio, arms linked and leaning on each other. They walk a few times around the pool where Ben-Hur's trireme was sunk, scene also of the naval battles of Lepanto, the Nile, and Chatham. They wander among the saloons of a town in the Wild West, down Viennese boulevards that lead past Brooklyn fire escapes to narrow Roman alleys that end at a forum with a temple like an iced cake. They sit down and stare out at the ancient arches of the Sette Bassi aqueduct and the blocks of flats on the Via Tuscolana.

"When Filippo was little . . . ," Maxim says after a while.

"Which Filippo?"

"Sangallo."

"The viscount. Why haven't I ever met that guy? Does he have something against women?"

"Why should he, when he's got so much in common with them? When he was little, he lived somewhere on an estate in the hills. In the early twenties. They didn't have a radio or a gramophone. His mother gave him scores. He read them the way we read books. He heard the parts in his head. Separate at first, then with another one, until in the hush of nature he could fill his thoughts with the complete symphony."

A small Fiat is approaching along the track beside the fence, throwing up an enormous cloud of dust.

"When there was a concert in town, Filippo's mother would take him. There, he would finally hear the melodies and harmonies. It was always a disappointment. The musicians were excellent, the conditions perfect. Yet it was never as beautiful as he'd imagined."

The car stops at the back gate and beeps impatiently until a guard appears, summoned from his afternoon nap. The coat of his uniform is unbuttoned.

"How long can we hold out?" asks Gala.

"Until New Year's, a few weeks longer if we only eat at the market. No more coffee at outdoor cafés, only standing at the bar, and definitely no more *stracciatella* at the Pantheon."

The car goes past. The driver is a small woman in a crocheted hat who can barely see over the wheel. She has to straighten up a little to cast a glance at the young people by the side of the road. Their eyes meet briefly before she disappears into the cloud of dust she's throwing up.

The realization hits them both at the same time.

"It's her."

"Gelsomina!"

"On her way to . . ."

". . . who else?"

They watch the car disappear behind the palisade of the fake forum.

"Gelsomina!" they scream together. They leap up. "Gelsomina. Gelsomina!" Gala kicks off her stilettos and starts running. Maxim scoops them up and follows. They take a shortcut over the cobblestones of medieval Paris and are just in time to see Snaporaz's wife get out of her car close to Studio 5. The film star opens the trunk and takes out a picnic basket, so old that the cane has forgotten it was once woven. The neck of a bottle of wine is sticking out, along with a leg of ham and a loaf of bread. While the woman rearranges it all, she looks up, accustomed to being pursued by paparazzi. Gala and Maxim, who have ducked behind the Sphinx of Giza, which has been put out in the sun to dry, can see her clearly. Gelsomina has grown old since her heyday, but she still has the features of a cartoon character: the big eyes and the stubby nose above that tiny body, the little clown from the film in which her husband made her a star. Carrying his lunch, she scuttles around the corner of the studio and enters through a fire escape hidden behind the garbage cans. Someone at a window on the top floor recognizes the sound of her steps on the concrete. He peers out through the Venetian blinds.

"Gotcha!" says Gala. She waves, but the man at the window steps back.

The blinds close with a clack.

Just then, they feel the security guard's hands on their shoulders.

. . .

Anything is permissible with the harbor in sight. The red-shirted Mazzini went to Pius IX seeking support for the revolution, and now the Dutch actors shed their final reservations. They apply for roles they would have turned their noses up at a week earlier, all in the hope of earning enough to stay in the city until casting starts for Snaporaz's film. The movie business may be in hibernation, but it's still peak season for advertising. There's plenty of modeling work, but there's also an enormous amount of competition. From high in the snow-covered Alps to the boot's dusty sole, Italy's most beautiful children come to Rome to capitalize on the New Year promotions and the sales that follow. Maxim and Gala go from one end of the city to another on their way to cattle calls, where the human livestock get numbers hung around their necks and are summoned in lots of fifty to be judged by the meat commission. Like shop-window dummies, they let impatient hands arrange them in all kinds of positions. The gleanings are meager, but enough to feed them. Gala poses as Mother Christmas for the post office, wearing a bag full of greeting cards and little else. Maxim shaves his upper legs and lower belly for the privilege of modeling a line of discount G-strings. Day after day they are appraised, discussed with bored gestures, and brushed aside. Gala takes it all in her stride until Christmas Eve, when things finally go wrong. The city is threatened by a shortage of male hands: sturdy wrists for watches and cuff links, strong fingers for pointing out prizes, sensual palms to offer engagement rings or boxes of chocolates. Gala, who loves Maxim's hands, takes him to a go-between, herself a former model. She has an office in a back room in the Via di Ripetta, but the woman has scarcely touched his fingers when she cries in disgust, "No, oh my God, Lord, no. No, no, no!" and drops them as if she's been offered two bloody stumps.

The insult cuts Gala to the quick. She vehemently defends the hands that caress her, but the witch insists that they are absolutely useless for promotional purposes.

"The knuckles are too broad."

"Too broad?" Gala jumps up. "How can a man's hands be too broad?"

The woman, used to keeping the desk between her and dissatisfied customers, rings a bell for the next hands to come in.

"Well, darling," she says, "I've learned to see things as they are. It was that or starve."

Maxim puts his arm around Gala's shoulders. They're already in the doorway as the woman, without looking up from her papers, quietly pursues her train of thought.

"Not that it wasn't wonderful, letting yourself be so blind," she muses, before energetically tearing herself away from her memories. "Ah, you're still so young, look at each other however you like, but don't come crying to me about how disappointing it is."

That night, they wander late through a city that seems to be theirs alone. As always, they have no need of other people. Lying languidly on the Piazza Navona, Gala decides to wet her face and neck with the water in the basin by the Moor's feet. She notices a man staring at them. With both hands, she scoops up some water and throws it at him to chase him away, but this only encourages him. Elated, as if reminded of a childhood game, he runs up, shouting that he wants to join in the fun. Gala and Maxim tolerate him. They pity his loneliness in a city overflowing with love. The man plunges his hands into the fountain, then thinks better of it. He lingers, hesitant, his cuffs in the water. He looks so sorry and misplaced that Gala and Maxim can't hold it in for a second longer and burst out laughing. Without a word, the stranger slinks off, whereupon they fall into each other's arms, grateful that they themselves are so alive.

"People used to let me know what they were up to, but now it's every man for himself."

The next morning, Geppi's grumbling wrenches them out of their deepest dreams. Sliding open the windows, she turns back the blankets, letting the cold air wash over their bodies, picks some clothes off the floor, and throws them in a bag.

"A trip, I predicted that, but not on Christmas morning itself. I always say blessed be those who deserve it and the rest will find out soon enough, but nevertheless he's waiting down there, a gentleman with a chauffeur who asked if he might try a sliver of my *panforte*. I took him some. And why not? Why the hell not? I like to see people enjoy themselves and I make my *panforte* from a recipe I got from the hermitesses of

Basilicata, just so you know, though the rest of it's none of my business. That baron out there is here for you."

She zips up the bag and puts it on the bed. When Maxim sits up, he has a piercing headache.

"Just one thing, signora, signor"—the concierge sounds unexpectedly humble—"as for renting out the room to . . . you know, third parties, how long do you think you'll be gone?"

"We're not going anywhere."

"But you will. They all do, sooner or later. How could it be any other way?" La Bimba Atomica casts a glance at their shamelessly young bodies and, for the length of a nostalgic sigh, imagines herself between them.

"Fine." She gets a grip and leaves. "Then I won't count on any more than this one Holy Day. I'll tell the gentleman you're up. *Buon natale*."

Sangallo is waiting on the garden bench, his gentle smile a balm to eyes having trouble adjusting to the daylight.

"I thought I'd take my children for a ride. It's extraordinary. A once-in-a-lifetime opportunity." He introduces himself to Gala. He hadn't counted on her, but doesn't let on. He bows his large frame and kisses her hand. Then he takes Maxim's and, wavering between awkwardness and charm, mischief and embarrassment, presses his lips against it. Finally, seeking refuge in Charlie Chaplin's apologetic expression, and not wanting them to feel neglected, he shrugs and kisses his own hands.

On their way to the car, Gala offers him an arm and leans against him, trusting him immediately.

"Onward, in the interest of science!"

They leave the city and take the autostrada south. By the time they're approaching Castelgandolfo, Sangallo has realized that his guests are hungover, observing the sun-drenched landscape through squinted eyes.

"We mustn't allow our view of the ancients to be troubled by the vices of youth," he says, ordering his chauffeur to drive into the mountains. He gets out in the woods around Lake Albano. Snuffling like a dog looking for a spoor, he shuffles through the brushwood. He pulls an herb out of the ground, roots and all. First he puts some leaves in Gala's mouth, and then in Maxim's: minty but sour and bitter as aspirin. He crushes another herb between thumb and middle finger, then rubs the white sap on their temples, first hers and then his. Their neck muscles relax almost immediately, while the pounding in their heads diminishes. At a nearby farmhouse, Sangallo asks the farmer's wife to make an omelet with ham and porcini, which they shovel down at the kitchen table. Beaming, Sangallo pours fresh goat's milk from a jug.

"To party and see the world," sighs Sangallo, "at your age! Your possibilities seem endless."

"Didn't you do the same?" asks Maxim.

"It wasn't the right time."

"But you were rich."

The old man looks at the goats grazing in the field.

"My mother wouldn't have permitted it. She wouldn't have trusted me with that much freedom. She would have cut off my allowance. Even given my circumstances . . . *I* wouldn't have had a penny."

You can hear the question hanging in the air, but Sangallo is too polite to ask it.

"We worked a bit," explains Gala, "but that extra money is gone. Now we're earning a little here and there."

"Our rent is next to nothing."

"Even so, Rome is expensive," says the viscount.

"Thank God for our allowance," laughs Maxim. "The Dutch state is a more bountiful mother than Countess Sangallo."

"A state allowance? You're not claiming that you've been sent here for reasons of state to enjoy the good life in Rome?"

"More or less," says Maxim. He does his best to explain the Dutch social security system. It's not easy. The concept of unemployment benefits isn't the problem—of course, the government doesn't abandon its stranded herring gutters and curdled milkmaids—but the old man twice mishears the amount they are receiving. The ease with which they've conquered a ship of gold like that gives rise to an array of new questions. He is most confused by the news that they never had to be employed in the first place, but became unemployed immediately, on their last day of school, when, like Maxim and Gala, they started getting paid for nothing.

"You could also call her a mother who is not terribly concerned about her offspring," Sangallo demurred. "She throws some money at them and turns her back, washing her hands of the problem."

It takes him a while to appreciate just how confident these youngsters are that they have a right to something they don't earn, never have earned, and have no intention of repaying, but once it's sunk in the astonishment on his face turns to increasing admiration. Smiling cautiously, then glancing from one to the other to make sure they're not pulling his leg, he bursts out laughing.

"An allowance from the state to do nothing? Masterful!" He slaps his thighs. "Only in the Netherlands!"

Sleeves rolled up, the farmer's wife comes out from behind her donkey to make sure he's not mocking her cooking.

"Not at all, woman," shouts Sangallo. "I've just been told something amazing, an unforgettable joke. You missed it. I can't possibly repeat it. Only in Holland, up in the far north. What can you expect from a nation that chose to settle in a swamp?"

The woman washes her hands at the pump and starts to clear the table.

"Hold on, seriously." Sangallo tries to keep a straight face but can't help chuckling, like a child who wants to hear a story it can't get enough of. "One more time: you get money every month and you don't have to do anything for it at all."

"Well, you do have to sign for it."

"An IOU!"

"No, just a form with a few questions about how you are and so on. You have to hand it in."

"And then there's an interview where they ask you about your answers?"

"You put it in a mailbox outside the building, so you don't have to go to the trouble of coming at office hours. And if you can't make it one time . . . or maybe a bit longer, a few months, or half a year . . ."

". . . you get somebody else to do it for you and you pocket the money!" guesses Sangallo. He is so overcome by the giggles that he has to walk over to the window for a breath of fresh air. "It's classic. This is, it's . . . I tell you, this is material for an opera, a comic intermezzo: tara-rom-ti-ra, the pranks of a shameless villain fleecing his master right under his nose. Pure commedia dell'arte: behind the count's back, the servants put on his most beautiful clothes and lord it over his riches. Pantalone in the polder. Piddelee, piddelee, piddelipom. Ah, Rossini is turning in his grave."

He pays the peasant woman for the meal, buying her wine and a woven basket of candied orange pieces, so sweet that the bottom is already in sight before the car has started heading south again.

"Les nouveaux pauvres," says Sangallo, his fingers touching Maxim's and Gala's as they try to scrape up the last crystalized droplets of fruit. "Cultural tramps, subsidized vagabonds. Traveling the world without a job and yet carefree. Beautiful, shameless people. That's how they do it, the new poor!"

Most of Vesuvius is hidden behind the clouds gathered on its slopes. They drive past Herculaneum, but it is closed for the holidays. They park beside the deserted supervisor's building—not out front, but around the back. Sangallo spreads a map out on the hood and decides to continue by foot over a donkey path. For a long time, it follows the fence, before turning off over extremely rough terrain. Sangallo explains that the tourist attractions are only a fraction of the archaeological treasures. On this side, where everything was buried under lava, there was more destruction than on the Pompeii side, which was buried under a rain of ash. But here too the grass grows over country houses, farms and basilicas, market squares, taverns, and theaters. The slopes they are walking over follow the roofs and terraces, galleries and domes of an ancient suburb. They leave the path for a roller-coaster route down steep declines and through unexpected pits, more and more slippery now that it has started drizzling.

A group of men in overalls has taken shelter beneath a tarpaulin strung between trees, waiting for their coffeepot to bubble above a gas burner. One embraces Sangallo. His name, Professor Baldassare, is not the only thing that reminds them of an old-style conjurer: he wears a monocle, has a Vandyke beard, and is followed by a blond assistant in a miniskirt. Beaming, she skips around him in the mud and hands him his props when he asks for them: umbrella, map, timetable, ballpoint, sketchbook, pointer. Hop-la!

They descend a short ladder to the excavations. Among the discoveries the professor points out, Gala and Maxim recognize an alley and the counter in front of the window of what was once a bakery. Next door, a stone phallus adorns the wall, a sign that this complex—which the professor has dubbed the House of the Bread Virgin—was once a brothel. They are standing on the round roof of what seems to be the most important discovery. The professor cannot mention it without beaming. The bathhouse, almost intact, must have been attached to the brothel. The concrete that has been hacked free from the lava is still covered with chunks of marble, and the rain is washing off the last clods of soil. The mud drips down the walls and over the petrified door, whose iron locks melted during the disaster in the year 79. Star shapes are slowly emerging in the damp cement beneath their feet. Inside, the bathers saw these stars illuminating planets on the ceiling of the dark steam bath, up to the moment that the lava filled the airholes and sealed the room in time.

The professor drums up his team. Grumbling, they leave their shelter and step out into the bad weather, where they meticulously follow the instructions of his assistant, who has put on a glimmering plastic rain hat for this number.

"Why are they working on Christmas?" asks Gala.

"In Italy, the past swallows an enormous amount of money. There are too many treasures and not enough cash, which gets distributed between two departments. First, the official one, from the government, which watches over and exploits excavated monuments and must make a profit, if only to pay its staff. So it's always in search of new star attractions, like an amusement park. Baldassare heads up its rival. It's made up of serious academics, a small but fanatical army who do their research as discreetly as possible. The government department tries to steal Baldassare's grants, but every cut just makes him more inventive. Officially, he works with archaeology students from foreign universities, but unofficially he works with grave robbers and bounty hunters. Their illegal expeditions carry out important preliminary work that is beyond his official ambit. He constantly struggles to keep them on his side so that the real treasures don't fall into the hands of the art collectors the professional grave robbers really work for. If he didn't cooperate, the damage would be much worse. As soon as everything's drawn up and recorded, he fills the site in again, before the government can turn it into an archaeological theme park. So he does his most important work when there are few prying eyes around, days like today . . ."

It clears up. The clouds part and reveal the volcano's quiet summit, but the improvement in the weather does nothing to accelerate the excavation.

"Sangallo's right," Gala says a little later. To kill time, she and Maxim are walking through the vineyards on the slope. "Is it humanly possible to be happier than we are right now?"

"I don't know. It feels like we're working our way toward something, but our lives are actually at a standstill."

"Happiness is never agitated. Don't you think? Whereas sorrow never stops." She hesitates. "Maxim, . . . this morning, what was that all about? Geppi hoping we wouldn't be back too soon."

"She rents out our bed."

"Our bed?"

"When we're not there, she rents it out."

"That's disgraceful." She laughs indignantly.

"Probably by the hour."

"And you let her?" she argues. "That's a great idea."

"We're living there for next to nothing, I can hardly complain."

"We have to look for something else."

"We can't afford anything else. Don't worry. It's just the mattress. The sheets are clean. For some reason, she's decided we're going on a trip."

Gala sits down. She closes her eyes and turns her face to the sun. Maxim does the same.

"Gianni asked me."

"What?"

"Yesterday morning at the market. All of a sudden he showed up on his *motorino*. Asking if I wanted to take a trip."

"With him?"

"Who else? I don't know. It took me by surprise. I didn't hang around, I just walked away."

"What a rogue." Maxim laughs.

"But what's it supposed to mean?"

"You're beautiful. This is Italy. All the men want to take a trip with you. Don't worry, I won't let you go . . ."

Gala looks at him.

"Never?"

In the fleeting instant in which they are nothing but each other's eyes, Maxim's head becomes a tumult, two scenarios playing out at high speed. He doesn't want to consider either one.

". . . unless you want to, of course," he answers, because what do you have left if you put beauty in a cage?

When they return, the camp is deserted, the pan boiling away on the burner. Everyone has hastily assembled in front of the bathhouse. Five strong men are attempting to pry open the door with a lever. Exhausted workmen are relieved by students who follow the professor's instructions, taking measurements and using scalpels and fine brushes to try to enlarge the gap between the door and the wall. It budges. Dust billows out of the chinks they've scraped open and swirls to the ground. For a moment, the door yields, then jams again. Each time it moves forward a little, it immediately sinks back into place, as if a rival team inside were pulling just as hard. The past refuses to let go, but the present is stronger. Unexpectedly, the grinding of stone on stone is followed by the sound of a powerful suction. Gala grabs Maxim's hand. She feels the change of pressure in her ears, just as she does with the onset of the epileptic aura that precedes her seizures. Maxim feels the same. Others reach for their ears too, briefly, or they swallow like people in a train that has raced into a tunnel. Then, as if the other team has given up, the door shoots forward with unexpected ease. The men stumble and fall, the petrified door atop them.

The first air escapes. A gust caresses Gala's hair, dry and poisonous in her throat. She gasps as if she's about to cough, drinking a full draft of the second wave, the air that wetly flies into freedom, soft as a sigh of relief, sweet as candied orange. Immediately afterward, as everyone present is sniffing for more of the same, this storm too has evaporated, the atmosphere calmed. In this stillness, Gala and Maxim look at each other, openmouthed, beaming with amazement. And then it happens. Emerging calmly from the bathhouse comes the smell of oleander, rolling warmly through the December air until it rises and is scattered.

Swirling through its midst comes eucalyptus and a dash of rose oil mixed with the powerful sting of birch, as penetrating as if the lids have just been removed from the pots of salve. Fearing that the slightest movement will disperse the shimmering cloud surrounding them, they stand motionless, but Gala sees that Maxim has closed his eyes, hand on his chest, head thrown back. Then come the perfumes, essences of geranium, honeysuckle, and vanilla, an acrid flood of musk. When these have been liberated, they fleetingly perceive the unmistakable hint of human sweat, as dull and dead as flakes of skin, sebum, and talc, immediately followed by oils, at first as soft as milk and then, sharper, sourer, the tang of fruit. Grasses arise, spicy, light as lilies, heavy as camomile and lavender. A few minutes after the capsule is opened, everything is gone. Only a little lavender, lingering close to the ground, wobbles up occasionally, as the people slowly begin to move. Sangallo stands immobile among them.

Inside, the bathhouse turns out to burrow deep under the hill. There are three large rooms, each filled for the main part with a basin—the hot, warm, and cold baths, separated by a series of cells for relaxing or dressing, all hurriedly abandoned. A stand that was knocked over. Earthenware salve pots in a niche. Lids lying broken on the ground. The outside light hardly reaches the second room, but even there the marble soaks it up and emanates a gentle glow. Some of the decorative panels have come loose from the walls. Earthquakes have caused damage. In two places where the ceiling has collapsed under the weight of the soil, roots push in from every direction, but as they wander through the rooms, Gala, Maxim, and Sangallo see them as they were. Their footsteps echo dully off the domes and round walls.

Gala lies at the edge of a bath to try to absorb the experience. Maxim goes over to sit beside her. They don't need words. They are both seeing themselves from a distance, not only experiencing the moment but seeing themselves in later years looking back upon it. Aware of themselves, of one another, breathing in that beauty, their diaphragms moving up and down to the same rhythm, just as when they're asleep. Watching themselves from somewhere in the distance, seeing how small they are there on the edge of the bath, they feel they should be weeping, crying, but they can't.

"You could touch her," says Sangallo, from the doorway. No one knows how long he's been watching. He whispers conspiratorily. "Why not? Just for a moment. Two bodies touching. Just for the image. The idea. In the interest of science."

"I touch her when I feel the need to," Maxim says, feeling gauche and strident, his voice hollow in the empty room.

"The body conquers eternity. Two young people. Here. In this light. From where I'm standing. Unimaginable, you together, and only me to see it."

"Come on, Gala," says Maxim. He stands and pulls her to her feet. And then, with gratuitous cruelty, "Before we know it, he'll pull out the shiny black coat."

"You're quite right," quips Sangallo, "tara-rom-ti-ra-ta-ta," but he looks as surprised as if he's just then realizing something. "I'm years older than you!" He gulps for air, twice, three times, deep and then deeper, as if the oxygen has only just reached him and he's catching up on something he'd forgotten.

Gala rests her hand on Maxim's neck.

"Come on," she whispers, "don't be like that," and she twirls a strand of his hair around her finger until it hurts. "We can do him a little favor in return, can't we?"

"You've been summoned."

"By him?"

"To his office. I don't know what's gotten into them. They want to see you. Unimaginable."

Gala is so shocked she drops the photos they've just had developed, one of herself and one of Maxim, immortalized at the entrance of Cinecittà. They float through the room on the breeze.

"Between Christmas and New Year's? Unheard of!" Fulvani screams into the receiver. "When all of Italy is eating and praying?"

Early the next morning, Gala and Maxim are at the gate. This time, a guard stops them, only to apologize after one quick call. The grounds look abandoned, but some people have turned up to work. They're hanging around in small groups, listless as cleaners at a train station hours before the first train is due to leave. The kiosk in the middle is open. Someone is drinking a cappuccino at the bar, but the chairs are upside down on the tables. Gala orders two vodkas. Maxim decides to ignore it.

The offices above Studio 5 seem deserted, but the low-level official is manning his desk. His face lights up when they come in. He takes their portraits down from the notice board and, holding the drawing pins carefully in his hand, opens the door to the next room, identical to the first. He pins the photos up again inside it and closes the door with a bow.

Before noon, this ceremony is repeated no less than five times. The same chairs and the same desks, but closer to the core. Only twice do they meet someone en route. The first is Giorgio Salvini, the casting director for this production, a friendly but absentminded man, who doesn't ask about their experience or photos but simply wants to know whether they too love the circus, at which point he starts reminiscing about his boyhood. After a while, Maxim cautiously interrupts to ask whether he knows anything about Snaporaz's film.

"Nobody ever knows anything about Snaporaz's films," he answers, surprised. "Not before they're shot. Anything can happen, each and every day, so even if you wanted to you could never say what's going on."

"And is there a possibility of a role for us?"

"Definitely. Until the very last moment, everything is possible."

"We were asked to come today . . ."

"See?"

". . . for an interview."

"Yes, and I'm enjoying it very much," Salvini says, launching into a story about how he hooked up with an itinerant troupe of *saltimbanques* when he was fourteen.

The next meeting is more formal. Gala and Maxim are in the last room, heads resting on their hands and backs aching from the cheap chairs, when a young blonde throws open the door, laying a pile of manuscripts on a desk marked with her name. Fiamella obviously wasn't expecting visitors.

"Who let you in?" she asks loftily, and their explanation fails to warm her up. "I have no idea who came up with such an idea. Someone's playing a joke on you. Snaporaz isn't even in the country."

She glances at their portraits on her notice board and shrugs.

"And even if he was . . ." She tears off the photos and gives them back, flapping them in the meantime like useless scrap. At last she opens the door, not to usher them into the next room, but to dispatch them into the hallway, steps away from where they'd begun hours before.

Enough already. They have a dream, and they're not going to let it slip away without a fight. There's no point in postponing the inevitable. They walk around to the side of the building, kick the garbage cans out of the way, and open the rear entrance of Studio 5. Nearby, they discover an iron fire escape, painted black to be nearly invisible against the black wall. As if on cue, their eyes glide up the stairs to the small glass room at the top. The old control room, built before the days of portable monitors, lightweight cranes, and radio microphones, protruding out of the wall eighteen meters up and seeming to float in the big empty studio. Thin blinds have been lowered on the studio side, but the low winter sun is shining straight into the office. Behind the glass, they can see the silhouette of a man pacing. That profile, that hair, that posture—straight back, weary shoulders: unmistakably Snaporaz.

He pauses in his thoughts, interrupted by the sound of feet ascending the iron stairs. He walks over to a window. With a snap he lets the blind shoot up, revealing him suddenly, like a lemon in a slot machine.

He pulls open the door. He's bigger than they imagined. And older, but his eyes are still bright. He scrunches them, and his narrow black eyebrows, which don't quite follow the line of his sockets, shoot up instead like tufts on either side and make him look angry. He's actually quite friendly. Without a word, he lets Gala and Maxim tell him their story. He looks at the photos they push into his hands.

The young man.

The young woman.

He examines their portraits. He examines them, first through his lashes, then stepping back a little and opening his eyes wide to take in their bodies. Especially Gala's. He comes up to her and does his best to look her in the eyes, but can't take his own off her breasts, which are high and half exposed by her plunging neckline. When they swell with her breathing, they seem to be coming to greet him.

It would be impolite not to return the greeting.

"Ciao, belle poppe!"

These are the first words they hear from his mouth. Between these and the next comes a long silence in which he takes Gala's hand and pinches her cheek as if she's a little girl. Gala beams, but lowers her eyes. Finally Maxim clears his throat. Snaporaz looks up, evidently surprised that someone else has come along with those breasts.

"Forget it," he tells him, already looking away. "You, I can't use in any way at all. Not now, not ever."

I was wrong about that. I have a use for Maxim after all. He's like the lantern in front of the teahouse. By placing him in the foreground in certain scenes, I can shape my picture of Gala, hidden behind him. Whether I like it or not, he is a part of her.

The doors are wide open. All kinds of things are blowing past. Images storm in, change shapes, melt down, fly off again. Everything is possible as long as you're still making up the story. This is the phase of waking dream.

People think that it demands concentration, but the opposite is true: it requires complete abandon. It feels like bewilderment and touches on insanity. You have to dare to step back, let everything go its own way: one who tries too hard to fall asleep spends the whole night tossing in bed.

Within these thoughts, special rules apply. They are sealed in time. Just as I am. Their images exist outside of reality. They show everything and nothing at once. One cannot exist without the other; you need nothing to imagine everything. From this basis characters emerge, hundreds at a time, some growing sharper, others blurring yet again. It makes no difference: a few are strong enough to stay. You begin to play with them, like a little boy playing with the bubbles of olive oil floating in his soup, but the more you stir, the more they take on a will of their own, fighting their way back to the surface.

This is the phase I love most. The stage of excess and irrationality, of unlimited freedom. Nothing matters, none of what you think, nothing you grasp of everything that comes your way. Everything can still be changed. You are uninhibited, because not even the most extreme choices have any strings attached. The characters are still free. You can make them do and be whatever you like, because though you know them you still haven't embraced them. You harry them with your imagination, like swinging a net at a butterfly, wanting to catch them but still enjoying their colors too much when they flutter away in fright. You keep putting off the moment you have to contain them, until at last you fear they'll escape if you put it off any longer. Make the story your own, or give it up altogether. So you catch them. One by one. In your cupped hands, separating them, confining them, assigning them boundaries.

Their wings beat against the palms of your hands.

This phase is now over.

From now on, choices must be made, if only because the producer insists and the people in the workplaces are waiting impatiently to start work on your dreams. Now I can no longer remain aloof. I get involved with my own material. I alter. Stop. Limit. Adjust. Limit again, more rigorously this time. Cutting back more, until the story, which could have been any story, becomes mine. The things I love most have to die, again and again. Until it tells my story, just as everything I have captured in pictures, in a different way every time, always tells of *me*.

"Forget it."

With these two words, I separated Gala from Maxim. The moment I spoke them was like the first blow of the clapper board announcing the first take of the first shot on the first day of shooting. With this line, the screenwriting phase irrevocably becomes the first step toward the story's materialization.

Air from the fantasy got mixed into reality. Two separate worlds, the invented story and its concrete filming, were mingled. In that single breath, I took responsibility for my characters. I walked into my own story. The dream dissolved in the day.

Part Three

Nüftes, Tüftes, and Grüftes

Now that we've made it this far, I have to tell you about my earliest memory. It's as important as it is odd, simple yet virtually incomprehensible, trivial, yet an apparent answer to essential questions. I understand what it was, but I can't explain it. It is highly improbable, but I experienced it myself.

It was like this. In the first years of my life, maybe even every night, just before I fell asleep, I regularly saw a bombardment of color. From the bombardment, a colorless core emerged, transparent and changeable as an air bubble in water. It was as far away as the moon in the sky, but when I stretched out my hand, I could grasp that strange planet between thumb and index finger. It had no mass, yet I could feel it. It resisted the pressure of my fingers in a way I recognized only much later, when I tried to push two magnets against each other. I succeeded at the same time I failed, an invisible tension both powerful and gently pleasant. The sensual feeling added to my joy in those moments, but the real pleasure was the sudden and fleeting realization, the knowledge, the absolute certainty, that, as long as I held this distant object "caught" between my fingers, I simultaneously had *everything* and *nothing* in my grasp.

This daily apparition became rarer once I started to talk and think more or less logically. I might have forgotten it completely if it hadn't suddenly returned twice in my midtwenties, before it disappeared forever.

. . .

Much to my mother's sorrow, I have a bad memory. I've forgotten most of my childhood. Toward the end of her life, when she said, "Remember when you did this or that?" I could never rise to the challenge. She brushed my doubts aside—"Oh, of course you remember"—before proving herself wrong by dredging up all the details. In the end, I'd lay a hand on her arm and pretend that it had all come back, and we'd smile at the fun we had together. Then she'd shake her head and start rummaging through her bag.

In fact, virtually all I remember from my childhood are moments that were captured in photos. I don't really remember them; I just know I experienced them. The pictures lead a life of their own. I think I recall something of that summer's day in the park, but I can't actually summon up a single feeling about it. From all those occasions, all I remember is the instant the shutter opened, freezing the light passing through the diaphragm.

Photography has changed our memory. The past used to be alive, and as people grew older, further removed from the facts, they were free to tone them down, to change them, forget them, embellish them, or fantasize them. Fact and fiction were equals, and neither had a monopoly on truth. The camera has deprived memory of this freedom. Our actions are captured. Pictures in a kid-leather album give the lie to the life we thought we led. All we can do is reconstruct a life from this evidence. The past has been pinned down forever; fantasy is confined to the future.

As indisputably as I remember a donkey ride on the beach, black and white with a zigzag edge, I remember the extraordinary apparition from my earliest childhood. I know that there was a clear perception and that it made me happy, but I can no longer call up the sensation and my understanding of it. All I know is that every night I held all of creation between my fingers.

From the moment I could capture the world between thumb and index finger, I understood that everything is limited. Indeed, this sense of limitation later became the determining fact of my life. Another child, exploring the world, might be surprised to find so many things he's never seen before, but I discovered the same thing everywhere—an edge, a border, a narrowing, an end—and if this surprised me, it was only because others seemed not to notice how limited were all the things around them. As long as I can remember, I've suffered from these limits. Well, suffering's not the word.

I'd wanted to discuss this with my friend Alberto in Sabaudia. He claims, in one of his books, that he's felt something similar with boredom, which made him suffer but also offered oblivion, alienated him yet placed reality in a new light. The limitations have the same effect on me.

For many people, they are simply the opposite of freedom; and for such people freedom means free choice, being carefree, unlimited progress. I don't see limits as the opposite of progress. I'd even say they resemble one another, since limits also take away worries, bring progress. I see it like this: infinite freedom offers infinite possibility. You rack your brains, worrying what to do next. It's impossible to choose, so you wait and see; ultimately, you do nothing at all. Limitations define a range for our possibilities. The more limits, the simpler the choice. Bold steps become easier the more we are closed in and confined, a constant contraction that helps us move ahead. Our true motivation is to avoid suffocation.

The development of civilization is like the route the water follows through the Acqua Felice, the aqueduct I see from my studio. Water from a placid lake in the Alban Hills is stored in a reservoir, from which only a single opening offers escape, into a stone chamber with converging walls. The pressure increases, forcing the water to seek a new exit and bringing it to the next stone chamber, from which it is pressed into yet another. Mile after mile, pushed through a system of tapering vessels, the confined water flows faster, always in the same direction, toward the center of Rome, filling pumps, pools, and horses' drinking troughs, turning mills, irrigating fields, and supplying fountains and bathhouses without ever losing its strength, until finally, through smaller and smaller pipes, it empties into the Moses Fountain. There, the sun glitters on the clear water flowing over the marble statues. It is part of a work of art, offering pleasure, beauty, and, on stifling days, cooling, to the people passing by.

That's what limits offer me: the possibility of channeling my reservoir of babbling thoughts until they begin to foam, gaining direction, speed, and power until, far from their source, they burst out in clear jets in the sun.

I

Gala and Maxim leave my office in silence. I could have watched them heading toward the bar, disappearing now and then behind the pines. She looks up at him, concerned, feeling his despondency more keenly than her own triumph. She takes his hand, but immediately lets go when she feels it stiffen. Her pity brings the full intensity of his humiliation home to him. Suddenly, he bursts into tears, as uninhibited as a child.

"I'm so happy for you." His shoulders heave as he gives in to months of tension. "Really, so happy," he manages to add. He waves Gala away. "The bar. Just go and wait for me. If you want to. At the bar. I'm . . . I need . . . just for a moment . . ." And then he turns away from her.

For the first time.

She stays there, standing in the middle of the road, watching him go. She calls out, but he doesn't answer. She's never seen him like this before. She shuffles from one foot to the other, nervous, wringing her hands, unsure whether to go after him. He's usually the one who supports her.

If I'd bothered to come out from behind my desk and walk over to the window, I could have seen all this. But a few minutes have passed and I've already forgotten the two Dutch kids. What's more, I've received a call from a Banco Ambrosiano office boy. He tries to bowl me over with compliments before offering me an incredible fee to make a commercial. For television, of all things!

It's not the strongest who survive, but the most foolish. There's no doubt Darwin got it wrong. Only people who delude themselves and then dare to believe their own delusion stand a chance in life.

And another secret: anyone can create art, but important art is only born from radical decisions, and those require a heavy dose of stupidity. Only a master can make essential decisions without a second thought—a master, or an idiot. So it is in all creative arts, and even more in the art of life.

It's not the strongest who comes off best, but the biggest fool. Self-deception keeps the human species going.

Gala watches Maxim until he walks into a saloon in the Western set at the rear of the grounds. With a flourish, she turns on her heel before the doors stop swinging.

"Snaporaz looked at me," she celebrates in her mind. "Snaporaz likes me. What a great man. What a monumental figure. True, he's blunt, and he didn't have to be so mean to Maxim, but that's only because he knows what he wants. What a man. What an artist. To think that I caught his eye. So likable, such sparkling eyes. And his mind! It's been tough, but it was all worthwhile!"

In the canteen, she orders a double espresso, boldly planting a red pump on the footrest of a stool and leaning an elbow on the cool marble bar.

For someone whose future has just been whipped out from under him, Maxim recovers with remarkable speed. He listens to the swish of the saloon doors closing behind him. He knew there wouldn't be anything behind the facade as he stepped from the outside to the outside. It was only a gesture, familiar from so many movies, but from a dramatic point of view it fitted his mood. He wanted to know what it felt like. But he's still sad to find things unchanged on the other side. There too raw emotion smarts in the pit of his stomach. Of course, he's disappointed, even indignant, at his treatment by the man he'd pinned all his hopes on, but that's not all. There's a reason his tears won't stop. Even now that he's caught his breath and stopped shaking, big round childish tears are still welling up in his eyes. This surprises him, and bothers him. He worries that he might be jealous, and the idea of being jealous of Gala repulses him, literally nauseates him, and suddenly, with two intense contractions, he empties his stomach. But while he's still bent over the vomit soaking into the red soil, he feels happy for Gala once again. She's been noticed. She's been chosen. She might get a role, make her mark, become a star, showing the whole world what Maxim's known for years: how different she is, how exceptional. His love returns as his hatred gathers strength, his hatred for the other side of the equation: Snaporaz, the nasty creep who, with the few mischievous words he spoke to Gala, has fallen from his pedestal forever.

Anger dries his tears. He squares his shoulders. He screws up his eyes like a spaghetti Western hero waiting for a shootout and studies the back of the set through his lashes, seeing it all in sharp focus: the nails in the canvas, the warped boards, the torn plastic over the windows. Moisture has crept beneath the tape holding down the roof. Things aren't the same on this side after all. Above one of the ponds, the former Sea of Galilee, seagulls are fighting over a toasted sandwich.

Calmer now, Maxim walks back. Being alone has done him good. It's starting to get dark. The neon lights in the bar flick on. The light shines through the windows. Between the sharp-edged shadows of the studios, the small building looks like a star that has crashed into the middle of the complex. At its center, Gala is standing at the bar, tossing her head back, shaking her hair, smiling at the men who have gathered around her hopefully, though they've got even less hope today than ever. And he suddenly realizes: before, he and Gala had been alone together in this city. Now each is alone separately. They've entered the set it's taken them so much trouble to build.

Relaxation after emotion. Maxim is sure that Gala will have an attack tonight. As soon as they get home, he tosses the *pizzette* and wine they picked up on the way onto the bed and heads into the bathroom to get her tablets. If she takes her dose right now, the convulsions will be less intense.

There is a box of her medication next to the sink, but it's empty. After a thorough search, he finds a new one in the bottom of her suitcase. Inside are three strips, enough for three weeks. As he's removing that night's dosage, the unknown Italian jar catches his eye again.

"Baby, what's this?" he calls, emerging from the bathroom with her pills in one hand and a glass of water and the jar in the other.

"Oh, that!" laughs Gala. She takes it from him nonchalantly, a bit too flippantly to reassure him. "I thought I'd need it with all the white bread here, but I haven't taken a single one." As if to prove it, she shakes the contents out onto the table. "Stupid. A waste of money. The olive oil does the job by itself." She takes her pills, then finds a station with Italian oldies on the transistor, pours herself a glass of wine, and dances across the room, hips swinging.

When the time comes, Maxim restrains her without much exertion.

"Sei un bravo ragazzo," sings Gigliola Cinquetti.

Maxim rocks Gala back and forth to the melody while wiping the dribble away from the corner of her mouth with his fingers.

"Sei diverso da tutti, e per questo ti a-ha-mo."

"You and every other beautiful young thing in Rome," says Sangallo.

Four days have passed without a word from Snaporaz, but Gala is still every bit as excited about their encounter. She realizes she's not in love, but the feeling of triumph is something very close. A voice inside her won't stop singing.

"They're all waiting for a call from Cinecittà." Sangallo is sitting between Gala and Maxim on the bench near the Temple of Venus on the Celio to see the sunset. "It doesn't come and it won't ever come, but they all sit in their rooms waiting for the phone. They forget to eat, they forget to live, and finally they die without a foot of film ever being shot of them."

He takes some prosecco from the antique traveling case he has lugged around all afternoon and passes around glasses to toast the moment he's been waiting for. In the distance, the sky above the old city glows an orange gold. The light ignites behind the clouds at sea, flares up over the suburbs, and spreads across the firmament until it reflects scarlet in the Tiber.

"Here, taste!" Sangallo opens a jar of lemon preserve and uses two fingers to spread a daub out over a slice of raw ham.

"How were you planning on surviving your success? You need to eat. Open wide!"

Gala snaps at the bait.

"You're no wiser than the rest, so I presume you'll be staying in Rome?"

"Of course!" says Gala, astonished. "Only a fool would leave right before the show."

Sangallo glances at Maxim.

"Definitely," he backs her up, "we're staying." The bittersweet preserve makes the pulpy meat the old man has prepared for him taste even more sickly. "Yes," he touches glasses, determinedly, "as long as we can, we'll stay."

"Then consider yourself hired, Maxim," Sangallo sighs. "I'm doing *La Clemenza di Tito*. There's a run-through Wednesday morning. First rehearsal's Friday. Extras. You and seven elegant youths are replacing the choir. They're too coarse and ugly to be permitted onstage. Let them sing from the wings. Appearances count for something too. There's no glory in it, my boy, and precious little money, but you can use it."

"Fine," says Maxim, "as long as there's time for everything else." No one asks him *what* else, but he explains anyway. "Auditions, screen tests, possible jobs . . ." But he hears the breath draining out of that last remnant of conviction.

Sangallo doesn't dare look at him. Their eyes are fixed on the horizon. Gala lays a hand on Maxim's shoulder and massages it gently while the last glow dies away behind the city.

All the while, she's thinking, Snaporaz, Snaporaz, Snaporaz. The old man pinched my cheek like I was still in diapers, but have I ever felt so clearly what a woman can do? He spoke to me like a father, but he looked at me like a lover. Do what you can, Snaporaz: I'll eat you up and spit you out. Just you try to humiliate me!

She feels Maxim's muscles under her hands and runs her fingers over them. He sighs and lays his head on her shoulder. Touching each other relaxes them both, makes both feel safe, but each in a different way. He is comforted by the complete lack of danger, but it makes her feel melancholy. He is returning to something familiar; she is glancing back at it one last time. Slowly, the evening glides over them.

"Ma chi è?" The woman who answers Snaporaz's telephone is as breathless as she was the first time. Gala found it very difficult to muster the courage to call, and now she persists, explaining that she met the maestro and that he was interested in her.

"I'm sorry, Signor Snaporaz *non c'è,*" the shrew snarls, and hangs up in the middle of Gala's next sentence.

Between Christmas and New Year's, the cold takes Rome by surprise. I haven't felt the warmth drain from my body so quickly since the day my school friends and I went to spy on Malena, the harbor whore, and ended up locked in the cold store by a tuna fisherman's jealous wife. Day after day, a freezing Russian wind pushed icy clouds over the Alpe della Luna and sent them rolling up the valley of the Tiber. There is ice in the Fountain of the Four Rivers and people fear for the lives of the palms on the Piazza di Spagna.

On the very first day of this assault, the heating in Gala and Maxim's room in Parioli is switched off. Geppi is implacable. She claims that the owner—no, not Signor Gianni, but his boss, an elderly count from distant Monterotondo—came by personally to seal the locks on the heating of all tenants in arrears. That same night she did knock on the door to give them a set of blankets and the advice to hand the rent over to Gianni before he came up with his own—and here she lowered her voice to a whisper—"proposal." Gala and Maxim cuddle up, but on the third day they awake so early, so chilled to the bone, that they have to find a hotel lobby on the Via Veneto to warm up in.

The way they stroll through the revolving door dissuades anyone from asking what they're doing there so early. They settle down in front of the fireplace with a couple of newspapers.

"At last, people with guts!"

Gala looks up.

A young woman, tall, blond, beautiful as a model, is standing at the silver dish with the warm cider that has been set out for the hotel guests. She scoops up a bowlful and blows the steam off it with pursed lips.

"I always say, if you're going to do it, then don't be ashamed of it."

"I have no idea what we should be ashamed of," answers Gala.

"Exactly, but if I had a dollar for all the ones who come in here staring into space and run off afterward with their heads hanging . . ."

"How absurd."

"The front desk doesn't like us hanging around, but if you ask me, between the three of us, we're the big hotels' most important attraction."

"The three of us?"

"Of course! They owe us at least one of those five stars."

"Why?"

"Do you think a single one of those businessmen would check in if we weren't hanging around?" She flops down in an armchair and kicks off her shoes. She stretches. Her fur coat falls open wide enough to show a skirt, probably designed in the Via Condotti, but definitely too short for the weather. A bellhop whistles. She pokes her tongue out at him.

"You're mistaken," says Maxim, trying to ascertain whether she's wearing panties. "We're only here to warm up."

"Warmth, friendship, longing for the womb, I've heard it all and nothing surprises me anymore."

"Just to warm up a little," Gala explains, "not to . . . well, not professionally, like you."

The young woman takes a mouthful of cider and tries to work out whether two old pros are trying to take her for a ride.

"Then you really must be mistaken." She shakes her head in regret. "You don't look like you need to be cold in this city. Unless . . ." Suddenly a bitter note emerges in her voice: "Unless you think you're too good to earn your living with pleasure."

Amid the rush of apologies that come tumbling out in response, Gala says, "I've thought about it."

Maxim looks at her.

"Big deal," he exclaims, not to be outdone, "we've all thought about it. That's not the point," but he stares at her to see if she's serious.

Gala averts her eyes.

"I've had offers."

"You?"

"Why not?" she adds indignantly. "Do you think I'm too repulsive?"

"From who?"
"I turned him down."
"Who??"
"I turned him down, but you know, in different circumstances . . ."
There is something provocative in the look they exchange. Gala knows he likes how she says such things. He knows she does it to get him going, and the dumbest thing he could do would be to act narrow-minded.
"I'm glad to hear it," the young woman interrupts them, "you're open-minded. People have such wrong ideas about our profession. Especially when you're operating in this class."
"This class?"
"Interesting men. Not just cheap tricks, but men who travel the world, politicians, guys with influence and opinions. They don't want a dummy, they want someone on their level. It starts as an intellectual challenge—fast, stimulating, and nine times out of ten that's as far as it goes. The cliché of call girls is complete nonsense. Most of us are students or have good jobs."
"I thought *that* was the cliché," says Maxim.
The young woman stands up. She belts her fur coat.
"Maybe I've gotten you wrong. This is only for the extras. Extra clothes, extra adventure. If it's a matter of paying the gas bill, the street corner will do."
She rummages through her purse and throws two of her agency's cards down on the table.
"Do yourselves a favor . . ." Before heading into the morning, she runs her fingers through her hair and puts on a pair of sunglasses. "There's only one thing worse than being used."

"Could you fuck someone you didn't love?" Gala asks on New Year's Eve, cuddling with Maxim in bed.
Shared warmth is twice as warm.
"Why not?"
They've spread their long coats over the blankets they've pulled up to their chins.
"Do you?"
"I don't fuck that many people," Maxim replies.

They're silent for a while. They don't often discuss these subjects. In the quiet room, it's easy to believe that people who love each other are each other's lovers. But things aren't that simple. Gala and Maxim grew up free enough to be able to believe one thing yet give themselves over to another. Those were times that virtually demanded that they develop separately in love, so that a chasm soon emerged in their intimacy, that unassailable dream, and what they got up to by themselves.

The rare occasions they mentioned these escapades were undeniably exciting. They had to work up the nerve to abandon the solidity of silence, and then to balance the desire to not wound the other with the need to match them. It's an odd game, and those who play it can't count on anyone else's understanding.

That afternoon Maxim filled two liter bottles with barrel wine. One has already been dispatched. He opens two paper packets from the *salumeria* on the *corso*. One contains Parma ham; the other, olives. Oil drips on the sheets.

"Yes," he brags, "I could do that. No problem. It'd be easier with someone who meant nothing to me."

"Sure. Maybe even better. Maybe that's it."

He briefly wonders whether this is what she wants to hear, and whether it's actually true.

"I've done it before," he says, to convince himself. Sometimes he longs so passionately for shamelessness. It wells up in him like warm sulfur in a cold spring, seeping through old cracks in the crust of his consciousness. "People I don't know at all, who don't interest me, whose names I don't even know. Without a single word. Sometimes without even looking at each other."

"Women?"

"People I wouldn't even think of talking to. Not even 'Hi, how are you?' "

"Men?"

"Would a woman do something like that?"

It's as busy on this festive night as it was quiet at Christmas. In every room, men are visiting girls. Gala and Maxim listen to their footsteps. In the hall. On the stairs. Above their heads. Doors.

Gala lays her head on his chest. She curls up and throws a leg over his. She's looking away from him. It's a game, but they wouldn't dare face its possible consequences. It's dangerous, like the trials of strength of her childhood. Maxim is a worthy opponent. She won't back off: instead, she ups the stakes, hiding her face behind her hair.

"So you really don't care if it's a man or a woman?"

He knows what she wants to hear.

"Not when I'm horny."

Gala doesn't answer.

"You've slept with women."

"A couple of times," she says curtly. "Friends I've known for years. It's familiar. It's not the same thing." Her head rises and falls with his breathing. She hears his heartbeat. Suddenly, she sits up, drinks her wine. She sits there with the glass wedged between her breasts and her pulled-up knees.

"Any man, any woman? It doesn't matter to you."

"Of course it does."

"A girlfriend, a complete stranger . . . You don't care when you feel the urge."

"Of course I care."

"So when you do love someone?"

"That's completely different." He sounds annoyed, but grabs one of the coats from the foot of the bed and drapes it carefully over her shoulders. She pulls it tighter. When he speaks again, it's gentler. Thoughtful.

"Friendship paralyzes lust. Love kills it. Being horny is wanting to own, take possession, be taken. Penetrating, forcing entry, imposing your will. That's hunting, not love. I want to worship the one I love, not spear them."

Gala looks at him over her shoulder.

"A lot of good that does her, the worshipped one," she answers laconically, flopping back on the pillows with a sigh, playful. She spreads her arms, lets the glass slip out of her hand to the floor.

"I want to look up to her," laughs Maxim, "not down on her!" He really means it. His own words have turned him on. He sits astride her, takes her wrists, presses them down.

"Loving, Gala, isn't about simply fucking, it's about admiring."

She looks at him.

"Not about real life," she says, "but about a dream." The mockery slowly drains from her face and she frowns, suddenly furious, shaking her head, trying to fight him off. Maxim only realizes the game is over when she shrieks and shakes her head so violently that it slams against one of the bedposts. Shocked by her ferocity, he immediately lets go.

"You can't enlarge people into idols. That's cruel."

"Why should I leave them small?" he splutters, grasping at a defense.

"The smaller you are, the bigger the world. The more imperfect a person is, the more chance he has to develop."

He lays his hand on her head where she bumped it.

"You're drunk."

They sit there, unsure what else to do, like children who have gone too far and are waiting for someone to rescue them.

"An ideal is a caricature. Instead of accepting the ugly parts, you blow the beautiful things out of proportion. How can anyone ever live up to that?"

For a second, Maxim thinks she's crying. Her head twitches against his hands a few times, but he doesn't say a word. He doesn't move, and when she continues speaking she's calm.

"It's awful when someone makes you prettier, or better, or bigger. His unconditional faith in you makes you all the more aware of your shortcomings. He doesn't see you as you are but as you could have been. That's where a lot of people's anger comes from. Only when you're soaring in someone else's eyes do you realize you're really stuck in the mud. That's the 'mire' in admired."

After New Year's, week after week passes without a sign of life from Snaporaz or even his lowliest minions. The disappointment lies like a boulder in the stream of Maxim and Gala's Roman life, collecting more silt each day. They don't talk about it, trying, each in their own way, to bypass the growing island of frustrated expectations. Maxim, as usual, takes the safe side. He can't yet admit it to himself, but he'd rather go back to the Netherlands. The wound of his rejection is not healing, and he's only remaining for Gala's sake. Since it doesn't look as if she'll end up any better than him, he wants to spare her further sorrow. If it were up to him, they'd spend their last lire enjoying the city and then go home at the start of springtime, a dream poorer and an experience richer. They'd be more satisfied with their Dutch lives, and in a few years they could look back at their adventure and laugh at their naïveté.

Gala, meanwhile, is consumed by doubt. Frame by frame, she runs through the scene in the office above Studio 5.

She keeps thinking that Snaporaz must have changed his mind. "I was too boring. I should have said something funny, witty, brazen. Something to stimulate him, even to annoy him, anything that would have made an impression. I had my chance and of course I blew it, 'cause I'm just a silly little girl, a born disappointment! But . . . well, the great man showed some interest. Yes, he really was interested. It might have been only for a second, but there's no doubt he was. So it must have been something later that made him change his mind. Too fat. Of course. I've got to go on a serious diet. But he loves voluptuous female flesh. Maybe not fat enough? Should I put on some weight? Or maybe I'm too ugly. Too weird-looking. My head is too big anyway. That's it, my head's just too big for my body. It's a little grotesque. I look like a cartoon woman, but, you know, he loves extreme characters. Maybe I'm not extreme enough? I'm probably just too ordinary. That's why he's not interested in Maxim: he's too handsome, and there's nothing special about being good-looking. But I'm not good-looking—I'm just too boring, is all, so he's shoved me aside with all the other dime-a-dozen actresses . . ."

She goes down a brambly path of self-recrimination, and when she finally surfaces, she's clinging to one overpowering, painful idea.

"I should have gone alone," she reproaches herself. "Without Maxim. Since Snaporaz wasn't interested in him, he's not interested in me either. He thinks we're a couple, of course, whereas if I'd gone by myself . . . He's an Italian man, after all. He doesn't notice you unless he thinks you're available. Maxim is a sweetheart, he means well, but in a situation like that he's a ball and chain."

The loneliness of this thought shocks her out of her weeklong reverie. She's disgusted with herself and pities Maxim at the same time. When she finds him again in the middle of the rapids, she seizes his hand as if she'll never let go; thus, after rounding the obstacle each in their own way, they are, temporarily, closer than ever before. But, strangely enough, Gala, unlike Maxim, never feels the slightest aversion to the man who caused all this turmoil.

In the opera house, Maxim goes through the daily rehearsals with the resignation of Napoleon confined to Elba forced to listen to his guard's lectures on strategy. Swallowing his pride, staring into space, determined to remain above the folly, he paces across the cardboard Forum in a crepe de chine tunic that leaves almost nothing to the imagination.

He spends the breaks in the telephone booth on the Piazza Gigli. He calls agencies. His dissatisfaction has ignited his old passion for acting, also known as "hoping for work." Anything is better than serving as human scenery.

In the afternoon, after going through the choreography—three steps forward, two to the side—he waits in the wings with the other extras until the stage manager calls. They are all tall, well-proportioned young Romans, dressed by Sangallo to bare their powerful neck and chest muscles and to expose their well-trained thighs almost to the groin. They all seem assured of their own worth. Enviously, Maxim watches their easy preening, their constant discussions of their own and the others' beauty. They have no other interests. They don't listen to the music. They don't discuss anything significant. At first, Maxim felt like a truffle on a pile of gravel. "They have their looks," he thought, "I have my talent." But he gradually realizes that the other young men see him as one of their own and judge him according to *their* standards. The first time he's asked to roll his chest muscles, he is so self-conscious that he is glad he's just put on his T-shirt. In these surroundings, he feels his intellect diminishing in value; he wants only to measure up physically. When the group compliments him on his thighs, he's flattered and explains the rigorous exercises that produced this result at the Amsterdam Theater Academy. When they ask him to stand beside the group's gymnast for a comparison, Maxim positively enjoys it.

I can't possibly be one of them, he thinks. It must be the bad lighting. But, well, I don't want to be shown up either . . . With a certain pride, he closes his book and lifts up his legionnaire's tunic.

The young men spend day after day like this, beneath the sweltering spotlights. Fresh air seldom penetrates the curtains that make an improvised room for the extras. Sequestered behind a set representing one of the Forum temples, they never appear before the choir or soloists without being summoned. In Italian opera, dominated by a hierarchy stricter than the Vatican's, these worlds have been separated for centuries.

Perhaps that explains why Maxim jumps at the fresh wind that blows across their scantily clad bodies halfway through the second week of rehearsals. Annoyed, he turns around to find himself looking straight into the eyes of Liliana Silberstrand.

"So this is where they keep you hidden away!" says the mezzo-soprano. "I was beginning to wonder whether I'd only seen you in a dream!"

Silberstrand is the Swedish court singer and, rumor has it, the Swedish queen's dearest friend. That would explain her style. Tall and slim, she is standing there with a hand on one hip. The light entering through the curtain she's holding open with the other hand has cast a reddish brown halo around her.

"But no, these men are real." She breathes in the smell of their sweat and closes her eyes with pleasure.

Silberstrand is singing Sesto, a role originally intended for a castrato. Until now, her man's role has been indicated only by the silver breastplate pinned to her costume, which is otherwise identical to the extras'. But she has more serious ambitions regarding her metamorphosis.

"All right, so tell me: how does a man walk? How does he keep his hips so still? I want to be convincing, so don't be shy, troops, make me one of you. What does a fellow do with his hands, and why must he sit with his legs spread? Is it the reason I think?"

The men couldn't have been more stunned if the soprano had turned up in a bikini. Half are flabbergasted because they've never seen an opera singer who wants to act, the other half because the opposite sex is attempting to join them in disguise. At any rate, within seconds it's every man for himself. Silberstrand delights in their attention.

"I already know how men drink," she says, producing a bottle, pulling the cork out with her teeth, and spitting it into a corner. She raises it to her lips and then passes it around, all the while maintaining, as under all circumstances, the grace of someone about to take her seat for the Nobel Prize banquet. She wipes her mouth on the back of her hand.

"O Dei, che smania è questa," she proudly sings, *"che tumulto nel cor."* She plants a foot on a stool and, like a childhood friend, puts an arm around Maxim's shoulders. "A leader, I thought, belongs with his men."

On the morning of the premiere of *La Clemenza,* Gala fishes her last anticonvulsant pill out of a traveling bag. The tablet is so battered that it could hardly be more than half a dose. The expiration date has long since elapsed, but she has no choice. That night, she watches the spectacle with her eyes half-closed. Erected from gleaming marble to Sangallo's design, the Forum Romanum is awash in light that hurts her eyes. Gala does her best to follow Maxim whenever he's on, but a piercing headache is coming over her. Maxim's outline blurs. She can just see him holding his hand out to the soprano dressed as a man and leading her up the stairs of the Capitol, two radiant figures who slowly disappear behind the black patch in the corner of her left eye. Gala breathes deeply with relief and lets everything go black.

"E chi tradisci? Il più grande, il più giusto, il più clemente!"

She listens to Silberstrand with her eyes closed.

The two women meet afterward in the limousine Sangallo has ordered to drive them and the young men through the winter storm to Ostia.

Waves wash over the boulevard and break against the terrace of the seaside hotel. Salty drops run down the glass wall of the dining-room extension. Inside it is warm and sticky. In the middle of the glass room stands an outsized torso of white marble, a fragment from a gigantic Hermes that once towered over the ancient breakwater. Robbed of its limbs, the muscular body is now surrounded by palms and orchids, and in its shadow, a table has been set for the group. Sangallo chooses a chair. The young men gather round him.

"You are the most beautiful reward for all my hard work," he tells them, though he generously shares their attention with the two women.

"I feel honored," Gala says, "to be allowed into your men's club," and she lets them flirt with her, languid and benevolent as a panther allowing itself to be provoked to a swipe, sure that no one could stand up to it in the ring.

Silberstrand is watching the circus with a smile of recognition and places her hand on the small of Maxim's back.

"Why do you think that men who would never really desire a woman are so keen to be surrounded by the most extreme specimens of the opposite sex?"

"How should I know?" Maxim asks indignantly. "That's just the way it is."

She appraises him with amusement.

"So you think I should accept it?"

"Either I love someone or I don't. All I'm interested in is whether they're exceptional. One of a kind. If someone wants to arouse my desire, they have to convince me there's no one else even remotely like them."

A little later: corks popping, Silberstrand and Gala surveying the group. Some of the young men roll up their sleeves to test their strength. Others cheer them on, passionately, as if something important were at stake.

"You've got it wrong," the singer whispers. "We haven't been invited to this men's club as women."

"No?"

"You and I are here to confirm their idea of women."

"And that is?"

"Exaggerated."

Gala shares her laughter.

"Real women, the ones you see everywhere, in the street, on the bus, even the kind that shake their thing on the TV here, everyday women . . . men might marry them, but they will never admit them to their fraternity. They fuck them, but they don't want them around in their free time."

"I can't believe anyone could be that primitive, not even a man."

"But their reaction to you and me is the opposite. You and I, we're larger than life. Not bigger than others, just more grotesque. Provocative, unattainable extremes: that's what men like."

"Are you talking about our tits and asses?"

"I'm talking about characteristics that are exaggerated like the characters in an opera, where you're either seduction or vengeance incarnate, passion or the heroine—never a complete person. That's why we're allowed here tonight—the more we make a show of our femininity, the more masculine they feel. They'll horse around and wrestle, but they'll think ten times before they lay a finger on us, before they'd actually touch us, really notice us."

They hear disco music: the hotel manager's attempt to drown out the rising storm. Some of the extras start dancing to dispel their boredom, and Silberstrand swings her arms around to show she's up for anything.

"Of course," she continues, "I put on airs. 'Crazy lady,' they say, 'just check her out, all independent. She's got no shame and she's free.' I've learned to give them what they want. They want more every year. In this game, it's not about what you look like, it's about how you're seen. Not the way you are, but how they'd like you to be. A goddess is a goddess because there's someone to worship her, so she conforms to the idea her worshippers have of her, because what would be left of her if they turned away?"

She catches the eyes of her troops. She flirts with a youth who soon seems to forget everything around them and dance just for her.

"In exchange for my efforts," Silberstrand continues, never taking her eyes off him, "I reap those glances one last time—though they're actually yours now. I used to get them without even noticing, and only when they disappeared did I start missing them. It's harder and harder for me to win them back."

She stands, pulling Gala behind her. For a while, ignoring the men completely, the women dance.

"It's only when you lose things," Silberstrand shouts in Gala's ear, "when life starts to contract, that you feel how vast it was, how spectacular it could be, one last time." She lets go and dances over to Maxim, who is talking to Sangallo.

"Fall in, centurion!" she commands. Without stopping the motion of her hips for an instant, the singer wraps her arms around his neck, pulling him onto the dance floor and stealing the show with swirling pirouettes and tango poses. Chest to chest, they catch their breath in what looks like an embrace.

"You've got a nice body, soldier!" she says in praise of her subordinate, pretending to inspect him. "Yes, I wouldn't mind celebrating the Lupercalia with you."

"Why not?" Maxim bluffs, elated by his success. He feels her breath on his neck as she nuzzles his earlobe. "You and I will celebrate the Lupercalia together. Except"—he reconsiders—"first you'll have to teach me what that is."

"That's not all I can teach you," she says, like a dirty old man talking to his secretary, planting her hands on his buttocks and pulling his groin against hers. "It's the feast where all the sexually mature young men of Rome are taken to the racecourse, stripped naked, set running, and pursued."

"By girls?"

"By women," says Silberstrand portentously, "and by their army officers, of course."

"You think you could catch me?"

"You think you'd run so fast?"

"That depends," he says as coolly and as brusquely as possible, but his answer is already throbbing against Silberstrand's belly. He can't help but admire her bearing, which remains just as superior, indeed almost regal, no matter how uncouth she acts. But he is most moved by her shameless exhibition.

"Young men like that were richly rewarded in ancient Rome," she pants. "When they lived up to their promise, their fortune was made."

"Those were the days."

"I'm mad about tradition."

Just then, Gala interrupts. She still has a headache and wants Maxim to take her home. Before he can leave, Silberstrand grabs his arm.

"Keep your promise, and I'll make the effort worth your while."

Back home, Maxim vainly rummages through cupboards and bags. There is no medicine left. He puts Gala to bed and sits beside her until she falls asleep. Then he leaves. He takes the tram to the Pyramid near Ostiense and from there jumps on the last train to the seaside, where he rushes through the storm along the lido toward Castel Fusano. The hotel's big lights have been turned off, and from a distance the winter garden looks dark as well. The tall windows of the conservatory reflect the rhythmic flashes from the lighthouse, but Maxim can see candlelight flickering behind the steamed-over glass. Sangallo and Silberstrand are sitting at the round table. And on the sofa at the foot of the ancient torso, the friends Griso and Gervaso are lying asleep, one with his head on the other's stomach.

When Maxim, drenched from the storm, steps into the oppressive warmth of the conservatory, Sangallo does not immediately notice him. Only when a delighted Silberstrand greets the young man does the director leap up like a worried father, taking off his jacket, wrapping it around Maxim's chilled shoulders, and drying his face with a napkin. He rings room service for a bathrobe and towels and dries Maxim's hair himself.

All this time, Maxim has scarcely dared to look at Silberstrand, but he peers at her from under the towel as the viscount rubs his head. Proud and tall as a queen on a throne, she observes him shamelessly, smiling slightly, with no doubt as to why he has returned.

She stands when Sangallo is finished. Using her fingers, she carefully combs Maxim's hair back as she studies his face. He feels his heart pounding the same way it does when he's standing in front of an audience, but he knows the techniques an actor uses to conceal it. He inhales deeply to slow the breathing that's making him light in the head. He even suppresses the blinking of his eyes as if for a close-up, because he knows the effort will moisten them and catch the light. He removes his cuff links before the singer unbuttons his wet shirt and takes it off. She wipes the drops from his chest with the palm of her hand, scraping her nails over a nipple in the process. Taking pleasure in his shiver, she slides the tip of her tongue across her teeth.

The director throws him a bathrobe and the singer helps him into it, turning up the collar and pressing a kiss onto his chest before closing the lapels. When she sits on the sofa beside the ancient Hermes' muscular flank, it seems only natural for Maxim to sit next to her, slumping down and placing his head on her bare shoulder. In the muggy conservatory, his breath feels cool on her skin. They listen to the wind as if a melody were hidden in the rattling windows.

"I think it was when we were casting *Ludwig,* Luchino and I," says Sangallo. He tops up their glasses from a new bottle he has ordered to celebrate Maxim's return. "At any rate, it was shortly after Helmut

Berger strolled in and ripped open our lives, yes, that must have been when we discovered that, when you get down to it, there are only three kinds of people. We christened them the Nüftes, the Tüftes, and the Grüftes. Presumably in honor of Helmut. Silly names to lighten up the whole suffocating situation. Nüftes, that's who I surround myself with, people like you: gorgeous, young, at the peak of their sexual power and beauty, almost unaware of their divinity, they light up the world for us, the others. The consolation . . ."

On the sofa, a groan goes up from one of the sleeping youths. He turns on his side, almost falling, but regains his balance without really waking, like a puppy nuzzling back into the rest of the litter. Sangallo smiles as if to dispel a melancholy memory and sips his wine.

"Then you have the Tüftes. Tüftes were once Nüftes. I'm one of them. You see: once a Nüfte, now a Tüfte. The Nüftes have grown old in style, happy that they have their memories, just a bit sad that they've lost so much."

"And the Grüftes?" asks Maxim, amused.

"You don't want to know." Sangallo shudders. "The Grüftes are ugly and unattractive. Always have been, always will be."

"And how do you become a Grüfte?"

"Ah, if only we knew . . . They are repulsive because they've declared war on everything good and beautiful. One day, perhaps in earliest childhood, they turned their backs on beauty. Luchino said they do it out of pure malice, but I think it's disappointment, some great sorrow, the fear of going your own way, which is the path that is essential to beauty."

"How awful."

Sangallo sits beside the sleepers on the sofa, dips two fingers in his glass, and sprinkles the wine on their faces. The young men wrinkle their noses and lick the moisture from their lips.

"Grüftes don't belong in our world, they're out there in the cold on the other side of the glass, and they are consumed by jealousy when they look in on the Nüftes and the Tüftes."

With great emotion, he stares at the misty conservatory windows, as if he could see their noses pressed against the glass. Then he stands up, calls to rouse his chauffeur, and orders him to take him home immediately.

He has the youths taken to a hotel room, where they can sleep it off together. Wrapping his coat around his shoulders, he bids goodnight and opens the conservatory door. The wind gusts in, tugging at the palms. Sangallo pauses in the doorway without turning back to Silberstrand and Maxim.

"The Grüftes take every chance they can to harm us, but we mustn't fear them. They can destroy our world, rob us of everything, but they can't touch us. Not really. They can't touch our souls."

While the old man walks away and the cold air spreads through the winter garden, Silberstrand bends over Maxim and kisses him. First his eyes, then his nose, then his cheek and mouth. She tastes of steel, her tongue and teeth sticky with wine. She pulls open the bathrobe, licks him on the throat, covers his chest with nipping kisses. She hardens his nipples between her teeth. Then she sucks them while impatiently squeezing his erection.

"I knew you'd come," she whispers. "You're made of the right, shameless stuff." Can she really be skillful enough to know exactly the words he wants to hear? The words to make him believe in his role?

He briefly imagines himself moving his hands over Gala's body during the first rehearsal of *The Mannequins' Ball*. Just like then, he's encouraged by the idea that he is acting. He juts his pelvis forward and feels his partner react. He now knows that it doesn't matter how you act as long as people believe you.

The singer's breathing quickens. Wildly, she shakes her locks away from her face, but when she drops to her knees before Maxim, she loses her balance and slides off the sofa with a bump. They look at each other for a moment, almost surprised to find themselves entangled like this, but the moment passes and they slip into their own fantasies. Growling, she bites into his jeans and claws savagely at his belt. He exposes himself and feeds her, leaning back, a shameless whore at last, his head resting on the ancient sculpture.

It's sweating. Drop after drop runs down the marble curves. Nothing holds them back on the muscular torso, but the drops all converge on the same place. Squinting, Maxim can make out the grooves from ancient chisels that lead the condensation down the abdomen to the groin and the amputated thigh. At long intervals, one tepid drop after another drips from the stone wound, straight down onto the furiously bobbing head of the woman who is fellating him.

It's his own disengagement that excites Maxim. Nothing else. More enjoyable than the sweet glow between his thighs or the warm sucking is the realization that he can let his body be used without the intervention of his mind. The discovery that he can separate the two enraptures him.

In his youth, his flesh and his soul had been fused by a searing sense of shame that was aroused within him; but now, in the steamy winter garden, they are soaked loose, liberated one from the other. This is why shamelessness is so addictive, so triumphant: it undermines the dictatorship of small-mindedness. As long as he can separate body and mind, Maxim knows, he can do anything. This realization is the sole source of his ardor.

He pulls Silberstrand away by her hair and takes charge in just the way he thinks she wants him to. She gladly consents, fighting her way out of her evening gown, letting him position her on the plush on all fours and, with a resounding groan, leading him into her from behind. She grabs him by the balls and tugs to her desired rhythm. Businesslike, she puts his hands on her breasts and shows him how hard to squeeze. Sex and love, thinks Maxim, cursing aloud with delight at his own hardness, how little sorrow there would be in the world if more people could separate the two. The singer tries a couple of times to look back, hoping to heighten her own excitement by seeing his pleasure in mounting her, but Maxim averts his gaze before their eyes can meet.

After they've come, tenderness wells up in him for the woman he's just fucked. She lies on her back. Her breasts don't look as firm as they felt, and flop to either side. He cups one in his hand and gently kisses a swollen nipple that still bears the imprint of his nails. He kisses her waist, rests his head on her well-trained solar plexus, and strokes her loose skin, which moves as his fingers caress it.

The difference between the two bodies could not be greater. Yet he is overcome with a trust he's never felt with another woman. Fucking without love; friendship without admiration: an equality that reminds him of two schoolboys lending each other a hand in the showers at the gym. They both know exactly what the other needs and can give. There are no explanations. No illusions. There are no games. No conflict. They know their desires and give what they can, neither demanding anything unavailable. They touch without being bound. Friendship.

The discovery moves him, as if it had brought him closer to something great.

Between him and the singer, there are none of the things that make men and women unequal. Pragmatism has eliminated any dishonesty. Their cards are on the table. She expects nothing more than what he's got to offer. There's no relationship getting in the way, and all thanks to the clear agreement they made beforehand.

But how clear has he really been? Maxim briefly wonders what they've actually agreed. She wanted him to come, and he came. Should he have set a price in advance? A time limit? The working relationship hasn't explicitly been discussed. But perhaps that would be too crude. And how would he describe his function? How much can you charge for something you like doing so much? And *when* should he raise the question? She'll probably do that herself; a woman of the world, unquenchable, a world traveler, must be an old hand.

Once again, that inexplicable emotion rises within him, and it annoys him, because it muddles his new image of himself. To get back into the role, he slips the fingers of the hand lying calmly between her legs into her, fiddling around inside. She wriggles a little, opens herself further, and pushes his head down. He briefly wonders whether this, too, is part of his duties, but when she pushes his face into her crotch, still swollen and dripping with lust, he no longer holds back, sinking his teeth into her with an intensity that hurts her but is nonetheless met with an astonished ecstatic scream.

No matter how coarsely he sucks and roots about, his emotion only grows. When he sits up, his eyes are as wet as the rest of his face. Silberstrand dries him off and kisses him, less fiercely now, tenderly. Gratefully. She presses her lips against his eyes as if to drink his tears.

In that instant, he disentangles himself. He walks among the bare tables and the potted palms, annoyed, indecisive, naked, trying to remember how they'd agreed on the payment. They did have an agreement, didn't they? More or less, even if it was partly unspoken. He'd have to learn to be clearer if he wanted to carry on with this kind of thing. But the longer he put it off, the less he could face it.

Silberstrand pulls on her dress and gathers his clothes. He looks through the glass wall while she drapes his shirt over his shoulders, pulls him against her, and rubs his sides, as if to keep him warm. He wipes the mist from the window to see something of the violence outside. The regularity of the lighthouse and the boulevard streetlights show nothing but the raging storm.

"Will you take me to bed?" she asks.

"I've got to get going." Maxim takes his clothes from her and starts getting dressed.

"At this hour? Don't be silly. How were you planning to get home?"

"I'll take a cab."

"You don't have any money."

"I will soon."

She shrugs.

"Either way, we're going to my room first. You can sleep for an hour or so, but then we'll run through the whole piece *da capo.*"

Maxim buckles his belt with exaggerated fastidiousness.

"That's what you want, isn't it, you hot boy?" Silberstrand kneads his crotch. "Maybe a bit calmer the second time around."

"Again?" he says, doing his best not to see her beauty and her pride in provoking him. "Fine." He takes a deep breath and speaks his lines as coolly as possible. "But then the meter starts running a second time as well."

The singer is still smiling, but he sees the pleasure slowly ebb from her eyes. She thinks she has misheard and shakes her head quickly to dispel a thought that seems so misplaced, but the truth comes crashing down just as she's about to ask her young lover to repeat his words.

"You want me to pay you." She says it quietly because it hurts.

Maxim feels it too.

"We're poor," he explains. "It's for medicine."

"You want *me* to pay *you*?" says Silberstrand, as if the reverse seems more plausible.

"You've seen the state Gala's in. If this weren't an emergency, it would never have occurred to me."

"Oh God!" exclaims the singer, almost motionless. Her eyes are frightened, wandering despondently to a point far behind him, as if she sees a terrible danger approaching. "Oh merciful God, it's come to this!"

For a second she stands there paralyzed, bewildered by the truth.

"I mean," Maxim corrects himself, shocked by the intensity of her reaction, "of course it would have occurred to me to want to . . . um, with you, together . . . but, of course, completely free of charge . . . who wouldn't want to be with a woman like you? But considering the shortage of funds. I thought . . . because you said, 'I'll reward you handsomely for the effort.' "

Her back is straight as she roots through her handbag, her head proud and upright throughout, though it's obvious that she can control her muscles only with the greatest effort. She finds a few notes and hurls them at his feet. Then she suddenly collapses, as if she's been kicked in the gut, sinking to the floor, slow and jerking, like an actor in a film that's coming off the reel. There she remains, curled up, almost lost in the puffy taffeta of the red dress, which spreads slowly over the marble, quietly shivering like Silberstrand herself. Maxim drops to his knees before her. He wants to hold her, soothe her with pleas for forgiveness, but she looks so fragile that he's afraid she'd fall apart at his touch. Slowly she raises her face. It is twisted with sorrow. She suddenly looks so old, so soullessly desolate, that Maxim shrinks back a few steps. He is the one who has broken this woman. She throws her head back like a wounded animal, opening her mouth wide, like a wolf about to howl, and she does, with all her strength, but no sound issues from her. Maxim, who was about to cover his ears in expectation of the voice that can normally drown out a symphony orchestra, drops his hands in astonishment. Her neck muscles are bundled in thick strands, her larynx is vibrating, and the veins in her throat are standing out, but the singer emits nothing but silence.

The only thing that swells is the storm, which fiercely buffets the glass construction with a number of quick gusts. Windowpanes bulge in their frames. They both feel the danger. The singer's eyes follow the roar passing over them, but this cannot dissuade her from her soundless shrieking: to the contrary, she fervently notches up the tension of her inaudible tones, as if to make the champagne flutes vibrate.

Just then, something slams against the top of the windows, five or six times, in quick staccato, before finally smashing through the glass with tremendous force. A large seagull, numb with fright and pain, falls into the middle of the room, trailing blood over the marble tiles. The sudden displacement of the conservatory's air rips doors open all around, rushing to the lobby, to the boulevard, to the beach. Glass shatters. The palms' heavy leaves are at the mercy of the wind. They wobble. One tree topples over, dragging a blossoming orange tree down with it. The gusts blow in seawater and sand that scours Maxim's skin.

Above all this, the gull is screeching. Silberstrand stands and walks over to the animal. She picks it up with two hands, strokes the head that flinches in fear and the beak that snaps at her. She presses kisses on the wounded body while combing its feathers for pieces of glass.

From the boulevard, Maxim looks back. All over the hotel, lights come on and people peer from behind curtains to locate the source of the uproar. In the distance, he sees the singer who was the beginning and the end of his new career. Erect in the storm, the white seagull's broad fluttering wings pressed against her heart, she stands among the glimmering shards of the winter garden.

2

"I know that girl," Gelsomina exclaims one morning. We're having breakfast on our balcony, and I'm sketching my dreams on a napkin. I always keep felt-tip pens within reach so I can scribble down the remnants of the night before they drown in the light of day. Gelsomina joins me under the parasol and slides my plate aside for a better view.

"Betty Boop perhaps?"

Like so many of the women I draw after they've appeared to me in the night, this character has a big head, high heels, and a small body with full breasts, but Gelsomina shakes her head.

"She's on your bulletin board at Cinecittà." She turns the drawing around. "Is she in our film?"

"Not as far as I know." I give her a plunging neckline and a yellow dress with black leopard-skin patches.

"Why the scarf tied around her head?"

"She's probably got a headache," I tease, "from all your questions!"

Playfully, Gelsomina snatches the napkin, even though she sees the drawing isn't finished. I try to grab it back, but she won't surrender it without a fight. She ties the napkin around her head and assumes the exaggerated pose of the young woman I've just drawn: one hand on the back of her head, the other on a hip she sticks out so far it looks almost deformed. She parades around, taunting me, and breaks into a run the moment I give chase. When I catch her, she demands a kiss in exchange for the napkin. I bargain with her until she allows me to give her three.

Gelsomina's eyes are closed and her lips pursed when I suddenly jerk the napkin off her head.

I dislodge her wig. Carried away by the game, I had lost sight of her fragility. It doesn't fly off completely, it just slides down the side of her head. I'm shocked. I always forget she's got it on. Enzo and the hair department at Cinecittà made it so beautifully, with so much love, that it's indistinguishable from real hair.

I apologize, but Gelsomina isn't embarrassed in front of me. She takes it off. Funny how those last strands are so much more precious to me than her full head of hair ever was. She replaces the wig as adeptly as the actress she is and kisses me anyway. But her face drops when she looks over my shoulder. The napkin has flown off the table. I make a grab for it, but it shoots up and swirls over the rooftops. Hand in hand, Gelsomina and I watch the woman from last night's dream blowing around in the sky. For a moment, it looks as if she's headed for the Pincio, but the wind shifts and the napkin falls at our feet like a dead bird.

A real cartoon character never ages. Unlike Gelsomina. She has been drawn by life. The skin droops, the lines have smudged on the page. She has weathered, and her colors have paled in the sun. The big head on that little body has become as wrinkled as a ball of newsprint in a wastepaper basket. I pick her up, unfold her, try to smooth her out with the palm of my hand. No one can ever have felt this much tenderness.

It is because they are decaying that we admire the frescoes of the great masters more deeply than the lords who commissioned them did on the morning they were unveiled. Only by choosing our own colors and completing the faded lines in our imaginations can we touch their essence.

I melt every morning when I wake up beside her, no less than I did fifty years ago. I feel her warmth. I touch her and pray that I might feel the same way in the hour of my death. Yet I am already dying. I lose consciousness. I sink away into the love where I myself cease to exist. I turn over and there she is: the spiky hair and those big, closed clown's eyes just above the blankets. I'd like to sob and squeak with joy, grab her, shake her, pull her out of bed, jump up and down together. No words can express it. I kiss her pert little nose, which twitches in her sleep as if I were tickling her nostrils with a straw.

I see her as a little girl, standing before a columbarium in the cemetery of the Ursuline Sisters in Bologna. The small tombs in the high marble walls bear no names, only years, one gleaming marble plaque for each year of her life. Ten columns wide, ten rows high. I bring her a ladder so that she can easily reach each age. In each tomb she opens, there is an urn with a copper plate marked with the year. When she lifts one of the lids, the ash billows up, and in the dust she glimpses herself as she looked in that year. She grabs one year after another, scattering it around. It's plain to see that never, not for a single moment, was she uglier or more beautiful than in any other. Because it has always been her, Gelsomina, my picture, my painting. The last tombs are still empty, gaping, unsealed holes in the wall. We crawl into one. Deep in the gloomy niche, I cuddle up to her and hear something rustling in the pocket of her coat. She has brought rum babas with her. We feed them to each other, sucking the liquor out of the cake. And that is how we wait, close to each other.

I wouldn't begrudge anyone this intimacy, but I refuse to believe that another couple has ever been, or ever will be, this close. There is not a moment when Gelsomina is not with me, not even when I'm in someone else's arms. How could it be otherwise? I exist inside her, and she in me.

It's strange how a love that keeps growing starts to hurt like sorrow. Perhaps because at the same time it grows you see the outline dissolving. You need to make haste to show the other how great your love really is. You can tell her every day how much you love her, but it gets to be like a nagging pain whose exact location you can never pinpoint when the doctor asks. Finally, you feel you have to scream your love out loud, because it's too big to capture in words, or even show in pictures.

Yet that's what Gelsomina has asked me to do. At first, I thought she was nagging me for a lead in my next film, just like all the other actresses, but then I realized that she wanted a memorial: a final testimony to our love. I'd done it before, celebrating my first rush of feeling for her, and then, in a subsequent film, my lust for her. Both came from within me. But recently Gelsomina asked for me to conjure a proof of my true love out of the light. I was stuck. If I can't tell the woman who's grown old with me what really matters, how can I possibly have anything to say to the world?

And just when I was starting to create this last monument for Gelsomina, Gala sashayed into my office at Cinecittà. At first I merely thought she might come in handy in a bit role in my homage, one of those anonymous and interchangeable girls like the ones Busby Berkeley arranged in geometric patterns to create his living kaleidoscopes. I sought figures—like the water nymph Bernini placed in the pedestal of a fountain to gaze admiringly at the towering Neptune above her—to exalt Gelsomina. Gala, if I ended up deciding to use her at all, would have simply been one of many tones that could lend color to Gelsomina. Why didn't I see how she would dazzle? I know it all too well, how passing time disintegrates the edifice until at last the nymph is fished out of the Tiber, then placed in a museum to be admired as a masterpiece. In every fragment the observers can, after all, guess at the whole.

And she's really there, hanging on my office wall, the girl I saw in my dreams, the one with the big cartoonish head. I pluck her portrait from the hopeful *fines fleurs* on my notice board. It's a close-up, but I can make out a leopard-skin print on the jacket flung over her shoulders.

I strain to recall our meeting, but can visualize neither last night's dream nor our encounter in the flesh. I lean her photo against the base of the office lamp in front of me and get to work. She keeps her eye on me all morning, and when I come back from my coffee break I read what's written on the back. Her name is something impossible that hurts my throat when I try to pronounce it. An address in Parioli is scrawled next to it, and the name of her agent.

"Just watching!" an astonished Fulvani exclaims. "Surely there can't be any harm in that?" He drops his chin to his chest and stares intently at the Dutch couple, scanning their faces for the least sign of consent, like a dog in front of a freshly filled bowl, trembling with subservience but incapable of hiding its tail-wagging excitement. Sitting across from him, Gala and Maxim clasp hands under the table. Each is waiting for the other to react, but minutes elapse without their moving so much as a finger. Their palms take on the same temperature; their fingertips become indistinguishable. Just when they turn to each other for support, they are so completely merged that they can no longer sense each other's thoughts.

"Unless," Fulvani pouts, turning away as if to conceal his disappointment, "unless, of course, you think that people should be ashamed of those moments when they're at their most beautiful?"

The scene is none too original and will fail to surprise anyone except those who act it out. It's a film-industry staple, and a hilarious new variant does the rounds at every party. Everyone hopes that things like this occasionally happen, but no one is personally acquainted with anyone villainous or naive enough to get caught up in such an adventure. Of course, Gala and Maxim have heard of these practices, but they laughed off the idea that decisions involving such large amounts of money could be made so frivolously. Soon, when it's all behind them and they're outside again, they'll run down the Via Angelo Brunetti doubled over with laughter. Still laughing, they'll run up the Pincio until they can no longer hold it in, whereupon they'll collapse in front of the Casina Valadier. There, giggling and spluttering while they order one expensive cocktail after the next, they'll slowly realize that, beneath their hilarity, which refuses to subside all evening, they feel no shame at all, but rather pride. Their bond has only been strengthened by this latest stunt.

When I called Fulvani that morning to tell him I wanted to screen-test Gala, I detected an ominous note beneath his usual obsequiousness. Was he annoyed that I was interested in one of his favorites? Impatient because he couldn't wait to use the lasso I'd given him to haul in his prey? At any rate, I remember I suddenly saw him sitting there on the other end of the line like a drooling Pantalone, bent over the telephone, sniggering as he used his spit to set a curl in his long goatee. That's how I'll show him when we shoot the scene.

After hanging up, I sketched myself as a big battleship bobbing up and down on the waves: the deck formed by my stomach is covered with bikini girls. Dancing wildly, they do their best to attract my attention, until I start shaking with pleasure. Then they tumble over my railings and plunge into the sea. My wake is full of sharks, feasting on everyone I've rejected.

There was a time when I couldn't sleep for thinking about everyone I've had to disappoint. I was young and recognized my own enthusiasm in the wide eyes that looked at me. "Where would I be now," I asked myself, "if no one had given me a first chance?" Then one night I ran through all the rejections I myself have received and awoke to the realization that those very roads, the ones that had been cut off, the chances I didn't get, were what made me who I am. After that, I slept like a baby. No rose flowers without being pruned. That may be why, less than a second after I'd pictured myself tossing a bouquet of Dutch tulips to Fulvani's shears, I'd forgotten Gala again, as if she'd never visited me, either in real life or in my dreams.

"Should you really come?" Gala asked Maxim after Fulvani had summoned her. She was sitting at the mirror, nervously adding a gold stroke above her peacock-blue eye shadow just to be on the safe side, something she normally did only before going to discos.

"We've come this far together. I'm supposed to leave you behind now?" He could feel that she didn't want him there. A few days before, she'd said as much, hinting—"Look, that's just how Italian men are"—that he was in the way. After a couple of nights, his initial sorrow hardened into stubbornness.

"I can't help noticing that this guy always invites you over during his secretaries' lunch break," Maxim said. "It's because they're like that, Gala, that I can't let you go there alone again." To make up for his insistence, he walked all the way to the bar on the Piazza Flaminia to fetch her a bottle of vodka, but when he got back he asked, as always, "You sure you really need it?" And, as always, Gala answered that she was more relaxed after a couple of swigs.

"Funnier."

"I don't believe that you could be much funnier than you are," he said. She stopped teasing her curls to look at him.

"That's sweet of you," she said, "but when I'm nervous I'm dull and boring; I get scared that I won't be able to say something funny, and that's enough to make me stare like a donkey."

"I've never seen you do anything but scintillate."

"Yes, *you*!" she snapped, as if he'd turned down a dead-end street. In a burst of impatience, she grabbed a pair of scissors and sliced off a troublesome curl. The results were so upsetting that anything else Maxim had to say was drowned out by the jeers of Snaporaz that already echoed through her head. She imagined the director stopping her screen test, face twisted with disappointment, so vividly that tears leapt to her eyes. And she was galled that Maxim still thought consoling words could ease her insecurity. He didn't realize that she longed for a scolding, a vicious gibe, to unleash her fighting spirit, to push her, in top form, into the arena.

"No, I don't have any taste," an aggrieved Maxim mumbled as he smoothed her wisps with a little spit, "to like you when you're not completely bombed."

Gala made a point of grabbing the bottle of vodka, sucking it half-empty in only a couple of swigs.

Even pressed against each other in the rattling elevator that was taking them to Skylight, their mood still hadn't thawed, though with every passing floor they noticed their breathing had synchronized, as it did when they shared a bed.

"He insisted on coming," Gala sighed to Fulvani, as if bemoaning the end of her career. The man opened the elevator door. To her chagrin, she realized she was trembling at the thought that he too might now be disappointed in her. Her shivering passed through the elevator cage, creating a short rattling inside the shaft. Fulvani's smile was wide and amiable, but she played it safe, raising her face to let the older man kiss her on both cheeks for the first time. But he scarcely took the time to enjoy it, apparently more interested in Maxim.

"I'm so glad to see you, my boy." He slapped a clammy hand on Maxim's neck and pulled him to his chest. "As if you sensed it . . ."

"Considering past experiences," Maxim said belligerently, "a chaperone seemed advisable."

"There's no doubt that two heads are better than one." Fulvani didn't seem to have heard his hostility. "United we stand, I always say!"

Maxim pulled back from the embrace, more leery than ever.

"I just called that house of yours to ask if you could come with Gala, my handsome young fellow, but you'd already left."

"You don't say," Maxim replied, so tetchily it earned him a dig in the ribs from Gala. "What a coincidence."

"Perhaps it was simply meant to be," Fulvani beamed, "and that's what it's starting to look like. I have good reason to believe that the Baby Jesus has lent me not one but two prize Dutch cows from His Christmas manger, but before I start milking, first tell me this, star athlete, how well can you ski?"

"Ski?"

"Or are you going to tell me you developed thighs like that just from riding in bed?"

"He danced," said Gala, coming to his aid.

"Nobody's perfect," Fulvani growled while measuring up one of the young man's legs by pinching it firmly from knee to groin.

"At Theater School. Every morning. Grands jetés in particular are . . ." Maxim stuttered, seeing Fulvani's face fall. "And skating, of course," he added, lowering his voice an octave to erase any suspicions of a pink tutu, "we skate whenever we get the chance."

"The Dutch!" groaned Fulvani. "When it gets cold, they head for the water. Who could possibly understand them?" Shaking his head, he released Maxim and turned to Gala.

"Darling, the moment has come. You know what I mean. Snaporaz is inordinately interested in you." His itching fingers floated in the air as if he were about to pinch her as well, but with a sigh of respect for so much beauty, he let them drop into his lap to get a grip on himself.

"Inordinately?" Hardly able to believe it, Gala seized the hand that Maxim extended as if to keep her from tumbling backward. "Inordinately? Did he really say that?"

"This is hardly the moment to bicker over one little word. The point is, he wants to use you. And can you blame the great man? Such fine specimens! And by the way," asked Fulvani, leaning back in his chair and studying Maxim as he lifted up Gala, spun her around, and planted a leisurely kiss on her neck, "do you ever do it in company?"

The elated couple grinned at him as if they had misheard. In fact, Fulvani's brazenness would have been swept aside by their jubilation if he hadn't taken the trouble to clarify. "Another man in bed with you, perhaps a woman? Even if just to watch. When you're that richly endowed, don't you have a duty to share with others? Just to watch, surely there can't be anything wrong with that?"

. . .

Maxim puts Gala down and in seconds is ready to drag Fulvani out from behind his desk, but the agent has already stood of his own accord, ignoring Maxim's threat so blatantly that the young man starts to wonder whether he's imagined the impertinence.

"All I have to say to you, young man, is that a major American studio is coming to shoot a TV film about an Olympic ski champion. We're talking about the lead here, so let me ask you again: do you ski, yes or no?"

"Like the best of them," lies Maxim, who has to wear crampons at the first sign of frost.

"He could slalom before he could walk," says Gala, to lend her support.

"Lovely." Fulvani observes Maxim's eagerness with a triumphant smile. "If you have no other objections . . ."

Silence descends. No one asks what they might object to.

"I knew I could talk you into it. The procedure is simple. I send Maxim to the Americans and I arrange an appointment for Gala. Tomorrow or the day after, as soon as possible. Probably at Snaporaz's office in his house on the Via Margutta. He'll chat with you, take a couple of photos, at the most a few test shots for the lighting. Don't mention the financial side, the maestro isn't involved in that and, anyway, negotiations are—as you've noticed—my strong suit. He wants you, and money won't be a problem. Yes, it looks like your adventure really is about to begin. Just one thing, I would like to watch . . ." His breathing gets heavier. He grabs Gala's arm and strokes the inside of her elbow with his coarse fingers. She can smell his breath. She feels herself going cold as she racks her mind to discover what she has done wrong. Has she given him a false impression? Feverish words race through her head—they always do when she panics—sentences from previous meetings, images from their last encounter. She grabs at her blouse. Should she have buttoned it up further? Either way, she's given the wrong idea. Now she's got to live up to it: otherwise, he'll be disappointed. Stay calm, she tells herself: whatever else happens, I can't let him think I'm childish. He can't think I'm out of my depth. What if he tells Snaporaz how I always back out of things? A man like that, a great director who hangs out with the world's most statuesque women like kids playing hide-and-seek in the street, what would he think if he heard I'm scared to play along? "I don't want an unsophisticated girl like that" is what he'll say! Now I've landed this role and I don't know if it's been forced on me or if I accidentally auditioned, but now that I've got it, I have to perform. I'm in a play again. With Maxim as my partner. We've done this piece before. We know what scene he's expecting, we've rehearsed it, we've got an eager audience, so what are we waiting for?

The idea that it's just a temporary role helps her relax. The stage fright will disappear the moment she steps into the spotlight. Fulvani feels her body yielding and pulls it up against his.

"Such a magnificent woman, such a handsome man. I thought that even the milkmaids in Holland didn't make a fuss over a little exhibitionism?"

"Enough with the innuendos!" Maxim puts his foot down, his eyes darting around in search of something he can knock over to punctuate his words, but everything looks too fragile.

"What innuendos? Babe"—Fulvani brings his lips close to Gala's ear—"did you hear any innuendos? I say exactly what I think, I'm open and honest about what I want, and I might have expected a little more gratitude." He kisses Gala's earlobe and blows his warm breath on her neck while keeping his eyes riveted on Maxim. "No, my only sin is that I'm a man. Just like you, my friend. With the same desires. If you want to condemn me for that, I plead guilty!"

Gala groans softly, almost entreatingly, but it's impossible to say whether she's pleading to be released or to be taken. Her head tilts back slightly, coming to rest against Fulvani's chest, the kind of movement a bird might make in a cat's jaws—a struggle will injure her, so she knows that hanging limp is her only chance—but both men see it as a sign of surrender. Fulvani's eyes glisten in triumph, still fixed on Maxim's. Encouraged, he inches her dress up her thigh until his stubby fingers touch her skin and glide in under her garters.

"What do you want?" Maxim hisses in Dutch so that the Italian won't understand him. Gala is shocked by his cold fury.

"Do you really want this, or do I smash his face in? Speak up for yourself for once, for Christ's sake!"

She doesn't, abandoned as she feels: abandoned by Maxim, but also, and much more intensely, abandoned by herself, just as in that brief moment before a seizure she always betrays herself, in that instant when she tries to grasp the last remnant of consciousness though she knows that within seconds she will so passionately long for the unknown that she'll voluntarily let go and meet the danger with open arms. And now, just as during her epileptic absences, she cannot reach Maxim. She suppresses the scream rising within her—she knows it won't help. Her consciousness is now separating from her body in a way that recalls her disease so strongly that she expects to see the fluttering red cape close around her at any moment. But this is no seizure. This time, there's no escape. She'll have to go through with it fully conscious. As she stares at the sun high over the rooftops, her pupils dilate, grow glassy, hide behind a layer of water, almost exactly as they do during the ecstasy of lovemaking. This is precisely what Maxim thinks he recognizes in her eyes.

"Then it's all up to you," he snaps. His annoyance has gone far beyond their earlier disagreement. She thought he was mad at *her,* but he's really angry at himself. He's a man: how can he know that the deepest resistance sometimes looks like acquiescence? All he sees is her breathing quicken as she opens up to Fulvani. He curses the godforsaken lust that, against his wishes and despite his abhorrence, turns him on, watching the man about to finger her. Fulvani doesn't miss it.

"See," he whispers into Gala's ear, sliding his fingers between her labia, "our ski instructor can't wait to join the fun. What do you think, shall we let him join in?"

She groans again, deeper now, more imploringly. This time it's clearer to all three of them, although it means something different to each: Gala is begging to be loved.

People say that fantasy expands our consciousness. I have learned that it contracts it.

And that contraction offers us an escape.

Throughout the whole scene, Gala stares at a tiny point in the distance. She's used the trick since early childhood. Few can hear the difference between cries of pleasure and cries of loneliness.

When her father was in one of his unpredictable moods and had her, in front of guests, do something impossible, or when he humiliated her for failing, she stared straight though the tunnel of recriminations she faced. Shining at the end was the reward of his love. She imagined herself an Indian, running the gauntlet through an angry mob. This was the way she'd found to survive the mercurial temper that could lame her mother and sisters.

Gala sees only through the corner of her eye what actually happens that afternoon at Skylight. Of the male bodies that caress her, that she caresses, she only experiences what she allows herself. She doesn't allow enough for fear, aversion, or sorrow, not enough for a sense of violation, but just enough to see how absurd it all is and burst out in gurgling laughter every once in a while. Meanwhile, her consciousness, far ahead of her, is waiting at the end of the tunnel. That's how she keeps her balance, and possibly even taking some pleasure in the men, in the excitement of the unexpected, in her own courage. And in the role she fantasizes to get her through it.

A tightrope walker doesn't look around. That is critical. He balances. It would be too much to look at the situation he's gotten himself into. He doesn't look at how far he can fall. He doesn't even look at the rope to see where to put his feet. His reality simultaneously exists and does not. In the same instant, he knows and doesn't know where he is. The equilibrist limits his vision to a small distant point. He concentrates on the destination. By constricting his consciousness, he reaches the other side.

This is my homage to love.

Pom, pom, pom, pom, pomodori
Juicy and red, in a sauce or on bread
Once on a vine, now they lie here instead
Big and sweet, juicy and red
If you bite them they're dead
Pom, pom, pom, pom, pomodori.

As soon as he recognizes me, the market vendor puts on a show. I feel like climbing up onto Giordano Bruno's pedestal and hiding under his bronze robes. While I hurry away, the man sings the entire jingle again by way of audition.

"I thought all your films were an homage to love," Gala says.

I've forgotten what we were talking about. That's been happening to me a lot lately. It's because of the people. Crowds always confuse me. I know they mean well, with the attention they pay me. I seek their cheerful faces, but I feel like running away once I've found them.

"An homage to love," she repeats.

I suddenly regret the whole thing. Why did I arrange to meet her in the busy Campo de' Fiori? Oh God, I'm afraid I know: to show her off, of course. And she knows it.

"I mean an homage to my love for a particular woman."

"Your own wife."

"Gelsomina."

"Of course, she is divine."

I look at the Dutch girl. She means it.

"She's the one who drew my attention to you."

"Gelsomina?"

We duck into a side street and choose a table hidden between flower boxes in a corner of the Piazza Farnese. I sketch her throughout the whole conversation, but none of my attempts resembles her as much as the picture I scribbled after my dream. She seems delighted—no, moved—to learn that I met her in my sleep. She refuses to believe it at first, but I pull the picture out of my pocket and show it to her. She looks at it in silence. I think she's about to burst into tears, but then she jumps up. She wants to leave without another word. I grab her wrist, but she won't yield, and I have to beg with the ardor I usually deploy to chase other actresses off.

"Now I can only be a disappointment!" Gala exclaims, shaking her head. The thought upsets her so much that she doesn't realize that she is proving precisely the opposite. "This real encounter can never be as important as our meeting in the night. I should never have come. What possessed you to ask me?"

"Roast chicken," is the first thing that occurs to me. "The best in Rome," and I order two.

I'm used to people laughing in my company. At the first suspicion that I'm trying to be funny, they slap their knees, buckle over, but not Gala. She worriedly keeps weighing the pros and cons of our meeting. She reminds me of a cartoon character racing full speed through the air because he hasn't yet realized that he's dangling over an abyss.

The birds are brought out. I tear off a leg. Before sinking my teeth into it, I kiss it, very quickly.

"What are you doing?" she asks, and I start to tell her about my grandmother in Castelrotondo, who once told me about a chick who was really a prince.

"Like the frog prince," I explain, "but with poultry. I was still young. That night we ate chicken and I got a terrible stomachache. I panicked. I thought my dinner was turning into a prince. Since then, I play it safe."

At that, Gala throws caution to the wind, planting her elbows on the table and plunging her fingers into her meal.

"There's just one thing I'm worried about . . ." She raises a drumstick to her mouth, pouts, and carries out the test I have applied automatically since I was five years old. She doesn't do it to impress me: she's completely natural, and as if a native had taught her a useful foreign custom, her tongue shoots out between her lips, gleaming with grease, to lick up a drop running down her chin. She slurps at the gravy while she continues speaking. "However random they may seem, images in the subconscious are more reliable than those registered by the retina."

Do I fall in love on the spot? Unlikely. Retold in this way, that's how it might seem, but I know myself. I lack the reserve of a northerner: the main thing is I want to go to bed with her. Preferably at once. I'm already adding her name in big elaborate letters to the bottom of a long list that I have, with great difficulty, fished out of the bottom drawer of my life. But as soon as I see myself appending her to the list of my conquests, I feel the paper tearing under my fingers. She seems so open and uncalculating that my horniness crumbles into endearment.

I let her talk. She is animated, intelligent, full of joie de vivre. I recognize and understand her insecurity, but she is so relaxed, so much in charge of the conversation, that my own doubts grow. I also feel the usual sorrow of age when faced with the young. Gala lets her eyes rest on me without so much as blinking. Piercing and ogling at once, that look forces me to shrink away until I'm crawling around inside my outsized body like a baby searching his playpen for a toy.

I find it in the skin around her eyes. It is remarkably bad. Probably because she uses too much makeup too often, makeup that is heavy and theatrical but not effective. She is perspiring lightly. In the course of the conversation, the color washes off and collects in premature crow's-feet.

I dip my napkin in water and wipe her cheek. It's our first touch. I keep dabbing, but don't really dare go much further. She takes the cloth from me and unquestioningly wipes the gunk off her face. Then I open the box of watercolors I take with me everywhere. On a saucer, I mix sienna and carmine. Using the butter that's on the table, I make a paste. I remove the gilded brush that Gelsomina gave me for my sixtieth birthday from its traveling case and apply the color around her eyes with delicate strokes.

As requested, she chatters on, amused, while I study the result. I draw her eyebrows as quotation marks, giving her an expression of surprise, and extend her lashes like sunbeams. Finally, I mix a color for her lips and apply it until she looks sulky.

She picks up a knife and looks at herself in the blade.

"But that's Gelsomina," she exclaims. "It is, the spitting image!"

I deny it, but Gala pulls a face that does indeed resemble the character I created for my wife in my first box-office success. It ruins my mood.

The first time I touched Gelsomina, I was making her up as well. I asked if I could cut her hair along the edge of an inverted flowerpot and she trusted me. She didn't even resist when I rubbed soap on the wisps to make them stick up. It was wartime, and there wasn't any powder, so I took a handful of flour and dusted her face by gently puffing on it. While I sought out her features with my white breath, she was pale as a kabuki actor. Her cheerfulness didn't seem exuberant at all, I told her, but restrained. She wasn't just showing off her mischievousness for effect, but expressed the loneliness of an entire life in a single smile. I saw a solitary tear well up in response, a tear that picked up so much flour on its way down her face that if only I'd had some boiling oil I could have easily made a dumpling of it by the time it fell from her chin.

I remember with how much love I then accentuated her upturned nose with a dab of red. That, more or less, must have been the moment when I swore solemnly that Gelsomina would never have to feel alone again. Yet over the years I've sent enough dough rolling down her face to serve a restaurant.

"What's the story with that friend of yours?" I ask Gala.

"Why?" She starts, because I haven't tried to hide my displeasure.

"That fellow who was with you in my office." I act surly. I'm used to taking my melancholy out on others. She flinches like a child expecting to have his ears boxed by the parish priest. I see it, but I can't stand the thought of her walking home to tell some guy I don't even know about the old man who made a fool of himself over her.

"Just tell me, do you live with him?"

I see that she's shocked; I can almost hear her brains rattling in search of a satisfactory answer.

"With that queen?" she asks airily, averting her eyes for the first time. I'd think she was lying, if the twist in her mouth didn't betray such deep contempt. "Where'd you get that idea? He and I are just girlfriends. That's all."

I like that, even if she's gone to the trouble of fabricating it. I stand up and tell her I've got work to do.

"See you later," Gala says, summoning up all her courage to add: "Maybe at an audition?"

"This was your audition."

As a gift, I give her the napkin with the drawing from my dream. She holds it up next to her face. The quotation mark eyebrows, the shape of the lips, the fanned-out lashes, the white linen. Gelsomina has already said it: "I know that girl."

I'm halfway down the Via Capo di Ferro when I think I hear Gala shouting something after me. She sees me looking back and waves with the napkin.

I think I hear the words "*Ciao,* little boy!" but I don't think her lips quite match them.

"I've blown it! I'm such an idiot!"

Gala flops down on the bed in Parioli.

"It was all there for the taking, and I missed every opportunity!"

Maxim tries to cheer her up, but she won't to be consoled.

In the Via Margutta, Gelsomina doesn't ask a thing until we're getting into bed.

"And was it the woman from your dream?"

"I couldn't help thinking of you."

When she sees that I mean it, she pats me on the cheek as if I were a child.

"A dream of a woman, then." She does a sultry impersonation of la Lollo to drive off her melancholy. "Those are the most dangerous, Signor Snaporaz, you mustn't forget that!" With that, she rolls over and turns off the light.

An hour later, I wake with a start. A drunk is staggering down the street. He's yowling out a song from my childhood, one I've never heard outside of my home ground. To keep him from waking Gelsomina, I get up to close the windows, but she doesn't notice a thing. His voice scrapes over the rooftops like the hooves of an obstinate donkey. I step out onto the balcony to catch every word. He crosses the Piazza del Popolo, and I try to make out whether his singing is headed for Parioli.

I've got a sweetheart living in Penna
And one on the plain of Maremma
One in the beautiful port of Ancona
For number four I have to walk to Viterbo
Not much further, the next is in Casentino
Then there's the one that I live with
And another in Magione
Four in Fratta, ten in Castiglione.

When I creep back into bed with Gelsomina, she, still fast asleep, wraps her arms and legs around me. This trust alone would be enough to make me love her. She presses her head against my chest, holding me tight, as someone who can't swim clings to an inner tube.

That's how I fall asleep. I search all night, but the only person I find is my mother.

"I do understand that," she says. We're picnicking on Rivabella, Rimini's lido, me in the sand, in knitted bathing trunks, and her on a boardwalk, seeking shelter in the shade of a deck chair. She peels an apple and puts the pieces on a napkin for me.

"When I was pregnant with your sister, I thought I could never love anyone as much as I loved you." Her toes play with the sand. She stretches out a hand to me, but I can't reach it.

"I already loved you so unbelievably, so incredibly much, that I thought it was physically impossible to find more love to give. You were everything to me. But the instant I saw her, it happened. Immediately. I loved her just as much without loving you a jot less." With a clack, she adjusts her chair to lie flat. She takes the napkin and throws it over her eyes. "That's how I learned that the love you share immediately doubles. No reason for panic. There's enough to go around."

A gust catches her napkin and carries it away. I try to see her face at last, but along the whole coast beachgoers from Bellariva to Rivabella have lost their napkins to the unexpected whirlwind. Hundreds swirl past. The fluttering white cloths hide my mother completely, and when they finally spread out over the sea, like gulls, she has suddenly disappeared.

3

First of all: none of what happened to Gala afterward had anything to do with me. I didn't even know about it. The few times I met her, I didn't notice anything. There were no signs of the outrageous things the poor child had to endure. To the contrary: she seemed to have blossomed, to have grown stronger, every time I saw her, prouder, more sure of herself. In my most enthusiastic moments, I even took credit for that, as if she were enjoying my reflected glory, rather than the other way around. Who would have thought . . . And even if I'd suspected it, what could I have done? Would I have gotten involved, or would I have been so shocked to realize how much havoc I wreak in other people's lives that I would have washed my hands of her? Perhaps I would have seen what now—now that I'm forced to look back on it all—seems so obvious: that her humiliation gave my own screenplay a perfect finishing touch.

In fact, I was having problems of my own. My Japanese backers unexpectedly pulled out. They were shocked by my failure to stick to agreements. I never stick to agreements, but apparently no one had told them. I'd ordered sets and costumes, only to reject them all afterward. We shot meters and meters of film trying to filter the light in Studio 5 to capture the glow I remembered on Gelsomina's face from a spring morning shortly after our daughter's death.

We thought our lives were over. We were staying in Borgo Pace, Marcello's country cottage, really no more than a shed with a well halfway up the Alpe della Luna, in order to mourn without paparazzi in the shrubbery. We'd scarcely slept and lay in bed, not daring to speak to each other as we waited for the morning. Finally, a blackbird broke the silence. Gelsomina threw open the shutters. There was a frost. The sun was low. Its rays were refracted pink by the ice encasing the blossoms. The effect came as such a surprise to my love, my brave darling, the meaning of my life, that she relaxed. After weeks of being twisted with grief, her mouth fell open. Blood streamed back into her lips. All those frozen buds, moving in the breeze, gave off prisms of light. The colors danced over her face and sparkled in her eyes. I wrapped a blanket around our shoulders. Cuddling together, we were standing at the open window looking out at the miracle when I suddenly realized that our love had survived, not despite the cold, but because of it. I felt Gelsomina's hand searching for mine.

Of course, I didn't tell Gelsomina that I was chasing the enchantment of that morning with my twenty-five thousand watts and forty-eight red filters, but it only took her one glance at the first rushes to guess. Without a word, she looked at me and nodded her approval. She's an old hand, and she stepped back into the light, without betraying her emotions in the least, uncomplainingly staring into the spotlights for four days, from early in the morning to late at night.

As soon as the technicians found what I was looking for, the reality paled so pathetically beside my memory that I dumped the whole scene.

Gelsomina was inconsolable, just like the Japanese. If they'd gotten their hands on Van Gogh, they would have made him paint those big yellow flowers from memory so they could save on florist bills. When the envoys from Nippon realized I wasn't going to use any of the footage I had spent a week shooting, with the entire crew on full pay, they thought I was throwing away their money. They couldn't understand that not filming is filming too. That a writer is thinking while drawing little characters on the page. That there's an electrifying tension in the silence before a composer jots down a note.

But even when I explained that my greatest successes had evolved just that way, they failed to warm to my working methods. Now they want me to write the script first, like everyone else, so they can calculate the filming costs. I patiently explained that I don't work that way. I only get distracted by thinking about what I want to make beforehand. Each thought sets off a hundred more. They still want me to lay out every shot in advance on a storyboard. Hundreds of precise images are worth more to them than one vague idea in my head: whereas that single image contains the whole.

I have a rough idea. When I go to bed, I try to focus on the thread of the story I want to tell, then I let my dreams get to work on it, and the next morning I know exactly what I want to see. Then I go to my studio. Everyone has to be ready, in full makeup, hair, and costume. I want them to be there waiting, just as a painter needs to be able to unscrew the caps of his tubes of paint before he can pick up a brush. Something comes of it or it doesn't. Try explaining that to a nation whose every smile is planned in advance. I felt the least I could do was try to convince them. For Gelsomina's sake. We flew to Tokyo, and our film was postponed indefinitely.

"Postponed!" Maxim exclaims. "Snaporaz is postponing your film?" He snatches the skis out of the prop manager's hands. "And he's only just telling you now?" He strides through the fake snow and strikes an athletic pose. He crouches to pretend he's zooming down a mountain. "Right when we're where we want to be!" For greater credibility, he makes swooshing and swishing sounds as he rounds the curves. That's about all there is to his screen test for the American ski drama, *The Billy Johnson Story*. The instructions are unclear, the lines are corny, and nobody knows anything about the background of the character he's supposed to be portraying. As if that's not bad enough, nobody has any idea how many weeks before shooting starts. Meanwhile, they're not even reimbursing his metro fares. The video camera is operated by the doddering Zoppo, who has been wandering around Cinecittà so long that people assume Mussolini included him in the original design. As soon as the tape is full, the old man removes it from the camera, sticks Maxim's name on it, and wordlessly departs to mail it to Los Angeles.

Maxim slides the goggles onto his forehead.

"Postponed? We'll see about that!" Except around his eyes, his face is made up in an orangey brown that makes him look like he's spent too much time under a sunlamp. He storms out of the test studio and marches threateningly to Studio 5, but everyone who has anything to do with Snaporaz's film has long since been sent home on leave.

"And what are Gala and I supposed to live off, Snaporaz?" he shouts, shaking his fists at the drawn blinds on the first floor. The students who have been employed to crawl around painting the grass red for the film adaptation of *L'herbe rouge* interrupt their work to applaud.

Less than a week has passed when Gala, who was reading in the Villa Borghese, comes back to find Geppi in front of her room, ear to the door.

"The signor has gone mad," she shouts. "Nowadays everyone's teetering on the edge, but your boyfriend finally toppled over just half an hour ago. Screaming, cursing, weeping, breaking things, ah, for a few happy minutes I felt like I still had kids at home!"

"But you told us you didn't have children," says Gala, searching for her key.

"So?" Geppi scurries off indignantly. "A woman's allowed to dream, isn't she?"

Inside is utter chaos. The cupboards have been emptied. Maxim has tried to shove their contents into the bags and suitcases that are heaped on the bed. Sitting in a chair with his back to her, he stares through the high window at the sky.

"We're going home," he says, without turning around. "I called your father . . ."

"You did what?"

"I called Jan. He's paying for our tickets. We can pick them up at the check-in desk."

"What did he say?"

"He loves you and would do anything for you."

(Old Vandemberg had actually jeered and exclaimed triumphantly that he'd always known this girl would cost society more than she was worth, which for him amounted to the same thing.)

Maxim holds up a letter. It's notification that his public assistance has been suspended pending a fraud investigation, and that he may have to refund the last three payments. It doesn't explain how they discovered that he was abroad. Maybe the friend who forges his signature each week got careless, or maybe someone jealous of their living the high life in Rome snitched. Either way, the cash flow has been cut and Gala's benefit check won't cover the rent.

"It's just money," Gala says to calm him down. "We'll think of something. What would Snaporaz say if I turned tail now?"

"Plenty of fish in the sea!"

"That's why I have to wait for him to start shooting again," she says without batting an eye. "If it's just that . . . I thought you'd had bad news from America."

"That too." He sounds so gloomy that she wraps her arms around him to cheer him up, just as she does after every rejection.

"I got the part." Irritated, he breaks free of her embrace. "A lead, with Martin Sheen. It could be my international breakthrough. So fucking typical: I get a lead on American TV, but I don't have enough money to survive till the first day of shooting."

"You've grabbed the ledge," says Geppi, who has stood waiting in the hall for Gala to come out. "Beautiful. Now you're hanging on. You're weeks behind with the rent. Should I stand here watching until your strength fails? I tell you: now is the time to call Signor Gianni, that's what I say."

As usual, Gala whisks by without paying any attention to the woman, but halfway down the hall she slows.

"He is the one who can lift you out of this pit," the concierge says emphatically, feeling a tug on her line. "Sooner or later, they all let Gianni help them up onto their feet. You'll see, the man's a saint!"

She picks up the receiver and dials. Gala wants to consult Maxim, but with her hand on the door handle she reconsiders. "A saint! One day pilgrims from all over the world will crawl to the city on their knees for the privilege of praying at his shrine."

Someone answers. Geppi holds the phone out. Gianni's voice blares impatiently. He couldn't possibly guess that it's Gala, standing there at a loss for words, scared to death that he might think she's deliberately making him wait. She accepts the receiver, but has no idea what she's supposed to say; she covers it with a hand. She feels tears rising, but pushes them back. She wants to yell for Maxim but gets a grip on herself. She feels helpless, as if for a moment she's small and shivering, back at the fair: her father whizzes past on a merry-go-round horse, urging her to trust him, to take the leap. She doesn't want to, but at the same time there is nothing she'd rather do.

If only I were braver, she tells herself. If just once I dared to jump, then nothing could stop me.

She looks plaintively at Geppi, who shrugs. "What can I say? There isn't enough room on all the walls of the Vatican to hang up the ex-votos from the foreigners Signor Gianni has helped out."

Gala only begins to sense the danger she's exposed herself to when she sees the smoke rising from Etna. During the flight to Sicily, first class, with champagne, she played the part of the international call girl. Now, in the train circling the base of the volcano, the moment she'll really become one is fast approaching. Gianni, who always delivers his best products personally, drops the mask of friendship, giving her final instructions like a company director talking to an errand boy.

"Don't be subservient, but don't get overconfident, either. Never be too cheeky, but don't be too childish, either. No unnecessary objections, but under no circumstances do anything you don't want to. If you remember that, you'll enjoy it more. If the client sees you enjoying yourself, he'll be satisfied."

He stops to glance at Gala, who removes an imaginary pencil from behind her ear and mocks his instructions by writing them down in shorthand on a nonexistent pad, the tip of her tongue sticking out of the corner of her mouth.

"Sparkle, the way you do so well, but be careful not to overshadow him. Never take the initiative, but don't be too compliant. Don't be scared. Relax. Set your pride aside and be yourself."

"What if my pride is part of myself?"

"Impossible. Pride is a refuge for people whose self-image clashes with the truth. A rickety bridge between dream and reality, unanchored on either side. Pride's the first thing you've got to get rid of if you want to learn to enjoy yourself."

Disliking his tone, Gala looks out over the Strait of Messina. Silently, she tries to list all the things she's proud of, but she's so insulted that even the most obvious elude her.

"Don't put on airs," says Gianni. "You're too self-confident to be proud."

The train arrives at the bathing resort.

"And from now on, stay away from me," he orders. "We can't give the impression that we're together." He dawdles behind on the platform, shaking his head in admiration at the sight of his protégée's swinging hips. Unaware of the structural defect behind this provocative miracle, the pimp says a quick prayer of thanks to Our Lady of Perpetual Help for sending him a personal retirement scheme, who is now disappearing slowly between the palms on the boulevard, the insides of her thighs gliding past one another.

At the appointed time, Gala stands atop the steps of San Leone. Down by the beach, a seated man is waiting under a parasol on the deck in front of a room hacked out of the rock on one side of the hotel. As soon as he sees her, he stands up to greet her.

Holding the railing, Gala's hand trembles. This surprises her, since she feels nothing but icy calm.

The man is wearing an expensive tailor-made linen suit, perhaps a bit much for a first meeting, but a hint, nonetheless, of how dashing he was in his youth. He thinks he sees the girl's eyes gliding over him approvingly. Gala is actually squinting, to force the glare of the sun on the waves into her black patch, so she can see more of his face. It is dark and manly, slightly troubled. She guesses he's around sixty. When he smiles, she sees clearly that he is nervous.

"That's a load off my mind!" she says, and means it, but he takes it as a compliment he must return. Afterward, they sit down. His butler opens the champagne and serves the first course.

Just before the *bomba bianca* is dished up in flaming maraschino, the man abandons his caution. He introduces himself as Pontorax, though that sounds more like a drug than a real name. He tells her that he is a neurologist, the head of a private psychiatric clinic in Catania.

"That's funny," laughs Gala. "Besides my parents, no one knows me better than neurologists." At that, she lays bare her medical history for him.

"Ah!" he cries in admiration, "the blessing of the sibyls!" And he tells her how the oracles of Apollo were chosen for their epileptic sensitivity. "They looked at the sun and provoked their trances by moving their hands back and forth in front of their eyes."

He shows her how. She imitates him, but he immediately grabs her hand and stops her, concerned. The touch lasts a fraction of a second longer than normal. To her surprise, Gala does not mind. The man is gentle and seems genuinely sympathetic.

"The flashing rays," he continues, "disrupted the temporal lobe of the brain, the center of creativity. The women fell to the ground in a convulsion and spoke in incomprehensible riddles. Now we treat it; in those days, kings traveled months to hear their prophecies."

After lunch, they board a small yacht anchored just off the beach, where she finds several brand-new swimsuits hung up, waiting for her. While they sunbathe, Pontorax's acquaintances come by in yachts, and when they sail on again, the *dottore* entertains her with anecdotes about his eccentric friends.

In the middle of one of his stories, Gala is overcome by an intense emotion she finds difficult to place. Her breathing quickens, and it's all she can do not to cry. It can't be true, she thinks. I can't be moved by a guy who pays to look at me in a swimsuit?

The *dottore* notices the change, but is tactful enough not to mention it. He pours her a cocktail and toasts her silently, just by looking at her, then resumes his story, allowing her to return to her thoughts.

What moved her was seeing the life in his eyes flare up when he looks at her. She quietly imagines the melancholy returning as soon as the old man turns back to the waves. The thought sets her mind at peace, inspiring a languid desire to give herself over to this game. She feels cheerful, and when she quickly closes her eyes, enjoying the warmth and the movement of the sea, she looks almost completely happy. Of course, it is the natural desire of age for youth that puts her at ease, though at first she doesn't realize that. She only feels that she'll never have to rattle off a poem or outdo him in cleverness in order to appeal to this man. She has won him simply by being who she is. Grateful, she rolls over to reward him with a better view.

The *dottore* is a gentleman who would never lay a finger on her uninvited, and who keeps his suit on all afternoon, though the financial nature of their encounter still makes their relationship unambiguous. She feels the inequality that obtains between master and slave, yet she couldn't say who was who. Until very recently, she would have recoiled from the situation, but rather than feeling alone, she is very much at one with him. Gala tries to remember whether she's ever been with a man in a situation like this before, with the cards so clearly on the table. It is new to her, but she can still predict all possible moves, as if she knows the game. Her role is as clear as his. This clarity makes her feel she's breathing again after a long period underwater. He's using me, she tells herself, but he needs me too; and that simple realization finally gives her the strength to reverse the roles.

The wood beneath her feet is scorching as she stands up and stretches. She walks up to her first client and kisses him on the cheek before running to the edge of the deck and diving.

The winner is not the little boy carrying the trophy, but the person who presented it.

They moor late in the afternoon, strolling down the main street, where branches of all the Via Condotti designers cater to the Mafia bosses' wives. The *dottore* suggests that she pick out a few dresses in one of the boutiques; she consents because it confirms the nature of their relationship. Afterward, they visit a jewelry store, where she points out the tiniest earrings available. After all, it's about what she is, not what she gets. Outside, he offers her his arm. That evening, they dance on the hotel terrace. Their bodies touch for the first time. She presses her stomach against his. Dr. Pontorax, who looks wooden, turns out to be surprisingly nimble to music. During the third rumba, Gala kisses him on the mouth, quickly but full of promise, and when he briefly closes his eyes with pleasure she gets an unmistakable sense that she's the one in charge.

When his chauffeur appears to take her back to the airport, Gala assumes there's been some mistake. She looks at the *dottore,* seductively at first, then pouting, but no matter how large the fish swimming around in his net, the fisherman has no intention of hauling it in.

Gianni is waiting for her in the back of the limousine. He tears open the envelope that is handed to him and pays Gala her agreed-upon fee. He then quickly counts the rest.

"Brava!" He pats her thigh approvingly. It's so much more than he expected that he slips her a tip as well. Despite the payment, she is overcome by such an astonishingly piercing sense of disappointment that she racks her brain for an explanation. She's had an exciting day and earned her money without a hitch. She took a trip, she shone in pleasant company. All this time, she's been the master of her fate. Her only frustration is that she's been relieved of the task she'd been dreading. Dismissed, why? The *dottore* had enough. Something obviously failed to please him, but what? Where did she fall short? She'd been feeling so strong, but the direction was snatched out of her hands just before the final scene. Her insecurities come rushing back. She is as surprised as she was seeing the flamingos—who had been flying off on the dry Sahara wind, one by one, all day long—settling down as a single flock in the bay that evening. And for the first time that day, Gala feels dirty.

A new Russia-leather suitcase containing the dresses and other gifts emerges from the trunk of the car. She is in time for the last flight to Fiumicino and will be back with Maxim before midnight. She's earned a month's salary in less than a day.

"How was it? What was he like?"

"Timid," she says, "as if I was the first."

"I've been bringing him someone every Friday," laughs Gianni, "for as long as I can remember."

Although she feels a pang of jealousy, it puts things back in perspective. It's commerce. Someone has bought a pound of tomatoes at the market and only a fool would give it a second thought, she tells herself, putting on a pair of headphones and closing her eyes.

"How about next Friday?" Gianni asks as he picks Gala's suitcase up from the carousel at the Rome airport and carries it to the baggage compartment of the bus that will take her back to the city.

"I'm busy," she says tersely.

"That's a great shame." Gianni stays outside, speaking through the window she slides open. "I bring him someone every week. Always fresh. Always someone else. You're the first he's asked back."

She looks at him through the window. He's serious.

"The first in all these years."

She doesn't answer. She couldn't have anyway. But once the bus has turned onto the autostrada, she gives herself over to tears so intense that the couple in front of her think she's just said farewell to a lover.

Maxim zips open the bag and fishes out the haute couture.

"Sicily?" he exclaims, throwing the frocks into a corner and studying the earrings. "Are you insane?"

"Nothing happened."

"As if that makes it so much better."

It is the anger of a father who finds his daughter the day after she's run away from home. First he embraces her, glad she's not hurt, and then he shakes her furiously, as if she's applied for a job as a white slave in Bahrain.

Suddenly he falls silent and looks at her. There is something in her face.

In all the years that he has loved her, he has hardly ever yelled at her. He's not like that. But on those rare occasions when it did happen, he always regretted it immediately: because she didn't fight back like a tigress, as she did with her father, but like a kitten pushed out of its litter, so entangled in excuses and rationalizations that he couldn't help but forgive and comfort her, taking her side so unconditionally that at the end of it he started to think she'd been right all along.

This time, however, she is calm and self-assured. She describes her experiences as if she has ridden on the back of a cricket to the land of Pinocchio. She smiles. It annoys him. All that drinking cocktails and floating in the bay! He should be happy for her, but the smile is too much. All crazy countesses and shabby American trust-fund kids buying up islands off the coast. A fabulous adventure, of course, and he doesn't resent it at all. But what's with the smile? He can't stand it. It just gets wider every time he speaks; there's something haughty about it, as if she'd just learned a secret about him.

That night, Maxim makes a point of turning over in bed, and they sleep with their backs to each other, but in the morning they breakfast together at Rosati with silver spoons and porcelain plates. In the Via Frattina, they buy new clothes—first for him, then for her—and at the optician's on the *corso* they both buy sunglasses with the classic slick Italian look. They hire a Vespa and spend the rest of the afternoon zooming around the Circus Maximus like Gregory Peck and Audrey Hepburn. Just before closing time, Gala goes into a bank and transfers the first installment of Maxim's debt to the Dutch state. From the few thousand lire that are left, they pay the admission and towel rental at Salvi's old Moorish bathhouse, hidden behind the facade of the Trevi. There, lying in sweltering rooms on warm sheets of marble, they rediscover each other in a feeling of bliss. Grateful for their regained liberty, they swap back rubs. But by the time they wash each other off in the cool water from the Acqua Vergine, fed by Agrippa's aqueduct from the mountains, their thoughts are already diverging.

Gala feels unexpectedly satisfied that she's blown every penny, as if doing so has lightened the shadiness of her previous day's activity and cleansed her taint of vague discomfort. A gnawing worry wells up in Maxim at the idea that now they're no less poor than before. Tomorrow morning, he won't be able to read the *Messagiero* until someone discards it in the street, and in the corner bar the *cornetti con crema* will stay in the glass case.

When the soap residue and skin flakes wash through the marble rosette into the drain, they bear not only the last of the day's euphoria but also some of the couple's reservations. Gushing through the old pipes to the square, they drain unnoticed into a corner of the monumental fountain, between the colossal statue of Oceanus and the seahorse to his left, rushing over the rocks and splashing into the basin, where they sink to the bottom. There they dissolve, only momentarily stirred up by a few sinking coins that a group of singing nuns from Salzburg toss over their shoulders in the hope that, after their yodeling concert in the Sant'Ignazio, they might return to the Holy City.

For almost a week, Gala and Maxim live the way they're used to living, hungry but with fashionable sunglasses. They don't mention Sicily. With every passing day, however, Gala's desire to take up the challenge a second time grows, as though she can face their daily tribulations a bit easier in the knowledge that a solution is at hand. Every day, she comes up with a few practical, financial reasons to return to the island, but in reality she can feel something much bigger beckoning her.

When she was small, death looked her in the eye, leaving his black window behind as a constant reminder. He drew a line around her life with thundering fireworks. Since then, she's known exactly how far she can go, and the price she will pay for transgression. But even in the frightened moments before a seizure, sinking away in darkness, not knowing whether she will ever return to the surface, she has never felt those limits as a threat to her life: to the contrary, they encourage her, just as thinning out a herd strengthens the stock.

When her life still had a chance to take off in any direction, the territory was limitless, so that she could only give any bit of it a quick glance. As soon as the safe area began to shrink, she got to know it thoroughly, deeply, intensely, discovering unsuspected possibilities in herself and feeling invulnerable within them. Her affliction gave her life a framework. Within it, she was shown to her utmost advantage, just as correct framing lends a film shot its tension.

Following her Sicilian adventure, she once again experienced the tension between limitation and protection. As long as her trip lasted, her duties were clearly delineated. All she needed to draw upon was one aspect of her nature: her femininity. And there, she needed to satisfy clearly defined standards. She reached the ceiling of her potential when constrained in this way. Or was it the floor? Either way, if someone had told her the day before that she'd ever let herself be so restricted just in order to please a man, she wouldn't have believed it. But compelled by circumstance, she had made herself docile, meekly doing what was demanded. Within these limits, she was astounded to discover a new, unsuspected freedom.

She loved Maxim because she felt completely at ease with him. He never asked anything beyond the familiar world they had built together. In that sense, they were equal. He looked up to her and admired her and took care not to challenge her in any way at all. He wasn't like other men. They always made her feel that they were superior, strong, self-contained, spurring her to constantly prove them wrong by surpassing them in everything she did. For them, she tried to be everything at once: witty and intelligent, wise and amusingly hotheaded, strong and sultry.

So the *dottore* was a revelation. He asked only one thing of her. The lines were clear. Within this terrain, she was completely free. She even had the upper hand. The clarity of what she needed to do to satisfy him pleased her. After all, a similar clarity had once saved her.

From the moment that little Gala came home from the hospital, Jan Vandemberg became the old tease she knew so well. To reassure his daughter that nothing had changed, he was pitiless, seizing every opportunity to castigate her, to force her back into shape. His taunting could even be nastier than before, but in one area he left her at peace: he never again asked her to perform with quotes like a circus act, not even for his most important guests. So great was his fear that his favorite daughter would again lose her footing in a pool of words and sink away.

No longer a frightening duty, the epigrams of Propertius became privileges she could grant or withhold. Her father learned to earn them. In exchange for a gift of some kind, she would grant him one of these favors. Now that she made him pay dearly, he was much more grateful for a few words of Cicero than when she gave them away to please him.

Maxim is one step ahead.

"I've been worried over nothing, haven't I?" From behind his dark glasses, he's been studying Gala's radiant expression for some time. In the last few days, she seems to be sitting straighter, talking with more confidence, prouder than ever before. This drastic adventure truly seems no more difficult for her than it was for him to put on Sangallo's black coat. And there's more, he tells himself. It hasn't just been easy for her, it even seems to have done her some good.

"If only I could be sure," he insists, "that you're not getting in too deep."

"I'm old enough and smart enough to know what I can handle," she assures him.

Maxim smiles at her. He's proud of his friend. Isn't this just what he's always seen in her, from those very first words: *Ah, movement!* That first sentence, which freed him from the dungeon of his past. He sneeringly thinks back on the moments he doubted her, when, out of weakness, he mistook her lack of inhibition for shallowness, folly, or blindness, just because his own mind was too much enchained to believe that anyone could be as free of scruples as Gala.

And today she surprised him again. What a woman! She tackles head-on something he'd never dare to, not after he made such a mess of it during that pathetic attempt with poor Silberstrand. He may have imagined himself to be liberated enough from his shame to undertake something like that, but all he has is borrowed freedom. His strength is nothing more than a reflection of Gala's open mind. That's why he always wants to be near her. She gives him the courage. Swept up by her, seeing her venture where he would never tread! He drinks in her presence like a magic potion, a life-giving elixir, without knowing or being able to guess its ingredients.

By the time he asks if she's planning another one of those trips, her mind is made up. She calls Gianni the same afternoon, and when they come home an envelope is waiting on the bed with a generous advance. They treat themselves to dinner.

This time, Gala flies alone. Dr. Pontorax has rented a villa for the weekend, one tucked away in the foothills of Mount Etna. His chauffeur is waiting at the Catania airport. Approaching the runway, her plane swings low over the crater, where molten lava bubbles and glows. The red of the fire colors the thunderclouds in the night sky.

It looks frightening, but the mighty volcano is reliably predictable, in fact: the treacherous ones are dormant. People build their homes against the walls of silted-up craters without realizing that the pressure is rising inside.

In that instant, the thunderstorm that has been building over the slopes of Mount Etna bursts around the descending aircraft. Fascinated by the violence, Gala looks out of the window. Blinding bolts of lightning shoot past on every side of the cabin.

Between the lightning, flashes of Maxim appear. It's unmistakably him. In that same moment, he walks naked through their room and gets into bed. He feels inexplicably afraid. Abandoned. He squeezes his eyes shut, pushes his scruples aside. They harass him from a land of terrors he has tried to leave behind. Fighting, he tosses and turns and presses his face into the pillow. He claws the wall. And now he calls her, now that she can't hear him: begging her not to go, shouting at the top of his voice, rattling off all the things he is afraid might happen to her, everything he was too scared to mention for fear she would laugh at him. The thoughts twist his stomach until he feels sick. He is so scared that she will love him less if she finds out how much he longs to keep her safe, tearing her away from the game of chance she craves and keeping her for himself, away from the unknown.

Now, drowned out by the crash of thunder, he finally screams it. That he misses her and won't sleep until she comes back. Now, only now, does he cry out, those few words that could have changed everything. But Gala can't hear them.

And so she takes the next step. It seems as if she is crossing a line, but she's actually drawing one at last, making a clear choice. Out of all the paths she could have chosen, this is the one she is claiming as her own.

I remember that one Sunday in the late autumn of 1934, when the elderly priest of the Chiesa del Suffragio announced that he had decided to exchange his beloved Rimini for a place in heaven, in order to spend the coming Christmas in the company of the Savior himself. Shortly after his death, he was replaced by Fra Cippo, a young Jesuit recently discharged from the strict Fossombrone seminary. He arrived before Advent and stepped into his new church just as the parishioners were busy decorating one of the side chapels as they had for decades, while everyone enjoyed a few jugs of altar wine and dipped into a basket of sweets. From the end of the summer, everyone looked forward to this old tradition, a popular celebration complete with singing and dancing. Too small to help, I was crawling around on the cool marble with the other children, but I can still picture the young mothers breast-feeding their babies on the wooden benches while their husbands decorated the altars under the artistic guidance of la Dumazima, the madam of the brothel in the Via Pisacane. As one of the few parishioners with a steady income in those difficult years, Dumazima donated a fixed percentage of her earnings every autumn to buy the most beautiful decorations the cane cutters of Imola could weave.

At the very moment that the young priest came walking up the aisle with his suitcase in one hand and his horsehair habit in the other, a group of young fishermen had joined forces to lift one of Dumazima's girls so that she could affix a garland between the arches of the chancel.

After the rigors of monastic life, Fra Cippo took their devotion for debauchery. He was so shocked that he hid his face in his hands, summoning the help of all the angels. His first deed was to ban Dumazima, her girls, and all who lived off their sins, from entering the church on Sundays and holy feast days. He would hear their confessions on other days, but for safety's sake he had a confessional moved from the church into the sacristy especially for them, to spare the Madonna and the Apostles catching even a whisper of the horrors that needed confessing.

The next Sunday, however, saw la Dumazima regally ensconced in her regular spot. Upon noticing her, Cippo covered the monstrance with a cloth and refused to remove the consecrated hosts from the ciborium in her presence. When he commanded her to leave so as not to endanger the spiritual welfare of the faithful, she stood up. Despite being a robust, sturdy woman with strong arms, she trembled now and had to grab hold of the pulpit.

"All I ask of Our Lord is what he offers us," she declared loudly, "His mercy."

"But, madam," boomed the priest, "the Christ child does not give his love away for nothing."

"That's what he's got in common with her!" someone shouted, to general hilarity.

"But fall on your knees," said Cippo, "show your repentance in the eyes of all and everything will be forgiven!"

"Are my sins so much worse than the others'?" she asked despairingly.

"The body is God's temple."

"That's true," blared squinty-eyed Minaccio, as drunk as ever, "and I've worshipped there." He was applauded from so many corners that Fra Cippo became even more implacable. He pointed at her, like Lot pointing at the burning city of Sodom.

"This woman lets herself be used," he cried. "Nothing in the world is worse than that!"

"Is that so?" said Dumazima. "We'll see about that." And with her head held high, she strode down the aisle and out of the church.

The following Sunday, her place was empty. It wasn't the only vacant spot in the pews that week. It wasn't enough to disturb Fra Cippo, but the next Friday he noticed that the faithful had rather a lot of legroom. A few little old ladies showed up on Saturday evening, and when he stepped up to the altar the next morning in his vestments, he discovered that his congregation had shrunk so much that he had to pinch an altar boy to make sure he wasn't dreaming. As the congregation left the church, he asked whether something was going around, but no one dared answer. Inside, however, he found Minaccio dozing drunkenly in the transept, and bribed him with a drink to find out what was going on.

Since her banishment, la Dumazima had grown bored, and since she had nowhere to go during Mass, she had started offering her services at a discount at those times. A significant number of her customers were taking advantage of a bargain too good to pass up.

Their wives, some incensed by their husbands' absence at Sunday breakfast, others troubled by their sudden appearance at times when they were accustomed to receiving their own lovers, blamed the priest for the disruption of their domestic lives. They resolved that until Fra Cippo repented, they would take their prayers and piety to Santa Rita's on the Piazzetta Castelfidardo.

The young priest was stubborn by nature; and although he chafed at the sight of the people standing on the cold square before the open doors of the crowded Santa Rita's for Christmas Eve Mass, he stuck to his guns.

That whole winter, his parish remained bare and quiet, and his fire-and-brimstone sermons echoed through the empty church with less conviction every Sunday. The collection bags were empty too, and he couldn't keep up his monthly contribution to the diocese. That spring, he was called to account before the canonical college and threatened with a return to the strict regime of Fossombrone.

Shortly afterward, he was seen walking down the Via Pisacane, where he asked for an appointment with Dumazima. No one knows what they discussed, but the very next Sunday the door of her house was bolted to those waiting outside. When she finally emerged, she was dressed for Mass. She passed among her admirers and, followed by her girls, headed for the church, attracting more and more attention on the way. Street urchins followed, and when she walked up the Corso d'Augusto people emerged from their houses. At the head of the procession, la Dumazima entered the Suffragio and took her place in the first pew. Fra Cippo, with a full house for the first time in months, said Mass without further comment. Dumazima was the first to kneel before the altar for Communion. When she stuck out her tongue, Fra Cippo closed his eyes before that instrument of the devil but laid the Eucharist on it all the same. Dumazima made the sign of the cross and let it melt. Only then did she rise, and for a moment—the story goes—the priest and the sinner smiled at each other.

She had worn him down; ever after, we called him Cippolo or Cippolino. When he ascended the pulpit on that day, the priest spoke to us for the first time from his heart instead of out of the commentaries.

"Such is the mercy of God," he said, "that He has told me that I was wrong: only one thing is worse than being used . . ."

At that, his congregation called out as one man, "Not being used!"

Snaporaz's Theory of Progress

Death is the border of life. If it weren't waiting for us there at the edge, we wouldn't realize that we're not just wandering around aimlessly but are heading somewhere. The border is what gives us direction. I see borders like that everywhere. They make us alert. They point to our limitations at the same time they show us all the marvelous possibilities within them. I have seen how a dictatorship unleashes new movements among the people. I have felt how oppression inspires the will to survive. I have watched our country flower forth from the devastation of war. I have seen love spring up from the ruins of hatred.

It is borders that keep us awake.

Limitation is what pushes us forward.

This is the engine of the world. This is the force that gives us life. Every cell divides. It makes itself smaller in order to grow. I believe that all of evolution, the entire history of man, can be reduced to this single principle.

Withdrawn in the immobility of my body, my mind flares up. I am ever more convinced that if fate so drastically cuts back our possibilities, it is only to make us bud all the more vigorously.

God Limits Man

At one time everything was possible. All was chaos. But one day God decides that enough is enough. And He immediately sets to work, as if already hearing the cavalcade of the whole circus approaching in the distance.

He first limits the free intercourse of the elements. He gathers them into two bodies: heaven and earth. Then He abruptly forbids darkness and light to play together as carelessly as before. To each He allocates a place: confining one to the day and the other to the night. He dams the waters too, separating land and sea. On the land, He draws borders and divides it into parcels. He gives a name to the most clearly fenced-off area, the Garden of Eden, setting it apart from the rest. He restrains time as well, making stars to divide the infinite into days and years.

Once the elements are thus secured, He creates living creatures, but gives them such feeble attributes that each must remain in its own environs: the fish are limited to the sea, the birds to the air, the mammals to the land. And even then He subdivides them. He creates each species according to its own nature and throws up barriers between them. He makes one group stronger and the other weaker, assigning each kind a place in a hierarchy that can only be abandoned at the price of expulsion and death.

At last He kneels on the earth, scrapes some into His hands, presses it firmly together, kneading and shaping it into the form of a man. He pinches the clay a couple of times to make a nose and then, just like that, blows breath into it.

He places this man in His Garden of Eden and watches him frolic around alone, aimless in so much freedom. Then God decides on a drastic measure. He creates a second person so that the first will no longer be free to flit around, willfully directing his attention to anything he likes. From now on, he'll have to take *her* into account, and learn to choose between her and himself. But even then, the two still skip about everywhere hand in hand. As long as they are unaware of any borders, they don't plan to go anywhere. Totally free and happy, the man and the woman are completely uninterested in any kind of progress.

God, who really has done His best to get it right and boil everything down to human dimensions, is so upset that He takes a day off to think things through. Surely the result of all His effort can't just be having to spend years watching them frolic aimlessly between the four rivers which He, to be on the safe side, has laid down around His paradise? As he ponders a way to force some development, God looks out over everything He has created. It's an obvious improvement. First there was only chaos; now He has a choice between heaven and earth, land and water, light and dark, man and woman. At first anything was possible; now, at least, a number of things have been set down. How weird really, He thinks, the more you hem things in, the more things come to be. The more limitations you impose, the more possibilities you create.

Only now, when He steps back to observe from a distance, does He discover a pattern: everything new comes from restriction! The earth arose by limiting heaven; land was created by pushing back water; darkness, by gathering light. As soon as you establish the one, the other appears. As if limits on the elements' freedom forced them to assert themselves against the rest. Creation, He now realizes, is nothing more than the continual limiting of things.

When things are divided, they multiply. They have less space, but that is exactly why they develop! This simple principle forms the heart of His new plaything.

Before, He did all the limiting and dividing by Himself, but once human beings learn to make distinctions, they can set to work, godlike, on their own. After all, He's got better things to do. What He needs is something to give progress a boost, something to get people moving on their own. The idea is so simple and so brilliant that He can't understand why it's taken Him so long to come up with it. Without further ado, He separates good from evil. By defining them, He creates them. Never could one have existed without the other.

Now all He has to do is let those two in paradise know that henceforth their joyful liberty is divided, that they have to choose between two new possibilities and be judged according to their choice. To play it safe, He points out a tree, one tree out of all the others, bearing the fruit of the knowledge of good and evil. At the same time—and this betrays a master's touch—He forbids the eating of it.

Lo and behold: His plan works. The ban itself immediately creates the desire to break it. Human thoughts are no longer free; they're limited to good and evil. He's hardly turned His back before these new powers join battle for the human mind. And when the man and woman can no longer stand it and taste the forbidden fruit, precisely as God expected, He feigns mortal offense and kicks them across the border.

Dazed, the people turn to look at the limitation imposed upon them. With paradise forbidden, they begin to long for it, and start to create their own.

"Well done," He shouts after them. "Go forth and multiply!" He tries not to laugh, because what He really means is, "Go forth and divide." That, after all, amounts to the same thing.

And so humanity gets its start. God's role in it is neither greater nor harsher than putting out a nightingale's eyes to make it sing.

Nor is the result less sweet to His ears. No sooner have the people had intercourse than their children are divided too, without any intervention from God. From now on, He only has to bother with them in passing—to relieve the boredom of a dull afternoon, for instance—and His interventions are invariably for their own good, limiting their freedom still more, in order to help them progress.

Like the time He forces all life back onto an ark. Bobbing around amid the deluge, mankind not only develops a taste for animal husbandry but also the will to survive. Or His contribution to Babylon, in which He splits the language everyone understands and limits each nation to its own tongue, making everyone learn to mime and gesticulate. From Abraham He takes food; from Moses, land. He is like the banks of the river through which the history of nations flows.

Finally, He decides the time is ripe to make mankind equal to the gods once and for all. He gives them ten commandments reducing everything to good and bad. For one, He tells them, they will be rewarded; for the other, punished. To make absolutely certain, He writes them down clearly, so that they can be referred to for all eternity without any room for misunderstanding.

The narrow constriction of everything human gives rise to humanity's realization of sin. Suddenly, people have a name for the things it has been their nature to feel. Now that emotions are no longer free, humanity is forced to think, and human nature is forevermore limited by reason. Dammed by the mind, the human heart will never overflow again.

And so, with disease, famine, and tyranny, He drives his creatures forward, according to the time-honored principle of the American action movie, in which each obstacle forces the fleeing hero to new feats that he never otherwise would have achieved. Our hero discovers new possibilities in himself and, after a messy adventure, sees the error of his ways, and stands on the threshold of a new existence, a happy ending that until then had been clouded in deep gloom.

Humanity does not shape its history from freedom, but by accepting each new challenge in order to shake off the fetters of the previous chapter.

He confines us in the smallest possible space in the hope that there, finally, immobile as Joseph in his cell, we will finally understand what we are dreaming of.

Man Limits God

Reason is what finally did Him in. Maybe God shouldn't have entrusted His commandments to stone. By recording His ideas, He gave mankind one for himself.

As soon as people became convinced that sin emerged from a contained, irrational part of their nature, a region not governed by the rules God had established, they started attempting to rationalize everything their mind couldn't grasp. Whatever was beyond their limited intelligence, they tried to cut down to size.

Of all the things that are all but incomprehensible to the human mind, the divine is undoubtedly the least tangible. Intangible is irrational, and the irrational leads to sin. So they tried to capture God in words.

His miracles, which they first heard in the sighing of the wind and saw in every budding tree, they tried to comprehend, a procedure akin to insisting on knowing the structure of the chemicals in which it was developed before sitting down to enjoy the film. First, in the heavens, they fix the hitherto mysterious stars, linking one to the other with lines that stretch like ropes and bind objects, one near, one far, that once floated free in infinity, compressing them into a constellation. Then, with these lines, they draw signs: no longer intangible, the stars now resemble animals, familiar objects. In this way, people appropriate the universe for themselves, as something that belongs to them, and no longer to another world.

But the signs of the zodiac still move too freely across the skies. They attempt to determine their paths and, like a tracker who has studied the habits of his prey, they capture the celestial bodies just as they snare wild animals with nets and lassos to tame them for farmwork. Finally, and for all time, they ascertain the paths the stars trace through the skies, interpreting them and believing that this is a way to read their future.

They treat all phenomena that arouse their curiosity just as they minimize heavenly wonders, reducing everything to proportions they can grasp. Even the birds of the air can no longer fly where they will. Unable to bear this reminder of their own former unboundedness, people cage them and gut them in the hope of reducing the incomprehensible to something that can be divined from a handful of innards.

Around this time, painters in the churches around Emilia Romagna reduce the features of the majestic Christ above the altar to those of a man in the throes of death. They change the radiant Madonna into a Mater Dolorosa. Now saints are saddled with the mug of the butcher or the baker up the street.

Yet the more they try to increase their understanding of themselves by reducing life to human proportions, ever smaller and ever more complicated, the less they see of the divine as they remember it, which was simple and overwhelming. Afraid perhaps that the memory of their own creation might elude them, they begin to reduce to words everything they can recall of the miraculous.

First, they describe their origin as they remember it, a smooth procession from chaos to order. Then, when that divine territory has been neatly contained in story, chapter, and verse, they are horrified to discover that nothing about it makes any sense whatsoever and that the rationale for everything is about to escape them like butterflies darting out of a cupped hand that is weary of chasing their capricious fluttering for so long and carelessly relaxes its grip.

They begin to interpret their writings, hoping to establish beyond a doubt the meaning of each word; but as they struggle to comprehend the unfathomable, diverse opinions arise. Discussion only makes meaning more elusive. They are terrified to discover that, unlike the stars or the entrails of birds, their own deepest wishes hold no clues to the future, and that everything is doomed to end without disclosing its meaning.

Though death means the ultimate reduction for the body, captured forever in the smallest imaginable space, scene of an ultimately glorious subdivision of the whole into increasingly digestible parts, the spirit, at the last moment, seems to escape after all, regaining its freedom. Mankind finds this unbearable. It would reduce the path of man's life to a channel through which everything is painstakingly squeezed, one that grows narrower and narrower, like the pipes under a fountain. And it would turn man into nothing more than a fisherman with a torn net, one whose prey, at the last moment, slips away, leaving him behind empty-handed to curse his fate.

So the wise men begin to determine the meaning of the writings. They resolve to split faith up into religions, and religions into movements, though all the faithful strive alike for a more precise image of their Creator. No longer simply present everywhere, He is reduced to representations that over the years grow more and more similar, until finally He's no more than a pair of eyes above a long white beard and an identical robe.

This process takes place more or less simultaneously among all the peoples of the world, each nation hacking its own portrait out of the rock of its faith, matching its own image. When His Essence, which just for the record is omnipresent, apparently resists capture by any of these images, they all choose a substitute to render the divine as visible as possible.

Once God's in the bag, they agree to cut the world down to size. It is, after all, too free, too big, for comfort. Just as they formed an image of Him, they now chart the world, initially dividing it along lines nature has provided, things like rivers and mountain chains, then according to grids of their own devising, ever finer, until finally borders become so precise that they pass straight through houses and over breakfast tables.

At the same time, people learn how to decimate themselves. Life was a gift from God, but once they've loosened the festive bow and torn off the shiny wrapping paper, they decide it's not as valuable as all that and start perfecting weaponry and cooking up ingenious methods of mass destruction. They realize that they need to drastically reduce their numbers at regular intervals, like lemmings hurling themselves off cliffs, if they are to make any progress.

Their next step is logical: to limit everything else about life in the same way. They assign the various elements and all of God's living wonders to their greatest thinkers, inviting each to study them, to ceaselessly ascertain more, to divide their subject constantly into ever smaller and, they hope, ever more comprehensible sections.

This is how they try to tame the winds and the ocean currents, by measuring and naming them; they fail to master them, but they keep them in such tight check that they can use them to navigate the seas, bringing the different parts of the world closer, making the globe seem smaller.

In a similar fashion, they apply their knowledge to the land, dividing it into fields and meadows in order to limit the plants that grow there to ones they find useful. Plants that grow wild in God's paradise are uprooted or poisoned. Instead of falling every which way in the soil, seeds are now sown in straight rows, separate one from the other, each in a fixed place, to guarantee that the shoots will appear at regular intervals.

They categorize most of the ideas they have caught hold of according to similar, clarifying principles. They build beautiful cabinets for the things they gather with their hands, storing away everything from seashells to butterflies, beetles to minerals, feathers to gems, according to its own category, in small drawers with clear labels. For the things they have mastered with the word, things like their concept of God, they erect enormous buildings in which to store everything according to rigid systems. Each item is given a fixed position in its own row, in a particular aisle, on planks not unlike those they use to contain their dead.

The harder mankind searches, the easier it is for God to elude them. The more they try to contain Him, subdividing His Creation into ever smaller pieces, the less they comprehend of Him. Meanwhile they're staring Him in the face, like the idiot Pazzotto, who tried to get a closer look at the film by pressing his nose against the screen during the matinee in the Folgor.

Man Limits Himself

The more you narrow the prism, the brighter the spectrum it casts. Maybe that's how the philosophers got the idea to call the encircling of emotion with reason the Enlightenment. They always remind me of the final moments of a Keystone Kops movie, clinging to the back of a wayward paddy wagon, swerving left and right down the road, their only hope the dark frame that slowly closes around them just before THE END appears on the screen.

Just as humanity develops by crossing off its possibilities, so does the individual progress personally. At birth, he is like Pico della Mirandola's Adam—beyond all limits. By exercising his own will, for he has nothing else, he must determine who he wants to be. He still has no fixed place in the world, no face, no talents. He must choose and master them himself. He has been placed at the center of the universe, the better to see everything it contains. He may shape his own mask freely, as he likes, inventing himself along the way.

There was a single perfect moment when all knowledge still lay within his reach. The *uomo universale* could, over the course of his lifetime, master every imaginable science and read and comprehend everything that was known. All things external to him were also within him. He was, very briefly, like God. They were both the same size. Being balanced knowledge. The created plumbed the depths of his creation and could look his Creator in the eye. As in a mirror, for a few seconds, they studied one another, the one more confused than the other, circling around, sizing each other up like equally matched boxers who prefer to avoid a fight doomed in any case to a draw. They went their separate ways, drunk with rage, heads spinning, unsure now who was who.

There is no strength without struggle. Perhaps because it's too frightening to countenance the idea of being God's equal, man decides to remove the arena to his inner self. He hopes eventually to produce the blueprint of a human, a single chart that explains and predicts everything, a precisely reproducible prototype that will confine all new humans to the limitations of their predecessors and banish the unexpected forever.

To expand his knowledge of himself, man starts making himself smaller.

First, he cuts others open to study their functions. Once he understands all the tissues, muscles, and organs, he cuts them into slices for viewing under a microscope, capturing ever smaller segments beneath the curve of the lens. Those who look through the microscope see an image round as a globe and animated as a carnival. You can keep zooming in on a part of the whole, over and over again, until you think it's impossible to dissect the cell any further, at which point you discover a whole new circus, complete with fire-eaters, juggling bears, and dwarves peddling nougat. In less and less, man discovers more and more.

The more answers he finds, the more questions are raised. He cannot seize, for example, his spirit. He clearly senses its presence, but he can't grasp it between tweezers or perform a biopsy on it. First, he tries to gauge personality from appearance, trying to read character from the shape of the head, and then he lifts the skull in the hope of discovering management behind a desk somewhere in the cerebral cortex.

Now, as always when he bumps against his limitations, a new branch of science blossoms: psychoanalysis. No need to explain that it immediately splits in half. One sage tries to reduce the mind's every surprise to a simple reaction to something else. The other reduces everything to the genes, declaring that every cell contains within it a complete memory. Each part suggests the whole, rather as, to me, eternity looms in a lump of ancient concrete beside a Roman autostrada.

As scientists and intellectuals narrow their vision in order to see more, ordinary men limit their abilities too. When I was small, the mountains around San Marino were still home to peasants and tradesmen who not only knew how to till their own land and feed and butcher their animals before cooking them in exquisite sauces in copper pots they had made themselves, but could also build their own houses from materials they had prepared themselves, after which they altered the course of streams to flow through their farmyards. They knew how and where to drill for water, and could keep the fire they sparked off two rocks in October burning until March. They wove their own fabrics and sewed their own clothes, designed and built furniture, and taught their children, born in the upstairs room without outside assistance, how to read and trade, how to bake pots and carve works of art from a piece of wood. They drank wine from their own grapes, which they pressed and bottled themselves. They made music on homemade instruments and told stories that resounded with the culture of the Etruscans and Romans. They were the last bearers of a long tradition that had been handed down from Italy's earliest inhabitants, but then they put their children to work in factories, where all their old skills were reduced to tightening a bolt or zipping up a bag. In less than a century, industrialization succeeded in reducing an autarkic man who conceived, built, and used his own machines to an interchangeable part in a production process, a cog in a machine. He forgot whether strawberries grew on bushes or trees, but was gratified to discover that he could produce more by working less.

They broke down their understanding of things as they lost their skills. The more knowledge a man acquires about something, the less he understands it. I remember a winter that was so cold that we had to go all the way to Verona to stay with my aunt Vitella, who had heating in her apartment. Her palazzo was one of the last in the old center to get electricity, after a concerted campaign by its residents. To entertain us, and only when we least expected it, Vitella would walk over to the switch by the door and turn her lights on and off and on and off again, eyes darting back and forth from the surprise on our faces to the miraculous lightbulb. It wasn't long before everyone was completely dependent on electricity: more comfortable, less in control. As man lost his knowledge of the things that determined his life, he seemed to grow bigger, more monstrous. He once knew the origin and use of everything around him, but now, without a clue as to how they work, he surrounds himself with the most wide-ranging devices, continually inventing ever more complicated things, just to keep surprising himself.

During my life, for instance, the computer has developed from an enormous machine with rotating parts that filled entire floors, lumbering objects that couldn't do very much. The memory took up many rooms. You could walk into a computer, wander around inside it. Now they are small and can do almost anything. They have become so minuscule that the day is not far off when they will be injected into your blood and wander around inside *you*.

Man now stores all his accumulated knowledge, far more now than could ever be gathered in libraries, on chips. For this, he reduces all the words he has ever spoken or written, all the sounds he has sung, played, and heard, every thought, every dream, all the images he has ever drawn or seen, everything he has felt and remembers to the numbers 1 and 0. The compression of energy sparks a new universe, just as this implosion of knowledge creates a new reality in which all this information will be accessible to everyone. His essence recorded on a bar code, his possessions on a cash card, man can withdraw behind the black hole of his monitor, where the last thing that still differentiates him, his unique facial characteristics, is reduced to grids and pixels on a screen on which everyone looks the same. Hidden behind it, reduced to no more than a name or, better still, its abbreviation, his possibilities for extending his range are unbounded. Thus limited, every person is linked to all others without ever needing to step outside, where it often can be a bit chilly.

Ultimately, I expect, man will order the last remnants of chaos by filing himself on a chip. Then he will be master over all humanity, with nothing more to fear than my aunt Vitella, who fiddled with the electric light switch to impress her guests in Verona. That last image will be the same as my earliest memory: I have something between my thumb and index finger, but I can't really hold it. I feel that it is everything and nothing at the same time.

As this whole show is being performed, God sits on His throne watching men, patient as Father Time in the cartoon, until Little Nemo rolls out of bed and wakes up with a start, because however big man grows by narrowing his perspective, he'll never manage to cut his dreams down to size.

Part Four

Roman Siege

Take a close-up. Zoom in on someone. You see less and less of him, yet he grows bigger, ever bigger, until all that's left of him is a single pore. It's nothing. You could spend a lifetime looking at that face without ever noticing that one tiny hole. That's how small it is, but you've made it enormous. The actor has hundreds of thousands of these pores. His dimensions seem dizzying. An ordinary person, but by showing less, by gradually making him disappear, you've turned him into a giant.

Galleon

> But that's the worst thing of all with my Rosita. Loving someone but not being able to feel her body; weeping yet not knowing who for; longing for someone you know isn't worth it; an open wound, bleeding incessantly, without a soul to bring you wool or bandages, or a handful of cooling snow.
>
> —Federico García Lorca

"You know what?" Gala says. "Let's go swimming!"

She is standing close to me in a cave. Behind her, the light is shining through a curtain of rain. I think she's got to be kidding, but then she actually starts stripping down! She snatches my hat off my head and throws it in a corner. I try to make out the expression on her face, but all I can see is a silhouette in front of a wall of pearls.

"It's raining. No one will see us. Let's go swimming!"

In a flash, I recognize the abandon of long ago. The thunderbolt strikes in Tivoli. I called her with a bit part in mind shortly after I got back to Rome. There was no glory in it and I could have asked anyone, but she had simply taken shape in my thoughts.

In Japan, she had appeared in my dreams again, more recognizable this time: wearing the same leopard-skin jacket but now carrying two buckets of milk on a yoke. "Gala!" I called. "Wait for me!" She turned. Fresh milk splashed out of the buckets and ran down her legs. It was steaming. And she said something. Probably in Dutch. I couldn't make it out. Then she walked on.

I'm well aware that people put their lives on hold for the privilege of filling out my pictures, yet for the first time in years I felt like I had to persuade someone to act in one of my films. Don't ask me why. I felt I had to convince Gala to do me a favor, instead of the other way round.

I had arranged a meeting in the *osteria* next to the Temple of the Sibyl at Tivoli. I told her about the project's progress, and her role. After lunch, we wandered into the valley to see the waterfalls. A spring shower took us by surprise, and we took shelter under the cliff. I thought she wanted to stay dry, forgetting that the Dutch are born in the rain.

"Yes," Gala decides, "I have an irresistible urge to swim. And right now." She kicks off her shoes and beckons.

And at that moment, nothing seems more sensible: come on, it's cold and wet, let's take our clothes off! No magic spell could have so utterly robbed me of my will. Suddenly they appear, all at once. As Gala walks through the veil of cold water, they leap out from the cavernous depths, the countless delicious fruits I have plucked throughout my impetuous life: Gelsomina on the frozen pond in Véviers, Gelsomina among the poppies on Testaccio and wading through the warm stream of Saturnia, Gelsomina on the train to Cannes, making love and not even stopping to show the conductor the ticket. And Gelsomina at yet another pond, frozen again, not far from Borgo Pace—together so much stronger than the rest of the world because we have no rational thinking to hold us back. We had the nerve to act without thinking about it. Of course every sentient being is anxiously sheltering from the storm, so let's run into the water buck naked: but of course! How could I forget that recklessness is one of our basic necessities?

She doesn't wait for me. Gala does her own thing. She's already forgotten me. While I stumble out of my shoes like an old fool and tug, cursing, at my garters, she's already frolicking around at the bottom of the waterfall. When I come running out barefoot, she waves to me as she kicks her feet. The movement sets off ripples and lifts her out of the water, slim and proud as a figurehead, her hair wet and clinging to her shoulders.

The years have made me suspicious. Actresses have thought up stranger ploys. But I know this is different. Those same years have taught me to see through their tricks. Gala is different from all those others, I can see: she's doing it for herself.

I remember this! Heedlessly, immediately plunging into everything that comes my way, just because. Meanwhile, she's not giving me a second thought, doing exactly what I want by thinking only of herself, not putting on a show for my benefit. Her only desire is to see herself swimming in the rain.

"Gala, wait, wait for me, Galeone!" I call, suddenly anxious that the naval review is over and she's about to sail. "Wait, Galeone, wait for me!"

And I don't fall in love with her, but I feel once again the possibility of falling in love with my own life.

At this stage, I wasn't officially aware of the poor state of Gelsomina's health. But I'm not blind. My poor clown! She keeps it to herself, of course. She never mentions her condition, not even now—she doesn't want to worry me. But her silence makes it obvious. Young filmmakers sometimes think they should announce the last act with trumpets and drums, but an end that approaches in silence is far more menacing.

I'm convinced it was the raw fish. You can call it coincidence, but I noticed a sudden deterioration after ten days in Osaka. If God wanted us to wrap everything in seaweed, surely He wouldn't have gone to the trouble of inventing olive oil?

During our trip, Gelsomina wore out faster than she did at home. I noticed because she kept jumping around, trying to look sprightly. Now and then, she would bend over suddenly, pretending to be looking for something she'd dropped, but I saw through her. She was trying to hide a stab of pain that might distract me from my discussions with the financiers.

When I asked her about it, she denied everything, but with eyes that big there was no point in lying. One morning, to prove that there was nothing wrong with her, she suggested climbing Mount Hotaka to see a monastery. I pretended I wasn't feeling well, but she ignored me. Once Gelsomina has set her mind to something, not even dengue fever or beriberi can dissuade her.

We drove to Matsumoto, but we had to walk at least an hour and a half from there. She became ill several times. I was afraid it was going to be too much for her, but I knew she would suffer more if I confronted her. She knew that I knew, but neither of us spoke about it.

"We shouldn't do too much," I said.

"A mountain is *not* too much," she replied.

Finally, we saw a monk working on the beehives by the roadside. He helped her for the last hundred meters and showed us into the vestibule to rest, opening the shutters of the dark room so we could see the courtyard where several old cherry trees were in full blossom. We sat there for a time to regain our strength, impressed by the breathtaking spectacle of the bright colors framed by the dark shutters and the walnut window frame.

Finally, she stood up. She had gotten a second wind and opened the courtyard doors to walk over to one of the trees. She stood like a child beneath the ancient giant with her head back, soaking up the miracle.

Suddenly, we felt God breathing.

A sigh of wind passed through the room. A draft entered the shutters and exited through the open doors to swirl around the tree. It tugged at the branches, just for a moment, rustling through the blossoms and making all the flowers let go at once. They were so light that they flew up for a second before fluttering down around Gelsomina. She spread her arms to pluck as many as she could from the air, standing astonished as a sea of color gathered around her ankles.

She stayed beneath the bare branches. In that instant we knew the truth. And she looked at me with a smile that was both radiant and lost; I hadn't seen anything like it since the death of our daughter.

"A mountain can never be too much," she said, "but a breath of wind . . ."

And less than a week later, I take to the water with another woman. At least, my big toe does. I stand at the edge. I was born to watch. The water is too cold for me. The moss on the stones feels funny under my feet. I am afraid I'll catch pneumonia. Big drops soak my shirt and singlet and water trickles down my chest, but I'm too happy to move. Grateful as a fern when a drought breaks, I bathe in my own folly.

. . .

"Good Lord, what's he done to you?" exclaims Maxim. Gala is standing in the doorway, trembling like a dog that's been thrown out of a moving car. My hat, which I put on her, has slid onto the back of her head. For a moment, Maxim is afraid that the event she avoided in Sicily has taken place in Tivoli after all, and he curses the carelessness with which he failed to see it coming. But then he sees how cheerful she is behind her running mascara.

"Snaporaz wants to use me."

"This is Italy. Every man wants to use you."

She rubs her hair dry.

"You're a man and you're in Italy," he hears from under the towel.

He fills the bath and washes her face.

"He can use me in two scenes. It's not much, but I'll be in them with Gelsomina and Marcello."

When she comes out of the bathroom, Maxim is ready to go. It's only the sight of his brand-new skis that reminds her that they're supposed to travel to Cortina d'Ampezzo this weekend. She's used the money she earned with her last Sicilian business trip to buy Maxim skiing lessons to prepare him for his American debut.

"I can't go," she sputters. "Snaporaz might call."

"Give him the number of the hotel."

"I can't bother him with something like that. He'll think I'm stalking him."

"He's used to people stalking him. I'll call him for you."

"Are you crazy! I don't want him to . . ."

"Think we're a couple?"

"I don't want to put him off."

"Why should I put him off?" asks Maxim, annoyed. "Does he want to cast you or fuck you?"

"He wants to cast me, but you know what men are like."

Maxim knows.

"Then tell him you're going by yourself," he grumbles.

"But what if he wants me today or tomorrow?"

"Then you're not here."

"That's what I mean. I have to be here in case he calls."

Maxim understands. Maxim always understands everything.

"It's the last snow," Gala says, "and you have to learn to ski." She takes him to the door, kisses him, and tries to make him smile by popping Snaporaz's hat on his head. It's much too small for him and sits on that Viking head like a miniature bowler atop a clown's wig.

That weekend, I get a call myself. It's the Academy of Motion Picture Arts and Sciences in Los Angeles. They've decided to give me another Oscar, not for a film—they're afraid no one will ever dare to invest in my undependability again—but for my entire oeuvre. They want me to collect it in person. I have no intention of doing so, but they think up all kinds of enticements to lure Gelsomina and me over the ocean. We can bring anyone we like. The first person I think of is Gala, but I immediately realize that's impossible. The press will be swarming. All kinds of festivities are planned. Some lunatic has even cooked up a plan for a theme park based on my films somewhere in the foothills of Santa Monica. Americans! I can't be bothered.

That night, I dream that they run a spit through a buffalo in my honor. The next morning, singing cowgirls serve me a plate piled high with its meat for breakfast. When I turn it down, explaining that I'm only used to eating a *dolce* in the morning, they pull out their lassos and chase me across an endless prairie. I don't look back, but I hear the swish of the ropes as they drive me on. In the barren, overgrazed landscape I can only find one place to take cover. It's a tall structure made of pipes. I climb it. At the top, I discover that I am standing atop a gigantic letter. It's a Y. In the distance I now see other letters, all just as big. Together they spell HOLLYWOOD. Around them there's a fence, the gate of which the cowgirls now slam shut.

Who would dare assert that it's only coincidence that Freud wrote his *Interpretation of Dreams* shortly after the birth of cinema?

Once Maxim departs for Cortina, Gala sits staring into space. She'd insisted, but she's still surprised that he actually went. This is her first night alone since they arrived in Rome. At first, she only feels emptiness, but then she discovers space inside it. Now, finally, she takes the time to think about her situation.

In her mind, she rewinds the scenes she acted out in the daytime in Tivoli with Snaporaz, replaying them from the beginning. She does it several times. With each showing, she concentrates less on their words and interaction, discovering instead new details in the environment: how bright the sandy color of the Temple of Sibyl and how dark the slime on the underwater stones; the frightened fish that shoots off as she swims toward it; how her slip clings to her body when she gets out of the water and how the old man reverts to his age in that moment—and here she rewinds a little to see Snaporaz forgetting himself for minutes on end, mouth open and relaxed, beaming like a child watching a procession. He even claps! This time, she notices that the handkerchief he uses to dab her dry shows an imprint of her face. Smudges of lipstick and mascara. The funeral shroud of a clown. He holds it to the light for a moment and then folds it up. Before putting it into his pocket, he presses the material to his nose, sniffing it. Then, suddenly, the severe look returns to his eyes and she's an actress auditioning once again. All candor disappears behind his eyelids. Reality slams down between her and the film director like a safety curtain.

The crashing sound rudely interrupts her musings, as if the auditorium doors have been opened too early. Alone in her room in Parioli, she is overcome by a great sadness. She still thinks it's because she misses Maxim. She stands up, paces. The streetlights shine through the small window, round and high in the wall like a porthole in a below-deck cabin. For the first time, she feels the oppressiveness of the basement, the weight of the house above it.

In reality, she's mourning the little boy she fleetingly glimpsed at the water's edge, delightedly clapping his hands just before the old man's features returned. That's the moment, when she stopped being a playmate and reverted to the role of actress, that oppresses her; the fourth wall closing between them, a curtain upon which the scenery artist had painted a mask of Snaporaz, heavy lids and dead eyes on either side of an exaggeratedly severe, hooked nose.

Snaporaz doesn't call, and still she stays up all night. The longer the silence, the more passionate her longing to hear from him. She dozes off now and then.

"Galeone, Galeone!" comes a stifled call from behind the curtain.

Even in this drowsy state, Gala knows that Snaporaz isn't thinking, It's the middle of the night, I think I'll ring up that Dutch actress. But that doesn't stop her from awaking, cheerfully hopeful, every time one of the house's nocturnal visitors hurries down the gravel path. More than for a role in his film, she longs with every hour that goes by for another chance to lift that severe curtain, even if that means hanging on the ropes with all her weight. Even if she doesn't yet realize it, she's no longer auditioning for his film, but for his life.

"The dew of love getting to you?" asks Geppi. Saturday is just dawning when Gala walks into the kitchen. Geppi fills the coffeepot and puts it on the stove.

"My mother always said that men spin their webs in the twilight, cobwebs so fine that you can't find them in the dark. But in the morning . . . ah! In the morning, very briefly, immediately after sunrise, just before the dew that clings to the threads has evaporated, you can catch a glimpse."

The big table is full of copper pots and pans that need cleaning. Gala picks one up and starts to polish it.

"It was her way of warning me. 'No matter how much you want it in the nighttime,' said Mamma, 'always wait until morning.' When you see the web, it's too late. The night has passed and you're trapped."

The pressure builds and the boiling water starts to press its way through the coffee.

"Ah, if only I'd listened to her!"

"I didn't sleep well," says Gala.

"It shows." Geppi presses the rattling lid down to hold in the steam and pours two cups. "Here, this'll take the rust off your edges."

Gala assesses the damage in her hand mirror. What if Snaporaz were to suddenly call? She couldn't let herself be seen like this, hair tangled from tossing and turning, her eyes swollen as if she's been crying.

"Surely that's not how you do it?" Geppi snatches the mirror, spits on a copper frying pan, rubs it with her sleeve, and holds it up. "A mirror can only show you who you are, just a woman, whether you're beautiful or ugly, but that's all. The dents in this pan show all kinds of faces. It splits you into different people like a funhouse mirror. I could be any number of women."

She sighs with satisfaction and holds the frying pan out to Gala.

"That's how I've looked at myself for years," Geppi continues. "I used to imagine all the women I might become. Now I think about the women I could have been."

Gala looks at the distorted faces staring at her from the dented copper.

"Why would I want a sharp image of a woman old enough to have to shave?" Geppi asks. "I'm free to put together something beautiful from this soup of distorted noses and melting chins."

Gala's portrait is constantly swimming through the copper.

"The less you see of yourself, the more chances you have to become something."

Waffle

Gelsomina and I spent much of the war in her aunt's apartment. All the men my age had been called up to fight for il Duce. To avoid this fate, I stayed off the street as much as possible. I never emerged before dark. I spent a lot of time drawing. I entertained myself by fantasizing about all the things I couldn't experience in reality. But I was impatient. I felt that life was passing me by. One day, I decided to go for a walk to the Piazza di Spagna. And there, of all places, the army was searching for draft dodgers. I didn't spot them in time, and when I tried to turn back I found the street behind me was blocked off. We were forced up onto the Spanish Steps, where German soldiers were interrogating everyone. It took a long time because they spoke bad Italian and everyone pretended not to understand them. I tried to think, but couldn't come up with anything. I didn't say a word and got packed onto the back of a truck. If I didn't do something, I was done for. The truck started to drive. I was very calm. "If this were a screenplay," I said to myself, "what would you have the main character do now?"

At that very moment, a young blond officer emerged from the Via della Croce, carrying a big packet of waffles under his arm, from Forlari's, the best in Rome. Delicious sponge pastry, icing all round, filled with brandied raisins—wonderful. I jumped off the back of the truck and ran up to him with outstretched arms. "Wolfgang, Wolfgang!" I shouted with great emotion, as if we had lost touch with each other a long time ago, throwing my arms around him as if I'd missed him terribly. One truck slowed for a moment, but no one opened fire. Then it drove on, the poor boys herded in the back like sheep headed for the slaughterhouse. The officer dropped his waffles in fright, trying to explain to me that his name wasn't Wolfgang. I apologized and walked into the Via Margutta as calmly as I could. I entered the first antiques shop I came to. It was a small shop, but I spent an hour frantically studying its wares. I think the owner understood. He didn't say a word. I just walked back and forth between mirrors in enormous rococo frames. The whole time, I could only think one thing: I'm saved, I'm saved!

Ever since, I've put my faith in the moment. The tighter a person is squeezed, the better his solutions.

Gala stays in her room for days, as if the war were raging outside instead of in her head. All this time, she waits by the telephone. She tries to read but can't concentrate. She tries to sleep but can't stop thinking. She tries to be angry with Snaporaz. She is angry with herself because she knows she'll forgive him the moment the phone rings.

It doesn't ring. Or rather, it rings only once. It's Maxim. He's made it to the mountains and wants to tell her all about his adventures. He detects agitation in her voice. He doesn't impose, wishes her goodnight, and hangs up, knowing she wants to keep the line free. At the end of day three, Gala finally thinks of food. There's nothing in the house. She dashes out to the supermarket just before closing time. Altogether she'll be gone for no more than ten minutes. The chance that the director will call in that time is negligible. Gala nonetheless panics in the checkout line. She pushes through in such a wild hurry that she can't find anything smaller and astonishes the checkout girl by throwing down a fifty-thousand-lira note and then running off without waiting for the change.

It's almost seven! What a ridiculous time not to be home. All Italians are at home at seven o'clock. If Snaporaz wants to call, of course he'll choose a time when he knows that every normal person is sitting in their living room. What possessed her to go out now, of all times? She takes off sprinting, only to teeter on her high heels. She kicks them off, stuffs them into a bag, and ignores the traffic to run barefoot across the Piazza Ungheria, all the while cursing her own stupidity and then

Maxim, who could have done this shopping if he hadn't been off sliding around on those stupid skis. While she runs, her panic becomes dejection, and though she doesn't slow down for the sharp gravel on the garden path, she is now so thoroughly convinced that she has missed Snaporaz's call that she sticks the key into the lock without listening to see whether she might catch a final tinkle. She flops down on the bed, opens a bag of chocolates, and wolfs them down without so much as tasting them.

She's sound asleep when the telephone finally rings. It's eleven thirty at night and she's lying fully dressed on her bed between the shopping bags. It rings seven or eight times before she wakes with a start. She shoots up. In two seconds, all the words she has spent the last couple of days rehearsing fall into place: a cool greeting, then a joke to give a relaxed impression, followed by something warm and affectionate before at last consenting to whatever the great man might propose. She reaches for the receiver but, just when she is about to pick it up, she hesitates. After all, she shouldn't seem too keen. She lets it ring twice more; she doesn't want me to think she's hanging around at home waiting for a call. Whatever the reason, when she finally answers, I have just hung up.

"I'm a silly old man," I tell myself. I'm actually relieved I didn't get her on the line and make a fool of myself with the guarded declaration of love I have been practicing before the mirror. I knew it: a woman like Gala doesn't sit home waiting for a bald old man. She's zooming around the city in an open sports car, pursued by a horde of admirers on *motorinos*. She's dancing to the rhythm of the bongos somewhere in Caracalla's baths, her silhouette visible under the arches, harried by the flames of a gypsy who is juggling with fire.

I've had fewer affairs than people think or the newspapers write. But they happened, and all were equally dear to me. Some must have been exceptional, but when I look back, they all start to seem the same. I was never heroic or shameless and self-assured like other men, but I was never cowardly or childish either. Self-confidence is something you expect in the young, but my relations with women have only grown simpler with the years. Romanticism aside, a man, as he grows older, does build up a certain routine. The awe and emotion you feel the first time a woman undresses before you is so miraculous that you assume that you will always feel it, no matter how often you are allowed to witness this mystery. You cannot possibly imagine a limit to the number of times that your lust will fight for precedence over gratitude and tears. But delight is finite. It slips surreptitiously away, and by the fiftieth or hundredth time, perhaps later, it's gone. It's not your desire that diminishes, just your astonishment that there's someone who wants to satisfy it. The love is no less genuine, only your surprise at finding it reciprocated. This is not an act of will: quite the opposite, you'd much rather feel that youthful unease, that piercing doubt, as if everything depended on the other. You can pursue it in the arms of one woman after the other, more passionately every time, but each subsequent embrace only makes its absence more palpable. This is the source of the vague sorrow behind our smiles.

It gets easier, requires less effort, every time. More casual, and you're less patient. If this is boredom—and I doubt it is, because it's still just as exciting and necessary—but if it *is* boredom, it's the same mild variety you cannot help but feel, as you grow older, observing new generations; the weary tenderness with which you watch their endless energy discovering everything you yourself have long known and experienced and seen too many times. It's not that you're inured to it; you just don't have the time. How many hours are wasted on doubt and diffidence, admiration and false modesty? With each passing year, I make less allowance for all that. Life just happens to be coming to an end, and that spurs you to get down to business. Why stand on ceremony when every creak of the springs sends you jumping up to make sure Death isn't sitting at the foot of the bed? With its impatience, death reduces all love to the essence.

But this time it's different. It's as if things are about to happen again for the first time. I'm so scared that I might miss out on the happiness being offered to me that everyone, even Gelsomina, becomes an annoyance. I'm rude, as if everything besides Gala were only a distraction from life. I lie awake nights, exulting in my nervousness. My heart skips beats, as if I'd embarked on a completely unknown adventure; as if I knew nothing more about women than that they have breasts like overripe pumpkins, like those of la Saraghina, who had to use both hands to lift them out of her blouse, one at a time, to show them to me and my schoolmates, who were waiting among the piled-up deck chairs on the beach.

It took the whole weekend for me to summon up the courage to phone Parioli. I spent three days imagining all possible reactions, from fury to scorn to pity. In one of my dreams, Gala was down on her haunches beside a gigantic telephone, wagging her tail like the dog from His Master's Voice, but as soon as I mentioned my feelings for her, she growled and leapt upon the phone and crushed the receiver between her jaws like a chicken bone. The only thing I hadn't thought of was the possibility that she wouldn't answer. Whereas that was the most obvious of all. A girl like her has better options than a man who keeps his teeth on the bedside table.

"Gala!" I shout. "Answer, please, Galeone, my delicious Galetta!" But there is no reaction on the other end of the line. I'm momentarily relieved to have been spared the indignity of a rejection. I embrace Gelsomina and treat her to dinner at Canova's. For ninety minutes, I tell myself that it was a close shave and all for the best. I order asparagus from Pozzuoli when she settles on gilthead bream from Lake Lucrino. We laugh and say how much we love each other and how happy we are that we bumped into each other fifty years ago. It is heartfelt and overpowering. She's convinced that it was the work of God; I say it was Pum Pum the clown, whose tuba exploded with such a bang at the Winter Circus that my sweetheart jumped up out of her chair and thereby let me wrap a protective arm around her for the first time. For dessert, they bring us one of those pyramid-shaped cheeses from Sarsina. As I cut it, I'm overcome by the intense meaninglessness of our lives—not in the usual way, but as a sudden paralysis that drains away all hope and vigor, as if a hole had been punched in my midriff. Gelsomina sees it, of course. She notices every twist of my mouth and every artery that throbs in my throat or temples. She grabs my hand and squeezes it to comfort me. She thinks that, in the euphoria of being together, my thoughts have turned to our daughter, plunging me into grief, just as she still mourns for our little girl every day.

"We'll see her again! We'll see her again!" she whispers, choking.

Amid this madness, my heart leaps at those words. Defying my judgment, it fantasizes about Gala. She emerges with wet hair and lifts her hands to wave hello.

"Until then, love is all that matters!" Gelsomina comforts me, so moved that tears are trickling down her cheeks. Panicking, as if about to be consumed by shame, I wriggle free from her embrace and reject the love I do not deserve. In the process, I knock over my wineglass. The cheese floats off the table. We take advantage of the consternation that follows to make our escape. Outside, Gelsomina wraps her short arms around my fat body and lays her head on my shoulder. Holding each other, we walk home like aging lovers.

As soon as I can, I call my friend Marcello. I'll explode just like that clown's tuba if I don't talk to someone about Gala. Marcellino is in Paris with his mistress and their daughter. Though I try to explain the situation as frivolously as possible, he takes it very seriously.

"When an extramarital relationship takes more energy than it gives," he says, "you have to stop it."

"But we don't have a relationship," I exclaim, telling him that all that's happened is that Gala wanted to swim in the rain.

I hear his tongue click against his teeth with concern.

"I've only heard you talk about a woman that way once before," he says, and we both know who he means. "Have you told her anything?"

"There's nothing to tell."

"That's the biggest threat to a wife, Snapo. You can't stop *nothing*."

I spend the rest of the afternoon trying to draw. I fill seven large pages with caricatures, sketches for a set, and ideas for a cartoon. One after the other, I tear them up. I can't do it, because, for the first time in my life, instead of wanting to create images, I want to dodge them.

Maxim now looks better than ever. It's insufferable. He's tanned as a stevedore and his hair has grown even blonder in the mountains of Cortina. He spent days skiing, and thanks to his training at the theater school he turned out to be a natural. When he walks into the room in Parioli, it's as if the sun follows him in, shining through the hall and gleaming around his shoulders like a halo; he looks like Ben-Hur arriving to visit his mother and sister in the leper cave. Nobody would be surprised if there were cellos and violins playing. He has missed his friend terribly and longingly calls out her name. He tears the curtains aside and throws open the windows, but our hero is too late. Mouth open, eyes rolled back, Gala is lifeless on the bed she has soiled.

He picks her up, not tenderly, but annoyed and impatient. He walks furiously into the shower, her limp body in his arms, and aims the cold water at her face. After a few seconds, he feels her chest expand with a jerk as she gasps for air. She seeks a foothold on the slippery tiles. She turns her face away to breathe, but he forces it back into the jet of water. She coughs, clears her throat, almost choking, but he is unrelenting. He's played this role so many times. He covers her mouth with his lips and blows his breath into her lungs. He doesn't loosen his grip until she's adopted his rhythm. She is still too weak to stand, and he is exhausted. The water streams down their cheeks. Embracing, they slip down to the floor. There they stay, shivering and shaking from the cold.

For a few days, it seems as if nothing has changed. Maxim and Gala are together all day long, just as they were in the first few months after their arrival. He spoils her in all kinds of ways. Until the pain has worn off and her wounded tongue can bear solid food again, he walks to Giolitti every few hours for a large tub of ice cream. She must have omitted her medicine for three or four days to suffer a grand mal of this magnitude, but Maxim doesn't make the slightest allusion to her negligence. I have to support her, he thinks, just as she supports me. After all, I can just as easily accuse myself of anything I reproach her for. He doesn't ask about Snaporaz, but she tells Maxim everything by doing her utmost not to mention him. And just this week, the director is on hundreds of walls all over the city. The news of his special Oscar has leaked out and they see him staring at them wherever they go from posters pushing the latest issue of *Gente,* whose lead article is a major interview with him. Every time Maxim sees one, he has to resist the urge to add vampire teeth, horns, and a forked tail.

To escape Snaporaz's eyes, Maxim leads Gala into subterranean Rome. Their days there are happy. They discover the Mithraeum beneath the San Clemente and explore the cellars of Caracalla. In the sacred catacombs along the Appia, they shake off the guide and the group and wander through endless corridors, as unruly as I was in '32, when I strayed from my parents there and got lost. Shrieking with excitement, they follow the flame of a cigarette lighter deep under fields until they reach the tenements of Tor Marancia, where they finally emerge through a trapdoor beside a *soprintendenza* shed in the Via Annunziatella.

Once their eyes have adjusted to the daylight, the first thing they see is the *Gente* poster, but Snaporaz's grin is already hidden behind a leaflet for Circus Orfei, whose current attraction is Mimil the clown. Gala seems indifferent to what's left of Snaporaz. To make sure he's got the old Gala back and that things between them are the way they were before, Maxim takes her out of town for a few days. Arm in arm, they wander through the excavations in Cerveteri, cheerful and carefree as the Etruscans portrayed there in their tombs, dancing and diving and swimming with dolphins. In Volterra, Maxim and Gala linger before one of countless urns on which a couple are depicted entwined on their deathbed, grinning with satisfaction, and as if reading their script my main characters whisper something to each other: that they would be happy if they too could enter eternity just as contented and united.

Little Chicken

"It's him," shouts a frantic Geppi. "In my house! He's inside, but he could walk outside any minute now." She's wearing a moth-eaten party dress that clings to her like a sausage skin. Copper mirror in one hand, rouge brush and kohl pencil in the other, the concierge patters through the basement searching for the best light. She elbows the raggedy Maxim and Gala, who have just returned from a long weekend among the tombs near Pitigliano, out of her way.

"One of your lovers visiting again?" Maxim teases.

Geppi lowers her mirror and looks at him solemnly.

"Not just my lover, but the lover of all Italian women." Her makeup gleams in a ray of sunshine. Her skills as a cosmetician date from her days supplementing her income with part-time employment in Testaccio funeral parlors. "Marcello's visited our bedrooms more often than our husbands, if only in our dreams."

"Marcello . . . *the* Marcello?"

"More often than our husbands, I tell you, and with more passion! Good Lord, just the thought makes me sweat like a whore in church."

She turns her back on Maxim and lifts up her hair. He gets to zip up the dress that fitted her in her youth.

"But why is he visiting you?" asks Gala.

"Not me, sunshine; no, the days that men were connoisseurs are gone forever. But it's almost as good: he's here for you. Just for you!

Imagine, Marcello here to pick you up! Oh, the things that Signor Gianni manages."

"Gianni's sent him?"

"Who else? Now tell me again that our benefactor isn't a saint?"

Gala grabs Maxim's arm. After the familiarity of their friendship, the idea of having to live up to expectations comes as a shock. She soon gathers her wits. The territory might not be safe, but she has long since scouted it out. She knows what to do. There's no time to waste. Her nervous frisson is what an understudy feels a few hours before the performance when she's asked to save the day by replacing the lead. She snatches Geppi's mirror, holds it a little to one side to coax her reflection out from behind her black spot, and sees her worst fears confirmed.

"He can't see me like this."

Gala nervously plucks at the wisps in her hair. The idea of appearing unprepared before a film star and heartbreaker like Marcello makes her forget that there's more hope for her than for Geppi.

"Just look at me, it's out of the question. What will he think?"

"Out of the question," Maxim growls, "and I'll tell him so." Her insecurity nettles him. Just when he thought he'd recovered the Gala he loves—just when she was finally becoming herself again! For the past few days, on their trip, he was free to be proud of her, as he always had been before. He's been showing her off. When they walked arm in arm, he enjoyed the looks of passers-by, and when they shouted *"Complimenti alla mamma!"* Maxim gloated, as if he personally had brought her into the world. And when, as happened several times a day, drooling boys climbed off their scooters, or middle-aged gentlemen got out of their racing cars, he didn't intervene but waited avidly for the shrewd and disdainful barbs Gala unleashed. As the rejected men slunk off kneading their crotches, he demonstratively claimed his love with a slow French kiss, arrogant and satisfied as if the compliment had been his.

Now, five minutes after they get home, Gala is already starting to dissolve before his eyes, like a dream in the morning light. He sees her courage, the only courage he has, ebb away as she allows herself to be intimidated by a name. Maxim is angry at the famous stranger for her sudden self-doubt, almost as angry at him as with Gala herself.

"Where is this guy?" he shouts combatively.

"When I said our princess wasn't in, the charmer insisted on leaving a note. I took him pen and paper, along with a slice of freshly baked onion tart . . ."

At that moment, the door opens and Marcello strides into the hall. His face is older than it looks onscreen—he is wearing glasses with heavy bone frames and a trilby to hide his balding spot—but his movements are as supple as on the morning he swung his legs over the side of the Trevi Fountain. The presence of a film star rarely fails to make an impression. Even people who've had time to steel themselves for the miracle tremble when the flat mask that's bombarded their subconscious becomes flesh before their eyes. All of them feel it, and a silence descends, as if one of the stone apostles in St. Peter's Square had just breathed in the Holy Spirit and descended among the believers using his robe as a parachute. After fifty years, Marcello is used to it, and patiently lets them catch their breath.

Geppi is first.

"Ah, Marcello!" she sings. "Marcello in my house." She puts one hand on her hip, the other behind her head, a pose she remembers from the days of burlesque. "When I was born did anyone think it would come to this?"

"Highly unlikely, signora," the actor answers so charmingly that the old woman doesn't feel slighted in the least when he walks by her to greet Gala with outstretched hands.

"I'm starting to understand what all the fuss is about," he says, Gala's nerves hidden as always behind a sultry facade. Who but Maxim could guess that her tongue is only darting out because her mouth is dry with fear, and that she bites her lower lip only to conceal its trembling? Gala will bait a man to keep him from attacking her. The same voluptuous terror once moved her to climb onto her father's desk. It's a nerviness that prays to be released from further daring. The result looks so provocative because every man senses that there is an anxiety behind the seductiveness, begging for reassurance. This is not lost on Marcello.

"That's why my friend wants to gamble it all at the last minute."

"Fine friends you have!"

Marcello looks at Maxim like a panda appraising an ant trying to argue its right to honey.

"If Gianni were my friend," Maxim says, backing down, "I'd at least want him to be a little bit discreet."

"Who's Gianni?" the actor inquires.

"The saint of the guesthouse!" says Geppi, crossing herself.

"A pimp!" roars Maxim.

"Well, then he's a colleague," Marcello laughs. "I too have the task of delivering the signorina to the harem of Italy's greatest living pasha!" Seeing the questioning looks, he adds, "My friend Snaporaz, the only man who makes work of his dreams. Work that will finally commence today." He looks at his watch and offers Gala an arm. "In forty-five minutes, to be precise. In Cinecittà. There's a lot of traffic on the Tuscolana around lunchtime, so if you're ready?"

"But I don't know a thing about it," she sputters.

"Neither does Snaporaz. He starts every film with a blank slate. We drift through the mist for days on end. It's terrifying to work in that void, but just when we start to despair, his genius blossoms."

"But are you sure he's expecting me?" asks Gala, walking through the garden.

"We'll surprise him." Marcello holds his car door open for her.

"No! He'll say, 'What's that girl doing here?' Maybe he doesn't even want me."

"Believe me, he wants you."

"He never called."

"Did you call him?"

"That's different."

"He didn't have the nerve." Marcello shrugs, pulling the agonized face Italians use to illustrate something they consider obvious. "He was afraid of spoiling his own surprise."

As soon as the car is out of sight, Maxim picks up their backpacks with a frustrated sigh and walks inside to unpack them.

"O Dio," exclaims Geppi, who can't stop waving, "if I still had my figure, the world would have nothing left to complain about!"

I have my arm around Gelsomina when they walk into Studio 5.

"Ouch!" she shouts when, from the shock, my fingers tense into a claw. To mask my confusion, I kiss my wife on the top of her head. For no reason. As if she were a child. Or a dog. It's ridiculous, but Gelsomina knows exactly what it means and looks up to identify her rival.

"Well, look what we have here!" she says.

I raise a hand to Gala and Marcello, mumble as if I've been expecting them, and quickly bend back over the table where I have spread out my latest sketches for the film. I pretend to be explaining my ideas to Gelsomina. In fact, there's only one thing on my mind.

I should have known Marcello would pull a stunt like this. He means well. He's my oldest friend. He gets into trouble and I help him out of it. I tell him what's bothering me and he smiles, brushing it all aside. I wouldn't have it any other way. I can do my own worrying. Our friendship is unconditional, deeply rooted in mutual incomprehension. Marcello thinks life is a big joke and believes that if only they made up their mind people could all bluff their way through it as carelessly as he does. Now and then, he tries to lend them a hand. This is not his strong suit. I ought to be grateful that he didn't get Gala to leap out of a giant tiramisu at a dinner celebrating my wedding anniversary. He undoubtedly believes he's doing me a favor, even though all I want at a moment like this is for the earth to split open and swallow me up. To make things worse, I can feel all too keenly how embarrassed Gala is. I could succumb beneath the double burden.

"And I get to waltz around in baggy pajamas?" asks Gelsomina. She snatches up a drawing that is anything but flattering.

"You're in a nursing home," I say. "You expect Versace?"

She flaps the drawing back and forth under my nose, as if it's stuck to her fingers like flypaper.

"This woman can't talk and her memory's gone. She's lost her past and her future. Her style's the last thing she'll give up."

When I'm too slow to give in, she actually threatens to shred my design: the very woman who, the moment I take my eyes off her, asks the grocer to return my shopping list so that she can save it for posterity in a calfskin scrapbook!

"Don't forget . . ." She grabs my wrist, pulls me toward her, and continues in a whisper, "This woman was born to the stage. She has emotions and sensibilities the other patients lack. She was used to expressing herself. When she was happy, she sang. When things went wrong, she fought her way back to happiness. And that woman is now standing eye to eye with her old love for one last time."

Our faces touch. I feel her breath as if we're making love. It frightens me.

"You should know that," she says. "You invented her. If she can no longer succeed in telling the love of her life what's going on inside her, she'll do anything to show him what he means to her."

And in that instant she lets go of me, casually straightening my jacket as if we were at a reception. She lays the drawing back on the table and continues, businesslike, "Her appearance is all she has left. It's the last language she speaks. I'm not saying she has to be beautiful, but she'll definitely want to spruce up, with the courage of despair."

For a half second, enough to make me shiver, she looks at me.

"Fine," I say. "Arrange it with wardrobe."

Her hand slides quickly up her neck to check her wig, and then Gelsomina walks up to Marcello, hugs him, and introduces herself to Gala.

Maxim, in Parioli, empties out the backpacks. He puts their underwear in a bucket to soak. He hangs up a shirt and a dress in the wardrobe. He pulls her diary out of a side pocket, runs his fingers over the Chinese silk, then replaces it in her bedside cabinet. He arranges his shaving kit in the bathroom and leaves her toiletries bag on her pillow. He lies beside it, maybe because he's worn out from the trip, maybe because he's bored.

One by one, my regular crew members arrive: Ruggero, Nicola, Fiamella with Tonino, Gianfranco, Alberto . . . Some of them haven't seen each other since my last film, three and a half years ago. The glory days, when our dream factory operated day and night, are over. Only the youth of the magnificent woman Marcello has brought gives us the brief illusion that nothing has changed. They reminisce, get a little something to eat, and together we raise our glasses to Vinzo, my faithful grip, who has left us, wishing him a beautiful spot in the wide frame up above. The whole time, I'm vainly trying to catch Gala's eye. She seems comfortable, chatting with everyone, animated but determined not to impose. I can't approach her immediately because I'm constantly talking to the people who, one after the next, keep coming up to me. They know I prefer these initial consultations informal—if I wanted to play the chairman, I'd have gone into politics. Anyway, there's not much to say. The film exists in my head and it will soon exist on celluloid. The two might be completely different and the journey from one to the other is as unpredictable and inimitable as life itself. I prefer to tell everyone my story separately, eight or ten times in a row. I open my notebooks, show them the portfolios with sketches. One points to this part of it, another to that, asking what it means. As always, I don't have a clue and make up something to save face.

That's how a squiggle that could have been anything acquires a meaning. It is given a place. Suddenly one idea belongs with another, maybe even inside the same particular scene. And just like that a certain development emerges from my chaos. The more I describe it, the more I have to make precise choices.

Finally, only a fraction of the visionary whole remains, but because the parts that are selected belonged to that whole, traces of the rest still cling to it, though these are different for every person. No one recognizes himself in everything; but everyone can see something of himself in smaller things—just as I sometimes enjoyed the posters and the photos of the stars in the glass cases outside the Fulgor more than the films inside. The posters let me make up my own stories. I don't say that my ideas improve with every choice, but they're none the worse for them, either. They're alive, if nothing else. The joy and sorrow I feel upon seeing my own work must be something like what God feels when he gazes down from His red, plush-lined box at a command performance of His Creation. My satisfaction with the little that has accidentally emerged is as great as my frustration about everything I intended to create but never got the chance to develop.

The meeting comes to an end after a couple of hours. Gelsomina goes off to Castelgandolfo to visit her sister. She gives me a kiss and wishes me abundant inspiration. The others follow, and Marcello, with a wink, leaves me alone with Gala.

"Galina," I say. "Galina, why on earth do you want to be an actress?"

I show her my plans and tell her I'm sorry I don't have a bigger part for her. She looks carefully at one sheet after the other. From the way she picks up the drawings and slides them across her field of vision, I can tell that she has eye problems. She offers no judgment but bursts into laughter at the sight of one of my caricatures. My heart leaps like a dog that's been tossed a bone.

"These drawings are only to picture things for myself," I say apologetically. For the first time, I'm embarrassed by my lack of technique, ashamed it's all so sketchy. "The film's always been inside my head, even before I knew it existed. Thousands of films screen there every day of the week, but the projector isn't on. All I have to do is make the light."

"Just as an untold number of sculptures in the marble of Carrara will never be freed from the mountain," Gala says. "The sculptor points one block out in the quarry because he sees its potential, but behind it thousands remain hidden forever." She shivers. "So many things will never be seen."

"There's always someone," I say, putting my arm around her reassuringly, "to think of those others when he sees that one . . ."

This is one version of the buildup to our first kiss. It's equally possible that those firm, resilient breasts of hers brush up against me every time she bends over one of the drawings. Feeling her stiffening nipples, at last I can no longer stand it and jump her. There's probably a little truth to both versions or—to stick to the philosophical jargon that has won me so many women—both images coexist and can be recognized in the other.

Either way, this is what happens next: her breathing quickens as soon as our mouths find each other. Her head tilts back to offer me her throat and she pulls her blouse open with both hands to let my lips descend. At the same time, she puts my hand between her legs, impatiently, grips it tight, briefly and fiercely rides it. It's over in two minutes. She's lying on the table, bare bottom on my drawings, shamelessly staying there as I nudge her legs apart for a better view of the glistening droplets pearling out of her. They roll down her thighs. Underneath, one of the little characters I've drawn from my dreams slurps them up, blurring with delight. I, on the other hand, am dressed impeccably throughout. Could there be any better proof that this is no fantasy? Quite the opposite! She makes no attempt whatsoever to please me. If I weren't enjoying the view so much, I would even feel used. She sits up, looks at me with big, moist eyes, and thanks me with a kiss. She takes my hand, presses it against her cheek, still sitting just the way she was. At last, she stands up, straightening her dress to show that playtime is over. As I wonder whether I've ever been the one to walk away unsatisfied, I try to look as aggrieved as possible, but that makes no impression at all.

She pours us both a glass of wine, clinks glasses, and beams as if we are equally sated.

"To love!" she says, but I have no idea if she means it. She soon insists on leaving. I walk her all the way to the gate.

"Maybe I act," she says, "because we've already had to leave so many possibilities behind in the stone."

"But that's the difference between sculptor and sculpture," I call out after her. "One has to wait for someone else to see something in it; the other is free to shape himself."

I walk to the bathroom to wash my hands, but at the sink I reconsider and decide to carry her with me for the rest of the day. In the mirror, I see the young man who fled into the antiques shop in the Via Margutta during the war.

"I'm saved!" he repeated to himself, walking back and forth between the gilded rococo curls. "I'm saved, I'm saved!"

Maxim wakes from his afternoon nap. The first thing he sees upon opening his eyes is Gala's toiletries bag. He picks it up and shakes it, a routine gesture after years of checking whether she has enough pills. He hears them rattling in their jars. Lots. More than enough. Reassured, he puts it back and turns over again. For five or six seconds he rests, then opens his eyes wide. He grabs the bag and unzips it.

Galley Slave

Gala is hardly through the gates of Cinecittà when the truth hits her, as abruptly as if someone yanked up the rear wall during a sensitive scene and let in the sunlight and the furious traffic on the Tuscolana. It can't be more than fifty paces to the entrance of the metro, but she suddenly lacks the strength to get there. The fury around her unleashes a storm inside her.

"What have I done?" she says out loud. Seeking support from the studio complex, she presses herself up against the wall like a child playing hide-and-seek just around the corner from the gate. She evaluates and examines words and caresses that happened without thinking at the time, and in so doing only judges herself. For each gesture, every sentence she uttered, she now comes up with ten others, better, pithier, more intriguing, more important, funnier.

The thought that Snaporaz might be standing on the other side of the wall at the same time, like her reflection, palms on the plaster, does not cross her mind. For her, everything the director has done or said is beyond dispute. The only reason she considers his behavior at all is to try to detect his ulterior motives. The more rationality she tries to impose on her sensuality, the more convinced she grows that Snaporaz could only deplore, deeply, her and her behavior. It must have been a tremendous strain for him to maintain his friendly facade; now, at this very moment, he must be on the phone telling Marcello what a deep and horrific disappointment that milkmaid was. Her intellect tells her that you couldn't find a man in the world who would not look favorably on a young woman who has just thrown herself at him, but in her heart she knows that she has fallen short again. She had come so close, only to see her big chance go up in flames.

"What possessed me?" she asks herself, weeping with impotence and rage. "For God's sake, how could I have let it come to this?"

Until the day I grew too fat to wear a swimsuit, I was always too skinny for one. For years, they called me Gandhi or Beanstalk. When I was sixteen, I watched the others impress girls by parading virtually naked over the beach in Rimini. I didn't dare. In response, I began dressing exorbitantly in three-piece suits with scarves and summer gloves. I studied pictures of Leopardi and D'Annunzio, men who never bared so much as their Adam's apple yet attracted women in droves. On even the hottest days, I strolled up and down the boulevard with a flower in my lapel. Under my arm, I carried a pad on which, for thirty lire, I would draw caricatures of the seaside visitors.

On those summer evenings, the Grand Hotel was like an enormous gleaming oasis between the peeling pavilions and the bleached awnings. The people who stayed there were rich and glamorous. Like me, they avoided the beach: you could not only be too scrawny for it, you could also, it seemed, be too stylish. The suitcases the bellboys carried into the hotel bore stickers with the names of fairy-tale cities and regions, and when the lights went on, the hotel, with its domes and towers, was transformed into a palace like the ones I imagined in Cairo, Lebanon, or Las Vegas. There was no way we local boys would be allowed in, but I spent hours sitting on a wall across the road, fantasizing about suicides and nights of insane passion, about duchesses who had lost everything playing faro, about the blackmail and rapes going on behind the drawn curtains on all those floors. When guests came out on their way to limousines or the casino, I would accost them, but it was unusual for anyone to take the time to pose for me. I didn't mind not earning much because it cost me nothing to listen to the band on the terrace play American songs all evening, or to watch characters who matched the ones in my dreams appear at the balustrade: men in tuxedos, women with plunging necklines whose curves gleamed in the light of the lanterns. I sketched them. They held champagne glasses or each other, and the women offered the men their lips.

On one of the warmest evenings of August, I was sitting in my regular spot when a lady beckoned from the terrace. She probably wasn't yet thirty-five, but in my eyes she was old. She asked if I'd like to draw her. While the headwaiter looked on as if perfectly aware of how scrawny I was under my padded shoulders, I started sketching. This was the first time in my life that I had entered the Grand Hotel, and as far as I knew it would be the last. I took my time. She asked me what I'd like to drink and ordered it. I took more care with the drawing than I did with the usual caricatures of traveling salesmen's girlfriends I did on the boulevard. Her eyes were deep set and melancholy. Twice we were suddenly forced to stop. She asked me to look away, and I heard her cough painfully several times. She was wearing jewels, and I echoed their gleam in her eyes and lips. The effort with which I looked at her brought a smile back to her face. Her eyes revived, and I felt them studying me. She burst out laughing at the way the tip of my tongue showed between my teeth when I concentrated. For a moment, I thought I could see her as a girl, dancing all night with admirers, her head back, her full blond curls bouncing in time to the music.

When I showed her the result, she took the pad from my hands with surprise. She studied it for a moment, then, without warning, leapt up and ran out into the garden with it. I found her in a bower of jasmine. She'd been crying, and she seemed about to start up again when she saw me. I didn't know what to do and on impulse I kissed her. She could have screamed and had me arrested, but instead she let me go on. And I went on. In her room, we made love without stopping to think and for hours were familiar in a way I had not thought a man and a woman could be. After these perfect hours, we reluctantly disentangled, but even before I reached the lobby I felt the blood draining from my legs. A bucket of shame doused the flaming euphoria from one moment to the next. The sight of her happiness and the intimacy of our union were still vivid in my mind's eye, but I was convinced of my own inadequacy, sure I'd made a fool of myself in every way. Till my dying day, the choir would chant "Gandhi!" My mind tried to reassure my wavering heart, if only long enough to get me past the hotel staff and to the revolving door. I ran straight to Marcellino, who even then was my bosom buddy. He spent the rest of the night assuring me that it was all the other way around, that the woman I described could usually only dream of a young lover like me, that I had done her a favor, that she would be the one worrying that she had failed to give a youth the passion he needed. It didn't help. I lay on my bed for days, heartsick thinking about everything I should have done differently. Not until I met Gelsomina did I recover my confidence in bed.

Only now, my face hidden in the fingers from which Gala is slowly fading, do I realize how intimately, how equally, age and youth yielded to each other long ago in the Grand Hotel.

Today I am the town's most famous son. There is an enormous bronze bust of me beside the elevators in the lobby. I've finally discovered what it commemorates. The most moving thing about intimacy is sharing not your pride but your shame.

If only I could explain all this to reassure Gala, my Galeotta, who moves away on the far side of the wall before descending into a metro filled with commuters. She wouldn't hear me above the voices shouting in her own head. Maybe later, when my monument to her is complete.

For now, her panic is strangely resigned, as it was that time she was riding the pastor's wife's knee while desperately searching for Homer's words: she knows she's going to fail and accepts the forfeit of love and the merciless punishment. That kind of certitude almost feels like security.

"You haven't gone into business for yourself, I hope?"

The metro doors are closing as Gala feels the hand on her neck. She tries to turn around, but Gianni tightens his grip, briefly, with a false playfulness, and when he lets go he leaves two bruises. With a grin, he flops down on the seat across from her. Gala slaps his face viciously. An old man takes his granddaughter by the hand and leads her to the next carriage.

"Either you and I work as a team," says Gianni, "or you'll never work again."

"Fine," says Gala, "I'll never work again."

"That's not how it works."

"I don't know what you mean," Gala answers. She pretends to look out through the window, which, in a subway tunnel, is not very convincing. Gianni catches her eye in the glass.

"I invested in you because I believed in you. Our working relationship and your beauty are closely related." She looks straight at him. His smile is just as friendly as the first time they met, but his breathing is short and sharp. His voice lowers menacingly. "If I end one of them, I'll end the other as well." He suddenly shoots forward, grabs her face with one hand, and squeezes hard. "Then at least I can be sure you won't be whoring around behind my back."

The injustice brings all the power back that love has squeezed out of her. After all, when a man lashes out at her she's on familiar territory.

"You're insane!" she says, planting her nails in his flesh and wrenching his hand away. He studies the cuts on his hand, lifts it to his mouth, and sucks out the blood.

"Am I? Geppi was kind enough to tell me that you were here. You were picked up and delivered."

"For a work meeting."

"Everyone has their own little name for it."

"You're fucking jealous, aren't you?" She doesn't doubt for an instant that she's got this man's measure. "Of Snaporaz!" and she laughs in Gianni's face.

"Just a director's work meeting with a starlet . . . all the better," says Gianni scornfully.

He gets out at the next stop.

"Don't forget," he calls from the platform before the doors close. "Sicily wants you."

And yet—incomprehensible—a smile glimmers through her anger when she hears those last words.

Laxatives. Everywhere: pots, powders, strips, enough milk of magnesia to flush out a whole regiment. The room in Parioli is strewn with them.

Gala freezes in the doorway. She couldn't wait to tell Maxim about her adventure, but now it dries up on her tongue. He's lying on the bed reading Billy Johnson's autobiography. He says hello, casually engrossed in the ski champion's life. She kicks off her shoes and sits down next to him.

"You're nuts," she says while quietly studying the display. "How much did this little joke cost you?"

"You use so much of this crap," Maxim replies spitefully. "I thought you might need a reserve."

"You shouldn't look through my things."

"You shouldn't hide things from me. How long have you been using this crap?"

When Maxim realized what it was he'd discovered in Gala's toiletries bag, he kept searching in disbelief, just to confirm his conviction that that was it. But there was a second jar of laxative pills in a handbag she rarely used. He found a third, with a heavy dosage and a huge list of warnings and side effects, between her mattress and the head of the bed, as if it had slipped down by accident. It was only when he found a small supply of an emetic that Gala had secreted under a loose plank behind the sink that he realized how serious things were. His first reaction was pity. He wanted to fetch her, hug her, rock her, whisper that she could always trust him with everything, that he'd understand whatever the problem was, that they could work it out together. At the same time, he blamed himself. He remembered holding one of those pots in his hands. Why hadn't he looked more closely when he had the chance? He'd wanted to look at the label, but had simply shrugged and put it back. On the other hand, he thought to reassure himself, what was all the fuss about? Laxatives are hardly heroin, after all. No, what upset him was that Gala was keeping secrets from him. That she was ashamed to tell him something. She, of all people, the very person who had taught him shamelessness!

Years ago, she'd walked in on him sitting on the toilet. She apologized and was about to turn on her heel, but he thought that two people who were so intimate should share everything. So she sat on the edge of the bath and acted out a Franca Rame monologue she was learning for an audition. He had never seen *her* shitting, but until a few months ago he had never given that a second thought. They had just eaten. He was getting into the bath when she entered to say that she had to go urgently. He nodded, splashing around unperturbedly, forcing her to request some privacy. He refused because he thought it ridiculous and couldn't be bothered to get out of the tub. She stomped off angrily, crossing the whole Borghese in order to take her time in a marble toilet in one of the hotels near the Trinità dei Monti. She didn't return till evening, at which point she felt no need to explain her behavior. He brushed off her absence as yet another of the idiosyncrasies he loved even when they annoyed him. How could he have guessed that she was already vomiting up any meal that was too heavy? That day, he'd interpreted her peculiar behavior as her usual spontaneity and lack of inhibition, though it was instead merely compulsive. And she didn't trust him enough to tell him. He felt a pang of reproach. And he grew angrier the more he thought about her deception. She hadn't just shut him out, she had deliberately misled him. If she wasn't who she seemed to be in that most intimate area, what else could he be mistaken about?

He took the bottles to the pharmacy in the Via Scipioni—according to the labels, that's where she bought them—slammed them down on the counter as if the owner were on trial, and haughtily demanded an explanation. The chemist shook his head and said that they were medicines that should not under any circumstances be taken in combination or alternately. Two were even only available by prescription. He looked them up. They had been prescribed by a clinic in Sicily. The doctor's name was difficult to decipher, but when Maxim suggested Pontorax, the chemist agreed. So she'd taken a complete stranger into her confidence; Maxim almost fainted with rage when he madly imagined her sitting back with that guy in an old-fashioned privy. He asked the pharmacy for all the laxatives he stocked. Initially the man refused and explained the state that someone who took all those drugs would end up in—dead intestinal flora, internal bleeding, loss of sphincter control, and colonic adhesions—but when Maxim insisted that it was for him and his family, seven children who ate nothing but white bread, the man gave in, especially when it became clear that Maxim was paying cash. He spread their last money out on the counter. He regretted it as soon as he was back on the sidewalk, but now there he is, lying there with Gala, in a room full of suppositories.

She blushes. He didn't know she could. He'd rather not have known. Now she looks like she's about to cry. He doesn't want her like this. He wants the Gala he's always known. He takes her hand.

"Can't you get off them?"

She shakes her head.

"How long has this been going on?"

She shrugs.

"The camera adds two kilos," she says quietly. "I wanted to get them off in advance."

"You're gorgeous."

"It's not how beautiful you are, it's how beautiful you feel."

"If you don't feel beautiful, who does? Can't you see everyone watching you on the street?"

"Fulvani thought I was heavy."

"Fulvani?"

"And Snaporaz definitely will. You know how particular they are in this business."

"So you throw it all up? After every meal?"

"No!"

He confronts her with a label he has found.

"Every once in a while," she admits, fixing her big eyes on him, just as she does during seizures.

"How could I not have noticed?"

"Because I'm so much smarter than you," she says, smiling cautiously.

"Can we cut it out?"

How can she explain that the skinnier she feels, the better she can face life?

"Let's not talk about it any more. I'll cut down."

"Why didn't you tell me at the beginning?"

"You? You're the last person I'd tell," she says, astonished, as it were obvious. "You love me too much."

When I was four years old, I went to the nursery school of the nuns of San Vincenzo. I was used to my mother's low neckline and big bare arms, but the sisters were covered from head to toe. I'd never seen anything like it. As soon as they lifted me up onto their laps, I started searching for skin between the folds of their robes, only to get tangled in their habits like a stage comic who can't find the opening in the curtain. I was astonished to see how all their delight in life gathered in their faces. Bound between collars and borders, their full lips and flushed cheeks all but exploded with femininity. I imagined the life bulging out of them, like air trying to escape a squeezed balloon. They wore wide wimples that bounced up and down with each step, like storks testing their wings in the nest, awaiting a favorable wind that would let them choose freedom.

A procession was held on the eve of the feast of San Vincenzo. They put me in the middle of a long row, gave me a candle, and lit it.

"Make sure you don't let it go out," they said. "If you do, you'll make the Mother of God cry!"

I'd once made my own mother cry by falling in the water. If I'd upset her so much by doing something I couldn't possibly help, how much grief would I cause the Holy Virgin Mother of God by messing up something I was carrying in my own hands? There was a brisk wind on the church square. We'd soon be out of town and cross the bridge along the Marrechia, where nothing could check the sea breeze. I grew dizzy with fear. The responsibility weighed so heavily on my shoulders that I was sure I couldn't possibly move. I looked imploringly at my mother, who was standing off to one side, but she just grinned and gave me the thumbs-up to tell me how good I looked in my new suit. All the while, the wind was tugging at the flame as if wanting to wrench it from the wick.

At last the statue of the saint was raised and the procession began to move, dragging its feet like a caterpillar, inching forward, then marching on the spot, then moving forward a bit more. Unable to think of anything except my candle, I kept bumping into the girl in front of me. The wax ran down my fingers. They were cold and the hot wax cut into them like a knife, but I didn't care: my scalding tears were undoubtedly less anguished than those of the Mother of God, who had already suffered so much, and I felt the pain as proof that I had at least managed to keep my flame burning for her.

By the time we reached the Tiberius Bridge, I had almost no feeling left in my hands. One of the nuns walked by, encouraging us. If she had seen the state I was in, she certainly would have intervened, but I held my candle away from her because her flapping cape could only make things worse. The farther we left the city behind us and moved toward the silent gloom of the valley, the more obsessed I became by my task. I had been asked to do something impossible but, almost miraculously, I was managing to do it. I believed in myself as never before. Everything else, especially the pain, was of secondary importance. Somehow, the rocking saint above our heads, the rhythmic hymns, and the flaring lights hypnotized me.

I rose above myself. I couldn't think of anything but my candle. The shorter it grew, the more important it became to let it burn all the way down. It didn't matter how long it had been burning, only how much farther it had to go. The less I had left, the more it mattered—just as an old man takes more care with his life and health than he did when he was younger, even though he has considerably less to lose. Strangely enough, I began to dread the end of the march, even though it meant the end of my ordeal. The longer my trial lasted, the more important it became.

Never in my life had I done anything as weighty as preventing the Madonna's tears. There was nothing I wanted more than to see it through, though at the same time, I could no longer imagine a purpose for my life afterward. Most of the other children's lights had already gone out. Mine was still burning. Or rather: I was still burning, completely identified with that candle. The wax melted. The flame floated in my cupped hands. The fire burned my skin. I could smell it. Black blisters appeared on my fingers. I could see clearly that I was carrying on like the idiot Pazzotto, yet I believed that I would cease to exist when the light went out. The meaning of life seemed to be contained within my suffering. I was ready to offer myself up to the Madonna for her helping me to surpass myself. My blisters burst open. I embraced the pain and the exhaustion because they proved what I could do. The strength that I felt at that moment was enough to last me the rest of my life, though I have never felt it since.

I have no other explanation for Gala's lack of appetite for food. Almost casually, the thought took root that she could control the uncontrollable. She began to deny her body food. The whole process was gradually set in motion, a few steps forward, sometimes grinding to a halt, then creeping forward again. The result mattered less than the deprivation she had to undergo for its sake. The more she persevered, the greater the challenge. Each fainting fit, every bodily weakness, buttressed her spirit, activating an inner strength she never called on at any other time. By burning herself up, she increased her own value to herself.

People with a limited understanding of women explain this as an attempt at self-punishment. All they are trying to do is reward themselves.

I only know this: in the procession of the nuns of San Vincenzo, my happiness was nothing more than a guttering flame in a storm. As long as I kept it going, I was in charge of the whole world and, more importantly, of myself.

No one knows better than Gelsomina how badly truth and I get on. When I come home that afternoon, she just looks at me. That is enough for both of us. She doesn't talk to me about her illness. Why should I worry her with Gala?

On the way home I bought a big present. It's wrapped in shiny cellophane. It's for Gelsomina. It's her birthday tomorrow. I love her. I want nothing more than to hear how she's doing—Is she in pain? Does she have hope?—but I still can't bring myself to ask. She's sitting by the window reading. I look at her. I think of how little time we have left together. We'll grow a bit older. Then immeasurable sorrow will come; the days will ebb a little longer for one of us. A surge of affection washes over me.

But while I am filled with one thing, the other is there too. Behind my love, in the distance, Gala lights up like a dazzling beacon, making all shapes disappear. I hear myself fantasizing like an old fool about a possibility of giving my life a new direction.

"Last year, I celebrated my birthday in Berlin," says Gelsomina, looking up from her book. "This year here. Where will I be for my next birthday?"

I don't know, but I'll do everything in my power to be with her. I don't tell her that. No one knows better than Gelsomina how much love it takes to keep your mouth shut.

The world of Gala and Maxim's youth most resembled the final scene of a fairy tale. Evil was vanquished. Nothing was impossible. The harness of rules their parents had grown up inside was like a suit of armor cracked and dented by war. Their children stretched, shucked off the pieces, and an entire generation left the nest with more hope than humanity had ever known. Youngsters meeting in the streets of Amsterdam flew into each other's arms, regardless of whether they'd ever met, and celebrated their freedom by throwing off their clothes. They rolled naked over the lawns of the municipal park, smoking, dancing, and drinking, overseen by police officers with colorful tulips in their caps. Young people embraced free love with the partners of their choice and without any risk of the snare of parenthood, thanks to new discoveries; and when, toward evening, they grew tired of enjoying themselves, they leapt into the canal and swam to the city square. Astonished people saw this new generation on television screens all over the world, sleeping unembarrassed at the base of a phallic marble monument, heads resting on each other's stomachs, flanked by two stone lions who watched over their dreams. In their songs, they praised freedom and love as if the two were inseparable. They tossed roses to soldiers and kissed their enemies, as if love had never caused a war.

When Maxim and Gala reached adulthood, this idyll was at its peak. For years, they had observed freedom weaving around them, fantasizing about the party that was going on everywhere, like children lying in bed listening to the music and laughter downstairs. When each of them, separately, was finally big enough to join the conga line, it turned out that it came easier to Gala than to Maxim. She shot out of her father's embrace like a piece of soap from a wet fist. His strict upbringing produced exactly the effect he had intended when, to her astonishment, she discovered that her contemporaries saw the provocative attitude and impregnable erudition that had always been her defense against him as overwhelming and charming. She slipped effortlessly into student life and breathed deeply of the recognition and freedom she had so long lacked, two qualities that, for her, would always remain irretrievably linked.

Maxim had never really missed freedom. He was born in a big house, the only child of frightened parents whose lives had been laid waste by the war.

After their meeting, his father and mother agreed that happiness and Holland were incompatible. They swapped the country where war had devastated their lives for Italy, and married in St. Peter's. The cities of their dreams were pale green, watery blue, pink; in the photo album, Maxim's mother colored in the black-and-white life of Naples, Locarno, Rome, and Florence with Ecoline ink. Things couldn't have been more beautiful. One photo shows her beaming, leaning out the window of Pensione Gasser in the Via San Nicolò da Tolentino, just behind the Piazza Barberini. Triumphant, she holds up a hand. In the setting sun, it casts a long shadow on the Roman wall, visible as a gigantic thumbs-up.

"That," she always told Maxim, "was the moment we knew you were on your way."

Soon after, winter won out over the wall heater. The parents had to think of their child. They went home and learned they were right.

Back in Holland, they shut themselves up in the house. In the hope of sparing Maxim their pain, they seldom took him out and only rarely invited people in, though other children almost never appeared. His father died young; his mother went out in the daytime, to earn a living; and Maxim had the house to himself. Isolated in the enormous attic, he constructed his own image of others and the world in which they lived. For a long time, this satisfied him. The possibilities of his own inner world seemed boundless, and that was why he took this for freedom. It was only much later that he realized that the real party was outside. When he threw open the shutters, he was so shocked by how violently real freedom attacked his imagined freedom that he recoiled and tried after all to creep away into his fantasies.

Despite all the students' claims, they still valued the collective above the individual, in a way you otherwise find only in isolated mountain villages. Among them, Maxim's behavior stood out as much as Gala's, though he encountered incomprehension where she reaped admiration. If the others had been less self-obsessed, they could have easily coaxed him into their world. But they shrugged him off, announcing loudly that it was each individual's duty to develop as an individual, regardless of how much lonely despondency might result.

Just when Maxim was about to commit himself permanently to this peculiar path, his eyes met Gala's. She had always been kept on a tight rein, so she seemed free of all constraint; he, who had never been held back, despaired as to whether he'd ever dare to make a move.

"To flit from place to place! What a joy it is to move," she said at that moment. "I would give my life for a night like this. To move!" And in these words, the two extremes recognized each other.

. . .

On the bed in their room in Parioli, Gala confides to Maxim the details of how she gave herself to Snaporaz: from the emotions that overwhelmed her when she felt the old man's desire to the contractions of her lower body around his fingers. She laughs like a naughty child, shaking her head, blushing and gasping for breath, when she realizes that something she'd thought was impossible really has happened. A moment later, she shrugs off the realization, giggling at her own shamelessness. And all the while, she seeks reassurance in Maxim's eyes, always wanting to know exactly what was right or wrong.

Maxim tells her everything is fine, though he can hardly take it all in. He struggles against a sorrow he can't explain as his jealousy wrestles with his awe. This recklessness is precisely what he's always admired in her, the thing he's tried to emulate, which gave him the courage to face the world. How can he reproach her now for the very thing he's always encouraged? Isn't this what he's always aspired to? He is so preoccupied with himself that he can't hear what she's really asking.

"See?" he says after a while. "We can't keep secrets from each other."

"No," Gala says, and decides not to upset him by recounting her meeting with Gianni.

Lightweight

People think that a man who loves more than one woman must divide his love between them. As if it's a bottle that can fill only a certain number of glasses. The opposite is true. Love simply doubles itself. And again. And yet again. And every time there turns out to be enough for everyone. It's a miraculous multiplication. But that's the way it is with miracles: you don't believe it unless you see it yourself.

One of the plans I peddled for years without interesting a single producer was for a film about a polygamist. Gérard Philipe in the lead. He's constantly running back and forth between the families he has to support. Eleven, twelve, thirteen . . . He tries to cut back, but he can't escape it. The more love he gives, the more he receives. Because that's just the way life is. And the more love he receives, the more he can return. And sure enough, soon there's enough for yet another family. So why not start a new one? He loves them all equally, and there's still enough love to go around. He drinks of love as the sea consumes water, from all sides, all the while pouring it back into the rivers. Finally, his confessor officially declares that it is a miracle of charity. The whole thing comes out when it's reported in the *Osservatore Romano,* but the women forgive him, because none of them has any cause for complaint. In the final scene, the poor man ascends to heaven before the assembled ecumenical council, lifted upon the hot air from the kisses blown to him by his lovers.

. . .

I call Gala first thing the next morning to discuss the film. We start seeing each other every day. She comes to my office or I pick her up. We have lunch. We laugh. Mostly that: we laugh for hours on end and then kiss like children who've been playing together and have to go home for dinner. *"Ciao, Gala Galla! Gallalina, ciao!"* I call after her, because she has made my life so light, waving both arms above my head, and when she's almost out of sight, I jump into the air a couple more times to see her that little bit longer.

We don't make love during those first weeks. We both want to, but I don't have the nerve. How often has my interest in a woman started to wane after doing the deed? Almost always. Giving in is the surest cure for adultery. Of course, every minute I'm with her I'm on the verge, but fear restrains me. Everything will be over if I stumble. I shall never have another new love. And so we kiss, innocently, granting our love the time to gather strength. If I lose Gala, then I'll have lost everything.

Every adulterous episode in my life was followed by profound calm and intense desire to be faithful to Gelsomina. My old love would flare up, burning like a wound desperate to heal as quickly as possible. I used to think that guilt was the reason for this increased intimacy. Or was it gratitude for the memories I retrieved? It may even have been relief, like that of a tearful schoolboy coming down from the mountains after his first mission with the partisans and making out his village in the first light of dawn. But it's none of these. It's not even faithfulness. It's simply weariness, temporarily sated by adultery. Surrendering to something sure. Part of me, secretly, longs to return to that certainty at once, just as in the night before battle a recruit in the trenches considers fleeing homeward. He doesn't do it, because he considers courage more important than survival. In the end, in my life, that's how I've pursued all my adulterous encounters.

Our restraint becomes unsustainable by springtime. Unnoticed, love has besieged us, and Gala and I feel it edging closer with each passing hour.

I pick her up one day at the end of May. The moment she gets into the car, we burst into laughter, because it can only be a matter of hours before the mounting pressure forces us to rip the clothes off each other's bodies. I drive straight to the Appia and park at Cecilia Metella's tomb. We keep up the charade a little longer, walking at least a kilometer hand in hand, me lugging the picnic basket, her wobbling down the ancient cobblestones on high heels. Finally, between the tombs of Marcus Servilius and Seneca, we head into the field. For the first time in my life, I love someone because there really is no other option left. Then we eat and drink and start over again from the beginning. At last I take the napkin she's used to dry her lips and draw a caricature of the two of us: me pursuing her, aroused to priapic proportions, she already casting off clothes in preparation. "Phew, finally!" she shouts.

If I could only be like Marcello! He follows his heart. If I ask him about his conscience, he shrugs, answering that each of us is responsible for his own life. Unfortunately, I don't believe this. Quite the opposite. In love, each is responsible for the life of the other.

Throughout the spring and summer, Maxim seldom crosses my path. He holds back and I wait in the car to avoid bumping into him. But when I pick up Gala and she opens the door of the villa, I sense him waiting in the shadowy hallway. I imagine him before our meetings: picking out her clothes, ironing them, laying them out for her. She is nervous about seeing me and he says something to reassure her right before I arrive. On two separate occasions, I even see his hand give her bottom an encouraging slap, as if spurring a horse on before a hurdle.

He loves her too, but he can't be a man for her in the Italian sense of the word. In this country, a man who doesn't want to possess his woman fully can't count on much sympathy. Every once in a while, I bring the conversation around to their friendship, usually because I'm jealous and want her to bend over backward to assure me that it can't compare to her feelings for me, but sometimes because I really do want to understand how people can become so completely one that they let each other go.

The second weekend of July, I decide to take Gala to Rimini. I feel the need for her to see where I come from. She needs to know where I played and loved, and I want to introduce her to those of my childhood friends who are still alive. I only wanted my previous mistresses to love the man I've become, but it's important for me that Gala love the boy I was as well. It's too hot to travel in the daytime, so we arrange to eat at Mario's on Friday afternoon before taking advantage of the cool evening to drive to Pennabilli, where we can spend the night at my friend Tonino's.

We've just taken our seats when Mario comes to tell us that a young man wishes to speak to Gala. It's Maxim. Out of politeness, I invite him to join us, but he refuses to sit down. He talks to Gala in their own language, but I understand that the small package he gives her contains the pills she needs and has once again forgotten. Is it any wonder I can't stand him? I don't like dogs or missionaries who work with lepers either. Why don't they ever think about other people? I'm only human. That much dedication makes me feel small but aggressive. Something about martyrs arouses my contempt. Maybe Maxim annoys me because he's so horribly reminiscent of Gelsomina. Is he religious as well? I wonder. I wouldn't have felt more uncomfortable if she herself had appeared at our table. Thank God, the saint of the pillboxes retreats again without further ado.

"Do you know what it is, more than anything else?" Gala sighs, watching him with eyes overflowing with love. "Maxim and I are too alike to be a good couple."

I can't compare my love for Gala to any of my previous infatuations, except with the first, the love of my life, Gelsomina. Each gesture, each touch of the one recalls the caress of the other. I don't think this has anything to do with Gala. I don't believe that her love for me is any different from the love the others felt. It has to do with me. Each whispered word resonates with fate, as dramatically as it did that very first time. Then, because I knew that everything was about to begin; now, because I know that this is the end.

"You know what?" she said after that first lunch in Tivoli. "It's raining. No one's under the waterfalls. Let's go swimming."

This will be my last unbridled passion. There cannot possibly be any doubt about that. My last chance to experience the tempestuousness of youth. It exhausts me, this passion of hers, but I do my best, I put on a bold face. And when I finally lay my hand on hers, as subtly as I can, trying to restrain it when I feel its caress beginning its descent from the gray hair on my chest, I do so with a sorrow that tears me apart, and the thought always flits through my mind: Ah, shall I let her have her way with me, because who could ask for a more beautiful death? But I stop her and tell her she's wearing me out. She smiles, kisses one of my nipples, and lays her head against mine.

"Of course!" I exclaim. "Galla, come on, it's cold, wet autumn weather, let's take off our clothes!" It's astounding to do what you want without a second thought, surrendering completely. That's what I want. No shame. Together you're so much stronger than anyone else, because no amount of reasoning can hold you back. That is what I am granted one last time.

That's my only excuse.

One day, as we lie beside each other after making love, she suddenly bends over to kiss me on the forehead.

"You've always been a little boy!" she whispers.

I bury my face between her breasts, hanging full and heavy. I kiss them, bite them, put my lips on them and blow as if I've got hold of a tuba. Like an idiot, I make all those mad noises so that she won't see that I can't hold back my tears. My immaturity is my joy and my curse. My pride and my downfall. The treasure I draw on, my daily source of the will to live. I stride forth like a child, with the idea that the really important things are just about to begin. But it's also the reason I could never be completely one with Gelsomina. She was like me, irresponsibly maladjusted to life. We saw that in one another and played together until the day she realized that the thing we'd always expected would never come. From then on, she didn't need a playmate. She needed a man. Especially after the loss of our daughter. I couldn't be that man for her. Since then, we still play the game, but she plays it like a parent with a child: Gelsomina puts on a show of false naïveté, seeing through my every move and letting me win. I accept my victory, but it gives me no pleasure because I feel that her love is so much greater. For her, winning is not as important as seeing me happy.

I would take it as a reproach from Gelsomina, but when Gala calls me a little boy, I think she means it as a compliment.

It's not for nothing that so many women compare their husbands to worms. Each new love splits a man in two. Both halves live on separately. Again and again they strengthen and grow to their full length. Love revitalizes by dividing. For me, this is the most important temptation, the most honest justification, perhaps even the only reason, for adultery.

I may well be as insignificant as a worm, but despite the Church and public morality, I feel very clearly that I am not failing either of my loves. To the contrary, the one animates the other. It must be human nature, because why should I be different from anyone else in this regard? I only know that I can lead different lives and keep them separate, easily, and with genuine and complete commitment.

And then suddenly this: early in August, Gelsomina has to fly to Taormina to open a retrospective of her films. I drop her off at Fiumicino and am standing on Gala's doorstep before my wife has left the ground. I throw open the door, race down the stairs two at a time, and we're in bed before I feel an unexpected pang and start to cry. The thought of lying in someone else's arms while Gelsomina is hanging in midair is too much. I can't take it. What if she came crashing down?

"If the heavens open for God's wrath to descend upon someone," Gala laughs to reassure me, "it'll be you, not her. She's innocent."

Gala's young. How much has she loved? How could she realize that even for Him, it would be exceptionally merciful to singe me with a divine thunderbolt? It would be much more devastating to take Gelsomina and leave me to live on without her.

You can only be sure you really love someone when the death of your lover is more terrifying than your own.

But the moments you realize how precious such unconditional love is are remarkably rare. Perhaps it would be too much of a burden for the soul to be reminded, day in, day out, of how fragile the thing is that has been entrusted to it. It forgets its value. It starts to appropriate the happiness it's been granted. Like a boy who has bought his first *motorino* on borrowed money and forgets, after just a couple of rides, that it's not really his. He does a wheelie in the schoolyard to impress the convent-school girls. As soon as it's reached the peak, the heart gets used to it, and starts to look around for new challenges.

. . .

Soon after Gelsomina's return from Sicily, I receive news from my producer that not a single insurer is prepared to accept her for the duration of the film. They all consider it too great a risk that my wife won't make it to the last day of shooting. I make an enormous scene in vain, ranting and raving into twenty phones, but when they offer to show me the conclusions of the medical experts, I refuse. I have absolutely no desire to know what life has in store. I just want to live it to the full.

I don't say a word to Gelsomina, but the first chance I get I pour my heart out to Gala. Before I've said a word, she's already guessed, as if miraculously, what it's about. Her sensitivity moves me so much that I make up an excuse, run off without any further explanation, and don't get back in touch with her for days. I can't. If I spoke the truth in her presence, I might catch a few snatches of it myself.

Instead, I don't let Gelsomina out of my sight. We flee to Venice for a few days and make love all night as if we're twenty. I give her gifts and fuss over her as if there's something to celebrate. One night, I invite all kinds of old friends I know she likes. I watch her laughing all evening and dance with her every time the band plays. It's to the rhythm of a rumba that she says, very sweetly, "That's enough now. I've got the idea."

She dances away and when we come back together I don't dare ask what she meant, and she's relieved not to have to explain. The next morning, we pack our bags.

My producer suggests giving Gelsomina's part to another actress. I refuse, even though it means that our film will almost certainly never be made. That day, I call the Banco Ambrosiano and agree to make a commercial for them. In search of ideas, I open the book where I record my dreams. I can't help but notice how light and cheerful they've been recently.

My love for Gala makes me feel so much younger—sometimes we spend hours sitting on the sand between the deck chairs from which my mother and her friends discussed the lifeguard's thighs and the price of purslane—at the same time it makes me feel older, about 123.

For years now, I've been overcome by immense sorrow every time I see a beautiful young woman. For two reasons. One: I want her, followed immediately by two: what for, actually?

In itself, there's something depressing about the unbridled male attraction to any woman who walks by. The deed must be done, you feel, and preferably as soon as possible, but you don't actually know why. It's an animal compulsion, a strategy to ensure the survival of the species. The instinct's most melancholy form is an old man's forced reaction to the full breasts and broad hips of a woman like Gala. Why? Surely it's no longer the urge to propagate his creaking bones? Heaven forbid. In the elderly far more than in the young, this desire is simply atavistic. His time has passed, yet he still wants to plant his seed in those hips, no matter how much his mind groans. This sorrow now accompanies my every desire for a woman. Just for a moment. The next instant fills me with idiotic abandon.

If I am a worm, let me at least have as much pleasure as imaginable. Because I now have the love of my life *and* someone to strengthen inside me the love for my own life.

Ladybug

"People have less and less imagination," the monsignor says. "It's emptying out of them like air from a leaky tire." At his desk, in his vestments, he's flicking through my drawings and ideas. Every once in a while, he picks one out and emits a wistful sigh. "With your films, you are one of the last holdouts against the human desire to rationalize."

"Ah, your reverence," I reply, "I might as well make films opposing gravity."

The head office of the Banco Ambrosiano is at the rear of the Vatican, between St. Peter's Station and the Via Duodo. From the advertising department window, I gaze over the Leonine Wall and see the sunlight shining on a fountain in the Papal Gardens. Below us, a train full of pilgrims sings at the tops of their voices to let the pope know they're on their way.

On the pages before us, I've sketched out some twenty dreams, the last few weeks' bizarre nocturnal inspiration. Why should I do things differently for a commercial rather than a feature film? I tell the monsignor that instead of a single ad, I want to make a short series for his bank. In each film, Paolo Villagio will play me. He's a slightly anxious, corpulent comedian I've often worked with. Each ad will consist of one of my foolish nightmares and end when Villagio awakes with a bang to discover that he's fallen out of bed. While he lies on the floor, trying to untangle himself from the sheets, a woman's voice will sound from downstairs. "You should've listened to me," she snaps. "If you'd taken your money to the Banco Ambrosiano like I told you to, the saints and the angels would be watching over it and you could get a decent night's sleep!"

The monsignor nods. He's not impressed, but he's seen stranger miracles and thinks I might just pull it off.

"Let's make *one* to start off with. Then we'll see." The monsignor slides the sketches back to me. "Choose one. You have carte blanche."

Astonished to have found such an accommodating Jesuit, I gather it all up, including the fat prostitutes and the sketch of a masturbating Romulus suckling at the teats of the wolf.

"But Reverend Father," I say, standing at the door with my folder under my arm, "why on earth did you ask me? All my life I've made fun of the Church. I've shown topless nuns and priests on roller skates. I dressed them in absurd robes and pushed them up onto the catwalk. I've done nothing but sin my whole life long, and I don't believe in anything."

"You've always claimed that dreams seem more real than reality."

I can't deny it.

"Our request comes from His Holiness himself," explains the monsignor. "How do you think we can convince people that God exists if they can no longer recognize truth in the improbable? You, Snaporaz, are our last hope. Imagination is the only erogenous zone that the Faith applauds."

Gala screams when she sees Gianni. This only seems to entertain him. He was simply sitting in the corner, in an armchair, when she entered the room in Parioli, but in her blind spot. He didn't speak. And since she wasn't expecting anyone, Gala closed the door behind her, kicked off her clothes, and climbed into the shower without noticing him.

She tries to regain her composure as she watches him approach. It's only two blows, but they're so hard that she loses her balance and bangs the back of her head against the tiles. Gianni knows where to hit a woman without leaving bruises that might compromise her market value.

"Sicily is growing impatient."

He looks down on the naked woman, turns off the hot tap, and walks away as if he had lost all interest.

Soon afterward, Geppi comes in. She finds Gala lying on the tiles, shivering under the cold water. She turns off the tap, wraps a towel around her, and rubs her hair dry.

"I'm sorry," she mumbles. "I'm so sorry."

I do feel that Gala's upset, but she won't admit it.

"But what is it, my Gallinella?" I ask several times that evening, struck by the distant look in her eyes and her forced smile. After dinner, I lure her into the Palazzo del Freddo and have them pile a banana boat high with scoops of all the fruit flavors. Gelato never fails to console, and sure enough, by the time she reaches mandarin, her eyes close with pleasure. Her will power is back when she opens them again.

"It can't go on like this," she says. I immediately assume she is referring to our love and get a sinking feeling in the pit of my stomach. I automatically think that the moment I've come to dread more with every passing day has arrived: that final shot, when the last love raises her hand and walks offscreen with a simple *"Ciao."* Words fail me and I can't look her in the eye. I concentrate on the ice cream, but the little scoops keep rolling off my long silver spoon before I can get them to my mouth.

Then, thank God, she continues. "I have to get away from Parioli. There's no other solution. As quickly as possible, but don't ask me why."

The apartment is no more than a convent cell hidden at the back of the church, squeezed between the transept and the roof above the altar. It winds around two buttresses, splitting the living space over three levels. One has room for a bed, one for a desk, and between the two is an awkward corner with a simple chair next to a side table with a telephone on it. Fortunately, it has a small terrace, closed off on one side by the colorful stained glass above the holy of holies, a large window depicting the Madonna and Child. The terrace looks out on a secluded courtyard with a gargoyle and the tall windows of the Teatro Argentina dressing rooms. On this warm afternoon, they're open. Several ballerinas are sitting at a row of mirrors, twisting their long hair into buns beneath the glare of the makeup lights.

Meanwhile, the cagey priest who is showing me all this is inspecting the cardinal's seal on my letter of introduction. The Vatican moves in mysterious ways. Nowadays, the Church's greatest miracles are reserved for those with the right contacts. The monsignor is a man of the world. When I explained matters to him, he immediately understood their importance and, with a smile confirming the open secret that celibacy is taken much more seriously outside the Vatican than within its walls, gave me this address. The church stands in the middle of the old Campo Marzio, its foundations resting on the Curia Pompei. It is one of the holy places that is almost forgotten amid the frantic city's traffic. The shepherd of this parish recognized me immediately, and appears to take a less frivolous view of my work than his superiors. He nonetheless shows me around, just as the monsignor's letter requests, and when I suggest a princely rent and immediately slip a generous donation toward the restoration of the confessionals into the collection box, the steely cast falls from his face, as if he's suddenly aware of the challenge before him. In the twilight of his life, hope dawns, that he might yet convert a real sinner. Wrapping his hands around mine, he slips me the key without so much as mentioning a lease, telling me that from now on his congregation would be honored to welcome me to Sunday-morning Mass.

I return with Gala that same evening. The front door is halfway up a stone spiral staircase. It is low. She has to bend to enter. Gala can hardly believe it and I am delighted by her astonishment. She throws her arms around my neck and for the first time since the war I make love on a bare floor, which my knees and back will remind me of for days to come. Immediately afterward, her doubts set in: she doesn't want me to think she's rewarding my efforts with her love. I have no way of knowing why she's making such a fuss and brush her reservations aside. Downcast, she sits on the floor of her new apartment, tugging her clothes on as quickly as possible. I'm getting used to her mood swings: she acts so impulsively, shocking herself so much in the process, that she forgets everything else around her. She can freeze in the middle of a busy street, hands in her hair, running through all the possible consequences of her actions. Horns blare, cars dart past on every side, but she's paralyzed with horror, and I have to try to drag her to the sidewalk. At such moments she drops everything, sometimes literally, because her fingers spread as if to fend off a suddenly looming disaster.

As if she's due some punishment and someone's about to give it. I've seen this brand of seductive impotence in cartoons, but never before witnessed it in a living creature. The effect is irresistible: both funny and touchingly foolish, like a comedian's double take, when something the whole audience long since realized slowly dawns on the performer. But Gala's delayed hesitation is not an act. I recognize it. It's the same eternal doubt that always overtakes my pleasure after the initial sprint. It doesn't show with me, but Gala's panic is so hopelessly direct that it freezes the laughter on your lips. All you want to do is take her in your arms and rock her.

No matter how desperate she is to escape Parioli, she'd rather stay there than accept this little bolt-hole as a gift from me. I assure her that the rent really is quite modest, mention a third of the actual amount, and tell her she can repay me as soon as she can afford it. She relaxes, takes my hand, and has a closer look at her new accommodations. We step out onto the terrace. The lights burning inside the church shine through the stained glass to throw colorful illuminations on the terrace.

"Oh God," she says suddenly, looking at me in horror. "Now you must think I'm ungrateful."

"Why would he think that?" says Maxim. "He's the one who should be grateful."

"All the trouble he's gone to . . . and I don't even have the grace to accept it without grumbling."

Gala walks into the bathroom in Parioli for the last time.

"You let him fuck you, didn't you?" Maxim calls. "Take it from me, the man is satisfied."

He's folded and packed her clothes. Then he fills her toiletries bag, lays it on top of the clothes, and zips up her bag.

"But it's still a mystery to me why you want to get away from here so suddenly." He pulls his own clothes out of the wardrobe and starts to fold them as well.

"The rent is too much for me."

"Fortunately, we can always find our way around that." He laughs.

"I said, 'It's too much for *me*,' " Gala shouts, louder.

Maxim pulls his suitcase out from under the bed.

"Oh well," he says, "it *is* a rat's nest, but I've been very happy here with you."

"Yes," she says warmly, "I've been happy with you too." A little later, she says, "I'll miss that terribly."

He has just picked up a pile of shirts.

"You'll miss it?" he asks. "What do you mean?" But as he stuffs his clothes into his suitcase, her meaning sinks in: she's moving alone. She says something else, but his surging grief drowns it out.

Then Gala flushes the toilet. He grabs the bag and tries to shove it back under the bed before she comes in, but now that it's full it won't slide so easily. She catches him.

"But, sweetheart," she says, laying a hand on the back of his neck. "Surely you didn't think . . ."

"Of course not," he says in a futile lie.

Giacomo, who is working with me on the sets for my commercial, measures Gala's convent cell and turns my sketches into technical drawings that I can take to scenery. It's not the first time the men there have done a little work on the side fixing up one of my love nests, but I can tell from the surprise on their faces that it's been quite a while, and they set to work with a certain degree of admiration. Mirrors are the essence of my plan to make everything seem deeper and wider, and the utmost attention is paid to the color and quality of the fabrics. The floor is tiled according to a pattern from the Domus Aurea and the walls are marbled in sections. The props department provides a sofa that dates back to the feast in my adaptation of Apuleius, and the artists of Cinecittà use cushions and mattresses to transform it into a three-quarter bed. I'll have to hang on to her to avoid ending up on the floor, but there's no room for anything bigger. They also design a desk that fits perfectly into a corner, leaving enough space for a minute dining table. Finally, they gild the telephone chair and upholster it with a thick layer of purple velvet. A trompe l'oeil based on Boromini's colonnade in the Palazzo Spada is painted on the blank wall of the terrace, so that at first glance it looks twice as deep as it is. It's all done as carefully as my film sets and within three days these deceptions have transformed the cell into a mini boudoir. Finally, I have spotlights mounted outside so that, at the press of a button, a suggestion of moonlight shining through leaves can be achieved. I'm not saying it's tasteful, but it is atmospheric.

The work is almost complete when Gelsomina strolls in during my final discussion with the carpenter. She looks at the drawings spread out on the table.

"What's that going to be, a doll's film?" she asks, referring to the dimensions of the rooms that are almost bursting out of the church.

The carpenter lends me a hand by pretending that it's just a suggestion for the commercial, when in fact I'm already halfway done with it, and I explain, most plausibly, that the Banco Ambrosiano budget simply doesn't stretch to large sets.

"The whole film is set in a cellar," I explain. "I'm dreaming I'm in a cell."

"Finally a dream that might come true," she teases. "But I can't believe it will be solitary confinement!" She says it with her sweetest smile, which could mean anything to bystanders, giving me a hard pinch on the cheek.

"By the way," she calls on her way out, as if it just popped into her mind, "the Academy in Los Angeles wants a definitive answer on that Oscar. I told them we're thrilled and will absolutely be there. That's all right with you, isn't it?"

The thought makes me ill. She knows that. I don't like traveling. My arthritis acts up. I suffer fits of dizziness. But Gelsomina doesn't wait for an answer. I'm too guilty to refuse her anything.

The first time Maxim enters Gala's new apartment, she's sitting on the chair next to the telephone. She's only been living there for a day and a half. He walks around. If he's impressed, he manages not to let on.

"It's ideal," he says. His voice is so cold it might as well be a reproach, but Gala seizes it like a drowning man grabbing a buoy.

"Really?" she asks. "So you think I've done the right thing?"

He suppresses his annoyance.

"Darling, it couldn't be better."

He wonders when she got into the habit of needing constant confirmation. Surely it hasn't been that long since they both followed their whims. Absurdities took them by surprise. Outdoing each other and themselves, they grew steadier, more confident. And whenever something threw them off balance, they held on to each other until they could get back on their feet.

With the melancholy surprise of an old man trying to find the fields he played in during the long summers of his childhood or to pick out the course of a stream in the suburbs that have grown up around his village, Maxim's eyes meet her face.

"You think it stinks," she says. "Be honest."

He searches his memory for the last moment he admired her, really admired her, for throwing herself into something that he would have flinched from. There must have been a last time, but he can't remember when it was.

"I miss you."

"But you'll come every day, won't you?" says Gala. "You have to. You must. I need your wise advice. We have to see each other every single day!"

"We won't miss a day. How could we?"

She smiles with relief.

"It's gorgeous here," he goes on. "It's a dream. Who would have thought it a few years ago? Us. Here. You. Snaporaz . . . Me." To snap out of this gloomy train of thought, he jumps up and tries to pull her up off the chair. "Let's go celebrate your new place. Come on, let's go eat somewhere."

She shakes her head.

"He might call."

"Then he'll call back again later."

She doesn't respond.

Maxim goes out and comes back with *pizzette* and wine. During their meal, the phone rings. From fright, Gala spits the mouthful she has just taken into her glass. Her hand is already at the receiver, but she waits. She lets it ring twice. Three times. Four.

"I don't want him thinking I'm sitting by the phone waiting for him to call."

"But you *are* sitting by the phone waiting for him to call."

"I don't want him to get the wrong impression."

The telephone rings for the fifth time. And again.

"Which wrong impression?"

"That I'm available on call."

She lets the phone ring twice more. Then it falls silent. They resume eating.

"I don't understand," Maxim says at last, "if you were already planning not to answer, we could just as well have gone out."

"And how would I have known if he'd called?" she asks, as if it were obvious. When she sees the incomprehension on his face, she brushes aside her embarrassment. "You're a man, you wouldn't understand."

He tries to think whether he's ever failed to understand her before.

"You must be a woman then, I guess," he says with bitter irony. "How strange that we never noticed the difference."

He kisses her on the mouth, as always. Before leaving, he sticks his head around the corner one last time. She hasn't moved from the spot all evening.

Now she's waving to him, a little girl waiting big-eyed next to the lifeguard for her parents to come and fetch her.

Out on the street, Maxim realizes that he could go back to smother her with kisses, but he doesn't.

It only takes him a few days to realize that he misses her more when he's with her than he does when he's alone.

Milky Way

My life is built around the pursuit of my dreams. The last thing I want to do is catch them.

That's why I don't call very often. I was determined to have her, but now that I've got her, I let days go by without even contacting her. All the trouble I took to create a place for us to hide from the city and write our own story, only to balk at the prospect: who could understand that? Her, maybe. Yes, in the end, maybe her. Years later, when she looks back on me, Gala will probably be the only one who understands. Because in this we are one. That's what's so creepy about it. That's what makes our relationship different from every other one I've ever had.

Gala constantly defied her father in order to stir his love. She preferred burning herself in the flames to doing like the others and warming herself with them. For the same reason, he badgered her, harassing her tirelessly with his impossible tasks.

"Pursue an endeavor, live forever," he made her rattle off, "but he who takes the prize, dies."

As soon as I am in danger of getting hold of something, I retreat. I am a coward. Running away is second nature to me.

And this is the only way I can contain the universe between my thumb and index finger. To keep from pulverizing my happiness or letting it slip through my fingers, I keep it floating there.

. . .

People everywhere call themselves my friends, but I hardly have any real friends. There are very few people I'm comfortable with. Two or three. And I don't see them all that often. It's one of the things that used to worry Gelsomina deeply. She doesn't really understand it, but she finally had to accept that I carry everyone who really matters to me with me in my heart. I don't make it easy for people to get to my heart, but once they succeed, I enclose them there forever. Within that isolation, our friendship is perfect. When they seek me out again, I feel warm and grateful, but I have no need of visitors. This feeling, so secure to me, is not always mutual. I find that hard to accept. Some turned their backs on me, unable to tell from my silence how much I loved them. This crushed me every time. And though my mind knows where I failed, it's still impossible for me to feel it. The people I care about are simply closer to me in my thoughts than when they're slurping up chicken soup at my kitchen table.

I think social interaction is just something people use to compensate for their lack of imagination.

For the first few years, Gelsomina persisted in trying to invite friends over, but I was too shy and suspicious and she soon gave up hope. Recently, however, she's taken to turning up now and then with someone new, introducing them to me with a look in her eye like a matchmaker trying one last time to pair off a shriveled old maid. Now that she's ill, she worries about leaving me behind alone. And she's afraid that *my* loneliness will be lonelier than anyone else's.

"You won't hate me for it?" she asked recently, out of the blue. We were at an outdoor café in Frascati. It was a perfect evening. I couldn't bear to have her suddenly explode the little bit of happiness that was left to us. I tried to laugh off the remark, but she wouldn't let it go.

"Promise you'll never blame me when I . . . well, if I deserted you."

"Are you mad?" I exclaimed. "First you tie me hand and foot and then, as soon as I'm totally devoted to you, you're going to dump me?" (All this in a tone that unmistakably meant the opposite.) "That is unforgivable!" When I saw her forcing a smile on my behalf, I immediately addressed her seriously. "Don't worry. You're the light of my life. Wherever you're planning on going, you'll always be shining deep inside me."

But I've never been able to dupe her with empty phrases. She didn't say another word. For a while, we looked over the lake, the headlights of the cars in the mountains rippling over the water. Finally, she shook her head, slowly but firmly.

My friendship fails to match any norm, and my love unfailingly falls short of the way I imagine it. Take my days now: I am in love. She is omnipresent in my mind, that delightful milky way, my Galassia! I discuss my every thought with her, present her my every idea. If they make her smile, I brighten; I feel dejected if she shrugs and try feverishly to think up something new that will impress her. I run everything past her, not just the big things, but also the question of whether to put Unghrese or Parma on my sandwich. I don't decide a single thing without her approval. I simply couldn't, since I exist only by virtue of her attention. Wherever I look, I feel her eyes turning the same way. When I walk, she takes me by the hand. I smell her presence in my every breath and when I exhale I see it ruffling her hair. When I have to speak to someone else and must, ever so briefly, turn my back on her, I feel her as clearly present as if her hand were resting between my shoulder blades. I spend every hour of the day with her.

Then evening comes.

Gelsomina is expecting me at home.

That's when it becomes extremely difficult to reconcile the euphoria I've been feeling with the reality that I haven't seen or spoken to Gala all day. I grab the phone and dial her number to explain that every hour has been dedicated to her and that I *must* see her the next day. Sometimes I find the nerve. More often I don't, and I drive home with Gala stretched out on the hood, waggling a reproachful finger.

This is how we squander weeks of our happiness. Many days find her world confined to the chair beside the telephone. She waits for me to call. When I finally do, she calmly pretends that she hadn't really been expecting me, pleasantly surprised, pleased, ever so briefly, to interrupt her hectic activities to speak to me. She herself never once tries to contact me, which only confirms my doubts. How could I know that this requires supreme will power, and how could I possibly guess at the shenanigans she gets up to trying to track me down? She regularly asks Maxim to dial the number of my office.

"I don't need to talk to him, I just want to know if he's there."

After the first few times, Maxim has learned that resistance is futile. He calls and gets a woman on the line. He makes up an excuse: once he was from *Vogue* and wanted to schedule an interview, another time he asked for material for a BBC documentary.

The high, pinched voice invariably answers, "Signor Snaporaz has left the office," and hangs up.

"See, he *is* there!" Gala exclaims angrily. Her eyes flood with tears, as if silence were more villainous from close by than from a distance.

She's right. That voice is me. I don't have any staff in my city office. She knows that. I answer the phone myself and pretend to be my own secretary. If I don't feel like talking to someone, I say I'm not there. How could I know that it's her? My heart would leap. I'd skip through the room like a little boy. Why doesn't she call herself to let me know that she really does care as much about me as she does in my dreams? Adultery is so much more complicated in practice than in theory.

Thank God, there are days when we do see each other and lap up our happiness, divine hours that prove all our fears unfounded, even if their perfection only feeds our folly in the days to come. How does a fool know that everything is really as perfect as he thinks it is?

And then, suddenly, amid the chaos that is love, I am ambushed by the suspicion that my difficulties in relations with friends and lovers are due not to their incapacity to live up to my image of them, but to my failure to measure up to the image of myself I present to others.

The night before I leave for Hollywood, something strange happens. Gala and I are eating at La Cesarina in the Via Sicilia. It has been a jovial evening. We are going to be far apart for a few days, but I promise to call as often as I can, and tell her that, with the appropriate discretion, of course, she can call me too. I take a card and write down the number of the Beverly Hilton. When I'm about to hand it to her, I see that she's turned as pale as a ghost and is staring horror-stricken at someone behind me. I turn around to see a fellow standing by the cloakroom. He's no oil painting, that's for sure. He waves.

"Who's that?" I ask, but drop it when I see the pained look on her face. We talk some more, but less than five minutes later she says she has to powder her nose. Her excuse is so transparent, it's charming.

She heads off to the toilets and I see the fellow follow her. He is too ugly to be her lover and too stupid to be dangerous, so I bear with her for a few minutes and gesture to Cesarina to bring me another bottle of wine.

That fellow is Gianni, of course, but at that moment I don't have the slightest inkling of his existence. Right after she moved, he traced her address by simply following Maxim on his daily pilgrimage. Then, for a long time, he left her in the delusion that she'd gotten rid of him.

"Sometimes you have to let a woman ripen," he informed Dr. Pontorax in Catania, not without a certain pride in the method he had developed over the years, "like leaving wine in the cellar to age until it's ready to drink."

Not long before, Gianni had called Gala. The way she answered betrayed that she was in love, a fortuitous circumstance he could use to increase her willingness. She hung up the moment he said his name. He knew that all he needed to do was to appear when she was in my company.

Gianni opens the door of the women's bathroom.

Gala is standing in front of the mirror.

He kicks open the doors of the cubicles to make sure there aren't any eavesdroppers. Then he blocks the entrance with a garbage can.

He has respect for his prey. Imperturbably, she puts on her lipstick, licks her teeth, and wipes a small smudge off a front tooth. As if alone, she starts combing her hair, a superior smile playing on her lips. He knows how to deal with that. He likes a challenge.

When Gala comes back to the table, I can't tell what's happened. She's excited about the upcoming Oscar presentation and promises to watch it live. I tell her how much I'm dreading it. Of course, she's noticed the slight deterioration in my health of late. I bluff to friends that the long, wild nights with Gala are taking their toll, but in these last few weeks we've actually spent more time lovingly holding hands than rolling ardently through the grass. I think something's pinched in my back and is cutting off the blood supply. Whatever it is, Gala is no more impressed than Gelsomina and thinks I should stop worrying about it, not just for my sake but for Gelsomina's. We go to her apartment and make love to say goodbye.

. . .

That night, when I crawl into bed beside Gelsomina, she ascribes my irritability to my aversion to our trip. I mutter something and turn my back. Why am I so much nicer to my wife after a whole day of being adulterous in my thoughts than after the one hour in which I actually give in?

The next day, around the time we're taking off from Fiumicino, Maxim's eyes are opened once and for all. It's the weekend before his first day of shooting. He has packed his bag and awaits the summons to the set near Cortina d'Ampezzo. He knows his lines by heart. He's rehearsing one of the key scenes, checking his slalom in the mirror, when the call comes from Cinecittà. It's the assistant of an assistant. He's terribly sorry, but the American investors have found a cheaper location in Romania. Maxim calmly answers that he doesn't mind the extra traveling.

"No," laughs the voice, "you don't get it. We're only taking the star. We'll get the rest from Romanian casting."

That evening, Maxim climbs the high steps to the Ara Coeli. The square in front of the church is tiny, but the whole city is at your feet. He and Gala have often come here to escape the traffic, enjoy the glow of the sunset, and sit close together, waiting for the first stars to appear over the city.

This time, he has come alone. He called her and told her his news. She sounded genuinely upset, but she was impatient as well. She wanted to comfort him, but couldn't wait to get off the phone. He knew why, and that only made him sadder.

"Come straight over," she said in a caring voice. "Venom must be drowned in wine! We'll eat and dance!"

He turned down her offer, and though she heard the catch in his voice, she didn't suspect that she could be its cause, telling herself that he was mourning the death of a career that was stillborn. She was incapable of seeing herself as pitiable. After all, she was at her peak. One of the most famous men in the world, a man who could have any woman he wanted, longed for no one but her! These might be the most perfect months of her life. Even if she spent most of her time holed up at home she was alive inside as never before.

"Or should I come over to you?" she finally asked, feeling that a happiness as great as hers carried certain obligations. But her question was so hushed and reluctant that Maxim pretended not to hear. She was glad when he hung up, because Snaporaz might be trying to get through to tell her that he'd arrived safely. If the line was busy, he might think she was trying to reach him.

Maxim has given Gala a good shaking. He has cried for her and with her. He's pitied her and told her off. He has listened to her and consoled her, but he's also come out and told her that she's definitely not the only broad Snaporaz has got filed away somewhere in the city for his enjoyment. He's shouted that the man is a son of a bitch and that she deserves better. But seeing her sorrow after the director has once again failed to contact her, he's defended him with equal ferocity and concocted explanations for his silence, just to comfort her. Before each meeting between Gala and Snaporaz, he has tried to calm her nerves. He's fetched vodka when she asked for it and bought condoms even though he was sure that she would never dare get them out. When she opened the door of her church to go out, he insisted on checking her makeup. He gave her that encouraging pat on the bottom or sometimes a kiss, which she accepted as greedily as a pearl diver takes one last breath before the plunge. Then she walked out beaming, quickly closing the door behind her, to throw her arms around Snaporaz's neck. Meanwhile, Maxim was shooting upstairs to the bell tower, four steps at a time, so that he could look out from the church roof and see the car squeeze through the narrow streets along the San Andrea delle Valle before disappearing in the traffic on the Corso Vittorio Emanuele. More than anything else, Maxim was gratified to know that Gala was finally happy, and in moments like these he hardly stopped to wonder why that happiness also made him sad.

He only gave in to his sorrow once she came home and returned to her position beside the phone. He did everything he could. He invented excuses to lure her out and even dragged her by the arm. In all those weeks, he only once succeeded in getting her to go out for a cappuccino at the corner bar. She knocked it back and was so anxious to leave that he pretended he'd forgotten another appointment. She kissed him gratefully, snatched her bag from the bar, and raced back to her cell as fast as her high heels and the double-S curvature of her back would let her.

After that, Maxim resigned himself to her lunacy. For a long time, he came more often, so that they could see each other for a few hours, at least twice a day. They discussed virtually nothing but Snaporaz, but he put up with it. He sometimes brought a book to read to her, as if she were sick in bed, but her thoughts were with her lover, so Maxim finally had to settle for reading on her terrace by himself.

He finally realized that he'd come to accept this bizarre situation as normal. The moment came when one of the actresses behind the windows of the theater across the courtyard began her singing exercises. Maxim, startled, looked up from the story he was completely absorbed in. For a second, maybe less, he didn't know where he was. He immediately recognized the colors the stained glass cast on his page, but he couldn't say whether Gala was at home or out somewhere with Snaporaz. He went to check. As always, she was sitting next to the phone. On her lap, she held a few sketches the great man had made of her. She lovingly ran her fingers over them, though Maxim had told her to be careful because a collector would pay good money for them. When he stuck his head around the corner, she greeted him with a broad smile. Maxim sat down and they chatted a little. Once again, they looked at the drawings; once again, Maxim told her how clear it was that she was tremendously important to Snaporaz. It was still terribly difficult to conceal his concern. He'd been with her for an hour and a half, yet was completely alone. He'd evidently walked in without being infuriated by seeing a woman like Gala waiting by the phone. To the contrary, he'd walked right past, as if she were a lavatory attendant with a coin-filled saucer, never stopping to think about how someone like that slowly fades, day by day, into the background.

At that moment, Maxim realized he'd lost the battle for Gala. Snaporaz had encircled her just as the Romans had done it since time immemorial: in rings that squeezed tighter every day, so that the besieged city hardly noticed that its territory was constantly shrinking, or that its citizens were being pressed ever closer together. At last, they gave in, not to external violence but to pressure from within.

Now Maxim withdraws to spare himself further injury. He'll be present to Gala when she needs him, he decides, but he can no longer expect anything from her.

. . .

The same cannot be said of Gianni. He has invested in her. This weekend, she's going to pay. To get rid of him, that's what she promised in the La Cesarina toilet: "As soon as Snaporaz is out of the country." He had come up from behind her and held her face so tightly that her words were almost impossible to understand. He made her repeat it.

"As soon as he's out of the country, I'll do what you want." She was prepared to promise him anything as long as Gianni disappeared without mentioning it to Snaporaz. "I'll do Sicily one last time, all right, one last time, damn you!" Then she sank her teeth into his hand and kicked with her high heels until he let go. She panted like a wild animal, bending forward with her hands on the sink. "One last time and then we're even!"

Tonight, he enters unannounced. Gala is on her terrace listening to the music coming from deep within the theater: a performance of *La Fanciulla del West*. She doesn't know the story of Puccini's opera and can only make out snatches of the libretto, but she enjoys the passion in the distant notes that resound so loudly in the empty courtyard that they sometimes make the glass in the church window shake in their leaden frames.

"Che faranno i vecchi miei
là lontano, là lontano,
che faranno . . . ?"

It takes a while before she notices another sound she can't place. Someone is fumbling at the door. She briefly imagines it's Snaporaz, but he's on the other side of the world. Before she knows it, Gianni is standing right there. Gala feels an urgent wave of panic, which she suppresses. She knew he'd make her keep her promise, but she had no idea that he knew where she lived, let alone that he'd found a key.

Determined to maintain her dignity, she walks inside to pack for the trip.

"That can wait," he says, pushing her back onto the terrace. She backs up until he's pressing her up against the church window. He kisses her on the neck. She gasps for breath. He kisses her on the mouth. He pulls her dress up and her underpants down. He grabs her wrists and spreads her arms against the enormous stained-glass window. He'll deliver her tomorrow; today he's sampling the merchandise.

"Il mio cane dopo tanto,
il mio cane mi ravviserà?"

Under the pressure of the bodies, the colored panes groan in their grooves. One breaks. Gala feels splinters. They fall on her bared shoulder, fine as sugar crystals. Rather than looking at the man who is having his way with her, she looks up. Despite the city lights, the stars are shining.

Close by, on the Ara Coeli, Maxim sees them too. They stretch in a long winding line from the Gianicolo to the Aventine. He was on his back looking up at them until it got too cold. He walks down the stairs on his way home. He passes the Largo Argentina. He passes the theater and turns into Gala's street. He wonders if she's lonely with Snaporaz on his way to the States. Then he does something he could never have imagined until recently, walking past her church without even ringing the bell.

It's after one by the time he goes to bed. He's just fallen asleep when Geppi arrives in her nightgown to tell him he's got a call.

"Why are you still up?" Sangallo blares down the phone. "Go to sleep at once, there's something very exceptional. I'll pick you up before dawn."

Tunnel

I always forget how much I like Los Angeles. The city reminds me of one big seaside promenade, and its inhabitants seem to be on permanent vacation. No matter how far you wander from the ocean, you still see people strolling around in shorts and flip-flops with newspapers tucked under their arms. Tanned and muscular, they walk down their boulevards like my boyhood friends in Rimini, who would parade along the Lungomare showing off for a class of Austrian schoolgirls.

We arrive early in the morning and are met by a limousine apparently designed for stilt walkers. The windows are armored glass, but we open them to let in the smells of jasmine and honeysuckle, which are flowering everywhere. On the leather of the backseat, Gelsomina's hand seeks mine. She squeezes it. I can tell she's trying to keep a secret because whenever I look at her she bursts into laughter, hiding her face in the collar of her coat and giggling behind it. I do what I've done for the last fifty years: pretend not to notice. As always, she seems to believe it.

It's done her a lot of good just to have this trip to look forward to. I was afraid the excitement would wear her out, but in fact she's actually recovered much of her former zest. For the last few days, she was leaping around the Via Margutta like a doe, getting everything packed and arranged. Gelsomina doesn't know it, but despite my insistence that it was the Roman taxi drivers who talked me into it, I have come for her. I always sit in the front of the cab. I don't tell them how to drive, but they tell me how to make movies. In the last few weeks, they were grinning behind the wheel until I let slip that I wasn't planning on traveling to Hollywood. At that, they stamped on their brakes and told me that I had a duty to the nation to collect that Oscar in person. Otherwise, they added, I could get out and walk.

I don't feel well. My arthritis is worse than ever. I don't know what's wrong with my body. It used to be my friend and we worked together, but now we've lost touch. These days, it has its own unpredictable will, and one that constantly overrules me. There's nothing as difficult as standing before an audience when you're not feeling well, especially with the whole world watching. I'm only doing it for her. She doesn't have much time. And I can already see her beaming. Over the years, Gelsomina has always enjoyed my honors far more than I have, and I realized only recently that she feels more honored when I receive a prize than she does when some film festival somewhere bestows an award on her. For my four previous Oscars, she was beaming in the front row, as if it was all thanks to her.

I also forget how much I dislike Los Angeles. Bewildered by the time difference, we sit down to a dinner being held at what feels like five a.m. It has been organized in my honor by the Academy, so I can't possibly get out of it. All night, I'm surrounded by producers wearing gold chains who find everything about me extraordinarily fantastic and brilliant: not just my films, but my wife, the color of my skin, the cut of my suit, my garters, the way I hold my little pinkie a bit crooked when I raise a glass to my lips. When I get up to go to the toilet, the whole flock shuffles along behind, and when I overlook a glass door in all the kerfuffle and bump into it—not hard, mind you—I have to kick and lash out to stop them from sticking me in an ambulance and carting me off for a brain scan at the Cedars-Sinai hospital. No matter how much I snarl at them, they offer me a fortune to come to America like Forman and Polanski and make films here.

I explain that I already tried that in '54, after winning my first Oscar. I received the same invitations and signed a contract committing myself to Hollywood for twelve weeks. I was very well paid, though all I had to do was hang around and think up some ideas. Secretaries, chauffeurs, and a house in Bel-Air were placed at my disposal. Cooks and gardeners were provided, along with journalists, pets, masseuses, and a daily supply of fresh flowers and new friends. I used the time to get to know those idols of my youth who were still alive: Mae West and Buster Keaton, George Raft, Joan Blondell, and Douglas Fairbanks Junior. I loved America because it was a ready-made film set. I became fascinated by how Americans erect their own facade and then start believing in it with all their heart. The myth of unlimited opportunity encourages Americans to think not only that dreams *can* come true, but that they *should*. I found this gullibility moving. Hoping, even though you know better! I imagined that no other place would suit me as well. The result was a flood of ideas. I laid one after the other on my producers' desks. They leapt up from their chairs. "Magnificent!" they shouted, and "How extraordinary!" while simultaneously looking like they'd bet on a crippled horse. Not until years later, when I was leafing through my notes, did I realize that not one of my ideas showed the American dream. Instead, they were aimed at the army of the dissatisfied watching that dream in the dark theater, on the other side of the fourth wall. Among those smiling faces, I zoomed in on the odd characters who live their lives underwater, awaiting their one big chance to surface, to take a deep breath of air, just once, in a spasm of terrible clarity.

Since then, I've turned down all offers from Hollywood, but now, for the first time, I consider them. For Gelsomina. The Americans could find the money the Japanese have refused. It's so tempting: a few concessions, and I can make another film. But just when I'm about to start explaining my plan to the assembled herd, the dining-room doors fly open and in walks Marcello! My friend, my soul mate! People nudge each other. I look at Gelsomina, who is watching my reaction to her surprise with moist, twinkling eyes. "Marcello!" I shout, "Marcellino, Marcelloto!" I hug him and I don't let go. The surprise of seeing his familiar face makes me realize how unfamiliar everything here is. He tells me that he has come to present my Oscar tomorrow. Just a few words of his voice, and the roomful of people who are staring at us dissolves. For a moment, the glitter of sequined evening dresses becomes the afternoon sun catching the waves in the harbor, and suddenly we're at an outdoor café halfway up the hills of Riccione, discussing the girls strolling under the plane trees with their mothers. I'm overcome by an emotion as unexpected as the one that once overtook me in the Garden of Forgotten Fruits, where my friend Tonino cultivates the endangered plants of the Maremma, when I recognized the spearmint my mother used to perfume her laundry.

Italy is my world. Its images are my language. If a man wears his hat at a certain angle, I can see that he comes from Livorno. The accent with which he greets me tells me that he was raised on potatoes with lard and fennel, and a gesture conveys the sorrow he feels about a choice he made in the war and has ever since regretted. I don't know everything about my country, but her myths are my myths. I share her collective anxieties and fantasies. When I close my eyes, I see our church statues and the hostesses of the lotto show, I hear the songs and the slogans, all the things an Italian recognizes instantly.

I'm too old to learn how to talk all over again. Gelsomina and I spend the rest of the night huddled at a separate table with Marcello, far from the big shots. We just come from a different world. In America, everyone is the same because the opportunities are unlimited; in Europe, every person develops into a unique individual because new possibilities are constantly cut off. No matter what the producers offer me that evening, I turn them all down, and my only excuse is an amiable explanation that it's much more important to me to have a dream than to see it come true.

Meanwhile, Gala is landing at the small airport of Catania. Gianni hasn't even come with her, that's how sure he is that he has her in his grip. After the previous night's assault, the sight of Pontorax is a relief. The *dottore* is waiting and raises a hand in greeting as soon as he recognizes her, beaming impatiently.

"I missed you," he says, driving off, and she'd like to believe it.

"I'm sure you found others to console you."

"Others?" he snorts. "Who could want others after he's had you?"

She's not entirely pleased by the way he puts it, but something within her is aroused and begins to pray that it's true. At any rate, he seems anxious for her to believe him.

"Didn't Gianni tell you that I immediately canceled his deliveries after you?"

She lays a hand on his knee.

"Others!" he says, as if the mere word pains him. Neither speaks for a while. He's driving himself this time, so badly that even the Sicilians notice and beep their horns. All at once, he pulls onto the shoulder of the highway, too agitated to wait. He turns to face her, staring at her intently. "Others! You staying away so long . . . I suppose that was because of *others*?"

She gazes at him and strokes his face.

"No," she says, and, though it's something only an actress can understand, she believes it herself. "No. There hasn't been anyone since you."

Trucks flash their lights as they bear down on them. Dr. Pontorax drives on. He doesn't take the exit to the beach and the luxury hotels, but heads to his clinic instead. It's a fortress-like building, constructed from blocks of lava from Etna, like the rest of the bleak city. Most of the staff have the weekend off, and the male nurses who see her walking down the corridors alongside the doctor look unsurprised. It is not an open institution. At every corner, Pontorax unlocks a barred door he closes again behind him.

"My wife suspects something," he says. "She's noticed a change since I met you. She's paid the hotel staff at all my regular addresses to report on my activities. You're staying here."

He opens a cell. The walls are padded, but otherwise the furnishings are remarkably luxurious for a hospital. Gala remembers that once, when he was drunk, he boasted that influential Sicilian families sometimes asked him to get rid of bothersome family members, all legally, of course, and only after an official declaration of non compos mentis.

Muted light from valuable bronze lamps illuminates a luxuriant bunch of tulips, fresh from the Dutch flower auction. Beneath them, an expensive box of chocolates with an extravagant bow, and there's a bottle of champagne in a cooler. On the accompanying card, the *dottore* declares his love again. He opens a steel wardrobe. Hanging inside are twelve magnificent dresses, with various pairs of high-heeled shoes beneath, all her size.

"For you," he whispers.

It suddenly occurs to her to wonder how a doctor got so inordinately wealthy.

In the same instant, Pontorax closes the steel door, slips off her shoes, and slides his tongue between her toes.

. . .

On the day of the Academy Awards, Gelsomina and I can no longer escape the madness. The circus starts early in the afternoon, when you're expected to appear in front of the Dorothy Chandler Pavilion in evening dress and stroll down an endless red carpet. Journalists and camera crews are positioned to your left and right behind crush barriers. They're not interested in us at first, since I'm bald and Gelsomina has never had a face-lift, but as soon as our names are called they start yelling to attract our attention, and when we're awkward enough to look in their direction, they ask about our favorite cocktails and who designed the handkerchief in my breast pocket. Hundreds upon hundreds of cameras flash until my head is spinning and I have to cover my face with my hands. Gelsomina, whose English is even worse than mine, mistakes this attention for admiration and wants me to stop and respond in detail, but I answer them all in Rimini dialect to discourage further questions. In this manner, we effortlessly overtake Clint Eastwood and Meryl Streep and are the first to reach the VIP lounge. I collapse into an armchair in a fit of petulance, so dizzy from all the lights that I resolve to stay there and not speak to another soul until it's time for me to ascend the stage in the evening.

Gala gets into an argument with her *dottore* over dinner. As she tries to make him realize that this will be her last visit, he does his best to convince her to come and live in Sicily as his mistress.

They finally patch it up and make love for the second time that day. She does her best to cushion the blow, but he remains resentful and goes home to spend the night with his wife.

Gala is left alone in the hospital room. Where else can she go? He hasn't given her any money. She doesn't even have enough lire for a bus ticket into town. She lies down and tries to sleep. Only after an hour does she realize that she doesn't have any medicine. Normally Pontorax provides it, but this time, in his anger, he forgot. She calls for help, but this wing is not in use. She tells herself that she's making a fuss about nothing, that everything will seem better in the morning. She falls asleep, only to be tormented hour after hour by demons that are too terrible and too dangerous to stir up in that cell. One moment keeps replaying in her mind: Pontorax saying, "I want you to be my wife." He is on his knees beside the hospital bed.

"You're already married," she says, full of compassion.

He slowly rises to his feet. He straightens his coat. He is trembling with disappointment. Suddenly he storms out into the corridor.

"I've broken stronger people than you!" he bellows, locking the heavy steel door from the outside.

Just before the presentation, the VIP lounge is full of stars. I'm slumped in an armchair, seasick from all the swaying bottoms and glittering diamond spangles, when a skinny man accosts me. A fat cigar is protruding from the corner of his mouth, but because of the California smoking ban he's only sucking it. He's wearing an enormous cowboy hat with his tuxedo and introduces himself as Philastus Hurlbut. To my surprise, he speaks in a singsong Italian full of archaic expressions. Like all Americans, he greets me as if our mothers used to bathe us together every Friday night. Beaming with pride, he reveals himself as the brain behind Snaporama. I congratulate him without having the slightest idea what he's talking about. While he showers me with compliments and treats me to a lecture on the decisive influence my films had on his adolescence, I signal for Gelsomina to come to my rescue, but she's talking to Jack Lemmon on the other side of the room. Even gestures that a harbormaster could use to steer an oil tanker into port only elicit from her a cheerful wave. I am thus obliged to listen politely to how the young Philastus Hurlbut of Dripping Springs, Texas, located a copy of Dante's *Purgatorio* in the school library and used it to master my language, which explains why he offered me a drink as if he were sitting in the council chamber of San Gimignano, trying to sway the Ghibelline faction. If I'm to take him at his word, his whole life has been nothing but one big buildup to the day he would meet me, and—he declares as if I've just won the lottery—"Today is that day!" I can't get away from him. The room is hermetically sealed by security men and the only escape route leads back down the red carpet, past all those cameras. I don't mention that I meet people who tell me this same story every day, and raise my glass to the Texan's great moment as if the excitement were mutual. Then he starts off again about Snaporama. While he rattles on, I dredge up a vague memory of a piece of mail that I filed with all the letters from stalkers and other fanatics, the ones I save for a day when I might need something to light my barbecue. Like all the rest of them, he has mistaken the lack of reaction as encouragement and set to work. His Snaporama turns out to be a high-tech carnival attraction for one of the massive amusement parks that have arisen around the city's big film studios. Like the rest, it will have a cinematic theme, and the theme, in this case, will be my work. If all goes according to plan, a ride will soon be whisking twenty visitors a minute—twelve hundred per hour—through my world. In keeping with the requirements of the age, it will loop the loop no less than three times.

I stare at Hurlbut as if I'd experienced the whole torment of the ride just by hearing about it. When I flatly tell him that I'm not interested, he insists on describing every detail of the insane enterprise.

The spectacle begins on the Via Veneto, where the visitors are seated on little red Vespas. As far as I can make out, they'll then plunge into subterranean Rome, zooming down catacombs and zipping through Petronius's bacchanalia. They are catapulted from the alleys of Casanova's Venice to Rimini, where they'll ride across the snow-covered square and into a brothel, where they'll be treated to a ride past, over, and under the women from all my films, who have been re-created with the latest technology and are indistinguishable from the real thing. This dizzying roller coaster ends on the rolling hills of a gigantic replica of the breasts of La Saraghina, between which the poor visitors finally disappear in a free fall, at the end of which they shoot out of the Trevi Fountain, scooter and all, ending with a big splash in the pond, where a Marcello lookalike is waiting to pluck them off their Vespas. In this way, pleads Hurlbut, a whole new generation will be familiarized with all my ideas in less than three minutes.

"Three minutes, sir?" I exclaim, insulted, leaping to my feet. "I've spent my whole life stretching those few minutes into an entire oeuvre. I'd have to be mad to let you condense them again!" I think I must have stood up too quickly, because I start seeing stars. Everything is spinning. I try to drop back into my chair, but I can tell from the shriek that Gelsomina lets loose from the other side of the room that I'm not going to make it. I'm not hurt, but there is enormous consternation. Between all the faces bending over me, mainly lawyers wanting me to sue the organizers for inadequate air conditioning, I can no longer make out Philastus Hurlbut's. Later, too, once I've shoved them all aside and am sitting calmly holding my darling's hand, he's nowhere to be seen. I must have given him an awful shock.

Gala awakes in the clinic. She hasn't slept well. But the first thing she sees is a delicious breakfast set out with a fresh rose. The sun is shining. There's nothing wrong, and the fears of the night have evaporated. Yet: the place still worries her. She spent enough months in hospitals when she was a child. Gianni can't complain. She's done what she said she would. Now she wants to go outside. What's more, she's got to have her pills. She calls out again. First just "Hello!" Then, a few times, "Pontorax!" Then, suddenly, she loses her nerve. She walks barefoot to the door. She wants to open it but doesn't. She stands there paralyzed.

How often has she stood like this over the last few months, longing to talk to Snaporaz: next to the phone, staring down at it, but incapable of picking up the receiver or dialing the number. She knew he loved her, but she was still terrified of discovering he didn't. Now, too, despite her firm conviction that the door is unlocked, she doesn't dare reach out to reassure herself with a simple gesture.

You'd have to be crazy to want to know the truth when it might confirm what you've been dreading. There are so many more possibilities in delusion.

And now she hears them in the distance: the insane, hallway after hallway of them, jiggling the steel handles of their cell doors. Their disappointment redoubles inside the building. It's deafening. The sound of their fumbling at all those locks is like a murmuring sea. The noise builds like a wave.

Gala jumps away from the door. She prefers not to know so she can hold on to her hope.

"I need my medicine!" she screeches. "Who's got my medicine?"

But it's too late. The wave is approaching from behind. She feels a presence. Her head is drawn to the left. There, she sees the bloodred lining of the cape being wrapped around her.

"Yes!" she calls out blissfully. "Yes!" As if there salvation lies.

. . .

They save me till the last, like cream in a *cornetto*. In the auditorium, they show a compilation of my most famous scenes, which, from behind the screen, I see as ghosts. Marcello gives a speech, listing the others who have been granted this rare honor: Chaplin, King Vidor, Hitchcock, all men I admire deeply. I feel very clearly that they are with me. Not only with me: they take me by the arm, they push me forward. When I stroll onto the stage, a standing ovation erupts. It feels like it's never going to end.

"Sit down, please!" I shout at the audience when I've had enough. "Make yourselves comfortable. The only one who needs to be uncomfortable here is me."

"For you, Snaporaz," says Sophia Loren, who is holding the Oscar. I have always found her breasts less astonishing than her muscles, which are also exposed this evening. "In appreciation of one of the silver screen's greatest storytellers. Congratulations. May I give you a kiss?"

"Yes, please!" I exclaim eagerly, making the audience laugh. Then I turn to face them. I have a speech prepared, but I can't be bothered. I curse myself because I'm afraid of being overcome by emotion. For people of my generation, in my country, "America" and "cinema" were virtually synonymous. Standing here now . . . My silence sets off a second ovation. I cut it short and do what everyone always does in this situation. I start thanking people.

"I cannot thank everyone," I say. My eyes seek out Gelsomina. "But one name, the name of both a great actress and my wife . . ." She beams just as I expected, but she's crying as well. The cameras seize on her. She appears in close-up on the enormous screen behind me. She bites her lip. Big fat tears roll down her cheeks. The director keeps her in the shot, so that I appear all over the world as a tiny little man at the chin of a weeping giantess. Two rivers stream out of her eyes and threaten to wash me away.

"Thank you, darling Gelsomina," I manage to gasp, then add, "and for God's sake stop crying."

Then I take my Oscar from Sophia and walk away.

Meanwhile, in Rome, the next morning is dawning. The door to the Sistine Chapel is unbolted. Sangallo and his young friend are admitted.

The viscount can't stop grinning about his exceptional surprise. It's Sunday. The museum is closed to the public and it's the Japanese team's day off. They are midway through their project. Their scaffolding bisects Michelangelo's masterpiece. On one side, the colors are bright and warm; on the other, somber and sooty. The elderly viscount ascends in the freight elevator; the young man climbs the scaffolding with short, supple movements. The guard stays below and opens the latest issue of *Oggi*. At the top, both men need to pause, less to recover than to realize where they are.

High up, near the ceiling of the immense space, atop the scaffolding, a plank floor has been laid. The planks bounce with every step, reinforcing the sense of floating in space.

They have a good view of the more distant paintings. The nudes and the prophets are gigantic. Between them, the sibyls. Sangallo squints to study the one from Cumae.

"She wrote the future of the world in nine books. Then, disguised as an old woman, she took them to Rome, where she offered them to King Tarquin for three hundred gold coins. He thought that was a bit steep, even for the fate of humanity, and sent her away. Every few weeks she came back, each time with one book less, but always for the same price. Not until Rome was plagued by disease and mysterious omens, when a newborn babe screamed 'Victory!' and ships sailed through the clouds, did Tarquin relent. For three hundred gold coins, he bought the three remaining books, which contained all the foreknowledge that would make Rome great. Everything predicted in those books, from the death of Caesar on the steps of the Curia to the birth of Christ, has happened exactly as foretold. Imagine," sighed Sangallo, "what mankind could have achieved if the sibyl hadn't burned the other six."

"Why didn't the king have her rewrite the lost volumes?"

"What do you think? He asked her, of course, but she refused. 'This has taught you,' she said, 'that whenever something is of real importance, the smallest fraction is as valuable as the whole.' "

Despite the impression it gives from below, the ceiling is anything but flat and smooth. The plaster has been dolloped on so roughly that it sags in places, so much so that the two men, much taller than the Japanese, often need to bend to avoid hitting their heads. They move cautiously toward the middle of the scaffold, trying to make out the figures above them, but that's impossible. They are so close to the paintings that their perspective is completely distorted. Maxim realizes he's looking at a face, but only because he can make out the color of skin against the blue of the sky and God's purple robe. Then he spots an eye. And a mouth, which looks twisted, stretched out like an anamorphosis.

Maxim and Sangallo walk to the center of the chapel, where, at the moment of Creation, God and Adam are floating opposite one another. Not far away are two of the high, wheeled platforms where the restorers lie as they work. Maxim and Sangallo hoist themselves up to see the work of art just as Michelangelo saw it while he painted, no more than an arm's length away. Maxim lies there, being solemnly impressed. For minutes on end, awestruck, he studies the brushstrokes in the plaster. He discovers a hair caught in the paint. It's sticking out a little. He wonders whether to pull it out and keep it as a relic. He imagines the emotions of the old viscount, who has spent a lifetime looking forward to this windfall, and lies as motionless as possible to avoid disturbing him. He's enjoying a few pink strokes in the purple, but when he finally dares to look to the side, Sangallo is already on his way back to the lift.

"What are you lying there for?" he says impatiently. "There's nothing to see."

"But what about the hand of the master?" Maxim splutters.

"Sometimes a miracle is so great you can only see it from a distance."

"And the power of his strokes? The sureness of the touch of . . ."

Sangallo clambers into the elevator. He presses a button and slowly descends out of sight.

"If Michelangelo wanted us to lie around with our noses pressed up against it, he'd have painted the whole thing on the floor."

Now Maxim is alone. He wonders whether he should go back down immediately or stick it out a little longer. He'll never be this close again. Procrastinating, he recognizes God's finger. It's as big as a man, but unmistakable. Here is the fingertip, a fold of skin around the knuckle, the nail. It's bent and looks relaxed. Maxim looks to see where it's pointing. There's Adam's finger. It is more forceful and extended, longing for that touch. From this distance, it's impossible to see who is giving life and who is receiving it. Is man born of God or does God come into being because man needs Him? Does the Almighty create the insignificant or vice versa? Contrary to what Maxim always thought, the two fingers do not touch. They strain to reach each other with all their might, but fail. There is a strip of sky between them. Their enormous fingers press against it in vain. Maxim measures the gap with his hands. It's nothing. A bit of air—as unbridgeable as the invisible magnetic field between two like poles.

"That's what happens when you relax after a stressful period," Pontorax explains. His face has come so close to Gala's that their noses brush. "That's still the best recipe for a grand mal." She feels his breath on her eyeballs. She wants to blink but can't. Her upper and lower eyelids are held back with little clamps. Leather straps hold her head down on the examination table. When she tries to feel where she is, she can't move her arms, either. Her wrists and ankles are attached to some medical apparatus, and a tight belt is chafing around her hips.

As soon as she opens her mouth to scream, he inserts a hardwood bit to stop her from biting herself.

"Take it easy, now," the doctor says solicitously. He mixes a liquid at a tall granite counter. "Fortunately, you're in the best of hands."

She rolls her eyes in every direction to try to make out the obsolete devices she is at the mercy of. There are wires going to her head. Now she can also feel the moist paste that attaches the electrodes to her scalp.

"You understand," whispers Dr. Pontorax, who is approaching with a pipette. "Above all, I blame myself. I don't know who caused you so much stress, but I'm the one you dared to relax with. There you have it, even a man with the best of intentions can unleash something awful."

He presses his lips against her forehead.

"Yes," he sighs, "a man who loves has a lot to answer for."

He drips the local anesthetic, which he has prepared lovingly, into one eye and then the other. Gala is shocked by the cold drops rolling over her dry eyeballs. Now Pontorax positions her directly before a battery of lamps and pulls a lever. She tries to look away, but her muscles have already stopped responding.

"Take it easy now, my little darling, it won't be long now."

The flashes begin at unpredictable intervals, slowly at first, here, then there, but soon, from every direction, there comes a barrage of light.

I break off the obligatory post-Oscar photo session because all that flashing is making me sick. As the tension fades, I start to feel my body again. I don't have a headache, but my head feels like an overinflated balloon. I feel like returning to our hotel immediately, but Gelsomina looks beautiful and, more than anything else, I want this to be her night. I realize it's not quite responsible, but we plunge into the festivities anyway, along with Marcello and the mother of his daughter, a great French actress who needs cheering up because she was nominated but didn't win. People come up to Gelsomina all evening. They compliment her for having such a wonderful husband and claim they could feel our love when I addressed her in my thank-you speech. They are invariably Americans, but it doesn't occur to Gelsomina to doubt them, and I know how important it is to her to show our love once again, indisputably, before the eyes of the world.

It's already morning by the time we get to bed.

"Ah, my Snaporaz, what a life we've had!"

I take her in my arms. Too happy to make love, we listen to our breathing. It's been synchronized for half a century.

"Can't you believe in God now," she asks, "after all this?" She soon falls asleep. I kiss her once again without waking her, but almost in the same instant Gala springs to my mind. I can't compare them, but she too will be proud. I send her a kiss and have no doubt that it will reach her. Even this far away, she will feel my love. I feel it myself, surging through my veins, as if trying to burst free. Love is pounding in my temples. The excitement keeps me awake. What can it mean? I jump out of bed, once again too quickly, and have to stand still for a moment until the room stops spinning. Then I pull open the curtain. A whole battery of lamps flash. When I can see again, I make out a crowd of paparazzi. I was the one who came up with them. I put those people on the Via Veneto. I hung cameras around their necks and used them in my film. They have pursued me ever since. Can there be any better proof that reality is no more than an imitation of the imagination? The journalists must be standing on a cherry picker, because our suite is on the top floor of the

Beverly Hilton. Someone is holding up a sign reading CONGRATULATIONS, SNAPORAZ! I wave, somewhat muddled, glad that, despite the heat, I'd put on my pajama coat. I pull it down as low as possible. My besiegers slide open the window and bombard me with questions. I try to close it again, but they're too strong for me. Someone steps into the room. It's Philastus Hurlbut. I tell him to leave, but he refuses and insists that I come for a ride on his Snaporama right now, in the middle of the night. I grab him by the collar and drag him to the door. When I open it, I see a red scooter waiting in the corridor. It's not a real one, but a carnival wagon, part of the attraction he envisages. There are another twenty identical wagons behind me, and all kinds of people, adults and children, are climbing into them with the paparazzi, shouting impatiently for me to hurry because they are curious and want to get started.

"Tiruli, tirula," they sing.

Their nervous excitement is infectious. Danger really *is* seductive; otherwise nobody would ever get on a roller coaster. I hesitate. In my entire life, I have never resisted temptation, so why would I start now, right at the very end?

"Pitipo, pitipa!"

I climb onto the Vespa in my pajama coat. The vinyl seat is cold on my bare bottom. I glimpse myself in the mirror. My head is a balloon. It's about to burst. I want to untie the knot and fly away, but the scooter is already moving. My life's work reduced to a couple of minutes. The paparazzi's cameras flash off the chrome. Pins prick my stretched skin. Blinded, I ride away from the room where Gelsomina lies sleeping and, with horrifying speed, disappear forever down the black hole of the hallway.

Part Five

Director's Cut

You see that it's dark.

You hear that it's quiet.

That's not to say there's nothing to see or hear.

It's a piece of unexposed film. The camera is rolling.

You see the *absence* of light.

You hear the *lack* of sound.

That's how I'm experiencing myself now. Where I am, I am no one. I still am, I'm just no longer someone. I'm not dead; I don't believe that. Dead means not living.

I'm just absent.

I'm not there.

I'm missing.

I've lost myself.

In me and around me is emptiness. Not that I have infinite space. The framing is very clear. Only through feeling my limitations do I experience the nothingness within and beyond them.

They are the first lines a cartoonist draws to divide up his page. His sheet of paper is no longer blank, but he has neither picture nor story.

Let me start again.

I'm lying in my own studio, Studio 5, where I shot all my films. Mounted on the wall behind me is an enormous canvas representing a blue sky.

I'm lying in front of it.

From the very first page.

Those are the facts.

I can't vouch for the rest, because where I am everything is equally true and untrue. I made up this screenplay from beginning to end and wasn't lying for a moment. The characters really existed. I was one of them. It is, taken as a whole, a faithful autobiography. The only question is: whose?

Something that didn't happen is not necessarily untrue.

That's cinema for you: you know it's impossible.

That doesn't mean you can't see it.

Dreams are exactly the same. That's why my life could never have happened anywhere except within these four walls.

After the Oscar ceremony, I apparently became unwell. No doubt. I always said I wouldn't enjoy the trip. I simply belong in Italy. So that's where they shipped me.

I opened my eyes in the clinic on Monteverde. I was lying in bed. On the ceiling above my head, there was an enormous painting of Gelsomina's smile. At least that's what I briefly thought, but it was Gelsomina herself, leaning over me, ecstatic to see my pupils constricting. She kissed my forehead and squeezed my hand, which she was holding as if it were an object whose ownership we were disputing, and which she had no plans to relinquish.

I wanted it back, but I couldn't get it to move. That squeezing was starting to hurt. I shouted indignantly that she had to learn to make do with her own hands, but I couldn't bring out a sound. I tried again, but couldn't move my lips or my voice box. I couldn't even expand my chest to give breath to my fury.

That was when I realized that the direction had passed to someone else.

It still took days for me to figure out what happened. I've always been used to the strangest dreams pressing themselves upon me, but this time it had happened in reverse. I myself had ended up in one of those dreams. I sit inside like a spermatozoon inside an ovum, surprised at his luck. It was an incredible journey, but he alone made it in. But once he realizes that the ovum has closed off behind him, he starts swimming whichever way he can. He can't believe that this is it. Happiness is always like that. The more he bumps into the cell's wall, the more he wonders whether there weren't any better eggs. Too late. The cell has already begun to divide.

With all my might, I struggle to awaken from my coma. But reality has closed around me. All I can do is bump my head against it.

I can't possibly say how long I lay in Monteverde. It could have been a week, it could have been six months. The most unbearable thing about a coma is that everyone else knows more about what's wrong than you do. They chatter away—"Watch what you say, madam, you never know how much they can understand"—but never think to tell you the time, the day of the week, or how long you have to go.

Besides Gelsomina, I didn't recognize a soul. Every day, a whole procession of nursing staff passed by my bed. They were always the same ones, but I didn't remember their faces. Eventually, I succeeded in remembering details, just as, in a circus cavalcade, you remember last year's acrobat less for her spectacular stunts than for the way the Lycra folds sparkle in her crotch.

I remember the calluses on the fingers of a night nurse and the goatee of a professor who did regular rounds with his female students. When they bent over me, the fabric around their buttons pulled so tight that I thought they were going to burst out of their white uniforms. I'm convinced that those girls didn't come because I was so medically interesting, but only for a chance to gawk at me. I hurled obscenities at them in Romagnolo, but they didn't hear a word and continued to practice catheter insertion.

After the official announcement that I had suffered a stroke, the clinic was besieged. People climbed trees in the hope of a heartrending photograph. A journalist from *Il Messaggero* disguised himself as a nurse to steal one of my electroencephalograms, but the editors found it too shocking to print. I couldn't care less. I see it as a compliment that a paparazzo like that wanted a souvenir of the brain from which he sprang. But I regretted the whole uproar for Gelsomina.

The sorrow exacerbated her own condition, but she still came to see me every day. She was veiled, to deprive the photographers of their entertainment. To make things even more dramatic, our fiftieth wedding anniversary arrived. On that day, she tried even harder to make herself beautiful, even though she had no idea whether I could actually see her. She bent over me and slowly raised her veil coquettishly. Perhaps she hoped that the shock of her beauty would succeed where the medical intervention had failed. The machines did not, however, indicate any increase in brain activity. Disappointed, she sat beside me, pulled the sermons of Antonio Vieira out of her bag, and seized the opportunity to read to me from them.

"It's your anniversary," I say every year, "not mine."

It's a joke, but she's never laughed. Because it's true. The marriage is hers, not mine. This year, of all years, I had resolved to surprise her by saying that this time, just once, since she insisted, it could be *our* wedding anniversary. Just to see her face. I did try, but it was too much. She didn't even look up from the holy words on her lap. I couldn't bear it and concentrated all the will power I could muster on my tongue.

"Spri bilissiti," was all I managed. "Spri bilissiti!" But it seemed to mean more to her than all the expensive jewelry I had given her over the years.

From then on, my memory began to recover. The first to come back in her full glory was Gala. She appeared with wet hair clinging to her bare shoulders. I regretted my paralysis more than ever. Every day, I tried to recognize hers among the faces appearing at my bedside. I saw many dear friends, but no sign of Gala. If everyone I had ever known was coming to visit, where was she? I eventually started to wonder whether she had really existed. It wouldn't be the first time I'd imagined someone so vividly that I accidentally set an extra place at the table. The sudden idea that Gala might not really exist made me depressed and lonely, which was so disastrous in my condition that I suffered a relapse and was forced to spend days in intensive care. That is where I began to concentrate on Gala's story.

Just as I build a feature film around a brief dream, I constructed a life from impressions. It was easy for me to summon up my memories of the episodes of our own love, but I added scenes from before I knew her, like her very first seizure at the flower auction, to understand how she came to love me so much. I effortlessly invented all of the foregoing, even the many scenes of Maxim and Gala, which I could not possibly have known about. Their thoughts popped into my mind perfectly formed, as if they were characters in one of my films. That's how close my camera got to them. When I saw them lying in bed, I saw their imperfections in sharp focus. I even discovered stretch marks on the side of the male body I have never seen naked. These young people have become so real that it's impossible for me to believe that Gala and Maxim are merely part of one of my innumerable unfinished projects. Much of what I imagine about them must be true.

Now, in the time I have left, all I have to do is synchronize their story with mine.

"If you expect something, you're just setting yourself up for disappointment," Sangallo explains on the way home from the Sistine Chapel. The experience has shaken the viscount so much that he has canceled lunch at the Checchino. In his apartment, he tosses his coat onto the sofa and disappears into the kitchen.

Maxim had to insist on accompanying the old man upstairs. He can't understand the viscount's sudden sorrow and feels like he needs to cheer him up.

"But what's so disappointing?"

"I had hoped to see more, but I saw less," Sangallo explains, returning with a lovely old Chianti. He clamps it between his legs but doesn't have the strength to pull the cork. The bottle slips out of his grip. He curses. He's hurt himself. He turns away to conceal his struggle to keep himself under control.

"You saw less of the whole, but all those details!"

"No," says Sangallo, "you don't understand. It's my eyes. They're deteriorating. Deteriorating fast. Soon I'll have to see paintings the way I listened to symphonies when I was a child: by imagining the separate notes and combining them as beautifully as I can in my mind."

"How awful," says Maxim. He picks up the bottle, opens it, and pours the wine, but the dislodged sediment has spoiled it.

"The cornea is falling apart like an old rag. That's all there is to it. I try to accept it. Some days it's easier than others. I have a little time left. I try to make the most of it."

"And then?"

Sangallo's mouth droops in an exaggerated frown. He slips a big flower into his lapel, lets his shoulders slump like a Pierrot's, and starts a Marcel Marceau impression. He sticks his arms out in front of him and measures out an imaginary room that is closing in on him. The expression of surprise on his scared face is so vivid that Maxim bursts out laughing. The viscount pretends that the laughter has attracted his attention in the darkness and comes toward him with his hands outstretched. The old fingers touch the young face. Engrossed, they glide over the forehead, down the cheekbones and the dimples in his cheeks. Then Sangallo acts out sudden recognition and curls his lips up into the widest of smiles.

They stand there like that, stomach to stomach, still smiling. The show is over but Sangallo's fingers are still touching Maxim's face. They start to move again. At first, just trembling. Then cautiously caressing, brushing through his hair and coming to rest on his neck. The old man's fragility is irresistible.

"I sat at so many long tables as the youngest," says Sangallo. "Between the courses, I was too impatient to remain sitting. I ran around and crawled between the legs of the adults. At so many parties and meetings I was the junior. What went wrong?"

There is nothing Maxim would rather do than comfort him. He feels a strong urge to accommodate him. It would be so natural. He could kiss Sangallo now. It would be easy to do and would make the old man so very happy.

But he doesn't. It's almost unforgivable, but he isn't yet strong enough to put himself to one side.

At that moment, the older man takes the initiative, pulling Maxim up against him and pressing his lips against his.

Maxim pushes him away gruffly.

"No!" he snaps. Then, when he's free again, more gently, "I'm sorry."

He walks to the corridor and presses the button for the elevator. While he is waiting, Sangallo appears in the doorway behind him.

"Don't worry," he says. "I'll stay the same person I've always been, it's just the world around me that's disappearing."

"Poor Rome!" sobs Geppi. "First Hannibal and now this!"

She has collapsed amid the potatoes she was peeling on the kitchen table when the news reached her. When Maxim comes in, she looks up and stretches her hands out to him. He has no choice but to hug and comfort her. She comes up to his navel.

"Like autumn leaves our loved ones fall from the tree. All the people I have lost: parents, sisters, brothers, and finally . . . ah, such is life. You know it's coming and if you can't take it you shouldn't have been here to begin with. One leaf after the other, until nothing remains but the bare trunk, not as lovely, but a lot stronger. And now this! This is really something else. What did we do to deserve it? Oh, Rome, poor old dear! This time they've taken an ax to the root."

She presses her wet cheeks against Maxim's stomach. He picks potato peel out of her hair. She assumes that everyone knows why Rome is mourning, so it takes Geppi a while to realize that the young man doesn't know about Snaporaz's stroke.

"Immediately after the Oscar ceremony! That's right, it was just on the news. Collapsed in Marcello's arms!"

Maxim can think only of Gala. He must get to her before she hears it from someone else.

"Ah, why didn't the angels take me instead!" Geppi laments, as he tries to extricate himself from her grip. "I'll pray for his recovery. The man has a Midas touch. And those gorgeous black curls of his!"

"Black curls? But, Geppi, Snaporaz has been bald for years."

"Bald?" She pushes him away with contempt. "Already they're sullying his name!" She raises a finger in the air and shouts after Maxim, "I tell you, our Snaporaz is tall and slim and incredibly handsome. Ah, our poor, poor dreams: who can save you now?"

Gala doesn't pick up the phone or open the door, so Maxim uses her spare key to enter her chapel. Has she heard already and left in a panic, or has she been away longer? Her bed hasn't been slept in. Her suitcase, along with her best clothes, is gone. Everything indicates a planned departure. When did he last see her? Why didn't he drop by yesterday evening? In less than five minutes, he has searched the room. He finds pieces of stained glass on the balcony.

The Monteverde doctors eventually decided I was strong enough for some recreation. I was hoisted out of bed, plopped down in a wheelchair, and pushed in endless circles around the hospital grounds. This ritual was repeated each morning and afternoon. En route, I feasted my eyes. A colorful group was convalescing in the garden. Some were sitting on benches singing simple songs with their nurses. Others practiced moving on the lawn, like jugglers warming up for a show, who keep going even when everything goes flying out of their hands. Most had suffered the same affliction as I had, and were recovering from a stroke or some other brain condition. Patients from the neurological and psychiatric wings entertained themselves together like healthy people on an excursion to an amusement park. Since I couldn't play ball games or fly a kite, I was regularly parked in the gazebo. Through the bars of the fence, you could just make out the dome of St. Peter's and the towers of the court. The other paralyzed patients were there to keep me company. We sat among the greenery like flowers gone to seed. Most of their mouths were agape, as if fate had struck them down in midsentence. Some looked around with big eyes, astonished that their film had become a photograph.

I knew that look.

As a young man, before I came to Rome, I briefly worked as a nurse. It wasn't meant to be. I can't stand the sight of my own suffering, let alone that of others. It was just to avoid military service. I was given a white coat and put to work in the psychiatric hospital in Bologna.

I had been there for less than a week and was starting to wonder whether I wouldn't be better off at the front when a colleague called me into his office.

"If you hear music a bit later," he said, "don't be surprised. It's a new patient."

As soon as I stepped back into the corridor, I forgot his words. It was Wednesday, my turn to give Signora Fèfè her bath. I'd grown used to the sight of her sitting outside her room, crying day and night, but I dreaded the prospect of actually touching her. I was eighteen and didn't know how to undress such a sorrowful woman. I talked to her as if she were a baby and tried to distract her by tickling her with the sponge, but nothing helped. Finally, I got so nervous that I could think of only two options: crying along or hitting her until she shut up. That was when she stopped and looked at me with surprise. She hadn't done that before. I was afraid she'd read my mind, but something in the distance had attracted her attention.

"Here comes the band!" she gaily blurted.

Then I heard it too. It sounded like a military drum fanfare. I wrapped a big towel around her and we ran out into the corridor to see it.

The music was coming from a single person, the new patient, a youth who could imitate every instrument with no more than his mouth and his limbs. He was a virtuoso, and his music sounded almost exactly like the real thing. He marched through the hallways, as blissful in his universe as Fèfè was miserable in hers. They had withdrawn into a facet of themselves, the place they had found to go on living.

I took the woman's hand and led her back to the bathroom, where I patted her dry. She started crying again. I decided to serve out my time as a nurse on that ward.

The insane are not slaves to fashion. The years don't change them. They have an individualism you don't find in the normal world. An individual is limited to a single self. The insane take it a step further and are limited to their obsessions. I have often been called mad. My obsessions are not only my reality, they are the basis of my films. I have drawn heavily on my experiences as a nurse. Later too, I often visited mental institutions. Everywhere I met the same characters. Their world terrified me, but it also inspired awe. It takes so much courage to let go of reality. I love their faces most of all. They hide nothing. That's why you see the same grimaces in institutions all over the world. They move me because they are eternal. Beauty is fleeting, but ugliness is timeless.

I used the boy who was an orchestra in one of my films, fleetingly. The actor played him brilliantly but couldn't hold a candle to the original, so we had to hire a military band to achieve the desired effect. I often think of him. He lets me know that the imagination is more than an escape. It is also a weapon. Even now, all I have to do is close my eyes to hear him approach.

He's playing the Radetzky March. Beaming just as he did fifty years earlier in Bologna, he marches down the corridors of the clinic in Sicily. He passes Gala's door. The noise wakes her. She thinks it's a distant circus parade. Then she remembers where she is. Somewhere where anything's possible. She is alone. She cautiously touches her face. Her head. She is no longer attached to any apparatus. She gets out of bed and feels the door. It opens. She sees the young man imitating the band at the end of the corridor. For a flash she catches his eye. The bliss on his face! She tries to follow but is intercepted by two male nurses, who escort her back to her room. That slight body between those two gorillas. The split in the hospital gown leaves her back exposed. Now that she's barefoot, the curvature of her spine is clearly visible. Her hair is tangled. Her mascara runs when she cries. The nurses are friendly and promise to alert Dr. Pontorax. The oompah-pah dies away in the distance.

In the meantime, more and more flowers keep arriving, making my room almost impassable. They've added stands in the corners to accommodate them, but it's not enough. They take them into the corridor at night. The white tiles, down the whole length of the hallway, are hidden behind tulips and roses. And a fresh load arrives every morning. With huge grins, the nurses carry them in: flowers, flowers, more flowers. Sometimes they read out the attached cards: some of the tributes have been sent from countries nobody's ever heard of by people whose names are meaningless to me. And so I lie here among flowers of every conceivable variety, like a float on the *corso,* surrounded by all the flowers of the world.

"Missing?" asks Geppi.

"There was a struggle."

"You think Gianni is capable of something like that?"

"You don't?" Maxim asks scornfully.

Geppi turns down the gas and sits at the table with him. He is nervous. She takes his hands, awkwardly, as if it's her problem as well. He pushes her away. He wants the pimp's address, but she refuses to give it to him.

"Go ahead, keep defending him, like always."

"I'm sure she's fine," she placates him. "Your Gala is enjoying a delicious dinner somewhere. By the sea. Under the palm trees."

"Look who I am talking to about what it means to love someone," Maxim says angrily.

She walks back to the stove and pours cream over the oyster mushrooms.

"That's not in the cards for everyone," she says calmly. "My Mario was even younger than me, and I'd just turned fifteen. One day, an uncle of mine showed up. He took me by the arm and led me away. My father walked with us until we'd left the village. I didn't think he'd let me go. He stopped eventually. He didn't know what to say. He held up his hand. Even before we'd left him behind, my father held up a hand and started waving. He stood like that until we reached a curve in the road and disappeared into the hills. I cried from fear. I screamed when they stuffed me into a wedding dress."

"Why didn't you refuse?" Maxim asks. He doesn't have time for other people's misery.

"Don't you ever go to the movies?" Geppi shakes her head. "I'm talking about Calabria! If you give someone bad directions, your parents get your left hand in a box." She dips her finger into the sauce to taste it, then wipes her hand on her apron. "Mario was a stranger. I was living in a town I'd never seen with a family who meant nothing to me. Then my baby was born. I gave him all my love."

"You told me you didn't have any children."

"I always hoped my son would do me proud."

She empties out a bag of tomatoes and tears off a piece of paper. She pulls a carpenter's pencil out of a drawer. She sharpens it with a knife.

"But no matter how tightly you keep your eyes shut, you can't pretend you're asleep forever."

"Did he . . . die?"

Geppi shakes her head.

"He finally found a way to get out of that village."

She licks the end of the pencil and writes something down.

"And he took me with him, the angel! Who am I to turn my back on him now? The way Gianni makes his money is nothing to be proud of, but it was our way out."

She slides the paper over to him. Pontorax's home address is written on it in big, rough letters.

That very evening, Maxim stands before a lava-stone mansion at the foot of Mount Etna. Only when he rings the bell does he realize that he hasn't told anyone where he's going. Why didn't he alert the consulate? He spent his last penny on the flight. He doesn't even have a plan. All he knows is that he's not leaving the island without Gala. He hears footsteps behind the door. He feels in his pockets in vain for something he could use as a weapon. To be on the safe side, he does what men do in the movies and clenches his fists. Bring it on, he thinks. Ready for anything.

Except a samba party.

The girl who opens the door shakes her maracas to the rhythm of the mambo. She is a mulatta, dressed in two half coconuts and a *filo dentale*. Swaying her hips to a rhythm of her own invention, she leads the way, as Maxim does his best to follow the string between her buttocks.

In the back garden, a Brazilian carnival is in full swing. On the hillside terraces, Sicilian high society is dancing to the music of two samba schools that have been flown in from Recife with all their members and costumes.

"Welcome to the world of *Cacão brasilão*!" Mrs. Pontorax greets Maxim with a caipirinha as if he's just another guest. She is plump, wearing the white bandanna and lace dress of a Candomblé priestess. "It's my husband's favorite TV show."

"I need to speak to your husband urgently."

"Is it about chocolate? Otherwise he's not interested. Chocolate breasts, chocolate butts . . . Since that show started, he can't think of anything else."

A conga line interrupts her.

"I'm looking for a woman."

"Well, feel free!" Mrs. Pontorax shouts while joining the end of the line. "There are plenty of beauties here tonight. The host of *Cacão brasilão* in person! Raffaella? Raffaella?"

Maxim forces his way through the guests, most of whom have opted for a colonial theme, which amounts to men in white linen suits and women with gold slave bangles. Wandering among them, naked extras are decked out as the indigenous gods of Bahia, wearing horns and skin painted red or blue. They jab at the merrymakers with tridents and hurry them along with thick leather whips.

Maxim finds the *dottore* near a pond at the bottom of the garden. He is unwinding in a swinging hammock, apparently drowning in the large open neck of his blouson. As soon as he realizes who Maxim is, he struggles to his feet, hindered by the hundreds of rustling, colorful ruches on his sleeves. The little man looks so unhappy in his gaucho outfit that Maxim abandons his resolve to use violence. What's more, the doctor seems to brighten up when he asks about Gala.

"I have bad news for her," says Maxim. "You must have heard. About Snaporaz."

"Oh, is she a film lover?"

"Snaporaz is . . . He's a friend of ours. I wanted to tell her before she hears it from someone else. Is she here?"

"She's at my clinic. You know about her condition?"

"Her seizures? Yes, of course, I know all about them. Has she had one?"

"Late yesterday. I kept her under observation last night."

"That was very kind of you, but it wasn't necessary."

"I thought it was."

"We don't need any advice." Maxim sounds annoyed. "We've lived with her illness for years. I take full responsibility for her health."

"Then you must blame yourself," says Pontorax compassionately.

"Why?"

"Because it's not just her neurological condition. Gala is malnourished. Haven't you noticed? There were even signs of dehydration, primarily due to excessive fluid loss in the feces."

"The laxatives. She's addicted to them. I know. I tried . . ."

"You failed," interrupts Pontorax. "Dehydration disrupts brain function. The body reacts as it would in a crisis. It manufactures substances to lower the level of consciousness. In combination with her other medication, it can cause disorientation, anxiety, and depression."

"I want to see her." Maxim seeks Pontorax's arm among the ruches. "Please. I have to go to her," he begs. "I love her."

The doctor appraises him.

"I can understand that," he says. He offers Maxim an arm and leads him through the crowd that has gathered on the terrace, where a group of street kids from Rio is launching kites. They've tied small paper lanterns to the tails to make the cheerful colors stand out against the evening sky.

"I'm sorry about interrupting your party," Maxim says as they climb into the limousine.

"I'm not," Pontorax laughs, exiting the parking area in the wrong gear. "My wife thinks I share her predilection for big parties. That is a misunderstanding. One of many between men and women. I love beautiful women, of course, but this whole Brazilian rage leaves me cold. My wife happens to have gone to all this trouble. I prefer not to disabuse her. That's less painful than the truth."

The wind is too strong. Some of the lanterns have caught fire in the sky. The tails ignite like fuses and the kites go up in flames. Smoldering scraps float down on the mountain road on every side of the car.

"The more we love a woman, the less we see her as she is," says Pontorax. "We think we know what our lovers want, but we could just as easily be wrong. Whose fault is that, the one who misunderstands or the one who no longer bothers to correct the misunderstanding?"

3

"I have to go to him!" Gala exclaims, breaking loose of Maxim's embrace. She leaps from the hospital bed and holds her face under the tap. In three minutes, she is dressed and ready to go. She takes the news that Snaporaz is in a coma as a general takes a mobilization order. No tears, no doubt. She wants only one thing.

Maxim recognizes it.

"Everyone loves someone," says Dr. Pontorax in consolation as he gives Maxim money for the return trip. "It's an endless chain. Sometimes we're lucky enough to be briefly coupled with one that fits. You have to recognize those moments and cherish them."

Back in Rome, Gala closes the door of her chapel behind her every morning and walks to the Castel Sant'Angelo. There, she takes bus 982 to the end of the line and walks the rest of the way through the fields. She registers at the hospital gate, where they ask her name and her relationship with me.

"We're close," is all she says.

Then they ask her to wait some distance from the main building in an external parking lot reserved for everyone who wants to see Snaporaz or hopes for news of his condition. The crowd grows daily, though none of them will ever be admitted. Beer and water vendors, pizza and ice cream sellers start showing up around ten. Even the Cinecittà souvenir stand, with its Snaporaz mugs, scarves, and key rings, has relocated here. Business is brisk, especially around noon, when the crowd swells with civil servants from the city who've come here for lunch and housewives treating their children to a day trip. Every Sunday afternoon, there is a Mass to pray for my recovery. Touring coaches have started to include the hospital on their routes, and ever more couples seeking an alternative backdrop for their wedding photos have been sighted. To ease the waiting, the hospital management has set up loudspeakers that constantly blast music from my films.

I hear the noise from my wheelchair in the gazebo. An elderly patient lifts her hospital gown like an evening dress and dances for hours on end, a blissful expression on her face.

The whole time I'm imagining Gala's out there waiting. It's enough to drive you mad. Her fingers through the wire netting. It cuts into her flesh. How can she know that there's nothing to worry about on my account? Nothing would make me feel better than to see her and reassure her, but I have no way of expressing that to anyone.

Interest fades as evening falls. The families go home, the vendors pack their wares, and around seven thirty, in midbeat, someone kills the music. Gala walks back to the gate, gives her name, and asks if there's any news. They tell her to try again tomorrow. At that, she walks off through the fields in the last light of the day.

Maxim is waiting for her at home. Since they got back from Sicily, his life has consisted of looking after Gala. He has taken on the task of feeding her properly. He brings bread and fruit in the morning for her daily trek to her lover. Then he combs the markets of Rome for grains and high-fiber vegetables, which he prepares in the afternoon according to a strict diet that gradually compels her bowels to start functioning independently, supported by a course of vitamins and expensive medicines prescribed by Dr. Pontorax.

The skiing debacle taught him that actors are completely interchangeable. Despite all their investments in their egos, they're easier to replace than a part of a set someone's spent a couple of hours hammering together. Maxim should have realized that when he saw the photos covering the walls of Cinecittà. He still couldn't go down a new path until the old one had been brutally cut off. As he recovered from that blow atop the steps to the Ara Coeli, he thought he'd reached a dead end. He mourned the life he had envisaged but, gradually, as his grief faded, the fog of his ambition slowly lifted too.

"And?" Every evening when Gala comes home, he asks the same question, "Did you get in?"

If she doesn't feel like talking about it, he serves dinner. When she starts to cry, he comforts her. This briefly makes him feel that he matters to her. Then she starts talking about Snaporaz, about how perfectly he's always understood her, how his genius reflects on her when she's with him, how it always makes her feel bigger than she actually is.

Maxim doesn't contradict her. Her sorrow hurts him, so why would he want to make it worse? He holds his tongue out of love for her. But his silence only helps prolong this hopeless situation.

Wouldn't it be more loving of me, he sometimes wonders, to tell her that the love between her and Snaporaz isn't all that unique? Shouldn't I grab her by the shoulders and shake her until she realizes that she's not the only beautiful young woman standing in the parking lot with her fingers in the wire fence, and that all those others think they've got the same right to stand by Snaporaz's sickbed?

But he loves her too much to hurt her. Or is he too cowardly to risk the truth?

So he says, "Yes, your relationship is unique, and every day it lasts is something to be grateful for," whereupon they turn on the television or sit out the evening with books until it's time for Maxim to return to Parioli.

Human reason can so strongly suppress imagination that, in all those nighttime wanderings through the city, Maxim only once comes face-to-face with himself. It happens on the Piazza Navona, just after the fountains have been turned off and the fortune-tellers have gone home. By the time he walks onto the square, it is deserted, except for a couple lying in each other's arms before the statue of the Moor, oblivious to anyone else.

Maxim has almost passed them by when he recognizes Gala and himself. He turns around. They look like they're in love. She's wearing her leopard-skin jacket. His head is on her shoulder. Maxim goes up to within a few meters of them, but the two are so happy, so absorbed in each other, that he doesn't seem to exist for them. New arrivals in the city, stretching out on the soft stones of the city squares that serve as their living room. They haven't committed themselves to anything; everything still seems possible. Then she stands and strips down to her slip. She washes her arms and shoulders in the basin. She bends over it and dips her face in the water. When she straightens up again, she notices Maxim staring at her from a distance. It makes her laugh. She scoops up water with both hands and throws it toward him. Encouraged, he runs toward the fountain. Again she tries to splash him. For a second, he looks like he'll go play with the young couple, but then he reconsiders and walks off without a word. He hurries away from the square. After all, Gala will be going out early the next morning, and he wants to be back at her place in time to prepare a high-fiber breakfast.

2

"Signora Vandemberg!" the man in the commercial shouts. He descends the dark stairs to the cellar. The woman he's following doesn't hear him. She is carrying a bucket of milk. In her long, spotted bathrobe, she walks past a row of cells. A bicycle stands behind the bars of one of them. The others seem to be empty.

"Signora Vandemberg," the man sighs, "from Holland. She was the most beautiful woman in the world. Signora!"

Now she turns around.

The man was not exaggerating.

"Signora, let me carry the bucket for you."

"Jij kunt het niet," the woman answers in Dutch, *"jij bent maar een jongen."*

He doesn't understand the words but seems to grasp her meaning. Suddenly, he realizes what he's got on. He's wearing a blue sailor's suit with a big white collar.

"But I'm the boss of a big company," he argues, astonished. "I'm feared and respected."

"Jij bent altijd een kleine jongen gebleven."

Now the foreign language is too much for him.

"I'm sorry," the man shouts desperately as she walks away with her bucket. "Can someone translate that for me?"

"I can," a lion says. He emerges from one of the cells and translates the Dutch woman's words. "You've always stayed a little boy." Then the lion lays his head on the lap of the man in the sailor's suit and begins to cry. The animal weeps slow, heavy, heartrending tears.

The whole thing takes less than ninety seconds and ends the way I wanted all the ads to end: the man wakes from his nightmare and falls out of bed with a thud. His snarling wife insists that he'd sleep better if he'd listened to her and entrusted his money to the Vatican bank.

I finished the cut just before I left for Los Angeles, but it hadn't been approved, let alone scheduled for broadcasting. Come to think of it: I haven't even been paid for it yet. In any event, the commercial suddenly appears on television. The timing has undoubtedly been influenced by the tremendous publicity surrounding my condition. A big advertising campaign in all the newspapers alerts people to "Snaporaz's Last Dream." That night, all of Italy is glued to the tube.

Gala watches with Maxim, completely unprepared. Finally, during the last commercial break in a game show, my ad begins.

The man descends the cellar stairs.

"Signora Vandemberg!" he shouts.

Neither of them realizes it straightaway. Gala doesn't react even when she hears her name a second time. She doesn't stir until the Italian actress does her best to render her incomprehensible Dutch lines.

"That's you!" says Maxim. "That's supposed to be you!"

"Jij bent altijd een kleine jongen gebleven," she says with an outlandish Italian accent.

"My hair!" says Gala. "My walk! Even the leopard-skin bathrobe."

"That is really too fucking much!" Maxim blurts. "The son of a bitch finally found a part for you, and he didn't even let you play it!"

"And welcome back to *More Is Less,*" the presenter coos, "the quiz where contestants . . ."

Maxim turns off the television, the better to hear his own indignation.

"He used me," says Gala quietly.

"He used you all right, but without really using you!"

"For the very last footage he ever shot."

Gala slowly stands and walks to the terrace.

"That doesn't mean we have to stand for it," Maxim bellows. "If you want, we can stop them from broadcasting it again. Or at least make them pay for using your name, for violating your . . ."

He stops in the middle of his tirade. He sees Gala standing there. The church lights are shining through the stained glass, covering her with color. She has clasped her hands before her breast, staring at the stars like Saint Catherine of Genoa after her vision.

"I have to give him his due," Maxim says darkly when he realizes that he'll have to surrender his place forever. "He really is the absolute master."

"His last ideas," whispers Gala. "He dedicated his last images to me."

They stand beside each other in silence. On the other side, the theater lights go out.

"I'm going home."

"Already?" Gala looks at him. "Come on, it's still early."

"No," says Maxim. "I mean I'm really going home." And after a long silence, he adds, "It's time."

1

Taking film reviewing to the next level, they declare me brain dead the morning after the broadcast. Overnight, two more strokes finished the job.

Gelsomina is very brave. She climbs into bed with me and throws one leg over my body just as she always does. Then, as if she's fallen asleep, she lies still. The nurses don't dare disturb her.

The medical director arrives around midday. As discreetly as possible, he mentions that in similar cases people sometimes opt not to prolong the patient's life artificially. With an exalted expression, as if trying to sell her a Caribbean cruise, he describes the process of natural dehydration. Shocked, Gelsomina summons her confessor, who sets in motion such mighty machinery that the medical director does not again show his face for the remainder of my stay.

Fiamella arrives to see Gelsomina, explaining that the journalists are at the gate and an announcement can no longer be delayed.

"Why?" asks my wife. "He's *my* husband."

"But he's their Snaporaz."

She insists on addressing the crowd herself and requests a few minutes to pull herself together. She walks out. She makes a short statement and answers questions from the press. She suddenly stops. She shields her eyes and stares into the crowd as if into the sun. Between the constantly flashing cameras, she has spotted Gala. With a wave of her hand, Gelsomina indicates that she can no longer go on and turns on her heel.

"How long have you been there?"

"Since nine."

Gelsomina stares out the window of the visitors' room.

"Every day," says Gala. "Since he's been here. I come around nine o'clock and stay until dark."

Now the two women look at each other. For a moment, the older woman's pain makes the younger forget her own. She takes Gelsomina's hands and presses them to her cheeks. Gelsomina sees her sincerity. Briefly, there is communion. Then the wife extricates herself and turns away.

"There are others," says Gelsomina. "He always managed to make them believe that they were the only one. We all wanted to believe it! Yet there were always others."

"Never like you."

"No."

"And no matter what you think of me, I never forgot his love for you."

Gelsomina still has her back turned to Gala.

"Why do you think we always believed him?" Gelsomina asks.

"Because he believed himself. He was completely sincere. Every single time."

"Yes," Gelsomina says. "Yes, he was always sincere. Even when he was lying. His imagination was his religion. And if he sincerely believed something, who are we to doubt him?"

"I never did."

"No," my wife says, somewhat surprised, "me neither."

"He just didn't love *real* life."

"He liked to observe it, as long as it didn't interfere with his imagination. That's very difficult for those of us who only have a real life."

Gala moves up beside her and they look out the window together.

Two silhouettes in front of the window.

"Go to him now, if you'd like."

Inside the frame: the outlines of two cartoon characters—one beginning, one rounding off an oeuvre.

They stare at the commotion in the distant parking lot.

"What do you think," Gelsomina asks, "are there any others out there?"

"Does it matter?"

Finally, they quickly glance at each other. Then Gala walks to the door.

" 'Everything gets smaller when you share it, except love.' That's what he said."

The old woman against the light.

"Do you understand that? Is our sorrow any less because we both feel it?"

The day before he leaves for Holland, Maxim walks through the city. Everywhere he encounters places where he was happy. He stands pensively before walking slowly on, as if he expects something to call him back, but hope has everywhere become a memory.

That's how he walks into the Galleria Doria Pamphilj, wanders through the rooms, and slumps down in an alcove opposite the *Apelles and Campaspe*. Just then, Sangallo enters, shuffling hastily, rushing down the corridors in his inimitable style. Maxim's spirits revive and he jumps up to greet him, but the viscount brushes past without noticing him. Sangallo touches one of the busts to make sure he has Innocent X before him. Just when Maxim is about to step up to him, a young man appears. He is as tall as Maxim and is wearing the long, shiny leather coat. High cheekbones, long neck, head thrown back with a certain arrogance. The new protégé even wears his hair in the style Maxim had when he arrived in the city. The youth laps up the viscount's anecdote.

Maxim knows the story.

He is overcome by a deep calm. The coincidence gives him an almost mystical feeling, as if the cycle of passion's death and revitalization had stopped for the slightest instant and restored everything to its proper balance.

Without announcing his presence, he leaves his old friend behind with his new pupil.

"Found?" echoes through the high-ceilinged room. "In a *hand*bag?"

. . .

"I left Gelsomina and walked down the hall to his room," Gala relates. "In front of the door, I changed my mind."

"After going to all that trouble?" Maxim asks incredulously.

"I went to all that trouble to see Snaporaz one more time. I only realized when my fingers were on the doorknob and I was trying to steel my nerves—I realized that whatever I'd find inside wouldn't be him. He wore a hat because he hoped people would think there was a full head of hair underneath it. That's not the kind of man who wants you to see him with tubes coming out of his windpipe."

Maxim leans back. This is their last evening together. They're eating at an outdoor café on the Campo de' Fiori. He studies the way she speaks, afflicted yet still calm.

"Everything I need to know about him is in my head. That simple fact struck me as if he himself were grabbing me by the shoulders, mocking me for being too dumb to figure it out sooner: Snaporaz is the last person in the world who would want to be seen as he really is. I pressed my hand against the closed door and then left."

Before, in her sorrow, she would have shrieked, flown off the handle, drowned her fears, danced herself into a frenzy. In Maxim's arms.

"Maybe, for once, you could see what he's brought us to," he says as coldly as he can. He's not looking at her, but keeps his eyes pinned on a group of buskers making music in the middle of the square, on the steps at the base of the statue.

"Devo punirmi," they sing, *"devo punirmi, se troppo amai."*

Two clowns illustrate the end of a love affair with the help of an enormous club, a broken violin, and jets of tears that spurt up high into the air.

Maxim blames me most for destroying his own image of Gala.

You don't have to talk to me about images.

Put an actress in front of a bare wall and with the help of a single light I can transform her from a goddess to a witch. I illuminate her from every side. I toy with the shadows on her throat, beneath her eyebrows, under her nostrils. I arrange her like a shop-window mannequin—however I like. Until I'm satisfied. When I'm done with her, she's exactly the same, but now she fits into the image I always had of her, even at night, when I summoned her in my dreams.

She is perfect because she looks the way I hoped she would.

That's it.

If the image doesn't match the one in your head, you've only got yourself to blame.

Gala was my fantasy, but she was the one who was ready to believe in herself. All I did was what I'd done to my city, Rome. I aimed the spotlight. I urged her to stay inside that narrow circle. I set her limits.

That is loving.

That is what makes two people lovers.

Within those narrow confines, I let her sparkle.

The characters in the commedia dell'arte wore no more than a single mask, but they could express everything—sorrow and joy, melancholy, pride, and despondency—with a turn of the head. The masks never changed, only the shadows. The actors spent a lifetime learning the nuances within a single face.

Now, in this light, Gala will discover all her possibilities.

"When I met you," Maxim continues on the Campo de' Fiori, still without looking at her, "I could hardly believe that anyone could be that uninhibited. That strong and self-assured."

"You thought so?"

"Your world was boundless. And you chose me, of all people, to take by the hand, to go off exploring together. Nothing held you back. You weren't afraid of anything! And you, of all people, made me feel that we were together, that together we'd do battle with the others, all the people I never understood. I just always assumed"—he looks at her—"I always thought that we'd stay on the same side of the camera."

"It's easy to be uninhibited when you're not aware of the danger," says Gala.

The clowns wrap up their show. One comes to their table to ask for money. In a single gesture, he raises his shoulders, his eyebrows, and the corners of his mouth by way of apology. Instead of tipping his hat, he thanks them by elegantly doffing his red nose.

Maxim and Gala spend the rest of the evening reminiscing. They declare how much they loved each other. They cry and drink and laugh and walk home the way they used to, arms entangled. In her apartment above the church, they kiss, collapse onto the bed, and tear each other's clothes off. They make love, no longer as friends, but, for the first time, as a man and a woman.

Maxim leaves at first light, without waking Gala. He has an early flight.

Camera!

My very first view of the world was through a shutter: the impressions were rushed, themselves as short as the exposure time.

In the following years, I was too busy growing up to think about it, but it came back to me when I was about six or seven. I was sitting next to my mother in the Fulgor watching a Buster Keaton short. The entire audience was roaring with laughter.

In the final scene, Keaton returns to his lonely existence on the prairie. He walks down a country road. He disappears in the distance as the eye of the camera closes slowly around him. The diaphragm contracts until everything goes black.

Suddenly I knew! That was exactly how the world appeared to me from the womb, just before I had to enter it. Right before I was born, the vulva opened several times. I clearly remember that round, pulsing frame around the walls of the room, the hands and faces in an uproar, everything drenched in a fierce white light that bounced off the sheets and stung my eyes. The preview was always very brief. The muscles contracted within seconds. Each time, the vagina's big black eye closed on the life that awaited me, just as, on that country road, the diaphragm closed around Buster Keaton.

THE END.

As soon as the lights flicked on for intermission, I told my mother. She whacked me on the back of the head, calling me a child of the devil who'd made the whole thing up. That taught me that the truth is not better than a lie. I bawled so much that Claretta, who carried her tray of sweets and cigarettes down the aisle during the breaks, slipped me an aniseed ball to shut me up.

From the hospital, I am driven to Cinecittà. The gate is wide open. Instead of the usual two security guards, there's a whole phalanx, including retirees and men who have the day off. They walk me into Studio 5, as if, after all these years, I couldn't find it myself. The big hall is empty. They lay me down in the middle and leave me alone, as if I were simply resting between takes.

Eventually, the light above the side entrance flicks on. Gelsomina enters, all in white. She is flanked by National Guardsmen with faces so long they look like they're escorting her to the scaffold. Fortunately, my sister is with her, and our best friends follow. They take up positions around me, and with that a procession of Romans that will last for hours begins to file past me. Most of them are strangers, but the men stretch out their arms and the women and girls blow me kisses. Why didn't they do that when I was eighteen and ready to abandon hope! Others I vaguely recognize. There are taxi drivers who once gave me a lift, the salesgirl from the Via Merulana who used to sell me my garters, the waiters from the Canova. Someone has brought along a harmonica to play me a tune and a girl releases a few balloons, but most are fairly nondescript, the kind of people that, on a normal day's shooting, I'd have sent straight to costumes for the full treatment.

The story goes that the Emperor Hadrian once had a spherical mirror hung in the Colosseum, a mirror that reflected the entirety of the world. Now I feel like I'm looking into that mirror, seeing everything at once: what lies ahead of me and what I've left behind, from beginning to end.

The two are rather similar.

The preview finishes and the diaphragm contracts.

The black eye closes.

I am heading toward the prairie along a country road.

I've seen enough of the city. The exposure time is up and the vulva contracts around me once more.

The intermission before the feature is about to begin. Claretta will be coming by any minute now. Chocolates, sweets, cigarettes! The older boys are lying in the aisle to look up her skirt. What wouldn't I give now for one of her lollipops!

All the commotion today was only a taste of what's in store for me tomorrow, in the Thermae of Diocletian. A media extravaganza, with Michelangelo's church as a free set. Inside, there's room for the government and a procession of celebrities the likes of which you'd normally see only on the Lido of Venice during the festival. Outside, thirty thousand people will cram together, overflowing from the Piazza della Repubblica into the Via Nazionale, watching the show on enormous television screens, where it will be regularly interrupted by ads for a postprandial liqueur and a new pasta brand that the sauce sticks to better.

Gelsomina will have to listen to one speech after the next. She will hold her rosary so tightly that it will cut into her palm and leave a wound. The president, who just a few years ago was calling me a godless pervert in the *Osservatore Romano,* will sobbingly claim that Italy has lost her favorite son. As always in this country, elections are just around the corner, so afterward the statesman will descend from the pulpit and kiss Gelsomina on the cheeks.

That will be the last straw. She'll start calling for me with heartrending cries. Behind her enormous sunglasses, that white turban hiding her bald skull, she will look terrible. Yet no one who sees these images will ever know a more beautiful woman.

Gala will be there all this time. At first, she'll be outside on the square, but Gelsomina will personally ensure that the young woman she had to share me with is plucked out of the crowd and given a place. She'll sit somewhere at the back of the church, where no one knows who she is, all alone, without a soul to whom she can confide the true nature of her grief. At one stage, Marcello will spot her from the front row and beckon her forward. She'll pretend not to notice.

After the hullabaloo is over, Gelsomina wants to touch me one last time. It's all taken a heavy toll on her and she will not survive me long. She needs support. Before the eyes of the world, she bends down toward me and whispers, *"Ciao, amore!"*

Thank you, darling, and for God's sake stop crying!

. . .

I've finally been reduced to the place in which I've always felt most at home: my imagination. That's all I am. I'm not even scared. What for? As long as you don't know what something is, it could be anything.

It's dark. Everyone's gone home. A pack of stray dogs lopes over the deserted grounds.

Must it end like this?

I can still hear the voice of one of the Japanese after hearing my proposal: "What!" he muttered. "That's it? It all just ends, without any hope, without a new beginning? The least you could do is a tree about to bloom. Anything, even just a budding flower!"

I'll see what I can do.

A door opens. Ciullo enters. He's my right-hand man, my jack-of-all-trades. I've worked with him since my first film. His footsteps echo in the empty studio.

"Hey, Ciullo! Good old Ciullo!"

He walks straight across the studio and pulls open the sliding door. The daylight shines in, a thin stripe that then widens across the full breadth of the studio. The panorama is blinding. My eyes are no longer used to it.

"Silence, filming!" someone shouts. "Camera?"

"Rolling."

"Sound?"

"Speed."

"Five, four, three . . ."

I invented Rome, Gala. Now you invent yourself.

". . . and action!"

AFTERWORD

Federico Fellini's funeral took place as described. The legendary Italian director died in 1993 after having lain in a coma for some time. Whenever Fellini inserted himself into one of his films, usually played by Marcello Mastroianni or Paolo Villagio, he gave himself the name Snaporaz.

His very last film footage was devoted to a short commercial for a Roman bank. "The Dream of the Lion in the Basement" turned out to be in honor of a certain Signora Vandemberg, and was just as described in this book, complete with the Dutch dialogue read by an Italian actress wearing leopard skin.

I recognized the leopard skin! And I knew the woman portrayed. She had a very similar name and was the friend that I had gone to Rome with in the mideighties, in the hope of landing a role in one of Fellini's films. When we arrived at Cinecittà she was wearing a jacket with that exact same print.

I'd met her in 1976 during the first rehearsal of *The Mannequins' Ball,* when we were both studying Dutch literature in Amsterdam, fell in love with her, and have loved her ever since.

I now believe that Fellini also genuinely loved her, but for a long time I didn't want to see that. I was too young, too disappointed, or perhaps simply jealous. I especially blamed the famous director for taking the magnificent, strong, independent woman who taught me, as a young man, to live without caring in the least what other people thought, and slowly but entirely making her dependent on him, to the point that she finally was reduced to living in a tiny cell above a church in which he had installed her, doing nothing more than sitting by the phone, waiting for his call.

I wondered how it was possible for love, which normally makes people stronger, to make someone weaker, her world smaller.

To answer the question I decided to write a novel. Along the way, as I was getting into the head of a character who had a lot in common with the Italian master, I started to better understand his great, childlike, genial mind, as well as his motivations.

Before sending the novel to my publisher, I, of course, showed it to the woman who had inspired one of the main characters and who is still living in Rome in the very same tiny room. She didn't ask me to change a word, even when she found her depiction unrecognizable. There was no need to. This is a novel. Certain facts from our lives, and people that played roles in them, were the basis of this fiction; I went to work with the facts just as I had in my other historical novels, but they are not the same as the people I knew, just as I, luckily, am not Maxim.

"When you tell people about your book," said my friend in Rome, "just say that you had a very different experience than I did. I remember it as a happy time."

A NOTE ABOUT THE AUTHOR

Arthur Japin, born in Haarlem in 1956, studied theater in London and Amsterdam and spent years acting on and writing for the stage, the screen, and television. He has sung with the Dutch National Opera and recently hosted his own television show.

Japin's first novel, *The Two Hearts of Kwasi Boachi* (the true story of a pair of ten-year-old African princes given as presents to the Dutch king), was made into an opera by the British composer Jonathan Dove in 2007. Japin has won many major literary prizes, including the 2004 Libris Literary Prize for *In Lucia's Eyes* (a novel about Casanova's first love). Both of these titles have been adapted as stage plays and are set to become major motion pictures. His work has been translated into more than twenty languages. He has taught at New York University and divides his time between Utrecht and the Dordogne.

A NOTE ON THE TYPE

The text of this book was set in Bembo, a facsimile of a typeface cut by Francesco Griffo for Aldus Manutius, the celebrated Venetian printer, in 1495. The face was named for Pietro Cardinal Bembo, the author of the small treatise entitled *De Aetna* in which it first appeared. Through the research of Stanley Morison, it is now generally acknowledged that all oldstyle type designs up to the time of William Caslon can be traced to the Bembo cut.

The present-day version of Bembo was introduced by the Monotype Corporation of London in 1929. Sturdy, well-balanced, and finely proportioned, Bembo is a face of rare beauty and great legibility in all of its sizes.

Composed by Creative Graphics, Allentown, Pennsylvania
Printed and bound by Berryville Graphics, Berryville, Virginia
Designed by Virginia Tan